What people are saying about FINDING FRASER...

"Jamie Fraser would be Deeply Gratified at having inspired such a charmingly funny, poignant story—and so am I."

Diana Gabaldon, author of the
New York Times Bestselling OUTLANDER series

"I loved this book. It transported me to a Scotland I wished I'd grown up in. Everything about it is a delight, and it's all authentic—the environment, the characters, the dialogue and the sheer enjoyment of it all."

Jack Whyte, best-selling author of, most recently,
THE GUARDIANS OF SCOTLAND series

"Finding Fraser is an absolute must-read for any Outlander fan. The story is both hilarious and romantic, as well as guaranteed to have readers turning the pages until the wee hours to discover if the heroine finds her very own Jamie Fraser."

Laura Bradbury, author of the
best-selling MY GRAPE ESCAPE series

"FINDING FRASER is for everyone who ever fell in love with a fictional character. Dyer blends humor, a love of Scotland, and romance into a page turner that will keep readers cheering on the main character and turning pages."

Eileen Cook, Author of REMEMBER,
and other books for teens and adults

Finding Fraser

a novel

other books by kc dyer

Seeds of Time
Secret of Light
Shades of Red
Ms. Zephyr's Notebook
A Walk Through a Window
Facing Fire

Finding Fraser

by kc dyer

Lions Mountain Literary

Library and Archives Canada Cataloguing in Publication

Dyer, K. C., author
Finding Fraser / kc dyer.

Issued in print and electronic formats.
ISBN 978-0-9940817-0-4 (pbk.).
ISBN 978-0-9940817-1-1 (kindle).
ISBN 978-0-9940817-2-8 (ibook).
ISBN 978-0-9940817-3-5 (epub).

I. Title.

PS8557.Y48F56 2015   C813'.6   C2015-902696-2
C2015-902697-0

This book is a work of fiction. Names, characters, places and incidents are products of the author's imagination or are used fictiously. Any resemblance to actual events or locales or persons, living or dead, is entirely coincidental.

Cover photo by Martin Chung of StudioImpossible.com
Published in Canada by Lions Mountain Literary.

Visit kc dyer's website at kcdyer.com,
or find her sweetly tweeting @kcdyer.
Visit Emma Sheridan at FindingFraser.com
or email her at EmmaFindingFraser@gmail.com.

This book is for Kathy and Pamela
who have been with Emma from the beginning,
and for Diana,
without whom there would be no Jamie to love.

FINDING FRASER

I met Jamie Fraser when I was nineteen years old. He was tall, red-headed, and at our first meeting at least, a virgin. I fell in love hard, fast and completely. He was older than me. He was taller than me. He knew how to ride a horse, wield a sword and stitch a wound. He was, in fact, the perfect man.

That he was fictional hardly entered into it.

I loved him then, and I love him now. Three boyfriends—one live-in—and an ex-husband have not changed my mind. Ten years have passed since I first met this man, yet somehow—somehow he is more important to me than ever.

And this is why, at twenty-nine years (and one day) old, I have decided to drop everything, to leave my life behind, and regardless of the cost to my wallet or my self-esteem, go forth and find my own James Alexander Malcolm MacKenzie Fraser.

About this Blogger

I've never been much of an adventurer. I'm pretty sure that's about to change.

EMMA SHERIDAN'S SCOTLAND

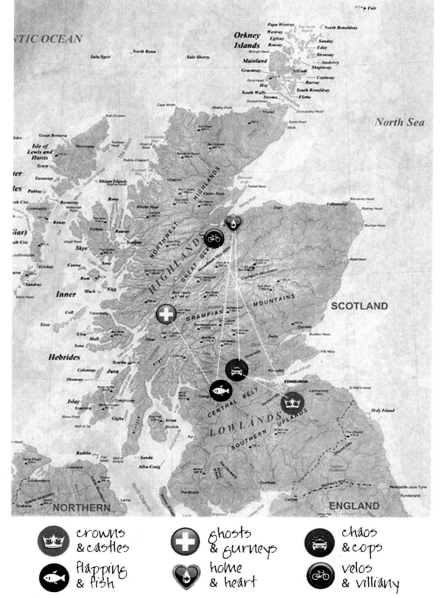

crowns & castles

ghosts & gurneys

chaos & cops

flapping & fish

home & heart

velos & villiany

PART 1: THE DEPARTURE

Facing the Future…
11:30 pm, February 15
Chicago, Illinois, USA

Well.

My first blog post.

I have to admit to being a little nervous. About the writing I mean. Actually, I'm nervous about the whole thing—this whole adventure. But the writing…I don't know. I've never been trendy, so maybe that's why this is working for me now. Now that the rest of the world has moved on to Twitter and Pinterest and Tumblr, it'll just be me and my travel blog. Yeah, that's right. It's a travel blog. Until yesterday, I was night manager at the Hitchhiker's Coffee Bar in midtown Chicago.

Today, everything has changed.

I've decided to go on a quest. A quest to find a living, breathing, twenty-first century warrior who will fight off every villain life can throw at us to remain stalwart by my side. And since I don't have anyone able—or willing—to travel with me, this is the next best thing. To share with you, my readers, all my adventures.

Let's see what happens, shall we?

- Emma Sheridan

Comments: 0

I closed the lid of my laptop. One post and I was sick of my online persona already. Who was this falsely cheery person? She sounded like she knew what she was doing.

Let's see what happens? More like "Let's document the debacle." Or … "Let's have some kind of a record so that the police know where to look when I disappear on this ill-fated potential disaster."

My birthday is February 14th. Which, this year, was yesterday. Now, when I was a kid, it was kind of a double-win. Cake, presents AND valentine chocolate all in one day? Total bonus.

But something changed as I got older. The first year of middle school, I was excited. I brought the usual bag filled with paper valentines to class, only to find some invisible force—one that I could not hope to tap into—had declared them uncool. High school was worse and by the time I made it to my twenties, I began to face the day with something like dread. If I had a boyfriend at the time, it was usually fine. Still, out of the nine birthdays I have lived through in my twenties, I've had a boyfriend for only two of them. I also had a husband for one, but that birthday was the worst of all.

Until now.

Yesterday, I turned 29. No valentine chocolate. Three cards: a birthday card from my sister, one from my friend Jazmin—and a valentine from my bank. Apparently they'd "love" to send me a new credit card at a reduced rate … 'specially for me.

As of yesterday, I also had a boss who went ballistic when he found out I was adding free shots of chocolate to people's mochas in honor of the day.

I guess I should say … Ex-boss.

Look, I know there must be other people in the same situation. Valentine's Day is a particularly lonely day to turn twenty-nine. It shouldn't be worse than having a birthday on Christmas, right? Statistically, at least 1/365th (which my calculator tells me is 0.274%) of the world's population must at least have a chance of sharing my birthday. But it doesn't feel like it's the case at all.

What it feels like … is something has to change. Something big. I'm not sure what this is going to look like. I'm scared.

But I'm going.

Fond Farewells…
7:45 pm, February 16
Chicago, Illinois, USA

Saying goodbye is hard. My parents live down south, but I have siblings in the city. *A* sibling, anyway. But farewells are just part of a new adventure, right?

Right?

– Emma S

Comments: 0

My sister loves me. I'm sure she does. But we come from practical stock: good, solid English grandparents, sensible and organized parents. She's true to her roots. My more — ah—*unique* ideas have never met with her approval.

The conversation we had earlier today did *not* go well.

"Emma, you are completely, entirely, without-a-doubt, batshit crazy."

"I'm not crazy. I just—I just need to do this, Soph. I'm not asking for your approval."

"You wouldn't get it if you were." She held up a finger. "In the first place, you've hardly been anywhere, and never on your own."

"Then it's high time I tried it, right?"

She glanced over her shoulder, pushed her chair back and closed her office door. Behind the glass walls, sensible people buzzed by, doing sensible, salary-earning work and living sensible lives. With Sophia that worked up, I was relieved I hadn't mentioned the whole searching-for-Jamie blog thing when I said I was leaving. No need to stir the pot even further.

Luckily, my sister is not an Internet time-waster. There are not, in her words, enough hours in the day to "squander a single minute reading the uneducated drivel produced by people with too much time on their hands." All the better.

But I digress.

My sister is a broker. (Funny, really, considering I've always been the broker one ...) Sophia's position as CFO of Angst & Argot was hard-won, and as a rule, she doesn't tolerate interruptions in her day. But when I'd emailed her with my plans, she'd called me immediately and insisted I stop by her office.

"Look," she continued, perching on the corner of her desk in her Ann Taylor suit, "I know you've been struggling at work. And ... I'm sorry the thing with Egon didn't work out."

I raised my eyebrows. "You're sorry? You were against my relationship with Egon from the start. *'He's a graphic artist, Emma. He drinks lattes, for Christ's sake. And what kind of name is Egon, anyway? It's the name of a flake. He's nothing but a latte-drinking hipster artist flake.'"*

She shrugged, and directed her gaze out at the 38th-floor vista. The Chicago skyline had the dark and lowering look it often has in February, reminding us resident mortals that winter isn't even half done with us yet. My sister blinked at me. "All I'm saying is that no matter how bad things are at home, it'll get better."

That made me snort. "I'm not struggling with my sexuality here, Sophia. I'm not suicidal."

"Egon was all wrong for you, Em. You just need to find the right man. If it's about a guy, why not try Internet dating again? Didn't you meet Egon online? You can find someone without leaving the country."

"This is not about a man," I said, waving my hand as dismissively as I could manage. "I'm just going to leave town for a while."

"On a fool's errand. A journey to nowhere."

"Scotland is not nowhere. It's a viable tourist destination."

It was her turn to make a disgusting nasal sound.

"Maybe in July. Take a look out there, Emma. It's the dead of winter, and *we're* in a civilized country. In Scotland, it'll be sleet and snow and no sun for six more months at least. If you're going to run away, why not head for the Caribbean? Maybe you'll meet a rich guy who'll make you forget all about Egon and his penchant for teenagers."

That was hard to take sitting down, so I stood up.

It was hard to take standing up, too, but by that time, I'd at least thought of a response.

"Tiffany's twenty, and he's welcome to her," I retorted. "Anyway, the whole thing with Egon was over almost a year ago. And I don't want to go to the Caribbean for a fling. I'm almost thirty. I'm embracing my agency as a woman. I need to see if I can have an actual life experience."

Sophia slammed her fist down on the desk. It looked like a gesture a CEO would make. I think maybe she'd been practicing. "I knew it! This idea has midlife crisis written all over it. Listen, Emma, what you should be doing right now is finding a decent job and solidifying your financial portfolio. You're half way to retirement age. You can't start ticking things off your bucket list when you don't even own a bucket."

She was, of course, depressingly correct. Half way to retirement, and I've never even held a job that offered benefits. But I was disinclined to remind her of that fact, and anyway, there was no arguing with my sister when she was on a roll. That she's two years younger than I am didn't help, either.

So I began to nod—and back away, slowly. "Okay, Soph. I'll think about it, I swear."

Her phone rang, and she held up a hand. "Wait a sec, I'll just put this on hold. *Sophia Sheridan, here—*"

But as soon as she picked up the phone, I waved back, smiled apologetically, gave her the universal finger-thumb gesture that I would call her—and bolted.

She didn't need to know that I hadn't exactly *quit* my job. Or that I was in the process of selling everything I owned.

Feeling Fine…
1:00 am, February 17
Chicago, Illinois, USA

Warm family good-byes are behind me, and preparations for the trip are well underway. Scotland, here I come!

- ES

Comments: 0

Feeling fine? Feeling freaked, more like. I wakened this morning after a night spent alternately panicking between "Oh my god! What have I done?" and trying to remember how to attain Shavasana. Since I attended my last yoga class when I was twenty-three, mostly the panic won.

In the end, I decided the best way to combat panic was action, so I dragged myself out of bed and headed downtown to have business cards printed up. Nothing says *Take Me Seriously* like a business card, right? By the time I got downtown, I'd decided on a design in my head and everything, but I spent a long time looking at the various fonts and so on to make sure it was perfect. When I placed the order, it seemed insane to have more than about twenty done, but the printers had a special deal for a hundred and fifty at half price, so I went for it.

FINDINGFRASER.COM
a blog
by EMMA SHERIDAN

A couple of hours later when I picked them up, I realized I had forgotten to specify any contact information on the cards. They were beautiful, all right; a creamy off-white with raised print and a serious-feeling heft to them. But no number. No email address.

This wasn't such a bad thing. My cell phone plan was ending in a week or so, anyway, and I wanted people to reach me through the blog. But—looking at those cards—god, things suddenly seemed so real.

So serious.

I hurried home before panic had me raving in the streets.

By noon I was lying on my back on my apartment floor, breathing into a fishy-smelling paper bag rescued from an old lunch I'd somehow forgotten in the back of the fridge. Which had never happened to me before. I cannot recall missing a meal for any reason since I had my tonsils removed when I was seven. It clearly speaks to the unsettled nature of my mind. Or maybe the fact it was tuna on rye. I *really* hate tuna.

I would have tried elevating my feet on the couch, but the guys from Goodwill had come and taken it away. The removal of the couch made it seem like everything was happening so fast, and the paper bag just wasn't cutting it, so I thought *fuck it,* and drank the last of the Chablis in the fridge. It was early, I knew, but I'd have to clean out the fridge at some point, right? Good enough reason on its own. Besides, the wine was in a box. Juice comes in a box and people drink juice at two in the afternoon all the time.

Right?

The paper bag smelled like tuna, okay? And there's a reason I hate tuna. All fish, really.

I haven't always hated fish. Barbecued salmon. Golden-fried halibut. Even oysters in the half-shell. Used to love 'em all.

Not any more. I lay on the floor beside the empty Chablis box and remembered …

The old clock by the front door had chimed eight that night as I set the shrimp cocktail on the table. It was our first anniversary and I was determined to do it up right. A veritable feast was lined up, ready to serve after the shrimp: creamy clam chowder to start, pan-fried trout for the main course and an enormous chocolate torte for dessert.

Egon showed up at eight fifteen with a pink posy in one hand—and his assistant Tiffany in the other. "Tiff's fridge broke down today," he said, setting the wilted flowers in the center of the table.

Tiffany wriggled between Egon and the table. "Oh, Emma, you are SO kind to include me," she gushed. "I SWORE I wouldn't disturb your special night with Egon, but he insisted you'd put on an enormous spread and I wouldn't be in the way."

That girl sucked those shrimp back like a Dyson. Egon had smiled indulgently and pushed the plate closer to her.

In retrospect, perhaps I should have taken the three of us eating our anniversary dinner as a sign. Because within six months, Tiffany was serving all-you-can-eat lobster dinners for two in my old apartment, and I haven't eaten seafood since.

Strangely, though, the break-up dinner didn't affect my feelings for chocolate tortes.

So yeah, I'd sworn to Sophia my plan wasn't about a man. Egon had cured me of Internet dating for life, but that didn't mean I didn't have a few good memories. Still, by three, the crying jag brought on by the old Chablis and the pictures of Egon on the mantle that I'd drunkenly begun to pack was over.

The crying was over, and so were the pictures.

Over the balcony railing, as a matter of fact.

That shattering noise glass makes on pavement?

Extremely satisfying.

I finished sweeping the entire parking lot free of glass by five-thirty. My building's Super is small, but she has great deductive reasoning—and she carries a big stick. (Literally. It's her son's old baseball bat. This neighborhood can be rough at night.)

She also had my security deposit check in her pocket, which she threatened to tear up if I didn't get my ass downstairs to clean up the mess I'd made.

When I dumped the last of my shattered memories into the bin, she nodded stiffly. "Men are dicks," she said. "They can't help it."

It was the closest thing to sympathy I'd received all week. I burst into tears, but she brandished the bat at me when I leaned in for a hug.

I figured I could live with that, seeing as she did give me the check.

Figure Four…
8:45 pm, February 18
Chicago, Illinois, USA

Less than a week before my plane leaves. I'm actually flying out of JFK in New York, so I'm going to have to get myself across four states in that time. I haven't quite sorted this out, as yet. But it is all coming together.

I'm really confident——and excited!

- ES

Comments: 1

SexxxyGrrl:

I very pleased follow love. Good to follow love.
Buy Gold watches here: watcherini.nairobi.com

It was *not* all coming together.

And with every day, the blog seemed to be rapidly morphing from true-life travelogue to creative non-fiction.

I decided I was okay with that. Reality TV notwithstanding, public humiliation is not all it's cracked up to be. Let the world see my best self, right?

And I had managed to find myself a killer deal on the plane ticket, even with the cost of the bus trip to New York tacked on.

My sister had left six messages on my cell phone, alternately haranguing me about shirking my family duties and reminding me to call our mother, so maybe *she* could talk some sense into me.

I did not call our mother.

Instead, I sold the last of my furniture. The worst was saying goodbye to my Xbox. No more dragon slaying in my future. It's like—well, it's kind of like saying goodbye to my youth. I mean, I didn't even have to give up the Xbox when I got married, for god's sake. And it's not like I've been playing Dragon Age anywhere near as much as I was two years ago.

But still. It hurts.

On the other hand, the Super's son paid thirty bucks for my old bed. I didn't tell him it was the same double bed I'd had since I was seventeen. Kinda sorry to see it go, but really? It's time. Everything has to go for this trip to even happen. And for it to mean anything at all? I need to make a complete break from the old Emma.

By afternoon, I found myself waiting at the passport office. I got there on time for my appointment, but they seemed to be running late and I ended up sitting in the waiting area, roasting in my coat and boots. My number was B48, and with only two officers on duty, the numbers crawled by painfully slowly.

A woman seated in a chair just in front of me was reading her Kindle, and I mentally kicked myself for forgetting to bring a book or a newspaper. With nothing else to do, I began killing time making notes for my next blog post. I was jotting a list of things I'd rather do than wait with fifty strangers for a passport when, out of the blue, the woman made a little involuntary sound.

I recognized that sound. Half gasp, half sigh. I had made it myself.

Over her shoulder I saw a single word, and I knew in an instant what she was reading.

One of the interview windows opened up, and the red digital number on the wall pinged as it changed. B47. No one moved. I gathered my papers together, hoping they'd just go to the next number when the woman in front of me suddenly jumped up. Her handbag and papers cascaded off her lap onto the floor

"That's me," she said loudly, pointing at the number on the wall, and scrambling to pick up her papers.

I knelt down and handed her two of the pages that had fallen near my feet.

"Thank you," she said, jamming the Kindle into her handbag.

I grinned at her. "OUTLANDER?" I said.

The smile on her face turned to puzzlement. "VOYAGER," she replied.

I nodded knowingly. "Oh, right. Must be the post-reunion scene?"

She stared at me suspiciously. "Have you been reading over my shoulder?"

I winced. "Not—not really. Claire's name just jumped out at me."

She raised a skeptical eyebrow and hurried off to the open window.

When my turn finally came, I paid the fee and picked up my passport. My photo looked like the face of someone who could drive a splintery wooden stake through a newborn puppy's heart.

So, just about like usual. A bit better than my driver's license, actually.

As I stepped into the elevator, mentally calculating if the money I got from the bed would justify a stay in a New York hotel instead of a hostel, someone touched my shoulder.

It was the woman with the Kindle.

"Are you a writer?" she blurted, looking pointedly at my notebook. She had one hand buried deep in her handbag.

I started to shake my head, and then re-thought it. "Well—I blog a bit," I said.

She narrowed her eyes and shot a look at my abdomen. "Mommy blogger?"

"I'm NOT pregnant," I said. "I just ate Indian food for lunch."

She shrugged, but didn't apologize. "So—book blogger, then?"

"No. It's more of a personal journal. About a trip I'm taking. A—a travel blog."

The doors opened. "Oh. Never mind, then." She turned on her heel and sped off toward the entranceway.

I hurried after her. "Wait a sec," I called, as she descended the front steps. "Why did you think—I mean, how did you know I'm a writer?"

She stopped on the stair below me. "*Only* a blogger," she corrected, and then paused for a minute, staring up at me.

"You were scribbling in that notebook, is all," she said, at last. "And since you knew the books, well—I thought you might be interested in this conference."

She dug deep into her handbag, and then thrust a flyer into my hands. It was heavily creased, and in the time I took to unfold it, she had her hand on the front door.

"What is it?" I cried out, unable to read and catch up at the same time.

I could feel the rush of cold wind as she opened the door below me. I heard her voice, borne on a wave of city traffic noise. "Love Is in the Air!" she yelled, the slam of the door cutting off her last word.

I was left standing in the entranceway, clutching my passport and a crumpled piece of hot pink paper.

Feet Forward...
4:30 pm, February 19
Somewhere past Cleveland on the I-90, USA

I'm on the road, at last. The journey begins with a bus ride. First stop: Philadelphia. Heading east, toward adventure. Forward!

— ES

Comments: 2

SexxxyGrrl:

I heart adventure. Adventure good to love. Buy Gold watches here: watcherini.nairobi.com

John Harrison, Houston, USA:

God's Love Pays. Earn 25 000 000. Learn MORE: watcherini.nairobi.com

Philadelphia. The city of brotherly love.
 Why Philadelphia? Why not straight to New York?

All because of one little pink flyer containing one significant piece of information. Something that could change the whole nature of this journey.

Some*one*.

I closed the lid to my laptop. The truth was, adventure was less exhilarating than it was actually nauseating. The original plan—admittedly made in the heat of the just-been-fired-on-my-birthday moment—had been to grab the cheapest flight I could find. That it meant a bus trip across four states (five, if you count Illinois) didn't even faze me. Part of the adventure, right?

And then Kindle Lady had come along and handed me a flyer that essentially said "Yes, Emma—this is the right decision. Follow your heart and you'll find your Fraser."

Amazing how reality can slide down your neck like a trickle of winter sleet.

My stomach was in knots. An hour earlier when I'd stepped off the slushy street and onto the bus, I'd remembered Sophia's jab. She was right, too. This trip would be the first time I had traveled completely solo in my whole life. Pathetic for someone teetering on the scary precipice of thirty years old, but true. Then the bus had pulled out and it was too late to turn back. I was on the road.

To commemorate the event, I posted to my blog using Wi-Fi on a moving vehicle for the first time ever.

That was kind of nauseating too, come to think of it.

The only good part was that I hadn't stopped to call anyone. Not my mother, not my sister, not even my friend Jazmin. I texted them all, instead. To say I was on my way. To say I loved them.

To say I was terrified.

I hadn't actually typed out the last bit. Sophia would have had the police searching for me if I had. As it was, I got a cheery "Have a great time, check in when you can!" back from my mother. Sophia's text held lower hopes for me. "Don't expect me to rescue you if you get into trouble." And Jazmin didn't reply at all.

That was okay, though because, before I left, I'd told her about the blog. She was a huge Jamie fan, too, and she'd sworn she would have come with me if she'd had the courage. She'd even promised to follow the blog. Now, I love my Jazzy-girl, but she doesn't know an RSS feed from her grass seed. (She's a landscape architect. Really good, too.) But since she is too much of a Luddite to even return a text, I have a plan. Once I get off this rocking bus and into Philadelphia, I'll find me some free Wi-Fi at a coffee shop, and link the blog to my Facebook page. Jazmin will be able to manage that, at least. She loves Facebook.

So yeah. As I sat on the bus rocketing past the brown slush-guttered suburbs of Chicago, my laptop and the sum total of everything else I brought was stowed in my backpack. I don't think I've owned so little property in—well, in my whole life. Growing up, I had all the comforts a middle-class home could offer. Even as a freshman, I lived in a college dorm packed with stuff: books, clothes and everything else. My hair products alone filled an entire closet. In those long-ago days, my life would have ended if anyone even suspected I had curly hair. What would the younger version of me have thought if she knew I'd actually sold my flat iron to help finance a trip to Scotland?

This was different. It felt real. It felt really … scary.

I leaned forward on the seat, clutched my stomach and closed my eyes. I tried talking myself through it.

Okay, Sheridan, focus. Selling everything means a fresh start. It means you can spend two full months looking for your Fraser. And anyway, it's only Philadelphia—you're not leaving the good old US of A just yet.

Deep breath. Deep breath.

Where was that damn tuna sandwich bag when I needed it?

The bus began slowing down, so I made a snap decision to just step out a minute and get a breath of air. Real, clean, not-very-far-from-Chicago air.

It had taken a few minutes, but in the immortal words my sister Sophia stole from a far better cause, things got better.

Really.

It had been a bit of a close one, though. I'd never had a full-blown panic attack on a public vehicle before. Once the screaming stopped, of course, things definitely improved.

That moment when the bus was slowing down? Well, it turned out the bus had only been gearing down to take a curve, and the driver had no intention of pausing to let one worried passenger out to breathe a bit of fresh air.

And to clarify? It wasn't me screaming.

My jaws were locked together in terror, just as tightly as my hands were clamped around the exit door, which apparently affected the driver's ability to control the vehicle, somehow. And maybe the radio to his dispatcher transmitted his screaming? At any rate, in the end the police were able to slow the bus down by maneuvering their cars in front of it.

The driver got the rest of the night off, so no need to feel too bad for him. And afterwards, when everyone had calmed down a bit, I had a nice chat with a very personable police officer, who told me he'd had panic attacks in his twenties, too.

"Twenty-nine was the worst," he said. "I freaked out one night and beat the shit out of this teenage kid. Thought I was going to lose my job. But, the kid turned out to be Muslim, so you know, in the end all I got was sensitivity-training and a transfer, and here I am today, helping talk you down."

Strangely disconcerting and comforting at the same time. Nothing like a cuddly racist to make a person feel better about herself.

The racist cop sent the first bus on its way once they'd dragged me off in Pittsburgh, and left me with his partner to wait for the next bus. The bus station where we were sitting smelled of urine and old socks, but it was pretty late and I was sitting with a cop, so I tried not to think about it.

"So, why Philadelphia?" she said, over our second cup of coffee.

I fished around in my pack and pulled out the flyer.

"Love Is in the Air, huh?" she said, glancing at the headline. "So, you're a writer, then. Well, that explains a lot."

"Blogger, actually," I said. "I'm on a bit of a travel adventure. This is kind of a side-trip. There's—well, there's someone at this event I really need to meet."

The officer returned to reading the flyer, and when she got to the bottom, her eyes snapped up to meet mine. "*Jeesely H*

Roosevelt Christ," she said, and her voice filled with a sudden reverence. "Do you SEE who's the Guest of Honor?"

I nodded slowly. "So—you've read the books?"

"Are you freaking kidding me? My husband gave them to me the year we got married. I lost a whole summer to, well ... to mmphm."

"Your husband? Whoah." I was impressed. "My ex wouldn't read a book to save his life. Only had eyes for the Blackhawks, that man. And his girlfriend, of course."

She nodded at me sympathetically. "Divorced, huh? Aw, you're probably better off without the bum."

"It only lasted a year," I mumbled.

She leaned across the table and pointed her spoon at me. "Well, in our case, that book is the recipe for a happy marriage, I tell ya. A man who aspires to be like Jamie Fraser is one in a million. My guy? Well, let's just say that the year AN ECHO IN THE BONE came out, he didn't watch a single playoff game. And the Penguins were going for the cup that season."

The things you learn from cops in bus stations.

She was one hundred percent right. I should have known Egon was wrong for me the minute he said he didn't read romances.

A. Historical fiction is NOT romance.

B. What the hell is wrong with reading romance, anyway?

And C.? He didn't read anything at all, really.

I should have known.

When my bus pulled up a few minutes later, the cop hugged me warmly and tucked an Ativan out of her own stash into my pocket to ward off any relapses.

"You'll love Philadelphia," she said. "But watch out for the ladies who are putting on your shin-dig. There's a romance writing group near here in Erie, and let me just say—we've been called out to a few of their parties. Some of those chicks are decently hard-core."

I waved through the window until she was just a teeny blue dot in the distance. Nice to know that even a cop could see the value of following a dream.

Fortuitous Fate...
3:30 pm, February 20
Philadelphia, Pennsylvania, USA

The most important news for today is that I have mastered the comment anti-spam function. Because, there may not be many actual readers out there, but holy crow—is my blog being followed by a lot of bots.

Okay, I'm lying.

Because the *most* important news is that I have actually made it into a special mini-conference, sponsored by an organization for writers of romantic fiction. Yes, the very conference advertised on a certain hot-pink flyer handed to me in Chicago.

Fate smiled on me that day.

Apparently, the conference has been planned to celebrate Something Special. (Also? I note that the flyer tended to Randomly Capitalize Important Items. Jane Austen, your influence has now extended into its third century...)

This particular Something Special is an industry award. And that it is an award given to someone who has never claimed to be a romance writer (nor an Over-User of Excessive Capitalization) is what makes it all the more interesting.

Yes.

It's true.

I have signed up to attend a conference where the guest speaker is the creator of the man I seek.

Herself.

Should I have skipped this event and gone straight through to New York City? What would you have done?

- ES

Comments: 0

So, yeah—it turned out the commenters on my blog had all been bots. When I checked back, there wasn't a single voice of support for my adventure. Nor a single vote of dissent, if you come right down to it.

But that's okay. I don't need external validation. Something — something larger than me is guiding this journey. Otherwise, how do you explain the presence of Herself in the very city I've ended up in?

Fine, so technically I didn't need to travel to Philadelphia in order to make my cheap New York flight. But it was pretty much on the way. I had to get to New York somehow. And the very thought of meeting Herself in the flesh made my hands start to shake. She was the woman who created Jamie Fraser, who built him up from clay—or from ink and paper, at least. She has gone on to beat him, wound him, torture him in every possible way, and still nurture his unending love for Claire over the course of the entire series.

The questions I had? Beyond number. The chance to meet Her, to talk with Her about Jamie, to ask Her where I should best seek out a real flesh-and-blood version of him? It was just too good to pass up.

When I'd finally made it into Philadelphia (with the help of the cop's Ativan), I discovered the station happened to be less than three blocks from the hotel where the event was being held.

It was meant to be.

The hike from the bus station had given me a chance to stretch my legs and allow the icy Philadelphia wind blow the last of the anxiety away. I'd made it. I was still on American soil, but the journey was truly underway. And as I stepped up to the hotel doors, a doorman in a top hat swept forward and held it open for me.

An open door held by a handsome man felt like an omen.

There was a small registration booth set up in the foyer. The special hotel rate offered to conference-goers was just about triple what I had budgeted to spend, but a hotel stay was not mandatory.

"We have loads of locals coming in," the lady behind the desk said. "In fact, the Belles are upstairs right now, planning a celebration for after the signing tomorrow."

I didn't know what bells she meant, but nodded anyway, mentally calculating the distance from the hotel venue to the nearest hostel. A mere fifteen blocks away. Nothing more than a quick and easy cab ride.

I was, however, required to join the romance writing group.

"Members-only event," chirped the ever-helpful lady behind the desk. "Are you a published writer?"

I thought about the little message that popped up every time I entered a blog post. *Please wait—post publishing ...*

"Oh, yes," I assured her. "That is—if published writers get a discount ...?"

They did indeed.

I handed over the thirty-five bucks for membership, and decided a city bus would do just as well as a taxi in the morning.

"... And as a member, you only have to pay twenty-five dollars to attend the conference!" she said, exuding charm and delight from every pore.

I've heard Philadelphia is a lovely city to walk through. Guess I'm going to find out soon enough.

Forever Fan...
Noon, February 21
Philadelphia, Pennsylvania, USA

Seventeen blocks through downtown Philadelphia in February. NOT for the faint of heart or the unscarved of face. And yeah, it was seventeen. Seems I miscounted on the local map yesterday. But I'm here at last. I have my lanyard declaring me a writer in good standing. I have my dog-eared copy of OUTLANDER, for Herself to sign. (Glory!) AND I have access to the hotel's free Wi-Fi on the main floor, which is where I am sitting as I type this. Literally. On the floor. Because the line-up for the signing was already three hundred people long when I got here at 9 a.m.

There are other conference events throughout the day, but the author, it turns out, will not be speaking here. She'll sign books, accept the award and be spirited away by sometime this evening.

Clearly, the gods of time travel shine on me today. Claire Beauchamp Randall Fraser might have been a somewhat unwilling inter-dimensional wanderer, but I am not. I plan to sit here on the floor and trace out Claire's journey on the map inside the cover of my copy of the book. It will be the blueprint for my journey. I shall walk in her footsteps.

For that reason, I will not be attending the panel on The Value of Vivid Verbs, nor the likely very instructive talk on Whipping up Sex Scenes by Adding Leather.

I am in line for a chance to meet the author of the man of my dreams.

The organizers here tell me I may only have time for one question.

The agony…

– ES

Comments: 0

Full Failure…
11:15 pm, February 21
Philadelphia, Pennsylvania, USA

Totally, totally blew it.

Complete and utter failure.

I don't deserve to live…

And now, she's gone for good. I saw the whole ~~ontourage~~ ~~entouraje~~ group pack up and leave over an hour ago. There was no sadness in her wake, however. All night this bar has been filled with cheery women bubbling with joy over their encounters with her. How sweet she is. How considerate. Great sense of humor——joking about her writer's cramp after five hundred signatures—— imagine!

My only hope is that the river of eager faces demanding signatures obliterates her memory of the encounter with me forever.

I wonder if anyone has ever managed to actually drown in a martini?

- ES

Comments: 0

W ell, that's a long face. Howie, I swear that's the longest
face we've seen tonight, wouldn't you say?" The woman
leered cheerfully at me as she balanced two beers in one hand
and slapped her companion on the shoulder with the other.

I smiled guiltily, swiveled my stool in the other direction
and slid my laptop into my bag. The woman was not put off by
my chilliness. In fact, she appeared to take it as a challenge.

"I'm guessing you got here too late for the autograph line.
Am I right? AMIRIGHT?" She nudged me with an elbow,
which had the effect of spinning me back into her presence.

I swirled the olive around in my glass, but there was no
escape. The woman downed her beer in a single gulp and
beamed at me.

I took a shaky breath. "No—no. She signed my book. She
was lovely."

The woman slapped the empty mug onto the bar, and,
using only that same right elbow, slid the other beer to the
man known as Howie with impressive agility. She was a bear
of a woman, six feet tall in her stocking feet—which I can
entirely attest to, since for some reason she was not actually
wearing shoes—with a halo of gray wiry hair that reminded
me somewhat endearingly of a dead dandelion. She wore an
enormous cross between a caftan and a housedress in an eye-
searing combination of green, purple and pink plaid.

Her companion was a tidy little man perhaps half a foot
shorter, with four or five strands of hair neatly pasted across
the crown of his head. He stood out not for his height or his
shiny baldness, but simply for his gender. Apart from the
busboy, he was the only male I could discern in the vicinity.

"Then why so glum?" the woman shouted, easily drowning
out the vaguely Celtic Muzak that had begun emanating from
somewhere in the ceiling. She slapped her hand on the bar.
"Give this lady another martini," she demanded. The bartender
had a new glass in my hand before my ears stopped ringing
from the command.

I fished around in my bag for my wallet, but a large hand came down on my own before I could pull it out. "It's on me, honey," she said, using her talented right elbow to lever Howie off the stool he'd been sitting on.

"Sharan Stone," she bellowed, and held out her giant hand for me to shake. "Not the movie star," she clarified, and guffawed loudly. "Though Howie thinks I am, dontcha, How?"

The little man crinkled his eyes at her and nodded, burying his moustache in his beer.

"I'd better be going," I said, standing up. "Thanks for the drink."

"Aw, honey, the party's just starting," Sharan Stone said. "And you shore look like you could use some cheering up. But never fear—you're with the Belles, now, and whatever's got you down is gonna be history fer sure. Check this out."

She stood up so forcefully the stool she'd usurped from Howie flew backwards and took out the busboy.

I was standing by this point, too, but one of those big hands clapped onto my shoulder and my knees gave out. I collapsed back down onto my stool, shocked into sobriety by sheer terror.

Sharan Stone put a finger and thumb into her mouth and blew the most piercing whistle I'd heard since grade school. The bar fell instantly silent.

"Belles!" she cried, and a cheer went up around me. I began to feel that I'd fallen into some bizarro-dream scenario, so I took a big gulp of the martini.

"BELLES," repeated Sharan Stone, "I do believe we've waited long enough."

Her voice, which likely had some decent staying power even at regular conversational levels, rose to a crescendo. "It's time for Ja-a-a-a-A-A-A-A-MIE!"

I clapped my hands over my ears as everyone around me took up the chant.

"Jaaa-MIE, Jaaa-MIE, JAAA-MIE!!!"

I say everyone, but in the sea of women chanting Jamie's name, Howie sat placidly, still sipping his beer with a gentle smile on his face.

"Jaaa-MIE, Jaaa-MIE, JAAA-MIE!!!" the crowd roared.

And in he came.

Over the previous week there had been many moments when the folly of my quest threatened to sink in and send me sensibly back to Chicago. Losing my shit on the bus. The fourteenth block of the walk from the hostel, when a massive truck splashed my legs with a wave of salty sleet from Philadelphia's biggest pothole. But let me tell you, NOTHING was as discouraging as seeing the buff guy in the kilt coming toward me along the top of that hotel bar.

His skin was spray-tanned to a shade of orange that matched the leather of his sporran. He'd leapt onto the bar like it was nothing, and strode the full length in a cloud of baby oil scent so thick it even cut through the smell of beer in the air. He wore nothing but a tiny kilt that I'm quite sure no self-respecting Scotsman would blow his nose into, and a plaid tam atop a vivid orange wig.

I think my heart broke a little at the sight of that wig.

The stripper pranced down the bar, jig-stepping over glasses to the sound of an electro-bagpipe drone. And the crowd?

The crowd went wild.

Even Howie was screaming as the Faux-Jamie gyrated and coyly lifted the hem of his kilt.

"Show us yer COCK, Jamie," screamed Sharan Stone out of one side of her mouth.

She was standing on her stool matching his every gyration, dancing along with him in her sock feet. Women scrambled over each other to jam money into his socks, his sporran, whatever they could reach. "SHOW US YER COCK!!!!"

I was pinned to my stool as the crowd of women surged toward the bar in a shining-eyed, sweaty wave. I dropped to my hands and knees and crawled for my life.

After what seemed an eternity of dodging legs of both the human and table variety, I accidentally smashed my face into an overturned chair, which knocked me back a little. But I realized I'd cleared the stampede, and somehow managed to escape alive. The knees of my jeans were soaked with beer, and I couldn't even bear to look at the palms of my hands, but I was still hammered enough to not really care. Someone reached a hand down to help me to my feet, and I found myself looking into a pair of calm, and clearly sober, blue eyes.

"Thank you," I gasped. "Sorry about the stickiness."

"No' a problem." He pulled a packet of antiseptic wipes from his pocket and cleaned his hands off. Then he won my heart completely by offering me one, too.

My rescuer stood about six feet tall, his rusty brown hair with a thread or two of gray at the temples. He had a messenger bag slung over one shoulder, and was in the process of winding a long woolen scarf around his face and neck.

"I've never seen anything quite like tha'," he said, nodding back at the melee.

I looked back, too, to see the guy on the bar had lost his wig, and had proven beyond a shadow of a doubt what a Scotsman wore under his kilt. As a matter of fact, the kilt was long gone. He had, somehow, managed to retain the sporran.

I nodded, too discouraged to speak.

"That's not Jamie," I managed, at last.

"No, you're right abou' that," he said, and he tapped his fingers thoughtfully on the back of a chair. "I'm fair certain his name is Steve-o, and he specializes in Cowboy or Disco

Dude, as a rule, but this was apparently such a big money-maker he couldnae turn it down."

I shot him a look.

"I heard him in the lounge earlier, talking on his mobile."

"You were listening to a male stripper talk on his cell phone?"

He smiled a little. "Aye. I was sitting in the lounge, working. I'm a writer. Eavesdropping is part of my job description."

"That's reassuring."

He shrugged, and I regretted the sarcasm in my tone. It wasn't his fault my night had turned out the way it had.

"Well, I'm heading to my hotel," he continued. "Sure you're all right? You've got quite a bump on your forehead, there."

I felt my face. There was a definite goose egg forming over my left eye, but other than that I seemed to have escaped unscathed.

"I think I'm good," I said. "Thanks again. It was scary in there."

We walked toward the entrance of the hotel when his cell phone rang. He smiled at me apologetically as he took the call, and I stepped over to the front desk.

Outside the windows, the snow swirled in a street-lit maelstrom.

"Is there a bus I can get from here to—uh—West Oregon Avenue?"

The girl behind the counter shook her head. "Not at this hour, I'm afraid. And our shuttle service is down—our driver, Nathan, can't get the battery to hold a charge."

Another long walk, then. I zipped up my coat and held a moment of silence for all the winter clothing I had sold at Second Hand Rose's the week before.

Beside me, my rescuer was just finishing his call. "See you soon, Becks. Dinner, fer sure." He turned and looked at me as I zipped my hood up like South Park Kenny.

"No bus then?"

Before I could do more than shake my head, the front door of the hotel opened and one of the doormen blew inside clutching his top hat, his face glowing frostbite-red.

"Share a cab?" my rescuer asked, and I didn't even check my wallet before agreeing.

It's amazing what you can learn about a person over the course of seventeen blocks. We exchanged cards, to begin with, and I managed to keep my mouth shut and not tell him that mine was the first card I'd ever given out in my life.

His name was Jack Findlay, and he had just wrapped up a freelance gig for the BBC, profiling several prominent American writers. He'd come to this event in hopes of asking a few questions of the guest of honor. When he learned she was not going to be speaking, he thought he might try his luck with a few of the local romance writers—and that was just about when things began to disintegrate in the bar.

"Apparently they're known as Beauchamp's Belles," he said, grinning at me as the cab bumped over ice ruts in the road. "The sort of fan club every author aspires to, aye?"

"I guess." I looked across the back seat of the cab at him, sitting with his messenger bag on his lap. "So, the BBC, huh? Are you English?"

His neck, the bit I could see over his woolen scarf anyway, took on an even rustier color than it had in the frozen air outside.

"Born in Fife," he said, stiffly. "Nowhere near England, as a matter of fact."

Great. I'd insulted him after he'd swept me away from the night's disaster. The first Scottish man I'd met in the flesh, too.

I studied his face for a minute as the streetlights flashed by. I'd seen no sign of a ring before he put his gloves on, but the phone call had marked him as taken. Besides – my Jamie would never share a name with Black Jack Randall. All the same, I didn't want him to think me completely ignorant.

"I'm sorry," I said, humbly. "Your accent is pretty soft compared to the ones I heard tonight. Are you here for long?"

He laughed. "Any accent you heard tonight sounded nothing like a true Scotsman, I'll tell ye that. And, no, America is finished wi' me for the present," he added. "I've a project at home I'll be finishing up next—should keep me out of trouble awhile. You?"

He'd added the last politely, but luckily at that moment, the cab pulled up to the hostel, and I wasn't forced to share my own plans. He waved away the five-dollar bill I thrust at him as the cab slowed to a stop, but I tossed it into his lap anyway.

"For your sporran," I said, still a little drunk.

The look of horror he gave me as the cab sped away led me to believe he didn't really get the joke.

Fall & Forget…
11:00 am, February 22
Philadelphia, USA

Well, I have to say the conference was a success for just about everybody who attended. Certainly the group of Belles I met in the bar seemed to be having a most excellent time. (Sharan, if you ever read this, say 'hi' to Howie for me, okay?) However, my own encounter with Herself was an unmitigated disaster, and I'm feeling very discouraged. I'm not sure if I can continue. I have resolved to never think of it again, let alone write about it here.

- ES

Comments: 1

SophiaSheridan, Chicago, USA:

I'm glad to see you have come to your senses, Emma. This whole idea sounds like a wild goose chase, and really? I'm not so sure you're not certifiable. Anyway, I think you'll agree the fun is over by now, right? (And yes, obviously I found your blog. Paul found it, actually. How can you waste your time with this nonsense?) Please don't make me read any more. The whole idea makes me nauseous. Come home.

Paul is Sophia's husband. They've been married two years, but they'd met in ninth grade. I have never forgotten what a little creep he was in school. It took him a long time to grow out of it. To tell you the truth, I'm not sure he ever did.

These days, Paul is a tech wizard—a geek's geek. He does some kind of work for the government, but all he'll tell me is that he is a *"white hat,"* whatever that means. And that he makes good money. *"Very* good money, Sis. *Very good."*

Asshole. And I am not his *"Sis."*

The morning after the disaster in Philadelphia, I had been all set to pack up and go home—cash the ticket in and maybe heed Sophia's advice and take a side trip to Mexico for a week, before deciding what to do next. However, a quick phone call reminded me the deal I got on the airline ticket was not refundable, not transferable.

And then I read Sophia's comment.

I threw myself down on the little hostel room bed—which was a mistake, as it was apparently constructed of baling wire and straw—and did what I always do when I'm feeling low.

I pulled out my copy of OUTLANDER.

Well, come on. Where do YOU go when your heart is broken?

This is not a rhetorical question.

Some people hit the bar. Some throw themselves into their work. Some just leap into the arms of the first non-homicidal-looking person they find.

Me? I go to the bookstore.

I mean, I've tried drowning my sorrows, but somehow—it just never works out well. Drunkenness invariably precedes regret, at least in my experience. (See the events of the previous night for a case in point ...)

My first boyfriend was beautiful. Dark hair, dark eyes. Achingly gorgeous bone-structure. I'd had NO idea what he'd seen in me, but when he'd asked me to coffee, I wasn't about to question it. We shared a second-year Grecian studies class, and he was one of only three males in the group. I was nearly twenty, and had resigned myself to undateable status long before. Who needed boys? After a painfully long dry spell in high school, I had thrown myself into my studies at college, and the middle-Renaissance period became my era of choice. NOT the best place to meet virile football players.

So when Campbell asked me to join him for our coffee break, I had a cup of Earl Grey in my hand before he could change his mind. He ordered a two-shot dark roast latte and we talked about my duties as a TA in a first-year literature class. How irritating it was to mark essays. How accessible the prof was in a kind of a Wolverine-era Hugh Jackman way. It was heaven.

That relationship lasted exactly thirty-seven cups of tea. Tall. With honey.

When it became clear to both of us that Campbell's long eyelashes were batting more at our hipster Hugh-look-alike professor than they were at me, he moved on.

And I went to the bookstore and bought the next Jamie and Claire book.

I don't mean to minimize my devastation, here. Only a woman whose first true love had left her for an older professor with mutton chop sideburns and penchant for reading sonnets aloud in class can truly understand the level of my loss.

Campbell was beautiful, he was perfect and he had been—so briefly—mine. For a week afterwards, I lay on the floor with my head awkwardly propped against my couch cushions. I could still smell the scent of him there in the living room; the place where he'd sat and endlessly Googled class ratings for our professor on my laptop. (And men's body-building sites. Hey—I was young, and a slow learner, okay?)

My friend Jazmin took me out for beers when it became clear that Campbell was lost to me. I sat at the bar and watched as she got progressively drunker, accepting Jager-bombs from a growing assortment of unsuitable young men. She finally left, her neck firmly ensconced in the crook of the elbow of the worst of the lot: a boy wearing a trucker hat emblazoned with the picture of a cup of coffee and the words 'Joe before Hos'. It was only 8 p.m., so I paid the bill and headed for the bookstore. Campbell might have been beautiful, but his back was unscarred by life, his hair was not auburn and he didn't roll his 'r's when he spoke.

That was not the first time I turned to the OUTLANDER books for solace. And it would not be the last. In my heart, I knew the story was really about a woman. A warm, funny, capable nurse who was inadvertently whisked through time and into the arms of a man who would—after a little initial trepidation and some complex plot twists—have and hold her for the rest of her life. Was it so wrong that I wanted him, too? And no less after the insanity of the last couple of days than I had after I'd lost Campbell and his long, perfect eyelashes.

So, there on my hostel room bed in Philadelphia, I re-read the wedding night chapter—my favorite—and then gently closed the cover of the book. Using my elbows, I propped myself back against the iron headboard of the exceedingly uncomfortable bed. Flipped open my laptop, logged onto my site. Typed.

Finks & Fortitude…
9:00 pm, February 22
Philadelphia, USA

I'm not ready to quit yet.

So the trip is on, bitches. And yeah, I'm talking to YOU, Paul, you rat-fink.

White hat my ass.

– ES

Comments: 0

As I finished typing, I noticed there was a comment on the previous posting. It was from someone named HiHoKitty, claiming to be from Sapporo, Japan. It read:

I believe is good you follow your dreams, even crazy.

"Take that Sophia," I muttered, as I closed the lid of the laptop.

And then I went to bed.

Flurries & Flashbacks…
2:30 pm, February 23
New York City, USA

Would you look at that? I've got a comment from someone who is neither my sister nor trying to sell me drugs to cure erectile dysfunction! At first, I thought it was just a bot, but I've decided to believe the goodness in human nature sometimes trumps the evil of the Internet. So, thanks, HiHoKitty of Sapporo, Japan. You seriously made my day. Though I have to say I'm not really sure if you are implying my dreams are crazy, or I am. Let's go with a sane woman following whimsical dreams and leave it at that, shall we?

I've made it to NYC, with nearly a full day to spare before the flight. I'm sitting in a coffee shop in Union Square. Last time I was here I was twenty-one. I came to visit New York with a few girlfriends, celebrating someone's birthday in August. The place had been ninety degrees of steaming and the Square was covered in tourists draped across every patch of available greenery.

Today the view out the window couldn't be more different. Last night's storm has stopped, and because it's Sunday, there's hardly any traffic. My coffee shop is across from a dog park, and I've spent most of the morning watching the local hounds playing in the snow. The dogs don't care that the roads are blocked. They really aren't blocked any more, anyway. When I walked here, the snow drifted nearly up to my knees in places, but now I can see the guys at the big grocery store across the square are out clearing sidewalks. A few brave souls are even driving, leaving long brown tire trails in the white streets.

I've got something special lined up for tonight. Will share more when I can.

- ES

Comments: 1

SophiaSheridan, Chicago, USA:

Let me get this straight. Your trip to England is not just to get over a broken heart, or run away from a real job. (Yes, I found out you got fired. Paul went down and talked to your ex-boss.) So, instead of facing things like an adult, you have run away to chase a man. And not just any man. A fictional character.

You are chasing a fictional character?

Emma, I am really worried. Can you please call? Call collect. Any time. Really.

The bus ride from Philly to New York had been orders of magnitude easier than the last one. Crankiness was a good motivator, and my frustration at Paul and Sophia had made the ride further away from home a bit easier, I guess. That whole worry thing that she played up in the comment section? A ruse. She just wants me home, doing whatever qualifies as normal in her world. Looking after her cat. Available at her beck and call. Standing in as the object of comparison against whom she is never found wanting.

So, right now, maybe the Big Apple is just what I need.

I'd woken up that morning and realized it was my last full day of having a phone plan, so I girded my loins (and all my other body parts) and called my mother to say goodbye. My mom and dad live in Florida now. They took Freedom 55 retirement a few years ago, and Mom told my sister and me that she intends to spend our entire inheritance before she dies. Sophia cheered this wholeheartedly, because at 28 years old, she's already got her retirement looked after.

Me, not so much.

But I love my mom, and I want her to be happy. Florida makes her happy. It makes my dad sleepy, so that might be a part of it, too …

Besides, living in the same city, Sophia and my mom were always at each other's throats. Two alpha females—it was painful. When my mom moved to Anna Maria Island, it was great news for my sister. But I kinda miss her. And if she was on Team Sophia for this one, I wasn't sure what I'd do.

Strangely enough, though, she hadn't laughed at me when I'd given her the run-down on the trip. I was pretty sure Sophia had filled her in with the—ah—less palatable version, but she didn't really make reference to it. Just didn't sound surprised. And not only that—she told me she wished she'd done the same thing.

"Honey, an adventure is just what you need. You and Sophia are such different creatures. Don't let her talk you out of it, okay?"

So—okay, mom. Thanks.

The morning had left me feeling more optimistic. It might have been the good call with my mom, or maybe the snow-draped statues—I don't know. My black eye from bashing into the Philadelphia hotel bar chair leg was almost gone. I had considered investing in some cover-up, but decided against it as too frivolous. A couple of people had looked at me nervously on the bus trip, but if a purple ring around my eye is going to buy me a seat by myself on the Greyhound, then it's a price worth paying, sez I.

Since I'd talked to my mother, and when I wasn't staring out the window at dog frolic, I had been surfing the Internet. Turns out 'Jack the writer' knew what he was talking about. Beauchamp's Belles have a huge online presence, and have been around forever. Long before I discovered my first Jamie and Claire book, anyway. They hold regular meetings and seem to be an enthusiastic and fun-loving group. I'm sure the gathering in Philadelphia was just an anomaly. Or maybe the Philly group just liked their fun on steroids.

Nevertheless, I needed all the help I could get, and those people were experts. They knew every scene in the story—every nuance of every scene. Further investigation proved that the Belles had begun their life in Canada in the '90's. That kinda explained it all, really. Every Canadian I've ever met has been nuts.

So, there I was, safely in New York, with time on my hands. Nearly a full day before my plane was due to fly out to Glasgow. And, on my screen, a small window opened as a link from the Belles' site. Some kind of a Scottish time-travel reading event was listed—for that night. Apparently the happening was not an official Belle's event, but still noted in their Fan Fiction section.

My empty calendar had suddenly filled up. I needed to be there.

The reading was scheduled to take place in a library meeting room. After the time on the road, my wardrobe needed a little work to be library-suitable. My New York hostel supposedly catered to backpacking travelers, but … well, it was pretty sketchy. I'd been planning to wash my laundry out in the sink, but looking around the hostel gave me pause. It was the sort of place where you don't want to leave your unmentionables hanging on the towel rack of your room, if you know what I mean. My first assignment on arrival in Scotland may well have to be a search for a laundromat.

Still, I had enough clean clothes left to gussy myself up for the reading, and I set out with as much confidence as I could muster. Unfortunately, the subway in this city is not for beginners, and I took an A train when I was supposed to take an E. By the time I got to the library and found the right room, the reading was already underway.

It wasn't really what I expected.

I mean, I'm not sure what I had expected. I'd never been to a fan-fiction reading before. I'd gone to hear John Irving read a few years earlier at the University of Chicago, and I tried (and failed) to get into an event with Neil Gaiman last summer. They'd oversold the venue, so I stood outside with a bunch of black-clothes-wearing dudes with floppy hair, and listened to the man read on a crackly loudspeaker.

Obviously, my reading-attendance experience was not vast. So when I walked into the library meeting-room, and four sets of eyes turned from the woman speaking at the front to gaze at me, it was a little embarrassing.

"Sorry I'm late," I whispered.

No one replied. Three of the sets of eyes settled back on the speaker, who was the only person in the room to look delighted at my arrival. The remaining set of eyes belonged to a dude dressed—interestingly enough—in black, with floppy hair. He stared at me, and only at me, for the remainder of the event.

"Don't worry," the speaker said. "I'm only five pages in. You want me to start again?"

"Not unless you want …" I began, but a resounding chorus of "NO!" from the remaining attendees drowned out my voice. The speaker shot me a glare, all goodwill lost, and rattled her page.

"… her trembling fingers reached for his member," she read in clear, ringing tones.

I had a sudden flashback to Sharan Stone.

The guy in black with the floppy hair rubbed one hand on his knee and gave me a slow grin. His teeth were all filed into points.

I scooted my chair next to the lady with the knitting basket who had looked so disapprovingly at me over her red reading glasses as I entered. She rolled her eyes and sniffed at me, but her knitting needles poked comfortingly out of her bag. Just within reach, if I needed one.

The woman reading was very fond of her character's member. That particular usage of the word just kills me. I mean—his *member*? I am a member of the World Wildlife Federation. For a while there, I was even a member of a book club. The use of that word to describe a man's penis always, ALWAYS makes me laugh. So I sat with my fist pushed up against my mouth and endeavored to look studious.

The speaker finished her reading on what you might call a climactic high point, and then it was Knitting Lady's turn.

She swished up to the podium at the front, and spent a little time fussing with the mic. After a scream of feedback, she settled into place.

"Now, my story is nothing like the OUTLANDER series," she began. "It features a blonde young dentist named Carrie who travels back in time through a Scottish cave to meet Braveheart. She seduces him and brings him forward to the present day, and … well, just wait until you hear what they get up to next!"

Scary-tooth Floppy-hair Dude perked right up at the sound of the word "dentist," and raised his eyebrows at me a couple of times. I decided not to look his way for the rest of the event.

"Ach, lassie," intoned Knitting Lady from the podium, "let me show ye what a real Scotsman hides under his plaid."

The readings carried on for more than an hour. Scary-tooth Floppy-hair Dude was the only person, aside from myself, who didn't read to the group. Each excerpt was met by enthusiastic applause from the audience, and when one of the librarians came in near the end to say the doors were closing, she applauded the last reader, too. It clearly was a rousing success as an event.

I picked up my pack and was strategizing how to get out of the library without being followed by Scary-tooth Dude when Knitting Lady came over to stand beside me. She was carrying a coat and had donned an orange stocking cap with an enormous pompom.

"You're new?" she asked.

I nodded. Scary-tooth Dude had jammed a black wool hat on his head and was nonchalantly leaning against the doorframe. "I'm just here for—for research purposes," I said.

"Writing a book yourself, then?" she asked, her eyebrows drawing together. "We don't hold with stealing ideas around here."

I shook my head hurriedly. "No—no. Just uh—very interested in the OUTLANDER books," I replied. "I was just at a *Beauchamp's Belles* meeting in Philadelphia last week, and thought I'd come and check out your reading."

Her frown relaxed and she shouldered her arm into the sleeve of a giant blue parka. "Oh my gosh—that group in Philadelphia are wonderful, aren't they?"

I laughed, and it seemed to be all the answer she needed. She stuck out the hand that emerged from her parka sleeve. "Genesie Anderson," she said. "We generally go for coffee after our readings. Care to join us? You can tell us about the latest from Philadelphia."

"Oh, I'm not from …" I began, but then I realized Scary-tooth Dude had somehow managed to manifest himself right behind me.

"I'm heading uptown. Want to share a cab?" he whistled in my ear.

"Uh—no thanks. Going for coffee with the ladies," I said, and hurried out the door after Genesie.

Maybe if the coffee shop had still been open, things would have been all right. I'd just like to clarify right from the start here that I only had one glass of wine. It was a cheap Merlot (half price for ladies' night) and I only drank it to be polite.

Twenty minutes after the library doors closed, we were gathered around a small table in the hotel bar across the street, next to the coffee shop.

Did I mention *nothing* good happens in hotel bars? But the place didn't smell too badly of stale beer and was fairly deserted apart from our small group, so I wasn't too worried. What could go wrong?

The Lady of the Members who had been the first to read, and whose real name turned out to be Marlene, ordered an

Irish coffee. I picked the wine, because it was on sale. Another woman whose name I have forgotten asked for a regular coffee, black, which made me inwardly cranky, because I hadn't thought of it before ordering the wine. I mean, I'd made my escape from Scary-tooth Dude, and I just needed to stall for a few minutes to ensure he was really gone before heading back to the hostel. Coffee would have been perfect. AND cheaper. But the server disappeared before I could change my order.

Genesie regarded me seriously over the rim of her red reading glasses. I suddenly felt as though I was sitting an exam. A very important oral exam, for which I had forgotten to study.

"Where is Nigel?" she asked.

I racked my brain. "I—I don't remember a character called Nigel," I said. "Is he in THE SCOTTISH PRISONER? I've only read that one through once, and it was on a borrowed Kindle with half the screen that wouldn't light."

She shook her head at me and tut-tutted gently. "Nigel. From our group at the library. You must have seen him—black jacket and long hair?"

"Oh! The guy with the—ah—dental issues?"

The nameless lady leaned forward. "I think he has lovely teeth," she said, seriously.

Genesie rattled her needles at me. She'd knit two rows since we'd sat down.

"Nigel is a sweet young man. Writes very interesting stories, too—usually in the Harry Potter genre, but occasionally in the OUTLANDER universe. And we try never to judge based on appearance in this group."

"Perhaps he'll join us later," Marlene added placidly.

Right about then, Genesie ordered two tequila shooters, and the evening took on a dream-like quality from that moment onward.

"So," she said, clutching me by the arm after downing the first in a single gulp. "You're a fan of the OUTLANDER books, are you?"

As I nodded, the table fell silent. It was like the group was collectively holding its breath.

"Betcha like that Jamie Fraser, then, do ya?" she said, pounding the second tequila and waving her glass at the server in a smooth, practiced move.

I nodded again.

Genesie slammed her hand on the tabletop. "What—and I'm looking for details here, mind you—just WHAT do you think some fictional character like Jamie Fraser has over a REAL man like Braveheart?"

"I—he —I guess what I really like is the relationship he has with Claire," I stumbled. "I love Jamie because he is such a manly man. He's a man of honor, but the love he holds for Claire is what really touches me."

Marlene sipped her Irish coffee, oblivious to Genesie's change of state. "I do enjoy the OUTLANDER books," she said, "but only in the way one enjoys the pioneers within any milieu. Certainly the series opened a door to the Scottish Time Travel genre, but it remains for those of us who REALLY care about the field to polish and improve upon the genre."

"Scottish Time Travel … genre …" I said, slowly. I'd never heard the expression before, and the idea that anyone could improve upon Jamie made me want to laugh.

So I did.

Genesie's face turned an interesting shade of plum, beginning with her nose and slowly spreading outward. The server scooped up her empty shot glasses and replaced them with full ones. The yellow liquid danced in the light as Genesie threw the first one down her throat.

"You think something's funny?" she said to me, after she'd swallowed.

I shrugged back into the sleeves of my coat. It didn't seem like I'd be doing too much research here after all. "Well, yeah," I said, taking a reckless slug of my wine. If she could shoot her alcohol, so could I.

The problem wasn't so much the wine, as the candor that came along with it.

"I think the OUTLANDER books show Jamie as a man who all men could aspire to emulate. And I know a cop in Pittsburgh who agrees with me, too."

Genesie's voice dropped dangerously low. "He is no man," she snarled. "He is merely a *character*! The truth, no matter how you cut it, is that Jamie Fraser may have made a good lad in a story, but he never existed."

"I don't know," I said, the wine making me bold. "I'd like to believe there is a Jamie Fraser out there somewhere. In fact, I'm going to try to find him."

Genesie looked at me as if I was insane. "You're going to find someone who's never existed? That's ridiculous."

"Look—Jamie's more than a character to me. He's—he's like a sort of blueprint for what I'd like to find in a man. He's smart and heroic …" I struggled to put into words all that I was feeling, but she waved me down.

"Heroic? Emma, if you want a hero, you need only look to William Wallace. He was a *real* man. A true Scot. Just one look at those wild eyes, the blue woad on his face, avenging his family and his country—now THERE was a man of honor."

Marlene tilted her head. "You've got a point," she said. "That Mel what's-his-member *did* cut a fine figure in a kilt."

"Oh, you're talking about the movie?" I swallowed the last of my wine in a single gulp. "I don't think you can rely on that movie as a reliable historical source. I heard they got a lot of the details wrong. By contrast, I happen to know the Jamie and Claire books are scrupulously researched."

Genesie stood up so suddenly that her chair flew backwards onto the floor behind her. Her voice, after four shots of tequila, had taken on a certain movie-variety Gaelic twang. "Are ye questioning the director's histor-r-r-ical accuracy?" she roared.

Now, in just about any other circumstances, I would have indeed questioned that particular director's veracity on any number of fronts. But I am no fool. And at that moment, I was pretty sure I could see steam emerging from the ears of the enraged woman in front of me. Also? She was in possession of knitting needles.

She began pushing up her sleeves.

"I—uh—I'm sure Braveheart was tremendously, uh— Brave," I stammered, scrambling quickly to my feet. "From— from his heart."

"Couldn't find a cab," came a hissing voice from behind my left ear. "Who's up for Jello shots?"

I grabbed my backpack and fled.

Fans & Fiction…
2:30 pm, February 24
New York City, USA

So, it turns out Sophia and Paul are right.

I am a novice. A lightweight. An abject beginner. A loser who gets her details wrong. And I am chasing a man to whom I have no right.

But not because he belongs to Claire.

The woman who set me straight is named Genesie. She's a knitter who writes. I'm fairly certain she'll never read this post, but, if she does…

Well, here's to you, Genesie.

She's a complete expert on all things Scottish, with a particular major in Braveheart.

But right now I'm typing this on the subway on the way to the airport, and I don't like the way a guy down at the end of the car is eyeing my laptop. I'm going to be massively early for my flight, so maybe I'll find someplace to write the whole story out properly when I get there.

- ES

Comments: 2

HiHoKitty, Sapporo, Japan:

You crazy. Dream not crazy. I, too, wish marry Jamie. I envy you, Miss Emma.

SophiaSheridan, Chicago, USA:

Know what? Your single, obsessed fan is correct. You ARE crazy. What kind of weird person takes off on a trip halfway around the world in search of a **FICTIONAL BOYFRIEND?** Give your head a shake, Emma. You're pretty critical of Paul, but at least he's a REAL man. And you know what else? Paul, who is a much bigger person than you, says you need to educate yourself about Internet memes. This HiHoKitty person is playing you for a fool, as if you aren't enough of one already.

WHY WON'T YOU CALL ME????

Holy crow. I am all set to go, with a boarding pass in my pocket and everything. I'm actually doing this. I can't believe it.

I feel strangely calm. Of course, right after I got here and checked in, I threw up for about half an hour in the restroom. My cover story involved copious amounts of drinking while partying it up in Manhattan the night before, but strangely enough, no one asked.

It wouldn't have been a total lie, anyway. I've decided never to enter a hotel bar again.

Fear of Flying…
9:00 pm, February 24
John Fitzgerald Kennedy Airport, New York, USA

Things I have learned since this journey began.

1. I am not crazy. Or, at least less crazy than some.

2. There are many, many people out there who know an encyclopedic amount about the world of Jamie and Claire. Most of them are warm and wonderful, but it is quite clear I will never know all they know.

3. It is not ever a good idea to get into an argument with said well-researched people. I always lose.

Perhaps the next time I try something like this, I should keep it to myself. The public humiliation element is perhaps More Than I Bargained For. (Resulting also in my growing need to Excessively Capitalize Items of Importance.)

I really hope this information is helpful, because these are probably the final words I'll ever write.

My plane is due to board in five minutes.

And…and…I have a confession to make.

The truth is that I haven't actually taken an international flight since I was in high school, when my Spanish class flew to Barcelona for a week. My financial situation has kept my travel pretty local since then. Not to mention the whole freaked out about leaving home thing.

Yeah—you know that little issue I had on the bus to Philadelphia? I'm fairly certain the feeling of being strapped to a seat at 40,000 feet has not improved since high school.

My earlier sense of calm has vanished. I'm pretty much in a state of dry-mouthed fear. There is no way I am going to make it to Glasgow alive. I've written a goodbye note to my parents on the back of my boarding pass, but it's really small and I ran out of space before I got to my sister.

And besides, looking back over these blog posts, I'm worried I've left the impression that I don't like my sister.

Therefore, now, as I face my death at age twenty-nine and ten days, it is the time to get real. The truth is, I do NOT dislike my sister. We don't hang out much and we don't agree on anything, really, but I love her, and in the event of my demise it's important to me that she knows that.

She's my sister. I *have* to love her, right?

So, Sophia——I do love you. Even when you invariably notice the rip in whatever I am wearing. Even when you point out the bags under my eyes from staying up all night playing Xbox. Even when you criticize my current quest.

Okay. I've done it. I've said all I need to say. Now I can go to my end in peace. I wish I'd talked more to that writer Jack about Scotland when I had the chance in the cab. And it kind of kills me not to ever know what it's going to be like to be thirty. I've heard the thirties as a decade really kick ass.

Goodbye. I love you all. Remember me. Thank you for reading.

- ES

Comments: 2

HiHoKitty, Sapporo, Japan:

It so brave to fly to find Jamie in spite your fear. I read your earlier posts to my book club. We all behind you, Miss Emma.

ParisiansLovePipers, Paris, France:

We love Jamie, *et nous vous aimont trop,* Emma. *Bon voyage!*

Part Two: The Retracing

Fantastic Flight…
11:00 am, February 25
Edinburgh Airport, Scotland

I'm here.

Can you believe it?

I can hardly believe it.

I am **HERE**. That is to say, alive, and on the ground in Scotland. Tired, cricked-of-neck from sitting frozen with fear for over seven hours on the plane, but with a weird kind of adrenaline-optimism shooting through my veins. I actually made it.

Not quite to the correct city, however.

My Glasgow flight was redirected to Edinburgh, due to a massive snowfall. And it was even touch and go here in Edinburgh, with some talk of dropping us in Manchester. Apparently they are not used to big snowfalls here.

But the pilot came on the p.a. system, and said he was going to give 'er a go, and for the three thousandth time I closed my eyes and prayed to a God I don't really believe in, and sure enough— whatever he gave 'er actually worked. We didn't even slide sideways on the landing, or crash into a snowbank, or anything. Not sure that the conversation with God helped. (But if it did— thank You…)

So I am here in a teashop in the airport, eating my first Scottish—REAL Scottish—shortbread, and trying to take it all in. The air is alive with wonderful accents and I don't know if it's jetlag talking but I. Just. Feel. Wonderful!

Because of the change of city, I'm going for broke and actually booking a hotel online through Sizzlespot. I've likely lost my deposit at the Glasgow hostel, I guess, but maybe I can get a note from the pilot and get my ten pounds back.

A note from the pilot? Yeah, okay, so maybe it's jetlag after all. I don't care a bit. Once I get some sleep, I guess I'm actually going to make a few changes to my plan.

But for now, I'm sipping bitter tea—just like Murtagh would make it!—and grinning like a fool at everyone who passes.

I'm here. In the land of Jamie Fraser.

I love it already.

- ES

Comments: 2

SophiaSheridan, Chicago, USA:

Okay, Emma, I quit. I can't believe you've actually gone through with this. There's no turning back now, you know. No one is going to come rescue you when things go wrong. I can't imagine your money will last long, so we can talk about this when it runs out. Then we'll see if you remember my phone number.

JackFindlay, New York, USA:

Hey, Emma. Used the card you gave me to find your blog. This is quite an adventure you've planned! It's nice to find you online after the odd meeting in Philadelphia, and I'm chuffed to see you've made it safely. Looks like I'm following in your footsteps, as I'm now in New York City, en route to heading home myself in a few days. My editor feels the final draft of the project I'm working on needs a fact check, so that's my next job sorted. Maybe we'll cross paths again, but anyway, just wanted to say it was lovely to meet you, and I wish you luck.

Jack

A h, jet lag.
I'd heard tell of it, but waking at five the day after my flight arrived, I marveled that anything could make such an early riser of me. While no one in the B&B was stirring, I took advantage of the 'Wi-Fi-included' option that I hadn't had the pleasure of enjoying while staying at the American hostels, and read the most recent comments while my tea steeped.

I felt an odd wash of pleasure at seeing Jack's name. I'd forgotten I'd given him the card. This was followed by a complete wave of embarrassment. The nice journalist or writer or whatever he was who'd rescued me from the mob scene in Philly now knew all about my trip to chase down a fictional character. From his home country, no less.

To make the embarrassment go away, I re-read Sophia's comment five or six times before shutting the lid of my laptop. Nothing like the love and support one gets from family. And, yeah—that was nothing like it. After my trembling-on-the-edge-of-the-abyss love note to her, too!

Standing up, I peered out the window of the tiny room in the Edinburgh bed and breakfast house. It was dark as a cell in Wentworth prison outside, so I was unable to even discern what the weather was like, though I did quickly learn that standing anywhere near the window guaranteed a swirl of icy-cold air around the ankles.

I drew the curtains across the window, counting on the heavy Scots wool to cut the worst of the cold. The heater was cozy, the kettle was efficient, and the lady of the house had even left me a little plaid packet of shortbread. I wasn't really sure of the era of manufacture of said cookies—or biscuits, as they were called on the package. They might have been made ten years before, for all I knew. The wrapper looked suspiciously old-fashioned.

I ate them anyway. The way I saw it, if they were old, maybe they were time-travel cookies. That had to help on this trip, didn't it?

The truth was that I had just spent the only night I would be able to afford in such luxurious circumstances, low-season discount notwithstanding. I had survived the flight and my first night in this gloriously brisk and brilliant country, and it was time to put my plan into action.

Yes. THE plan.

The one where I was to journey to Scotland, blink my eyes fetchingly and immediately meet a rugged, red-heided Scotsman who would endure any amount of suffering to remain stalwart at my side.

Reality wrapped its cold fingers around my heart. The actual hard details of how I would find this man, and what I would do next remained decidedly unclear in my brain. I sighed, and leaned back against the wall, my sister's words echoing in my ears in the pre-dawn light. And hers was not the only voice I heard in the gray of that Edinburgh morning.

Sophia had told me I was an idiot on a wild goose chase. Sharan Stone had been strictly concerned with faux-Jamie genitalia. And Genesie had been right, at least about Jamie. He was fictional. I *knew* that. I did.

But I also knew that right up the street was an enormous castle looming over the city. And wild goose chase or not, I could hear it calling my name. I pushed all my doubts aside, gulped the last of my bitter tea, and headed out to find my fate.

Firth of Forth…
4:15 pm, February 26
Edinburgh, Scotland

Twelve hours, ten flights of stone steps, eight misheard conversations, six cups of coffee, four shortbread biscuits and two sore feet later, my first full day on the shores of the Firth of Forth is winding to a close. I mean, it is only just after five in the afternoon, but I am seriously toasted. Not sleeping on the plane didn't help. But know what?

I actually have a plan. A sleep-deprived, caffeine-overloaded, adrenaline-fueled sort of plan, but a plan, nonetheless.

Remember the map on the inside of my copy of OUTLANDER? Well, that day—the day of an event I try very hard not to recall—in Philadelphia, while the lineup to have our books signed snaked back and forth for more than three hours, I tried to trace out Claire's route, with a purple Sharpie I borrowed from the lady behind me in line.

Apparently she used it to write poetry.

Perhaps I shouldn't have chosen an implement that would bleed through to the dedication page. But no matter. Because the map is now indelibly written on my soul. Or, at least the soles of my shoes, since I think I'll be walking a whole lot more than Claire ever did. In the end, the map-making proved a little difficult, as I had trouble locating many of the places Claire visited, but I did my best.

So, though I do not have a stalwart horse, complete with kilted horseman to hand, nor even the modern equivalent of car and driver, and though the ground is covered in ice and not likely to offer the joy of a summertime stroll through balmy air, and even though Claire's route as mapped from the story is strangely convoluted and several of the locations are entirely fictional, none of these things will stay me from the swift completion of my appointed rounds.

Or round, technically.

Because that's what the plan is. A circumlocution of this lovely country in which I find myself, with significant stopping points as visited by one Claire Elizabeth Beauchamp Randall Fraser a mere 250 fictional years ago. At each of these stops, I shall leave no stone unturned in my search for a Jamie-like man of my dreams.

I have splurged on one more night at this whimsical Edinburgh B&B. I plan to eat all the biscuits, in spite of the fact that it will bring my total to six for the day, thereby ruining the mathematical rhythm of the opening sentence of this post. And tomorrow? First stop: Inverness. (Actually, my first stop will be the Edinburgh bus station.) Shortly thereafter followed by a visit to the city where Frank and Claire second-honeymooned before she made her life-changing journey. I've found a hostel near the center of town that boasts hot running showers.

What more can I ask?

- ES

Comments: 37

HiHoKitty, Sapporo, Japan:

Book club members SO excited you are in the land of Jamie and Claire, Miss Emma. We re-read OUTLANDER in your honor.

ParisiansLovePipers, Paris, France:

Nous retenons notre souffle... We hold our breath that you might travel safe. Drone on, Emma!

(Read 35 more comments here...)

I closed the lid of my computer feeling completely gobsmacked (a word I picked up at the train station here and plan to work into conversation as much as possible). It had taken me a full twenty minutes to read the comment section of my blog.

Twenty minutes, because, gosh, it appeared that HiHoKitty had a whole host of friends who were ardent fans of Jamie-san. The idea that thirty-six Japanese readers cared enough to comment left me feeling delighted and heartened. I'd even picked up what appeared to be a member of a marching pipe and drum band from France. Take that Sophia and Paul, you naysayers!

But hot on the heels of the flush of success came an unexpected feeling of responsibility.

When I'd begun the blog, it was more or less a means to keep me focused on the idea of finding my particular version of Jamie. Clearly, I hadn't really thought things through, as evidenced by my sister's disdain. But less than three weeks after starting the thing, it had become a kind of ... addiction.

Finding Fraser was supposed to be a personal diary to my inner self. But in a way, it had also become my sort of version of a Canterbury Tale, situated slightly further north and some six hundred years into the future. The only difference being the object of the pilgrimage; not so much the shrine of a saint outside a big church as a contemporary Scotsman ready to pledge his heart to an errant American girl.

Practically the same, really, wouldn't you say?

Fortunate Foreigner...
6:30 pm, February 26
Edinburgh, Scotland

I've recovered a bit after the long day, and decided in honor of my collection of blog friends, to summarize my trip to Edinburgh Castle.

The trip started poorly, mostly because the place was so freaking expensive. But when I dug out my old student card from the University of Chicago, the girl behind the glass took pity on me.

"Ach," she said. "This is three years expired, Miss." She looked around in both directions and leaned in on the crackly mic. "But seein' as it's the low season and all, and as there are no stewards on at the moment to tour you aboot, we'll go with the student rate, shall we?"

I beamed at her.

"Jes' spend the extra in the gift shop, love," she said, and slid the ticket through the slot in the window.

As I stepped away, I saw she'd slipped in a bonus voucher for a self-guiding audio tour.

Moments later, I clutched the audio guide to my bosom and scurried off before she could change her mind.

And the castle?

Blew my mind.

I stood inside the blue sentry box at the front gate, and looked down the road they call the Royal Mile. The air was crisp and wintery, but most of the snow was gone for the moment. The bits that remained were crushed into slush between the cobbles on the street. It stretched all the way down to the Scottish Parliament buildings, just about exactly a mile below, though I couldn't see them, because the road leading away from the castle was not exactly straight. I did get a glimpse of the roof of a church I had passed on the climb up, its spire now below me; black against the gray sky. I caught my breath from the hike up and thought about the more than two thousand years of history that lay under my feet.

Two *thousand* years. I had no idea. But according to my audio guide—and I held that audio guide in the greatest authority—there had been settlement on this rock since at least nine hundred years before anyone thought of following a star to see a baby in Bethlehem. The first fortress had been built on the rock sometime around 600 AD and its walls were mortared in time and blood.

It was breathtaking.

Determined not to let the girl at the entry booth down, I listened to every option on the headset. I walked through every storied room, stared at every tapestry, admired every sharpened death implement. In spite of no sleep on the plane and severe jet lag, I spent the entire day prowling the grounds. I stood under the razor-sharp points of the portcullis gate, grateful that the thing appeared to be stuck open. I leaned against the studded iron door. I caressed the cannons, and even wept a little over the graves of the garrison dogs, buried in a tiny section of garden.

I don't know what I expected, but those gray castle walls won my heart completely. I wandered every inch of the place.

If Jamie (or his doppelgänger) was anywhere to be found inside that monumental building, I would have found him.

He was not.

I did spend a lot of time smiling at Scottish men, but most of them just averted their eyes and scurried off. My flirting technique clearly needs work.

But tomorrow is another day, and for now I plan to seek my dinner somewhere near the Royal Mile. Goodnight all my wonderful new blog friends, and (since I am feeling generous) goodnight to you, too, Sophia. Next time we chat, I will be in Inverness, the Highland location of Frank and Claire's second honeymoon.

\- ES

Comments: 67

OzziGrrrl, Brisbane, Australia:

Cheerin' you on Emma——root them plaid laddies!

HiHoKitty, Sapporo, Japan:

All Scottish men wear kilts, yes? Or not in daytime?

SophiaSheridan, Chicago, USA:

Are you inventing these so-called followers, Emma? I wouldn't put it past you. Anything to prove a point. But fake followers are not going to help you find a job. Come home. And listen—— there's this cute guy working IT in Paul's office. He's an actual human being, Emma. Better than some Scottish figment of your imagination, right? Come home.

(Read 64 more comments here…)

I thought long and hard about heading out for food after writing the last post. The lack of sleep and the over-abundance of exercise had combined to make me feel like a zombie. But in the end, the idea of eating yet another packet of shortbread cookies drove me out the door. The little bed and breakfast I was staying in was located in what the Edinburghers called the Old Town, just up the hill from the train station on Princes Street.

That was, apparently, to distinguish it from the New Town, which was the part of the city below the castle. The New Town was first built before America was a country, and once I knew that, it pretty much gave me a sense of the way Scots view the passage of time.

From the guide on my bedside table, it looked like all the cheapest places to eat were to be found in the New Town, just down the hill. It was a decent walk from my place, and after six hours of climbing stone steps and slithering along icy cobblestones, my legs and feet were just about done in. I had no idea if a bus could even take me in the right direction, and cab fare would have been five pounds at least.

I learned this because I asked the lady who took my audio guide back at the castle gate.

So, as I slid out of my little bed and breakfast place onto the Royal Mile, I steeled myself to pay the cab fare. But it was nearly seven-thirty, and night comes early to the gray Scottish lowlands. There was not a taxi to be seen in the dark. A block or two down, the road intersected with another that appeared to wind down toward Princes Street, and I headed that way on my very sore feet.

On the winding road however, my luck turned and I spotted a small pub, from which emanated the sounds of joy and frivolity. Surely they would have a phone I could call a cab from?

In I went.

It turned out the price of a beer was less than half the cost of a taxi ride to the New Town.

I learned this, because I asked the lady taking beer orders behind the bar.

As I sank down on what appeared to be the only open seat in the place, my feet screamed in relief. Or they would have, if they'd had little mouths. Which they did not, I'm grateful to say, because how weird would THAT have been?

The server who had so generously told me the relative price of beer and taxi cabs reappeared seconds later with a golden glass of ambrosia in her hand.

My table was a tall one and had a dangerous tilt to it, which may have explained why it was unoccupied. I leaned back against a wall in the corner and slipped off one of my boots. By the time I'd taken the first few sips, I'd forgotten that I didn't generally like beer, and had been transported into the strange euphoria of exhaustion, hunger and the ecstasy that came of being able to rub one's sore foot in secret under a table in a Scottish pub.

I decided to sit there for a bit and soak in the atmosphere, listening to Edinburghers enjoy their end-of-workday cheer; and when my feet had sufficiently recovered, I'd walk down the hill to find someplace to eat.

The plan was somewhat thwarted, though, when I knocked my entire beer into my lap.

In truth, it wasn't totally my fault. I'd been watching the ruddy nape of a neck at the table beside me and idly wondering if Jamie would drink beer in a place like this—if he lived in the present day, of course.

Whoever the guy with the ruddy neck was, I could only see the back of his head. It was a nice head. Well-shaped, and covered in a thick thatch of dark blonde hair, lighter at the tips and gelled a bit northward, from the looks of things. His shoulders were square under the cover of a heavy cable-knit sweater, and he was enjoying the company of a sweet young thing, very blonde and blue-eyed. His hand lay proprietorially on her arm as they talked.

A dark-haired girl beside the blonde who was quite clearly the worse for the wine she'd been drinking suddenly shrieked with laughter. "Ye slay me, Laoghaire," she cried, practically snorting wine out of her nose. "Ye fookin' slay me!"

Okay, okay, so I *know* she wasn't really saying "Laoghaire". *Lawrie* vs *Leery*, right? But, still, it's pretty close.

Close enough to make a person jump a little, bump the wobbly table and maybe spill their beer into their lap. I managed to grab the glass as it teetered, but not before half the contents washed in a golden wave that shone briefly in the low light of the pub before soaking the entire crotch of my jeans.

I may have let out a little cry of despair.

But I have to say, in retrospect, that this wasn't all bad. Because the young man Not-Really-Laoghaire had been talking to thought it was his fault.

One minute I was staring in disbelief as my only pair of jeans—with me in them—took on a look usually associated with severe incontinence. And the next, a large young man was swabbing my leg dry.

Very large.

With fair hair that might have been reddish before it was highlighted.

I had barely a moment to think that this was the closest thing I'd had to a sexual experience with a man in more than a year, when he spoke. "Ach, I'm so sorry, Miss. My chair must've hit your table …"

"It's—it's okay," I said, unwilling to cop to the fact I'd spilled my own beer onto my own self. "It's a wobbly table," I added, in a tiny concession to honesty.

He paused at the sound of my voice, handful of soggy napkins in midair. "Ach, worse still—and you a visitor, too." His forehead crumpled with concern.

"Really, it's okay. It woke me up. I'm massively jetlagged, and I need my senses about me to make it back to the place I'm staying."

"That may be true," he said, his big brown eyes boring into mine. "But let me at least buy you another beer."

I shook my head, but he was already waving at the server. She waved back and he placed his large hands on the table and shook it critically.

"Righ'," he said. "I'll just have a look …" and vanished beneath the table.

In a second he bobbed up again. "That's seen it," he said. "The ol' beer mat solution."

I peered into the gloom under the table, and sure enough, he'd folded a couple of cardboard coasters and jammed them under one of the table legs. I gave the table a shake. "I think you've got it."

He smiled and blinked both his eyes at me. "Trust me, Miss," he said. "Ah'm a mechanic."

I laughed. "Really?"

"That I am. And you—are an American. Are ye a student?"

I nodded, and glanced over his shoulder. The two girls he was with seemed oblivious to the fact he'd moved over to sit beside me. They were deep in conversation; the dark-haired girl who had, just seconds before, been shrieking with laughter was now openly weeping, eyeliner streaking down her face.

"Yes, American, but not a student. Just here visiting for a while. Is—is your friend okay?"

He waved a dismissive hand. "Ach, she's no' really my friend. Friend of a friend, yeh ken? And a wee bit pickled for my tastes, for all that. But tell us about yerself—whereabouts in America are ye from? New York City?"

"Chicago, actually. It's further …"

"West. Yeah, I know it. Jazz and blues, Charlie Parker and the Bulls."

I ogled him. "You follow basketball? I thought it was only soccer over here—and cricket."

He looked pained, and slapped a hand to his heart. "Ach, don't paint us with that brush. Pansy Englishmen's game, that one. Now, rugby—there's a game a man can sink his teeth into. But yeah, next to rugby, it's the NBA all the way for me."

He leaned back on his stool and looked at me appraisingly. If I hadn't been sleep-deprived and stinking of beer I probably would have fainted on the spot, but even as it was, I had to fight the urge to lick him. Tall, fair hair in an over-grown crew cut, warm brown eyes. The sleeves of his sweater were rolled back over well-muscled forearms. The server returned and dropped two fresh beer mats on the table, followed by a replacement of my half pint and a pint of Guinness for him. He held up the beer to me.

"To Michael Jordan and charming American visitors," he said.

I tried to look away from his forearms and clinked his glass with my own.

"So, what is it ye do in Chicago, Miss Yankee?"

"I—uh ..." I began, stalling a little, when suddenly the dark-haired girl's streaked face appeared over the shoulder of my new tablemate.

"Hhayymissshhhh," she said, draping herself across his back and wrapping her arms around his neck. "We're lonely, man. Who's your new friend?"

He shot an irritated look at her and pushed her arms off his shoulders. "Eilidh, behave yerself. We've an American guest here—first day, aye?"

I nodded. Eilidh looked unhappy at being pushed aside. "Ach, another tourist, no doubt."

She leaned on the table and waved a finger in the direction of my face. "I deal with the likes of you all shummer," she said, a trifle blearily. "I do the ghosht tour out of the Cathedral on the Mile. Twishe a day—three times on Shundays. All day every day, Americans, Japanese and the damned Germans. Always the damned Germans."

The very cute Scottish guy scowled at her again, and toyed with one of the beer coasters. He had a working man's hands, red and rough, but his nails were clean. His finger traced the logo on the coaster.

"Eilidh ..." he repeated, warningly, but she ignored him, shaking her head sorrowfully.

I held my breath to see if she would cry again, but her mood shifted abruptly and she brightened.

"It'sh only once a week, now though. Off sheason." She pointed the finger at me again. "Are ye comin' out to join us this week, then? We could use the coin."

Both sets of eyes turned to me, but the coherence that had returned with the beer dousing had begun to fade. "I—I'm not sure ..." I began.

"Jeremy's here, Hamish."

It was the blonde girl. Laoghaire. Laurie. My head was spinning with beer and tiredness.

"Just texted, he's stopped out front. We've got to be off."

The cute guy's face fell. "Ach thought we were stayin' for the karaoke," he said, patting his pocket. "Ah've got mah set list all ready—Mellencamp, The Boss, Marvin Gaye."

He leaned against my arm. "No one can beat my version of 'Sexual Healing," he said, waggling his eyebrows.

My internal organs rearranged themselves spontaneously.

"I'd—I'd like to hear that," I managed.

Laurie tucked her arm under one of Eilidh's and gazed impassively at me.

The cute guy—Hamish—shot me a crinkled, perfect and slightly regretful grin as he stood up. "Lovely talkin' to yeh," he said. "But I need to hop this pink Cadillac. I'd stop longer, but it's my only hope of a ride north, sadly."

My brain and body began to work in concert at last. "You're not leaving?" I began, but he didn't hear me.

He took Eilidh's free arm and circled around to lead her toward the door.

"*Hitchin' a ride*," she sang into his face, and giggled.

"Nice to meet you," I called out, a little desperately. I tried to get to my own feet, but my stool was jammed in behind the no-longer-wobbly table.

The blonde shot me a look over her shoulder at the sound of my voice. "Another American, eh, Hamish?"

She and Eilidh roared with laughter as they stepped out onto the street.

And that's how I met—and lost—my Jamie Fraser on the very first day in Scotland.

Fumbling Fraser...
9:00 am, Feb 27
Somewhere in the wilds of Scotland, North of Edinburgh

As you can see from the header, I've not quite made it to Inverness yet. As it turned out, the cheapest bus ticket to Inverness is what you might call a milk run. We stop at sixteen hamlets along the way. Choosing to look at the bright side, however, this allows me the opportunity to use the Wi-Fi provided on the CityLink bus and post to my blog.

I've also got the freedom to gaze out the window in search of red-heided warriors, and try not to think too hard about the one I met so briefly in Edinburgh.

It is to weep.

– ES

Comments: 43

HiHoKitty, Sapporo, Japan:

Miss Emma! How can you not say the whole story? Agony in my heart!

Burns' Bairns, Victoria, CA:

Checking in at a very late hour from the Wet Coast of Canada to cheer you on, Emma. Our poetry collective are all huge Jamie and Claire fans. Last night we toasted your journey with a dram and the leftover haggis from Burn's Night. *Slainte!*

(Read 41 more comments here…)

It had been pitch dark as I made my way along the street to the bus station the morning after losing my Fraser. Turned out there was a direct train from Waverly, Edinburgh's main train station, but at double the price of the bus ride, and after an unplanned two-night stay in Edinburgh, my finances were feeling stretched. Heading north at seven am by bus was my only option if I wanted to make it all the way while it was still daylight. When I checked the map, it looked like a fairly short distance compared to the journey from Chicago to New York. But even with no stops along the way, it would still be nearly a four-hour trip.

I slumped into my seat and dozed for a while, and then surfaced long enough to post the brief note to my blog. I tried several times to find the words to write more, but they just wouldn't come. The truth was, I mostly mulled over the loss of the cute guy. Already, in my mind's eye, I could see his face bathed in a kind of golden glow. Fair hair just verging on scruffy, and his crinkly smile as he sat down to talk with me. Apart from the whole blonde highlights thing, he was physically very similar to Jamie.

Kind. Considerate. Very, very cute. A spasm of something akin to pain shot through me at the thought that I hadn't even offered to stay connected by email.

I mean—it's not like I was about to hand him my card.

But there in the cold, hard light of a Scottish spring morning, on the bouncy back seat of a CityLink transit bus, the memory of the fleeting feel of those long, square fingers as they brushed mine was still enough to make my knees weak. I stared out the window into the darkness, feeling my face suffuse with heat. *Get a hold of yourself, Sheridan.*

The bus shuddered and lurched around a corner, and slowed to a stop at the on-ramp to the freeway – the MOTORway.

He was just a nice young man, welcoming a visitor to his country, I thought, brooding.

With his well-muscled forearms.

Reaching down, I yanked my pack onto my knees. I needed to think of something else. Time to look at the map again. I had just pulled out my copy of OUTLANDER from the bottom of the front pocket, when I felt someone slide into the seat beside me.

A merry face, creased as an old tortoise and topped with a greasy brown abomination of a hat, smiled into mine.

"Here from awa'?" he inquired, indicating the map inside the book with a nod and gently spraying my face with spittle.

I nodded back and fished a suspiciously crumpled napkin from my pocket to use when the old fellow turned away.

He didn't.

I smiled damply back at him, and scrunched a little further down into my seat as he began to stub his thick finger onto locations on the map and narrate the entire history of Scotland, beginning with the Picts.

Inverness in February is … well, safe to say it's pretty gray. Strangely enough, it was not terribly cold. Not seventeen-blocks-in-wintery-Philadelphia cold, at least. But now that I knew the complete history of the place from its role as an early stronghold of the Picts, through the likely-less-evil-than-Will-Shakespeare-would-have-had-you-believe reign of MacBeth, to the current standing of the Caley Thistle football club, it almost felt like I was returning home.

My seatmate, Alan MacLeod by name, squeezed my shoulder fondly as the bus slowed to a halt outside a downtown hotel.

"Ye know where to find me, lass, if ye have any questions. And mind ye keep that wee card…" he nodded at the scrap of paper I had safely clutched in one hand. "Jes' gi' us a call if ye need transport anywhere, mind. As I tole' ye, mah youngest son's got a Triumph he's fair proud of, and he hires himself out all the time ta tourists in the season who need tae get to the golf links hereabouts."

"Thank you, Mr. MacLeod. I'll remember that."

He reached a hand up to grasp the seat back, and groaned as he hauled himself to his feet, but the pretty much tooth-free smile never left his face. "Ach, it's just Al, lassie, or Alan if yer feelin' formal. Call anytime, love."

And with that, he stumped off up the aisle of the bus to the front door. I glanced down at the card in my hand. *Alec MacLeod*, it said. *Hired Car Service, Inverness-shire. Taxi, weddings, evenings out. No trip too small!*

Could Alan's taxi-driving son be another possible Jamie? I tucked the card into my pack and followed him off the bus.

Further Fieldwork…
5:00 pm, February 27
Inverness, Scotland

Arrived safely in Inverness.

The trip was much less eventful than earlier bus journeys, thankfully. I had a very informative seatmate who ensured I will never confuse Jacobians with followers of anyone but King James again! Perhaps the history lesson has cured me of my fear of traveling? I think it more likely that now I am here, in beautiful wintery Scotland, my sense of adventure has stepped back into the lead.

Thanks to all who wrote such kind comments about my time in Edinburgh. Many of you are worried I met and lost my Jamie Fraser on the first day in Scotland, and that I will quit trying. I want to set your minds at ease.

First of all, the man I met was blonder than Jamie. He might have been roughly the same size, and was quite kind and friendly—but—but, he's gone, okay? He's too blonde and he's gone and I have no idea where he lives. Think of him as a practice Jamie. I'm moving on, and I hope you'll do the same.

For now, I turn my attention to Inverness, the land of Frank and Claire's second honeymoon. The true beginning point of Claire's story. A chance for me to find the stones she walked through.

I promise to report in!

- ES

Comments: 15

MagischeSteinkraus, Berlin, Deutchland:

Sounds like a good German boy. *Hier finden Sie ein weiteres Jamie!*

HiHoKitty, Sapporo, Japan:

Did false-Jamie wear kilt, Miss Emma? How you find REAL Jamie?

KnittersNotQuitters, Corner Brook, NL&L, Canada:

Huge Claire and Jamie fans here in the wilds of Newfoundland. Hoping you find your boy, and knitting up a special scarf in honour of your journey!

SophiaSheridan, Chicago, USA:

I just want you to know that, of all the humiliations you have foisted on this family, this is the greatest. I only hope and pray our parents stay ignorant of this little experiment until it dies a righteous and terrible death.

(Read 11 more comments here...)

I tried to ignore Sophia's comment and focus on all the others cheering me on. But it was hard. Mostly because she was right. This was an exercise in public humiliation, no doubt. But it was far less painful than Internet dating had been. There, I'd even had to put a picture of myself online, and answer hideously embarrassing questions for the whole world to see. The whole dating world, anyway. In the end, all I got out of it was a husband who lasted just over a year—two, if you count the cyber-courtship period.

But it got me thinking. Until then, I'd thought of my blog as little more than an online diary of an adventure. Reading all the comments, though... HiHoKitty was certainly taking me seriously. And from what I'd learned from Genesie, nothing could be more serious to a knitter than designing a pattern.

It kinda blew my mind. If the blog was giving inspiration to others to go out and follow their dreams too—what could be the harm in that? Maybe it was time I started to take it more seriously.

So I pushed Sophia's voice to the back of my head and spent the next two weeks exploring every nook and cranny of Inverness.

I prowled through the quiet aisles of St. Andrew's Cathedral, with its strangely capped spires and beautiful stained glass. I laughed at the practical Scots, converting the rusty red Inverness Castle into contemporary use as a Sherriff's court. I spent days wandering the winding streets, in the rain and sleet, peering into the windows of tiny B&Bs hunting for ladies who looked like Claire and Frank's housekeeper Mrs. Baird.

Found lots of them, too.

But any evidence of Claire and Frank themselves was nowhere to be found. And on top of that? My cheap accommodation evaporated.

Football Fellas…
3:00 pm, March 14
Inverness, Scotland

In light of reader HiHoKitty's recent question, I've decided to open this post with a few words of wisdom on the subject of meeting Scottish men in the wild. In the spirit of full disclosure, I am forced to report that no, they do not wear kilts all of the time. [I would, however, be first in line to suggest that possibility, should a national referendum on the subject ever arise!] I am trying to not get caught up in cultural stereotyping of this particular sort. So far, the kilted Scotsmen I have come across have been strictly of the 'piping for the tourists' variety. This time of year is not a big draw for visitors from afar, so even those have been few and far between.

Rest assured, HiHoKitty, that I have, however, greeted every kilted man I have seen with a smile. Most of them have found it hard to smile back with the blowpipe in their mouths, but I remain hopeful.

I feel that the most important advice I can offer for travelers who seek to meet others is to set aside your computer and get out among the people. Situate yourself in locations where locals gather. Do a speed-dating event, if one is nearby!

In travel news, I've been staying in an awesome little hostel that was dead empty, because, as noted earlier, there aren't too many tourists strolling through the Highlands in March. The 'no tourist' situation has been definitely to my benefit, though, since the proprietors let me stay for five pounds a day, as long as I didn't eat. But apparently the local rugby club, Craig Dunan, has decided to put on a clinic, and players from a bunch of nearby towns are all converging on Inverness. The hostel manager said she felt bad, but she couldn't turn down the money from such a big group.

Anyway, I've seen all I can in town here, so it's time to turn my attention to finding Claire's standing stones at *Craigh na Dun*. I can't find a reference to precisely where the stones are in my copy of OUTLANDER, but at least from the name of the rugby team, they *must* be nearby.

Wish me luck!

- ES

HiHoKitty, Sapporo, Japan:

In the story, Mister Crook drive Claire on his motor-cycle a leisurely jaunt from Mrs. Baird's house. I am not sure how distant is a 'jaunt', but I think *Craigh na Dun* must not be far away. Luck to you, Miss Emma. Luck!

(Read 32 more comments <u>here</u>...)

B y the time I'd found a new hostel and sorted out my room, it was 'half five' according to the landlady, and I was starving. She tore a map of the city off the top of the pad on the check-in desk and directed me to a pub a couple of blocks away. This new hostel was going to cost me double what the last one had, but there was nothing to be done about it. At least it was a private room. I stepped inside long enough to dump my extra clothes onto the bed and then headed down the street to find food.

The rain seeped into my collar, so I yanked up my hood and thought about my blog post as I walked. In spite of my advice to HiHoKitty and the others, I was pretty certain there would be zero opportunities for speed dating in Inverness. The thought occurred to me that my friend Jazmin would have organized a speed-dating event with the rugby team. For the first time, I was suddenly grateful to be on my own.

It was early for dinner, so I managed to find a table in a dark corner. I'd noted with a brief, hungry burst of joy that there was a small 'Wi-Fi available here' sticker on the door, so by the time my sausages and chips arrived I was all set up with my browser open to the Tourism Scotland page. Next to it, my copy of OUTLANDER was propped against a bottle of something called 'brown sauce'. I turned to look at the map page inside the cover.

I searched until the last sausage was just a greasy memory on my plate, but I could not find a set of standing stones near Inverness that remotely matched the description of *Craigh na Dun*.

My eyes burned a little from staring at the screen so long.

"D'yeh mind if I sit here?" said a voice beside me, and I looked up to see a good-looking young guy with a tall sleeve of beer in each hand.

This was the first time I'd lifted my head from the computer screen since the server had brought my food, and I noticed with some embarrassment that the place had pretty much filled up since then. I was the only person hogging a four-seat table to myself.

"No—no, go right ahead," I said, flustered, and yet flattered at the same time that the offer to share a table had come with a beer. "I'll just move my stuff over."

"Nae need, nae need," the guy said. "I'm meetin' a mate here. We can both squeeze in and ye'll niver notice us."

Ah. So much for the free beer, then. Still, I smiled at him and wedged myself further into the corner of the bench seat. I slipped the book into my pack and slid it down onto the floor between my feet.

"Verra kind of yeh, Miss. Are ye a student over from America, then?" he asked, sitting on the bench beside me and placing the spare beer on the table across from us.

I closed the window to my blog page and shook my head. "Just a blogger," I said, and then because he appeared to be waiting for more, I added, "here doing some research."

He leaned back in his seat, nodding sagely. "Ach, yeah. I'm a big fan o' blogs. I read 'em all—news, sport, you name it. Yeh must give me the location of yours so I can read all about it."

At least he wasn't laughing at me. *And* he was pretty cute. I decided to risk a question. "Do you know anything about the history of the area? I'm looking for a set of standing stones that should be not too far away."

"Standing stones?" His face creased in thought. "Well— there's the stones at Balnuaran of Clava, up past Culloden. They circle an ancient gravesite."

I shook my head. "No, the ones I'm looking for should be on the side of a hill, in an area that was once wooded—I'm not sure if there are still trees there now."

"A hill, yeh say ..." He thought for a moment before taking a long swallow of beer. "Yeh know, my mate may be able to help yeh. He's an expert in everything. Won't be but a minute more."

"Okay," I said, and closed the screen of my laptop. My hopes of getting any work done were fading with each sip of beer he took. I finished my own cranberry juice and wondered if *he* could be my Jamie. A bit on the short side, but he seemed nice enough.

Clearly reading my thoughts, he stuck his hand out, his broad smile only slightly marred by a missing tooth in front.

"Name's Craig," he said. "And you are ...?"

"Emma," I said.

"Nice to meet yeh, Emma the American," he said. "And now, since I have the bladder of a wee girl, I'll be off to th' bogs. Keep an eye on me mate's pint, wouldja? Allus late, that lad."

As he walked away, I took the opportunity to slip my computer into my pack. It had become pretty noisy and crowded in the pub and was obviously not the place to do a little quiet planning. I was just sliding out of the corner when I felt a hand on my arm.

"D'ye trrrust me?"

An extremely small man stood beside my seat. His eyes didn't meet mine, but glared straight forward, which meant they were glued to my chest.

"D'ye trrrust me, lassie?" he repeated.

"I—I ..."

Craig walked back up, regarding us with a twinkle in his eye.

"Ah, Emma—I see ye've met Rabbie. Rabbie Rowanby, meet Emma the American."

The small man's hand remained in my face, so I leaned backwards and shook it weakly.

"The name's Rowanby by birth," he confided. "But everyone knows me as Rabbie the Gnome."

He smiled, favored me at last with a straight look in the eyes and hoisted himself up into the seat by the beer, which was thankfully across the table. Unfortunately, Craig slid back in beside me, effectively blocking any easy exit.

"Another pink drink for the lady," cried Rabbie, and then reached across the table to take my hand again.

Craig leaned over and poked him in the chest and I took his instinctive recoil as an opportunity to pull my hand out of his grasp.

"Never trust this man," Craig intoned.

Rabbie glared at him a moment and then the two of them broke into helpless laughter.

I leaned back against the seat and took a sip of the drink that had magically appeared in front of me. This cranberry juice had added to it a generous helping of something that tasted distinctly of alcohol.

I smiled as Craig chuckled his way through an explanation of what a true, old and dear friend Rabbie was. The individual in question was still doubled over, laughing.

I guess one beer goes a long way in a small man.

"Rab, Rab—ge' aholda yersel', man," spluttered Craig at last. "Now, this young lady is lookin' to find hersel' a set of nearby standin' stones on the side of a hill. Have yeh go' any ideas?"

"Ach, yeh can have a look at me own stones, lass," Rabbie replied, reaching under the table. "Fair fine they are, with one standin' tall between 'em right now!"

I tried desperately to unhear that sentence.

"Rabbie Rowanby, behave yersel'," scolded Craig. "This young lady has been kind enough to share her table wi' the likes of us. There's no need fer that sorta language."

The tiny man's face puckered in an entirely insincere expression of apology. But as much as he turned his mouth down, he could not still the evil twinkle in those eyes. I scootched a little further into the corner.

"Ah, yer right as allus, Craigy-boy. I see a beautiful woman and I cannae help mesel'."

He tapped a blackened fingernail against his chin. "Hmmm. To tell yeh the gospel truth—and I seen me share of faerie rings around the north—there ain't any circles on hillsides I can recall. Now, doon Fort William way, there's a couple a beauts, mind ..."

My bladder, by that time filled not only with my own cranberry juice, but also with this newer, strangely tastier concoction, suddenly made itself known to me. And as it did, the light dawned.

"Excuse me," I muttered, head down. "Just have to go to the ladies'."

Craig had to stand to allow me out. Rabbie jumped out of his own seat and advancing his leg, made a deep bow as I slid out of the booth.

"Jes' round the corner, there," he said, helpfully. And then not so helpfully: "Ye mus' have a bladder o' steel, lass! I'd a been t' the bogs twice wi' the amount of drink ye've got down yer gullet!"

I dashed to the washroom, the feeling of relief at escaping only mildly tempered by my own maybe less than steel-like capacity. There had to be a back door to this place—I could leave Craig and Rabbie to briefly mourn my passing before hitting on the next single woman they could find.

It wasn't until I was washing my hands that I realized I'd left my backpack at the table.

"Hey, yer hoggin' the sink, there. You mean tae vomit or summit? Ye look pale as a wee ghostie." A blonde with half her head shaved and the other half in purple streaks finally sighed impatiently and elbowed me out of the way.

"No—I'm fine, fine ..." I stammered, and jumped to one side. The paper towel bin was empty so I shook my hands off (which earned me yet another dirty look from Scottish Goth Girl), and headed back in.

The two men were deep in discussion when I arrived back at the table.

"An' the craic is," Rabbie said, his face pushed right across the table into his friend's, "her feet are bound so tightly they practically form a perfect hole."

He had his fingers held up in an 'OK' sign, which he quickly dropped when he realized I was standing there.

"Oh, ye know—all girls are lovely," he said, quickly. "Chinese, American—what's the difference, right? I love 'em all." He smiled into my eyes. "Truly, I do."

"I've got to get going," I said, hastily. "Thanks for the drink."

"Nae, nae—ye cannae leave yet," cried Rabbie. He slid over, and I could see my backpack sitting there on the bench seat. One quick grab and I could be off. "Look—here's another drink jes' waitin' for ye. One fer the road, aye?"

I leaned in to put a hand on my backpack and found myself bodily hauled back into my seat. That Wee Rabbie had some decent upper body strength.

I wilted into my seat and had a sip of the new drink, which, strangely enough, tasted even better than the last.

Upper body strength and magic potions—what was up with this guy, anyway?

"So," he said, placing both his hands cozily over mine. "As a woman, you might know this. Have yeh heard of anything more effective than a vinegar bath for chlamydia? Itches like hell, mind."

Just then, a dark-haired girl pushed her way passed our table, drink in one hand and backpack slung over her shoulder. Desperate, I hatched an instant, if slightly alcohol-befuddled plan. "Susan!" I called out to the woman. "Oh my god! I can't believe it's you!"

She kept walking, clearly having not heard me and focused on finding a spot to set her drink. It didn't matter.

"Sorry, guys—it's been … uh—fascinating—talking with you, but I've got to go." I stood up as much as the table would allow and leaned on Rabbie's chair a little.

His eyes lit up, and he peered at the back of her head as she walked deeper into the pub. "Ye know her, do ye? Well, invite her to sit with us! We can make room." He pushed his chair over, effectively blocking Craig from having any space to let me out. My heart sank. I started to babble.

"Oh, no—it's fine, really. She's—she's my cousin. I haven't seen her for years. I didn't know she was even in the country."

"No worries—she's welcome," he insisted, and then yelled "SUSAN!!!!" across the bar in a voice guaranteed to stop any sexually transmitted disease in its tracks. The entire pub actually fell silent for a moment as everyone turned to look at the source of the bull-sized bellow.

Everyone except the woman with the backpack.

"She's deaf," I said, and gave a single desperate hip check to my pack. It ricocheted uselessly off one of Rabbie's stevedore arms, but his beer slid perilously close to the edge of the table and he leaned forward to steady it.

That was all I needed. I pulled my knees up to my chest, planted my feet on the bench seat and vaulted over his head.

I cleared him by a full foot, I swear.

"Very, very deaf," I repeated, as if nothing had happened. "I'll just go catch up with her and bring her back to the table, okay?"

The surrounding pub noise rose up again, once it became clear there was no fight or other interesting occurrence about to break out. Both men beamed amiably and clinked glasses.

"Ach, that's brilliant, Craigy-boy," Rabbie said cheerfully. "Now there'll be one for *you* to take home tonight wi' ye, too."

He stood up in his seat and craned his neck back at her. "Look at that dark hair! She's not Chinese, is she?" he asked, hopefully.

I turned my back and fled.

Clutching my pack to my chest, I pushed through the crowd toward the back of the bar. My knee was killing me, having bashed it on the table as I took the leap, but I considered it a war wound, and well worth the outcome.

The young woman with the backpack had disappeared, but the girl who had served our drinks earlier was standing beside the bar, loading beer onto her enormous tray.

"Is there a back way out of here?" I hissed in her ear.

She grinned. "Had enough of our Mister Rowanby, have ye?"

I shot her a pleading look.

"Righ'. No' that I blame ye—he's a bit much to handle, sometimes. But ye likely should know…" she leaned over and whispered in my ear. "Forget the whole 'gnome' thing. He's also known as 'Rabbie the tripod,' and for good reason, luv."

She grinned at my look of horror. "Righ', righ'—I see he's no' for you. No worries. Just past the bogs there's a door marked 'private'. Inside's a flight o' stairs. Beneath the landing is another door that'll lead you out to the lane."

I dropped a two-pound coin on her tray. "Thank you!"

"Ta, yerself. And mind you don't go up them stairs. Office is up there, and I'll catch hell if any of the brass sees yeh, aye?"

"Got it. And thanks again."

She rolled her eyes. "Ach, you aren't the first and ye won't be the last to need an escape route from wee Rabbie. For all his endowments, the man's a menace to anything with a vagina."

"Or a bound foot," I muttered, as I pushed my way toward the door and my freedom.

It was slightly less crowded at the back of the pub, but even so, the door was located in such a dark corner it was hard to see. When I shook the handle, it felt like it was locked. I looked over my shoulder to see the server in conversation with Rabbie. Then they turned and looked right at me. I grabbed the handle with both hands and yanked it with all my strength.

The door swung open and I threw myself inside, only to come face-to-face with the brunette woman with the backpack, just coming down the stairs. She was no longer holding a drink, since her free hand was in her pocket, but the loaded pack was still slung over her shoulder.

"I—I ..." she began, but I interrupted her.

"You," I said, "just saved my life."

Her expression could best be described as somewhat confused. "I saved your ... what?"

"Oi!" came a man's voice from the top of the stairs. "That you, Helen? We're out of bluidy ink!"

She shot a look up the stairs and I held my finger to my lips. Behind her in the dim stairwell, a brass doorknob gleamed under a sign that said Door Alarmed. I took a deep breath and turned the knob. Icy night-time air swirled in, but no alarm went off.

"HELEN?" called the voice, and we both piled outside and hastily slammed the door behind us.

I set off in the direction of the hostel, and the girl kept pace with me, tucking her head into a voluminous wool scarf.

"Thanks," I said as we hurried up the street. "I owe you one."

"Yeah," she said, and shot me a grin. "Apparently I jes' saved yer feckin' life for yeh."

I grinned back at her. "You did. I've been held captive in there for the past hour by a sex-crazed gnome. Dwarf. I—I mean, little person."

She laughed. "An' here I thought you Americans were all about the political correctness."

"He called himself Rabbie the Gnome—I swear! Anyway, I told him you were my cousin Susan. Didn't you hear him yell at you? He practically deafened everyone in the place."

She laughed again. "No, I didn't. But it's funny, that—because me name *is* Susan."

I stopped in the street and stared at her. "Seriously?"

She nodded. "Yeah. Fer real, an all. Susan D—Susan O'Donnell."

She stuck out her hand and I shook it. "Emma Sheridan."

She nodded at my backpack. "Where are ye stayin', when yer not trying to avoid randy gnomes?"

I pointed up the street. "My hostel's up that way."

"Really? Mine, too. I'll walk wit' ye. Luckily, we Irish are good at protectin' ourselves from the wee folk."

I laughed. "Oh, you're from Ireland? Whereabouts?"

She inclined her head. "The Republic, o'course. Yeh evir been?"

"No. This is my first time in the United Kingdom."

"Ah, well, and you with such an Irish name, and all. I'm a Dubliner. Headin' north to visit family on Skye. When I'm not rescuing fair Americans."

I grinned. "Well, you know, his friend was cute, and seemed pretty nice until Rabbie arrived. He was an unbelievable horn-dog."

She laughed. "Horn dog, eh? I've niver heard that one, but I like it. *Horn dog.*" She repeated it with an American accent, and I laughed too. Her accent was terrible.

We walked up the street as the wind from the river tried its best to freeze every exposed bit of my flesh. I had my hood pulled up but was seriously envying Susan her scarf by the time we neared the hostel.

"This is me," I said, stepping into the shelter of the doorway.

She glanced up at the sign over the door. "Away wit' yeh! Me too!"

We had to step aside as a loudly chattering group of young males tumbled out the doorway. Susan gave me a thoughtful look.

"What're yer plans for tomorrow?"

I shrugged. "I—uh—just looking around for old stone circles, actually."

She jammed her hands further in her pockets. "Care to meet for coffee in the morning before you set out? I've a mind to see a few sights around here before I head north. If you're willin' to put up wit' the company."

"Why not?" I said, and opened the door, holding it for her.

But she stepped backwards. "Oh, I'm not goin' in yet. I've a fair few errands to do before I hit the sheets tonight." She grinned and pointed at a heavily shuttered cafe across the street. "Meet ye at nine sharp, yeah?"

"Sure thing," I said, and watched her stride off into the swirling snow.

Fate & Faith...
8:30 am, March 15
Inverness, Scotland

A few brief thoughts on having faith in human nature while traveling:

1. Just because someone buys you a drink in a bar does not mean his intentions are noble.

2. Have the strength of character to just walk away. If a situation feels bad, it probably is. Follow your gut instinct!

3. If you do find yourself backed into a corner, girl power can save you. I speak from experience—having faith in our sisters has saved many a woman trapped on the bench seat of a bar by a gnome.

And to finish, a public service announcement for anyone planning to come to this beautiful old city:

4. Do not accept cranberry juice offered by an odd little man with a penchant for Asian ladies' feet. Do not then go on and drink two of these drinks, no matter how good they taste.

You will thank me.

– ES

My room in the hostel was warm and snug, and had a bonus kettle, though no biscuits to be found. I'd slept like a cranberry-vodka-saturated log, and rose to find the day painfully sunshiny, with no traces of the tiny flakes that had blown so viciously through the gaps in my coat the night before. My knee was swollen to the size of a baseball, and my head felt even worse. Since I'd posted already, cruising on the house Wi-Fi, I left the laptop locked in my room and headed down the stairs with just my pack over my shoulder.

I made it over to the coffee shop, and was sitting in a corner when Susan walked in. The effects of Rabbie's pink drinks were far less desirable in the cold hard light of a Scottish morning, and it is possible I may have had to rest my head on the table once or twice. By contrast, Susan had a spring in her step and such a twinkle in her eye that I dropped my head into my hands.

"Oi—feelin a bi' rough, are yeh?" she said. I nodded and sipped my coffee.

"Well, we can't have tha now, can we? I'll jes' have yer cup, here, shall I?" She slid my coffee out from between my protesting hands and poured a dollop of something into it from a flask she whipped out of her coat pocket.

"Ohhhh—I don't think so," I whispered. Even the sound of my own words echoed painfully around in my head. "I've taken some aspirin. I'll be better soon."

"Nonsense. Drink that right up. Is it hot enough?"

She peered at the steam coming off the cup with one of her over-bright eyes, and pronounced it just right. "Go on. Drink it. We haven't all day for you to be scuppered now, do we?"

She pushed the cup back into my hands. The steam wafted up and fogged my glasses. I hadn't even the strength of character to get my contacts into my eyes that morning.

"Aren't you going to have something?" I asked, weakly, stalling.

The coffee shop smelled sickeningly of porridge and fresh scones. "At least let me buy you a cup of tea," I said, as she slapped a local map down on the table.

"Nah, I wouldn't think of it," she said, but when the girl came by to wipe down the table, she agreed to a hot drink, and then jumped up to have a look behind the counter.

Moments later, she returned to the table with two bacon rolls and a large cup of coffee. She stared sternly at my still-full cup. "Get that inside yeh. We've a day to plan."

I nodded obediently and took a sip. Whatever she'd done to the coffee made it taste like road tar. With insects in it.

Susan heaved an exasperated sigh and stood up. "Let me just give yeh a hand ..." she began, and before I knew what was happening, she had my nose pinched between two fingers. When I opened my mouth to gasp out a protest, she poured half of the steaming cup down my throat. The other half splattered onto my lap and across the table.

I have experienced my share of pain in my lifetime, but having my entire insides seared by a steaming cauldron of bug-tar was like nothing I'd ever known. My eyeballs immediately flooded with tears of shock and pain and my tongue felt like it had been cooked right inside my mouth.

"Right," she said. "Now a glass of tap water and you'll be fit for anything."

I staggered over to the counter, and apparently the expression on my face was enough, because the old lady who passed for the Scottish equivalent of a barista slid a full water glass across the counter to me without a word.

I gulped it down and then turned to face Susan. "What the hell?" I gasped. "You could have scarred me for life!"

She grinned at me. "How's yer head?" she said, and took a bite of her first roll.

I sat back down, feeling the charred insides of my mouth with my abused tongue. Everything seemed to still be in place, if completely singed. But my head—my head was filled with the buzzing of a thousand bees.

"So, you're looking for historical monuments, are yeh?" she said. "Yeh do know we're jes' a stone's throw from Culloden?"

I nodded gingerly, hoping the bees would quiet themselves. I watched her wolf down the first roll. "Yes, I was planning to go there, but a bit later in my trip. I'm sort of tracing a route I've planned out."

"Yeah, yeah, agreed. But if ye're planning to go, why not now? Save yerself a trip back to this godforsaken hole." She bit deeply into her second roll, and sighed before taking a long drink of her coffee. "I'm goin' there today, meself. Ye're welcome to join me."

"I guess so ..." I said.

The bees seemed to be settling at last, and she launched into a vivid description of all that could be seen and enjoyed on the nearby battlefield.

After about five minutes of that, she looked at me inquiringly, and I thought of my own carefully constructed plans. My explanation would involve admitting to the annotated map inside the cover of my OUTLANDER book. I decided I didn't really care to tell this very practical woman that I was in search of a mysterious red-headed warrior who was destined to sweep me away to happily ever after.

Especially after the episode with Rabbie.

"Let's do it," I said, making up my mind on the spot. "Is it a long taxi ride from here?"

She jumped up, wiping her face with the back of one hand. "Who needs a feckin' taxicab?" she said, grinning. "The sun's shining! We're goin' by bike."

And so as Susan went off to arrange for a second bicycle rental for me, I went up to pay for her coffee. Turns out she'd forgotten to look after her breakfast, so I added the bill to my own, thinking of the money saved on cab fare. After all, I'd planned to tour Culloden near the end of my trip, and Susan had promised to show me where the secret graves of a rogue band of Irishmen who had fought alongside the Scots lay. I'd never find anything like that on my own.

I stepped outside the coffee shop to find Susan already half a block ahead of me.

"Bike shop's just up the street here," she called, and I limped along as fast as my sore knee would allow, cursing her cheeriness every step of the way.

But damned if my head didn't hurt any more. At all.

She stood with a hand on the door to the shop. Outside three or four bicycles of assorted sizes stood propped in a rusting iron stand.

"Right. You have a look out here and decide which bike is the best for you. I'll go in and take care of the deposit, yeah?"

"I can come in—you shouldn't have to pay my deposit, Susan."

She waved me off. "Ach, it's jes' five quid to rent. Yeh pay the bulk of it when ye return 'em. We'll even it out then."

With that, she turned on her heel and marched inside to the tinkling of a little bell tied to the door. I slowly walked along the line of bikes, trying to judge which one would suit me best. My knee was pretty sore, so I wanted something that was the right size so as not to aggravate the weird knee injury I had acquired while escaping Rabbie. I had my hand on a flashy little green number when a young man stepped out the door.

"Right—yeh like that one, do ye? 'Fraid it's a bit too small a frame for a big girl like you—howse aboot yeh try this one?"

I dragged my big girl ass over and tried sitting on the black utility number he held out to me. "It's got a nice lamp on it for the evenin'," he said, encouragingly.

"I have no intention of riding after dark," I said, coldly. "But it'll be fine. I'll take it."

He smiled blandly back at me, oblivious to my attempts to cut him dead with my eyes. "Early in the year for you American girls to be out touring the country," he said.

I was about to point out to him that only one of us was American, when the bell tinkled again and Susan came out of the shop. She threw her leg over the green bicycle and the young man nodded. "Looks about right," he said. "See yiz later, eh?"

I declined to wave goodbye.

As the young man walked back into the shop, Susan wheeled her bike over beside me and nudged me with her elbow. "He were a feckin' looker, weren't he?" she hissed. "I'da bent my ass over the countertop with him if we weren't on the go today, I tell yeh."

"I can't see it," I said, but she'd already pulled out onto the street.

I jumped on my bike and pedaled after her. Knee or no knee, I was going to keep up if it killed me.

The ride to Culloden Battlefield was, according to the local map I had tucked in my pack, along a fairly straightforward route of only a bit more than five miles. Susan had been to the battlefield many times before, she assured me, and though it was her first time taking a bicycle, felt it would take us no more than a half an hour to get there. I found the first ten minutes to be pretty tough, negotiating on the left side of the road. Twice I pulled right into traffic, and the second time Susan had to literally reach out and grab my shirt to yank me out of the way of a speeding truck.

She stuck two fingers up at the rapidly receding back of the vehicle. "Feckin' eejit!" she screamed, not that it seemed to slow him down at all.

She turned back to me. "All right then, Emma?"

I nodded, hoping that the extra calories burned from my heart beating at twice the recommended rate would maybe qualify me for the smaller bike the next time.

"Not sure he knew you were mad at him when you only shot him a peace sign," I said, when my breath returned.

She laughed. "Ah, you Yanks and yer middle finger salute. This is our version—more of a Celtic Peace Sign, mebbe. Trust me when I say this one has just as ripe a meaning."

I nodded and filed it away. Susan was a veritable font of local culture, and I felt a moment of gratefulness that fate had introduced us at the pub. My headache had vanished, and now she'd taught me how to swear in sign language. The beginnings of a true friendship.

The ride was fairly uneventful after that. I'd clipped my room key to an outer zipper on my pack, and it jingled lightly as we trundled along the gravel verge of the road. Outside Inverness, there was still a skiff of snow on the ground, but the roads themselves were clear, and the sun and ride combined to keep me warm. I paused and looked both ways at every intersection, just in case, and Susan soon had us pedaling into the parking lot at the gate of the battlefield presentation center.

The road leading to Culloden circled near the actual battlefield before arriving at the entrance, and I peered across the brown lumpy expanse, sure that Susan must be mistaken. I could see sheep wandering about, but how could anyone possibly fight a battle on such an odd and uneven surface?

We rolled our bikes up outside, and Susan expertly locked them together on an otherwise empty bike stand. "Ye can niver be too careful, aye?" she said, tapping the side of her nose.

I tapped back. One more cultural lesson learned. It was turning out to be an amazing day.

11:30 am, March 15

Inverness, Scotland

Haven't got my laptop with me, so jotting quickly here in my notebook, and will copy to the blog later. Remember to make a short post to note the change of plan. I still hope to try to follow Claire's footsteps wherever possible, but this is a chance I can't pass up. The proximity of Culloden Battlefield, and the opportunity for a personal guide has brought me here a bit earlier than I had thought. I'm sure to learn so much, and it'll probably mean I save a bit of money, too, not having to double-back the way Claire did.

kc dyer

I jammed my little spiral notebook into my pack after making the notes. I'd post to the blog again when I returned to the hostel. By then I'd probably have a ton of interesting facts to add. Susan had turned out to be the best part of the trip so far; a walking Wikipedia of information.

But as I waited for her to come back from the restroom, I found my thoughts turning to the drop in comments from my Japanese fan club. I mean, this trip was supposed to be for me, after all. But my self-confidence had been really shaken by the sudden cyber-silence.

What did this say about me? Just who was I making this trip for, anyway?

I grabbed my notebook again.

Also, remember to leave a note to HiHoKitty and the other commenters from Asia: Make sure to say I'm truly sorry if Rabbie's remark about the feet offended anyone. To tell you the truth, it offended me, too, and I was just trying to get that across.

Hoping they don't give up on support for my "Finding Fraser" quest. I have to find some way to say just how important their encouragement has been to me. Whatever else comes of this trip, I've learned that I really do enjoy the writing. I'd love to find some way to keep it going, even after the journey...

Susan came marching out of the restroom and slapped me on the arm.

"Why so glum, chum? This place is amazing. And I've a few special treats in store for yeh, too. Just follow ol' Suzy and learn all about it."

For an Irish visitor, Susan's knowledge of this ancient Scottish site was almost encyclopedic. Within minutes, she had me choking back tears as we walked into the visitor's center at Culloden Moor. The course of history had been changed at this very location and the skirl of the pipes that greeted us as we entered was a reminder of all the Scottish lives lost on those fields so long ago.

I had to stop and take a deep breath. I was here in the very place where Jamie and his clan brothers had fought and so desperately lost against the English. Or—his real-life counterparts had, at least. I could hardly believe it.

We wandered through the displays describing the banishment and return of the pretender, Charles Stuart, known to all as Bonny Prince Charlie, and the lead-up to the battle as he rode through Scotland gathering support. I had to dig around in my pocket for a tissue as I read the displays, and by the time we sat down for a short film re-enacting the battle itself I was nearly losing it.

Susan must have sensed my emotion, as she moved away to give me some privacy. A few minutes later, as the lights went up between film loops, I could see I was not the only person wiping their eyes.

I walked into the main section of the visitor's center and Susan was there to greet me.

"Yeah—difficult to see, ain't it?" she said, her voice low. "Let's go outside and yeh can get a feel for the actual battlefield in person."

She hurried through the rest of the displays and I followed her outside. The sunny morning had clouded over somewhat, but the day was still bright. We followed the path that led out into the field.

"It's pretty mucky out there right now, but yeh get the idea of what it musta been like, yeah?" said Susan. She shaded her eyes and pointed off to one side of the field. "The fight had begun at Nairn, but hadn't gone well and the feckin' English chose this site to finish the Scots off. That flag over there shows where the Scots made their stand, and the English troops stood over on t'other side."

We followed the path as far as we could as it wound across the bleak moor. A collection of black sheep gathered to one side of the field, nosing at the frozen grass and nibbling the first tender shoots under the snow.

"I can't believe they could hold a battle on this land—it's not even remotely flat. You'd think they'd all be tripping and falling into the rough patches."

Susan shrugged. "Well, they had no heavy equipment, or even horses really," she said. "And it was likely not quite as lumpy as it seems today. Here, check these out."

She hurried over to one of the mounds under the snow and reached down to brush it off. Under her gloved fingers, words appeared on a surface of rough-hewn stone. *Clan Stewart of Appin*, it read.

"A gravestone?" I breathed. I could hardly believe it.

Susan nodded. "Indeed. These were put in place by the landholders after the battle and have been here since. And see over there?"

I followed as she hurried past a much larger stone to one side of the moor. "Is this another grave marker?" I asked, pausing beside it.

"Tch," Susan waved her hand, not even turning her head to look. "That marks the graves of the few English soldiers who fell here. Doesn't even bear a second glance. No—what I wanted to show you is away this side."

She stood well over to one side of the field, beside a couple of low rocks almost completely buried in snow. But instead of brushing them clean, she bent over almost on one foot, leaning and listening.

"Can ye hear it?" she asked. I paused and solved the problem of my winded panting by holding my breath. It had been a bit of an energetic day to that point.

After a moment, I looked at her. "Is that water?" I asked, and she beamed at me as though I had just passed an important test.

"Tis the Well of the Dead," she explained. "On'y source of water fer the poor souls on the battlefield."

I stood beside the spot in the snow and thought about the real-life version of Jamie and his lads, their lifeblood quenching this frozen ground. Heroes for their nation but doomed all the same.

"Emma. The mos' important bit is here."

Thinking of Jamie and the wrenching choices he and his family had to make, with so many lives lost, I wiped my eyes surreptitiously and turned to where Susan was standing. It was yet another snow-covered rock, and I marveled at how well she knew the geography of the place.

I bent to brush the rock face off, but she put her hand on my arm.

"There's no call for that. No words mark this stone," she said, somberly. "This is a place of our shared heritage, you and I. For this is the stone where the Irish fell—the Irish who came to the aid of their Scots brothers against the foul shared enemy."

"There were Irish battling at Culloden?" I whispered, feeling my fingertips tingle at the very thought. "I had no idea."

She nodded. "My very own family members fell here, and yours, for the bugler was a Sheridan."

I think my mouth must have dropped open. One of my own ancestors had fought with the brave, doomed Scots at Culloden? Where so many of the Frasers and MacKenzies had fallen? My heart swelled with a fierce pride, which must have shone through on my face, for Susan smiled and patted my arm.

"Aye. God's truth, though ye'll find it in no history book. It's a point of pride, passed down from Irish father to son in story and song."

I squeezed her arm. "I can't believe it—I am *so* lucky to have met you," I said. "How would I have learned any of this without you here?"

"Mus' be destiny," she said, with a grin. "Now, how about some lunch? I'm feckin' starvin', I am."

I couldn't talk Susan into going back inside for lunch. She refused to pay tourist prices, she said. I pointed out that as it was March, they likely still had the lower winter season rates in play, but she was adamant.

"I'll wait for yeh here," she said, brushing the snow off a wooden bench and pulling out a small sandwich. I left her there, went inside and bought two containers of warm clam chowder and a couple of ham sandwiches. She received my offerings of food with earnest thanks, and while we ate, pointed out the various strategic battle sites that were in view.

The day had assumed a kind of silvery-gray tinge, but Susan insisted there was little chance of rain. As she scraped the last of the soup from her cardboard container, my will broke.

"I have to tell you something, Susan," I said, trying to keep my voice steady. "I haven't told you the whole truth. I'm not just a normal tourist. I'm here—well, I'm chasing a fugitive."

She looked up at me, her spoon poised halfway to her mouth, a startled expression on her face.

"A—what …?"

"A fugitive from the past. A ghost. A person who has never existed, but is so real that I believe he must be here somewhere. Here for me."

Her startled expression gave way to what almost looked like relief before settling on full-out puzzlement. "What the feck are y'sayin', girl?"

So I started at the beginning and told her. I brought out the book, even opening the cover to show where I had drawn Claire's journey on the map of Scotland printed inside. I admit that her eyes widened several times as I went through the details, but to give her credit, she didn't laugh at me. Not even once.

When I was through she stood up and checked her watch.

"Well, it seems perfectly feckin' clear to me," she said, shouldering her pack. "Ye need to cross that yon field, and head to Clava to see the stones."

"Clava," I repeated slowly. "I think Craig—the cute guy in the pub last night—I think he mentioned Clava. But he said they were cairns."

"Jes' another word for an old grave site. There are three of 'em there, and the center one is circled by standing stones. They are the only ones anywhere near Inverness, as far as I know. If you're looking for stones hereabouts, y'must see the ones there."

"But—Craig did say they're not on the side of a hill, or even in a forested grove …"

"The side of a hill? Ah, girl, yer author lady there must have been using some of that there poetic license, righ'? The stones were for reading the sky—why would they plant 'em in the woods? But ye'd be crazy not to go today—it's jes' a mile or so ride from here, on t'other side of that road over there."

I nodded at that. I seemed to remember *Craigh na Dun* was in a clearing — and who's to say what had happened to the forests of Scotland since the 1740s?

"All right," I said, at last. "Let's do it. We've got the bikes for another couple of hours. Why not?"

Susan shook her head regretfully. "Ah, girl, I'd love to come and help ye find yer Highlander, but I have an errand or two to attend to this afternoon. I have to be ridin' back to Inverness, now. Ye mus' go on without me and have a look at the place. Who knows? Maybe the man o' your dreams will be there, ready to show ye what's unner his kilt, eh?"

She patted my shoulder to show she was just joking, and then drew a few lines on the local map the hostel lady had given me. "No distance at all, really. And there are road signs the whole way, to direct the tourists. Y'won't have any trouble findin' the place."

We walked past the entrance to the visitor center. "Listen, you," she said as the warmth of the building enfolded us. "I'll have a chat with that looker at the bike shop, eh, and tell him you'll be along shortly with yours. Y'can allus lock it up outside if the shop's closed by the time ye get back."

I pulled out my wallet. "Okay, but let me give you the money for my share, at least."

She folded the bills into her pocket. "If there's a late charge, I'll cover it and you can jes' get it back to me tomorrow, aye?"

"No—no—take five extra pounds, just in case."

That bill disappeared into her pocket with the rest. "Righ', perfect. And if there's no charge, I'll get this back to you in the mornin', then."

We were walking toward the exit through the gift shop, among the rows of plaid shortbread biscuit packets and stuffed Nessies, when a bit of a disturbance rose up at the cash desk. A man I recognized as one of the people who had been wiping his eyes at the end of the battle re-enactment movie was complaining loudly to the cashier.

"Look," he said. "My wallet is gone. I had it when I came in, because I paid the entrance fee. Someone's taken it."

Susan clutched my arm. "Didja hear that, Emma? Fella's had his pocket picked. Is yours still safely stowed?"

I felt for my own wallet, but it was safe in my pack, and then thought about Susan jamming my cash into the pocket of her jeans.

"Have you got yours?" I asked, as we walked toward our bikes. She patted her pocket and took a quick look inside. "Yep, it's there. Guess we got off lucky."

Through the front window of the visitors' center we could see quite a commotion brewing, with several employees milling around a group of clearly very disturbed patrons.

Susan swung her leg over her bicycle. "Ye'll have no trouble at all finding Clava," she said. "I'll see to the bikes and you can tell me all about it tomorrow, yeah?"

I walked my bike up beside her, my knee still stiff from the earlier ride. "Thanks for the tour today. I don't think I'll ever forget that unmarked grave of the bugler named Sheridan."

"Faith and Begorrah," she said, her accent deepening. "We need to keep the feckin' spirit of the green alive, yeah?"

I nodded and she wheeled around and headed down the road to Inverness. "See you tomorrow!" I called to her back, as she raced away.

She raised a hand in return. I could have sworn she flashed me the Celtic peace sign, which made me laugh out loud. I leaned my bike back against the wall, and paused to make a couple of quick notes before heading off myself.

3:00 pm, March 15

Culloden Battlefield, Scotland

Notes to self for later:

This place has everything I dreamed of, and more. The fields are rough and filled with memorials to the dead. My tour guide (Susan!) took me to a place where soldiers of my own family ancestry made their sacrifice in the name of the Bonny Prince.

It is a day I will never forget.

And speaking of forgetting, a note to HiHoKitty. (No, I'm not obsessing...)

HiHoKitty, to answer your question, no, Hamish (the young man I met) was not wearing a kilt. He had on a very nice cable-knit sweater, though, over his equally nice arms. I've thought about him every day for the two-and-a-half long weeks since I lost him.

Maybe I shouldn't include that last line... too desperate-sounding.

I threw my notebook into my pack, shouldered it and pedaled off in the direction Susan had pointed.

The circle.

It was after four by the time I pedaled up to the sign Susan had told me to look for on the road. The sky was low and gray—not quite rain, but a mist filled the air. I couldn't tell if it came down from the clouds or up from the ground itself, which as soon as I stepped off the road was dense and damp underfoot.

There was one of those mini-tour buses parked by the sign and I could see a small collection of people in heavy tweed coats and rubber boots snaking their way down though a thin line of trees. I leaned my bike against the sign and peered up at the sky. It didn't look like it was about to full-out rain, but the mist showed no sign of slowing, either. As the bike guy had pointed out, there was a light on the handlebars of my hired bicycle, but I didn't relish the idea of a ride back to Inverness along these bumpy roads alone in the darkness either. I was turning out to be a less intrepid traveler than Susan gave me credit for.

Deciding to make it a short visit, I leaned over the Historic Scotland sign to read the description of the site. Turned out the place was old—much older than the fields of Culloden. And though there were standing stones, something was not quite … right.

I leaned against a fence post and pulled out my copy of OUTLANDER, flipping through the early chapters. Some of the pages were beginning to feel loose. I was going to have to be careful not to lose any.

The last of the bus people—a pair of middle-aged ladies— stumped past me, chatting animatedly. I was scanning quickly through the middle of chapter three when I felt a tap on my sleeve.

"Best hurry along, dear. Angus gave us last call at least ten minutes ago."

Her companion giggled conspiratorially. "Evelyn and I wanted to wait for the dusk, in case a group of local women showed up with sheets under their arms. But I guess we're going to be disappointed *again*."

I blinked at them. It seemed so odd to hear American accents after nearly three weeks, that I had trouble taking in what they were saying. "I—I'm not on the bus," I said, sticking a finger between the pages. "I rode my bike."

The first lady—Evelyn—pointed to the book. "You're not on the OUTLANDER Tour?" she said. "But you have the book …"

A little clarity began to seep through. "The OUTLANDER Tour," I repeated slowly. "You're here on a tour …?"

"… Based on the television program!" finished Evelyn, triumphantly.

"And the book, of course," chuckled her companion.

"Ladies!" came a shout from below us on the road.

"I—I even didn't know there was such a thing," I stuttered, as the ladies each took one of my arms and marched me down the path. "Really—I came here by bicycle."

"I'm sure Angus will be delighted to add another participant, don't you think, Helen?" said Evelyn, as she hustled me down the path. "You can take Gerald's place—he's disappeared somewhere."

"*And* you have a copy of the book," said Helen, who was her friend's equal in energy and speed. "That should be enough for Angus. He was just saying today that he's almost never sold out on this spring tour."

"Plenty of seats, plenty of seats," said Evelyn. "Lots of space, even for the missing Gerald! Tonight we stay in Inverness, and there's a whisky tasting event. Tomorrow's Stirling Castle!"

"And the brewery!" added Helen.

I was beginning to feel a bit breathless at the pace the sturdy ladies were setting as they hauled me along. Since logic hadn't worked, I tried fruitlessly to extricate my arms as we speedily approached the waiting bus. The impatient bus driver stood inside on the front steps with one arm raised to his tardy passengers. Even at this distance I could see the puzzled look on his face.

"Look who we've brought you, Angus," called Evelyn, in a voice that carried the distance with no difficulty. "We've found a wee Claire!"

"She's got a copy of the book," cried Helen, not to be outdone. "And just look at that hair! She looks just like the actress who plays Claire!"

I put my hand up to find the ponytail I'd jammed my hair into that morning was, in fact, long gone. I could feel my hair cascading around my head in frizzy, damp ringlets.

"I sold my hair straightener," I muttered. But by that time we had lurched to a stop at the foot of the bus steps, where the astonished face of the tour driver looked down at us.

"I'm not on the tour," I said to him apologetically. "These ladies were hoping to change my mind."

The driver stepped down through the door. "Now, Evelyn," he said calmly. "You must stop capturing young ladies. This is clearly not Claire. For goodness sake, she sounds as American as you are! You must remember Claire was an Englishwoman."

For the record, I have to say I look about as different from Claire Beauchamp Fraser as is humanly possible. I'm taller, for one—five foot seven when I remember to straighten my spine. And my hair—on a summer day—could charitably be described as dishwater blonde, but is more often mousey brown. My eyes are green, but the contacts somehow make them come out a hazel color, too. I guess I share a certain paleness to the skin in common with Claire, but apart from that and the inclination of my hair to go curly in the damp—nothing.

Apparently this truth began to sink in with Helen. I could feel her grip on my arm lessen. "Her hair *is* a bit too fair, if you look at it carefully," she said, but I could hear the disappointment in her voice. Evelyn, however, was not prepared to give up yet.

"But she has the book—there it is in her hand," she said pleadingly to the driver.

"We all have the book, Evelyn. It's why we are here. But that doesn't mean every young woman we meet has to be Claire."

Helen gave it a last salvo. "Gerald's been threatening to leave all day," she said. "This young lady could use his seat."

"Gerald's sorted, ladies. Truthfully. Dinnae worry your heads about him. Now we must be movin' along."

Evelyn reluctantly let go of my arm and stepped onto the bus. "But what about the ghost we saw, Angus? What about that?"

The bus driver smiled at her and reached a hand to help Helen up the stairs. "That *was* very exciting," he said, and rolled his eyes at me. "Ye mus' tell me all about it again in th' pub t'night, awright?"

I stepped back onto the path as he swung the door closed. "*So sorry,*" he mouthed, as the door hissed shut.

I just smiled and waved as the taillights bumped up the road.

An OUTLANDER tour.

I felt strangely let down. It never occurred to me that anyone else would go in search of Jamie and Claire. I'd never even had the sense to look it up online before I'd come, but now that the evidence was before my eyes, I couldn't believe I'd not thought of it. The books are best sellers, and the televised version had brought Jamie and Claire to further millions — why wouldn't people want to investigate the mysterious Highlands for themselves? For all I knew, hundreds of fans flock to the sites from the stories every year. Why not? After all, Harry Potter had theme parks all over the world.

And yet … I couldn't help feel that a comparison between Helen and Evelyn and myself was—what? Not the same. Just not the same. I'd never watched the show, for one thing. I wanted to keep the pictures in my head of Jamie and Claire and the others intact. Helen and Evelyn wanted to see the land of the stories, yes, but were they actually looking for Jamie? Had they actually met him in the flesh—in the form of a young man named Hamish—in Edinburgh?

Definitely not the same.

I hurried toward the cairns in the rapidly gathering darkness.

There were three of them in total. The two outer cairns looked like piles of gray rock in the deepening twilight. I could see they were hollow in the center, though, like two giant, rocky doughnuts. The mist lightened a little as I approached the final cairn, and right away it was clearly different from the other two. Standing stones radiated around it like the numbers on a clock face, and there was a path running through to an opening in the center of the mound.

It was definitely too dark to look up details in my book, but I figured that fifteen more minutes at the site would still leave me with enough light in the sky to get back to the main road, if I stood up and really pedaled. In spite of Susan's advice, my gut instinct had been right about this not being anything like how I pictured *Craigh na Dun*. There were standing stones, yes, but the ancient graves were clearly the main focus of this site. Mammoth circles of piled stones, the two outer cairns each with a clear passageway to the center.

The Heritage Scotland sign had mentioned the presence of *cists,* which apparently were an ancient version of small, square coffins. The standing stones encircled the middle gravesite in a kind of sunburst pattern.

I wished there was less rain and more time. And maybe my laptop. I really wanted to know what had led people to leave these cairns here so many millennia ago. Long before Jamie's time, anyway.

But dusk was already falling, and I needed a restroom. Also, I was hoping for a half an hour's battery life on my bike lamp, so the whys and wherefores of this ancient place would have to stay on my to-do list for the time being.

I felt my hair lift a little off my neck as a thin breeze began to blow, and above me the heavy cloud that had shrouded the day began to break. This gave the brief illusion of a lightening of the sky, highlighted by the sight of a single star, low to the horizon.

The evening star.

How many times had Claire looked up at the stars, longing for her Jamie?

I made up my mind, dropped my pack near the path and stepped into the trees to relieve myself. It might cost me a minute or so of extra darkness, but it would make for a much less painful ride back into Inverness.

Moments later, I shuffled back toward the path, grateful for a pocketful of old Kleenex. Looking around, I tried to orient myself with the single, twinkling star. It seemed to be almost due east of where I stood, and I knew the road I needed to take would head almost straight north before bearing west and south down to Inverness.

I stopped for a minute, just staring into the darkness between the stones. What was I doing here? I mean, I know my plan was to retrace Claire's steps, but maybe I needed to rethink it a little. Much as I was enjoying every minute of this visit, I had made exactly zero progress toward my goal of meeting an actual, flesh-and-blood Scottish guy.

The day had been full of so much that was wonderful, but I needed to get back to my room and work on my focus.

I swung my pack up onto my shoulder and turned toward my bike when I saw a light bobbing between the Cairns.

I dropped behind one of the stones like a ninja, all thoughts of the return trip to Inverness gone from my brain.

The light must have come from somewhere behind the center cairn, because I could see the shadow of one of the standing stones nearby. I sidestepped back into the trees, carefully avoiding the small puddle beneath the third tree over.

All I could think of were Evelyn's words. *"But what about the ghost we saw, Angus? What about that?"*

What *about* that?

The light bobbed once more, and then vanished.

My hair lifted again in the breeze, and a light suddenly shone down on me. I slowly turned to face it. My guts twisted like a prisoner who had attempted escape, only to be caught at the forest edge by guards and a collection of slavering, killer dogs.

But there were no guards, and thankfully no killer dogs. Only a moon that had risen, pale yellow on the eastern horizon. It wasn't a spotlight, but it cast a strange glow across the trees. Across the cairns.

Ghosts don't walk in moonlight, do they?

I decided they didn't, and then I tiptoed closer to the standing stones in the middle of the site, to see for myself.

As I crept forward, I decided to use the stones themselves as camouflage. This place was so different from the mental image I had of *Craigh na Dun*. It was in a field, for one thing, not a mountainside. But the stones still formed an unmistakable circle, and drew me forward. They were mostly taller than my head, and the solid feel of the cold, hard rock under my fingertips was reassuring, somehow. The trees offered little

kc dyer

cover, as the area around the ancient site was in a clearing, and the stones circled the low, gray lumps of the cairns in the darkness. Unlike Claire's experience at *Craigh na Dun*, these stones did not scream when I touched them and for that I felt strangely—torn.

The sensible part of my brain knew that I hadn't visited this circle to find a ghost, and yet—Claire's life had been completely changed when she touched the stone. A wee small part of my heart told me I wanted that same thing. A different life. Something else to consider when I returned to Inverness.

But for now, I needed to find out more about that bobbing light.

I peered around the edge of the giant rock and scanned the area. The light had not flickered into view again since I had first seen it, and I began to wonder if the moon had been playing tricks with my eyes. Maybe it had glanced off a fleck of metal in one of the stones piled in the center cairn?

Whispering through the dead leaves surrounding the trees behind me, the breeze rustled just like the sound of shuffling footsteps in the dark. The hair on the back of my neck was standing at full alert. I took a deep breath, slipped out from behind the shelter of the standing stone and half crab-scuttled to the edge of the center cairn itself. The stones of the cairn had a different look and feel than those standing sentinel behind me. As I crouched by the low mound, my fingers traced odd indentations on the stone's surface—the strange, unexplained cupping that the information sign had told me helped date the site to its ancient origins. The hypothesis was that the marks were strictly decorative, but the texture under my fingers made me feel uncomfortable. Like I was touching the back of an ancient, sleeping guardian.

Just then, the moon shone out again from behind a tattered bit of cloud and flooded the place like a spotlight. And directly in front of me, standing, legs spread in the center of the opening of the cairn, was the clear silhouette of a Highlander.

I'm pretty sure I fainted for a moment, right there on the side of the mound of rock. My vision blurred and swam, but when I rubbed my eyes, there he remained. Clouds scudded across the moon, but could not obscure the unmistakable outline of a tall man in a kilt. He wore some kind of heavy boots on his feet, and the plaid was topped by something that could have been a substantial fur cape.

A strange feeling of unreality slipped over me. It was like in those dreams where I tried to run, but couldn't. My feet felt mired in mud. I must have been holding my breath, because right about then an actual wave of nausea washed over me. I had to close my eyes a moment to stop from delivering my clam chowder from lunch onto the dead grass beneath my feet.

When I opened my eyes again, he was gone.

I stood up immediately and stepped toward where he had been standing, but the moon dropped back under the cover of the cloud again and my sore knee made crushing contact with one of the ancient stones. I bit my tongue so as not to cry out, and my eyes filled with sudden, hot tears. I'm not sure if it was from the effort to keep silent through the pain in my knee, or from the reality that I had somehow misplaced my Highlander once again.

In a few short, limping steps I was at the entrance to the cairn. There was nothing—no one—there. Leaning forward, I peered along the pathway that led to the center of the burial mound, but it was open to the air, and I could see nothing. I spun outwards and looked around behind me, but the darkness had closed in again as the clouds drew their curtain across the full moon.

If my eyes hadn't deceived me and a man had really been there, he was there no longer. I slumped against the rock mound, completely at a loss. Had the nattering of the old ladies from the tour bus been the truth? Was wishful thinking making me see things? Or was I really losing my mind?

kc dyer

In the distance the wail of a siren rose up. Ambulance, or police or fire—I couldn't tell. But it was a purely contemporary sound. As I listened to it fade away, my heart rate slowed enough to allow logic to begin to seep back into my brain. He had been there—he had. I had seen him. I had seen the dark lines of his plaid moving against his knees in the light breeze. I wasn't sure what he had been wearing over the plaid—some kind of heavy cloak, certainly—but I *was* sure of the heavy boots.

I dropped to my knees. Perhaps the damp ground would give evidence of boot prints to prove I was not completely losing it. I glared up at the sky, willing the cloud cover to part at least enough so that I had a bit of dappled moonlight to see the ground.

In answer, tiny raindrops began to spatter my upturned face. I shook them off and concentrated on the ground. By feel alone I could tell the entrance to the cairn was not rock, but mud. Fairly frozen mud, to be sure, but maybe …

My bicycle lamp. I pushed all thoughts of low batteries and returning safely back to the hostel to the back of my brain. I needed to know if there were fresh boot prints, and for that, I needed light. I jumped to my feet and ran smack into the unmistakably solid body of a non-ghostly human male.

Just after midnight, March 16

Inverness, Scotland

Jotting a quick note while my co-ghost hunter (very kindly) pays the cabbie. Have had the strangest and most unique day of my visit. Perhaps of my whole life.

Back in my room, I didn't even turn on the light, just dropped my pack in the corner and sagged into my bed.

Stretched out, and fell asleep to the memory of the screaming …

Yes, there had been screaming, but not all of it had come from my throat. Screaming, slipping, falling, grabbing, slapping, snatching, pushing, recriminations and finally, breathless, panting silence as I'd stared at the man in front of me, bathed in the reflection of his flashlight.

"I thought you were a ghost," he said, at the very moment I blurted, "You're not a ghost." If we had been in a movie, we would have both laughed wryly and compared notes.

As it was, he glared at me, a streak of mud on one cheek and his left eye beginning to swell from its untimely meeting with my elbow. I stood, arms crossed, at the entrance to the ancient tomb, my heart sunk just about as low as it had been at any point along this strange journey.

Not taking his eyes off me, he bent to the ground to retrieve something in the dark. As he stood up again, I could see he held my book.

"That's mine," I said, reaching for it.

"Not so fast." His voice was laden with cadence from the American south, and marked with deep suspicion. "Mah copy has a blue cover. How do I know you're not one of them Irish gypsies who lie in wait in dark places to rob innocents?"

"Look," I said. "You can tell from my voice I'm an American. And you'll have to take my word for the fact I'm no thief. I'm sorry I bumped into you. I thought I saw something, and clearly you did too. We were both mistaken, obviously. Just hand back my book and I'll be on my way."

He leaned against the rocky passageway inside the cairn, tucked the book under his arm and re-directed the flashlight from my face onto his own backpack. After rustling about for a moment, he fastidiously closed the top and slipped the straps back over one shoulder and then the other. Not until he had carefully re-buckled the chest strap did he direct the beam of the flashlight back onto the ground between our feet and hand me my book.

"Mine's still in my pack," he said, in no way apologetically.

A light—not the flashlight—went on in my head.

"You must be Gerald."

His expression did a quick change from suspicious to startled, then back to suspicious again. "How'd you know that?"

I sighed. "I met Helen and Evelyn, earlier. They mentioned a man named Gerald had gone missing from their tour. They even invited me to take your place."

He sniffed. "I'm surprised they missed me, the old biddies. Always going on about 'Claire this' and 'Claire that'—*so* tiresome."

He shone his light at my face again.

"Would you please stop doing that? You're blinding me every time."

He completely ignored me. "It must have been the hair," he muttered viciously. "They love the ones with the curly hair."

I put a hand up to my head and surreptitiously yanked out a couple of twigs, dropping them on the ground behind my leg. "Well, yeah, I think Evelyn might have been inclined to think that way," I admitted. "But everyone set her straight."

"Then it's *all* Evelyn's fault," the man said, bitterly. "She was the one who swore she saw a ghost."

"You're on the Tour," I said, slowly, as the pieces began to fall into place. "And you were looking for—Jamie?"

"I saw him too," he declared, a trifle shrilly. "I woulda spoken to him, but for your interference."

"I didn't interfere," I said, hotly. "I just stepped closer to get a better look."

The man grabbed me by both shoulders and shook me a little. "Then you spotted him, too? In the moonlight?"

I nodded and he shook me again once more before dropping my shoulders. His face was exultant. "I knew it. I knew he was here."

I crossed my arms, shivered and considered the possibility that I had crashed into a madman. I mean, I didn't really expect to meet a fictional character from the past at the first stone circle I'd ever been to, but this guy clearly did. The light rain had wept itself away but the moon was completely gone, blanketed by the rolling fog. The thought of the bike ride back to Inverness was beginning to haunt me more than the ghost. Still, I had to know …

"You left the tour to stay here and look for a ghost? Why? What ghost?"

He gave me an impatient shrug and slapped the cover of the book in my hand. "*What ghost?* How are you even worthy to carry this around?"

"I—I just mean …" I stammered, at an almost total loss, "Of course I know the ghost from the story. It's just—why are you looking for that ghost? And why *here*?"

He sighed and shot me a sideways glance. "Let's get out of this rain," he said, and even somewhat gallantly stepped aside with a gesture indicating I should go first. I stepped gingerly onto the spot where I thought the path lay, and seconds later, his flashlight beam shone down to light the way to the road. The path was very narrow and rocky, so the going was slow, but unlike his earlier behavior, he showed no impatience. He walked behind me slowly, holding the flashlight high so we could both make out the way ahead.

"My name's Gerald Abernathy," he said as we entered the narrow band of trees that ringed the ancient site. "That is, my father was an Abernathy, one of the Georgia Abernathys, actually, but my mother's family are all old Scots. Her maiden name was Grey."

I thought about this as I stumbled along the path. "As in Lord John Grey?"

The flashlight beam bobbed a bit and then stopped moving. I couldn't see a thing without it, so I turned to face Gerald.

"I know it's fiction," he said quietly, his accent deepening as he spoke. "But it's almost like I could be a descendent of Lord John. He believed Jamie was the perfect fella..." He took a deep breath. "And so do I."

He raised his chin as he said this, looking at me defiantly.

I smiled up at him. "Well then, it appears we are both trying to find the same man," I said, and turned back to the path once more.

A few stumbling moments later, we stood at the same spot by the side of the road where I had watched Evelyn and Helen's tour bus pull away. A car stood idling in the drizzle, headlights cutting through the night and reflecting off the water droplets on my bicycle.

"You know," said Gerald, eyeing my wet bike. "I could really use a drink after seeing that ghost, and you look like you could use a lift into town. Care to share my cab?"

With the help of the cabbie we got the bike jammed into the trunk—the "boot" he called it—and slid damply into the back seat of the wonderfully warm taxi. The return to Inverness was not long, but enough time for us to both discover how much we had in common, not the least of which was a love for OUTLANDER and its most famous Highland warrior.

The cabbie disgorged Gerald, my bicycle and me at a pub just a block from my hostel and across the street from the place where Susan and I had rented the bikes. The store was dark, so I leaned the bike up against the front wall of the pub and decided to return it in the morning, safe in the knowledge Susan would have paid the bill earlier.

Gerald picked a seat right by the fireplace and I slid into the chair across from him. He sighed and gestured to the half-pint of golden liquid sitting in front of me. "Drink up," he said, and took a sip of his own. "It's a shandy. I've developed a taste for them on the tour."

"Thanks." I took a sip. I was fairly certain it was beer and ginger ale mixed together. A little sweet for my tastes, but a free drink was a free drink.

Gerald swallowed another deep draft of his drink and sighed deeply.

"I'm sorry," he said at last. "But I was so knocked out by the sight of that Highlander. It—he—took my breath away."

"Me, too. But, to tell you the truth, I wasn't completely convinced. It couldn't have been a ghost, right? I mean—there must be some rational explanation."

I took another sip of my drink, which was growing on me. "It's not the right circle, for one. And his cloak looked funny … I just needed to get closer."

He nodded. "I had no expectations, you know. I mean— Clava Cairns— it's nowhere near Fort William, and in spite of what everyone says, I'm sure *Craigh na Dun* is much closer to there than here. And I had those old biddies nattering on like fence birds the whole time. We argued about the site all the way down on the bus. Evelyn was convinced she'd see the ghost at Clava, and I was equally sure we would not."

"And then you did."

He grinned at me for the first time, completely transforming his expression in an instant from sour-faced to charming.

"Apparently, so did you. Anyway, I decided on the trip up from Edinburgh that I'd had enough of all the natterin' …"

"Claire this and Claire that?"

He laughed. "Yeah. I'm not a whisky man, either. Bourbon's more to my taste. In the end, as soon as my cellphone picked up service outside Inverness, I called and booked the cab. Had a private word with Angus the tour driver and it was all set. I had no idea what I'd see, but the lure of waiting by the stone circle had a certain appeal, which I'm sure you can appreciate."

I nodded and sipped. The glow of the shandy warmed my insides. "Not to mention ditching the tour-bus denizens."

He leaned back in his chair and looked me over from frizzy head to wet toe. "Definitely more Laoghaire than Claire with that fair hair of yours," he said, appraisingly. "I guess I should worry that you might just pull a Laoghaire and move in on my ghost, then?"

I tucked a strand of damp hair behind my ear. "Well, if it *was* him, it'll be the second time I've lost Jamie on this trip, so there'll be no stealing your man," I said. "Besides, I'm more anxious to find a modern version of him in the flesh than in apparition-form."

Gerald nodded. "What're you going to do next?"

I shrugged. "I met a friend here—her name's Susan. She said something about some other stone circles nearby. And I need to think things through a bit, I guess."

He waved at the server and counted a few bills onto the table. "It's Fort William for me," he said. "I've pinpointed a set of standing stones on a hillside down there that are pretty much derelict, and not on any of the tour maps I've read, anyway."

"Really?" I asked, intrigued, in spite of myself. "Where?"

His face closed up again, as suddenly as it had opened, and I could tell he was wrestling with himself. "You have internet access?" he said, at last. I nodded and he slid a small notebook and pen over to me. "Write your contact information here. If I have any luck at all, I'll tell you—afterwards."

I raised my hand to him as he walked out the door, convinced I would never hear from him again— and a bit relieved at the thought. That he believed in ghosts was odd enough— but that he was chasing down the ghost of a fictional character?

Demented.

8:45 am, March 16

Inverness, Scotland

I'm still pretty tired, and not really sure I want to blog about this anyway, but I can sum up, I think, by saying this trip is far from over.

I saw a ghost last night.

The circle was wrong.

The location was wrong.

And yet I saw a ghost. A ghostly Highlander.

I'm not sure what to make of this. I don't know what it means.

This trip is FAR from over.

I flipped the cover of the notebook closed and dropped it on the pillow beside me, too exhausted from the events of the day before to even grab my laptop and do the post properly.

Breathing deeply, I stared up at the ceiling, just taking stock. My body hurt all over from the bike ride, but strangely enough my knee seemed to be completely better. I tried to remember when it had stopped hurting—I'd bashed it again on one of the standing stones, but sometime after stepping into the stone circle— the pain had vanished.

I lay there as the sun rose slowly behind the thin white curtains in my hostel room window, thinking about the silhouette of the Highlander, standing in the moonlight.

What the hell was it that I had seen?

Something niggled at me, but I couldn't put my finger on it. Still, I knew in my heart the search wasn't over. Maybe the so-called ghost was telling me I was on the right track? Gerald certainly thought so. Wrong ghost, wrong circle. But if he did find the right one, the chances I'd ever hear from him again were pretty slim.

Feckin' slim, as Susan would say.

I flexed my knee again under the covers. Maybe the bike ride had done it good after all?

The thought of the bike suddenly had me sitting bolt upright in bed. I hadn't returned the bike! And not only had I not returned it, I had left it propped, *unlocked* outside the pub we'd been to the night before.

I threw on some clothes, grabbed my wallet from my pack and bolted down the stairs.

"All right, Emma?" called Mrs. Henderson, the hostel-keeper.

"Back in a minute," I gasped to her, as I ran past.

It was only a block to the pub, and miracle of miracles, I saw the bike almost right away, leaning against the wall just where I'd left it. I dropped my hands to my knees for a minute when I got there, panting and bathed in the feeling of relief washing over me. After I'd caught my breath, I rolled the bike over to the store, determined to be kind even to the man who'd made remarks about my size relative to the little green bicycle the day before.

I pulled the bike into a stand at the front door and headed inside.

The bike-renter guy sat atop a high stool, doing some kind of puzzle in the newspaper.

"Hiya," he said, looking up. "Brought me bike back, have yeh?"

"Yes. I'm afraid I returned last night after you'd closed."

He strode over toward the cash register. "Nae worries, nae worries. Didja have a good ride?"

"Yes. We made it to Culloden, and then I carried on to Clava."

"Ach, the stones at Balnuaran. Lovely, aren't they?" He leaned on the glass counter-top. "I've heard they're a wee bi' haunted. Didja see a ghost, then?"

"I'm not really sure, to tell you the truth," I said quietly, but he was hitting buttons on his cash register, and the ringing may have drowned out my response.

"Righ' then—it'll be fifty quid altogether, with the VAT, an all."

I was sure I hadn't heard him correctly. "Fifty quid—that's fifty pounds, right?"

"Righ' you are, little lady!"

Hmmph. Suddenly I was a *little* lady? I decided to let it drop, and deal with the more worrisome issue first.

"I think there's a mistake, somewhere. My friend should have paid for me yesterday when she dropped her bike off. They were twenty pounds each, to rent for the day?"

"Aye, they were, plus tax, o'course. But your friend left her bike as promised, and said you'd be coverin' the costs when you returned."

The skin of his neck had gone an interesting shade of red when Susan's name came up, but I didn't have time to think about anything but the fact that the last of my cash was going to have to go to this man.

I looked through my wallet. "I'm sorry—there must be some mistake," I repeated. "I gave her the cash to pay you yesterday. I've only got forty-five pounds on me—will that do until I can find her? I promise I'll bring the rest back when I do."

"Aye," he said, slowly. "I reckon that'll be awrigh', but ... well, be as quick as ye can, aye? Me boss is in—ah—a bit of a mood t'day, and I'd rather stay on her good side, ye ken?"

I handed over the last of my cash and hurried back to the hostel. Mrs. Henderson sat at her place near the front door. She lifted her head as I walked in.

"Ah, there ye are, dear. Ready to pack up and head on wi' yer partner, then?"

I held back an impatient sigh. The last thing I had time for was a leisurely discussion of how she had mixed me up with another patron.

"No— no, I don't have a partner, Mrs. Henderson. I'm here on my own, remember? Listen, have you seen Susan—ah— Susan O'Donnell this morning? She's staying in one of the other rooms here. I need to find her to straighten something out."

"The other American girl? Well, o'course I seen her. She checked out this mornin' bright an' early. I thought ye were off after her."

"No— not an American. This girl is Irish. Susan O'Donnell. Short, dark hair, about this tall? The one I ..." Surely Mrs. Henderson had seen us riding off together the previous day?

"Aye, she's a bonnie one, isn't she? But she left long before breakfast. Did she no' leave ye a message?"

I stared at Mrs. Henderson's face, and a terrible feeling of unease began to sweep over me. "Just a sec," I said, and took the stairs up to my room two at a time.

"Got all the time in the world, luv," she called up the stairs after me.

And there, with the warm light of a Scottish morning shining brightly through my window, I saw what the darkness and my exhaustion had hidden from me the night before.

Everything I had brought with me was gone.

Everything I hadn't carried in my pack, anyway. My laptop. My travel cash cards. Even my contact lenses. My little coil notebook and pen still lay where I'd dropped them on the pillow.

I felt like I'd been punched in the gut. What kind of depraved thief steals someone's contact lenses?

After a few moments of anguish, it was clear there was no use standing and staring at my empty room. I trailed back down the stairs.

"Mrs. Henderson," I said slowly. "All my stuff is missing from my room. I think it's been stolen."

"Ach, nonsense, girlie. It was yer partner 'at gathered it all up for yeh. She said ye'd decided to stop hiding and let the world know the truth."

"I don't have a partner, Mrs. Henderson. I came here alone, remember?"

"Aye, and a sad-faced thing ye were, too. I was delighted to see ye perk up when yer friend arrived." She leaned across the desk and whispered, "There's nae shame in it, luv. She's a dear one, that Susan. The two of yeh make a sweet couple. She told me all about your plans to return to California and set up a bed and breakfast there."

"We are *not* a couple!" I spluttered, and a light came on in Mrs. Henderson's eyes. She nodded understandingly.

"Aye, I see the way of it then, luv." She touched a finger to the side of her nose. "I were young once meself—had more one night stands than I'd care to have Mister Henderson know!"

"Oh my god," I said, slowly. "It was *not* a one-night stand. I just went out sightseeing with her. We talked about the Battle of Culloden all day!"

"Weel … as you say, o' course, as ye say," she said, still smiling. "Our customers allus have the right to complete privacy, o'course. But ye know we are verra broad-minded here. No prejudices at all, for anyone."

"I'm not gay!" I practically yelled. I realized my fists were clenched and the kind lady had actually been quite startled by my outburst.

For the first time, her face darkened. "Aye, there's no call for homophobia, either," she said warningly. "I'll hold no truck with that sort of thing under my roof."

"Mrs. Henderson," I said, trying to keep my voice calm. "Let's just take the whole sexuality thing out of it, okay? I believe Susan stole all my things. Did you allow her the key to my room?"

Comprehension was beginning to dawn on the woman's face, but I could see where it was still at war with what she had clearly believed was a sweet little love story unfolding before her eyes.

"My laptop and my cash card were in my room. I need them to pay your bill, Mrs. Henderson. And they're missing."

She stood up and brushed her hair back nervously. "I—I, well, she said you wanted discretion, and I saw the two of you head off to the battlefield together. It just made perfect sense— two dear young American girls, and yerself clearly lookin' for love. You tol' me so when you arrived! And she was just so ..."

"Convincing," I said. I slumped in a plaid chair that looked far more comfortable than it turned out to be in reality. "You thought she was American, I thought she was Irish. I wonder which is the truth? You *did* give her the key, then?"

I looked up at the horrified expression on the hostel-keeper's face. "I think I need to go talk to the police, Mrs. Henderson."

She nodded. "Aye. I can see that's the way of it, now. Try not to fret, luv. The station's not far. Gi' me a quick moment to lock up and I'll walk wi' ye there."

She shook her head sadly, pushing one arm through the sleeve of her coat. "Tis allus worse when they love ye and leave ye," she said.

I followed her out through the door. "There was no loving, Mrs. Henderson, okay? NO loving."

"'At's what they allus say," she said, turning her key in the lock. "Accordin' to Mister Henderson, anyroad."

11:00 am March 16

Inverness Police Station, Scotland

<u>List of stolen items</u>

- Laptop

- Visa Cash cards, total value $975 US

- 6 prs underwear

- 6 prs socks

- 2 white t-shirts, One with Grateful Dead logo, one plain

- Sweatpants

- Shampoo/conditioner, toiletries

- Contact lenses, case, solution

The police officer was kind, but preoccupied. Mrs. Henderson was ushered away, and I was brought into see Sergeant Milton Garda in his diminutive office. He looked my list over, and then slapped a pen on the paper in front of me and had me write the whole story down. I did my best, leaving out the bit about the hunt for Jamie, of course. Afterwards, he read it over silently before setting the page gently down on the table.

"She said 'Faith and Begorrah' and you bought it?" he said, incredulously.

"Well—yeah. I've heard it before from Irish people, I'm sure of it."

He shook his head. "Well, mebbe in a cereal commercial …" he muttered.

"She called the truck driver who nearly ran over me a *feckin' eejit*," I said, stubbornly. "*That* sounded Irish."

He nodded. "Mebbe so. But it ain't the truck driver who's the feckin' eejit here, is it?"

I had to agree with him.

He picked up my statement again. "So, ye spent most of the day at the battlefield, aye?"

I nodded. "We headed over around ten o'clock or so, and stayed until after lunch. Maybe mid-afternoon?"

The officer leaned back in his chair and flicked the door open with the tip of one finger. "Allie!" he bellowed. "I need Dav!"

By the time he returned all four chair legs to the floor and clicked his pen once, another young officer was knocking on the door.

"Emma Sheridan, meet Special Constable Dav Dosanj. Dav, this young woman has been taken in by some besom going by the name of …" he checked my statement, "… Susan O'Donnell. A young, brunette woman. Robbed her blind, ye might say. AND the two of them spent the day at the battlefield."

The second officer shot a look at his Sergeant. "Is she clean, sir?"

He nodded. "Aye. Got rube written all over her. The perp stole all her money, laptop …"

"Contact lenses," I muttered, hanging my head.

I looked up in time to catch the sergeant rolling his eyes at the new guy.

"Well, what kind of a weirdo steals a person's contacts?" I asked. "Maybe it's a part of her M.O., and it'll help you track her down."

"Whatever you say, Miss," said the sergeant. "Now tell the special constable here anything you can remember about your trip to the battlefield."

"Look, I don't know what this has to do with anything," I said, my exasperation growing. "I don't remember anything special. We rode over there on the rented bikes—which I ended up paying for twice, thanks to Susan—and toured around the place."

"Were you with her at all times?" Dosanj asked.

"Yeah … or maybe, okay, not at *all* times," I said, slowly, remembering. "Someone had their pocket picked, just as we were leaving. You think she …?"

"With your permission, sir?" said Dosanj, and his sergeant nodded. The special constable stepped over to a side desk that held a computer with an ancient monitor. He flipped the on-switch, tapped a few keys and stepped away from the screen.

There, in grainy black and white, was a closed circuit view of the visitor's center gift shop. A few people milled about including— the back of Susan's head. She'd pulled up her hoodie, but there was no mistaking the backpack she had slung over one shoulder.

"That's her!" I cried, involuntarily.

"Wait for it …" Dosanj said, then leaned forward and hit the space bar. The picture froze with Susan's hand slipping into the back pocket of a man bent over examining a collection of snow globes. The officer tapped a computer key several times, and each time the picture moved forward a frame, as Susan smoothly pulled something dark out of the pocket and slipped it into the open zipper of her pack.

"Her name's not Susan O'Donnell," said Sergeant Garda. "And she's as Irish as I am Indian. No offense, Dosanj."

"None taken, sir."

"The bike guy told me she was American," I whispered.

"Well, we're not sure. We reckon she may actually be a Canadian national, or p'raps a dual. At any rate, she's travelling on an American passport, under the name of Gail Lee Duncan."

"Gail … Duncan?" I repeated.

"Aye. That shot from the CCTV camera was taken yesterday morning," Dosanj said, snapping the computer off. "We have a dozen more like it."

"I must have been in watching the movie. You know—the one about the massacre on the battlefield? I thought she'd left to give me some space, because … well, just because," I said. "So it wasn't just me she stole from?"

The special constable shook his head. "She pretty much cleaned out the pockets of everyone in the place," he said. "She's good, I'll give 'er that. No one felt a thing." He nodded at his colleague. "She lifted a wee trinket for herself, too—a Celtic cross on a necklace, was it?"

"An anklet," said Garda. "I'm surprised she took so little, but there wasnae much time, aye?"

"She didn't want to go back inside for lunch," I said, walking through it again in my mind. "I went in, and bought us both lunch—she'd given me such a good tour and I felt bad when I saw how little she'd brought to eat."

I looked over at Sergeant Garda. "You're right. I even bought her lunch. I *am* a feckin' eejit."

Dosanj's eyes widened, and Garda held up both his hands. "Now jes' a minute, lass—I niver said …"

I smiled weakly. "You didn't say I wasn't."

He shrugged. "Did you keep the paperwork from the cash cards, at least?"

"I wrote the pin numbers and everything all down. I knew I was supposed to keep the information separate from the card in case I lost it. But I had it in my …"

"Let me guess," Garda interrupted. "In your sponge bag wi' the contact lenses?"

I nodded miserably. "Do you think I could put a stop-payment on it online?"

The senior officer shrugged. "You can try, of course. We have Internet access at the outer office desk. But if she's cashed it out already, you'll be out of luck."

He stood up. "I'm right sorry, Miss," he said, formally. "We'll do the best we can to catch her. This is a small country, and as a rule the Americans stand out, particularly in this season. With luck we'll nab her. But the truth is, she'll likely head south and become a thorn in the side of the Yard."

"They're welcome to 'er," muttered Dosanj. He held the door open for me, and I left without another word.

Filthy Fiasco…
1:30 pm, March 16
Inverness, Scotland

Last day in Inverness. I'm sorry to report my trip is at an untimely end—in an unfortunate incident, I have been robbed of my cash, my contact lenses and all my faith in human nature. I'm typing this at an Internet cafe, as my laptop was taken, too. There's nothing for it but to see if I can move up the date of my ticket home.

Thanks to you all for your support. This trip would not have been the same without you.

- Emma

Comments: 0

I typed the last word, and logged off with a sigh. Forty-five seconds to spare on the hour-for-a-pound deal they had for out-of-season webheads like me. Just me, actually, since there was no one else in the place, except the granny who had taken my money. When I walked in, she had barely looked up from her book to accept my coin.

"Good book?" I had asked, automatically.

She crinkled her eyes at me and held up the cover. THE SCOTTISH PRISONER.

"Ay loveth the short ones," she lisped, a result of there not being a single tooth remaining in her head. "They keep me fired up for when the next good thized 'un comes along."

I slung my pack over my shoulder and headed for the door. Inverness had its own small airport, and I needed to catch the bus out there to talk to an airline person about trading in my ticket. The granny at the door didn't lift her head as I left. She chuckled and muttered to herself as I opened the door.

"'… I swallowed a gnat.'_Ach, Jamie my boy—I do love ye so."

"You and me both," I said sadly, and headed out onto the muddy street.

I had to put the cab fare to the airport on my credit card. So, yeah, yeah, I knew there was a bus I could catch. Right from downtown Inverness straight out to the airport. But after spending my last pound coin on Internet access, I literally did not have any cash on me. I'd have had to go to a bank machine for a cash advance on my credit card, anyway. And if I was going out, I might as well go in style.

Fortunately, the taxi driver had nothing to say. He grunted when I asked to be taken to the airport, and sped off so fast that my head snapped back and bounced off the headrest in the rear seat.

Tiny beads of sleet spattered the window as I slumped against the door, watching the river Ness wind away into the distance. Flowing away. Like my money. Like my once-in-a-lifetime trip to Scotland.

All my losses, though, paled against having to face my sister when I got home. I took that thought and tucked it in with what happened the day I met Herself, and resolved never to think of either of them again.

The taxi driver disgorged me at the airport with a handwritten credit receipt and a grunt. I scampered inside to get out of the weather and looked around for the correct airline desk. The airport was a fairly small one and there was hardly anyone to be seen. I finally found the desk I was looking for. A young man stood behind it, lifting a bag of trash out of a bin. A tag pinned to his lapel read: My name is Matthew. How can I help you?

"Hi," I said, gloomily. "I need to change a ticket—can you do that here?"

He shook his head. "Sorry, Miss. I'm just closing down. Ye'll have tae come back tomorrow." He finished tying a knot in the trash bag with a tidy little snap.

I stared at him, completely without words. Everything in me—every drop of plasma, every cell, every follicle—wanted to scream my frustration into his neatly groomed face.

Instead, I did what I have vowed to never do since I read Gloria Steinem's autobiography in seventh grade.

I burst into tears. "Everything-I-own-was-sto-ho-ho-len," I sobbed, "and-I'm-living-on-my Vi-hee-hee-sa-card."

"Oh dear," Matthew said, looking desperate for someone to take the sniveling wreck off his hands. Unluckily for him, the place remained pretty much deserted.

He took a deep breath and pulled a pristine handkerchief out of his pocket.

"I'm afraid we're out of tissues," he said. "I've just thrown away the empty box."

I accepted his handkerchief, wiped my eyes and then took a deep breath. It seemed to help. "I'm sorry," I said, shakily. "I've had kind of a rough week."

"Look," he said. "I can see you're very upset and I wish I could assist. But I am not authorized to reschedule flights. You can try doing it online …"

"My—my laptop was stolen, too," I said, teetering.

"Deep breath," he said, hurriedly. "Try another deep breath."

By this time my glasses had completely fogged up. I pulled them off and used the only dry corner remaining of his handkerchief to wipe them. "I don't even wear glasses in public, as a rule," I said, pointing at my face. "But she even stole my conta-hac-hact lenses.

"Your contact lenses?" he said, sounding truly horrified for the first time. "What kind of monster steals someone's contact lenses?"

Exactly. I sniffed and held up the hankie enquiringly.

"Go ahead," he said, looking resigned. "You can keep it."

I blew my nose into his handkerchief and took several more deep breaths. Something inside me felt broken. I had no idea what to do next.

A steady clicking noise coming from the other side of the desk made me look up at last. The young man's fingers were flying across his terminal, his brow furrowed in concentration. After a few moments of unbroken typing, he smiled, and leaned over the desk.

"Look," he whispered. "I'm not authorized to change your flight—I just don't have the codes. But I can at least do a quick refund of your return flight cost, so you can rebook on your own. Do you have your credit card?"

I did. Still in my hand from paying the taxi driver. I slid it over the desk at him.

"Not that way, not that way," he hissed. "Down here." One of his hands emerged from around the back of the desk, out of sight of the CCTV cameras.

Trying to affect an innocent face, I slipped the card into his hand.

"This is the card you paid your initial booking on?" he whispered.

I nodded.

"And you swear you'll rebook your return flight with our airline as soon as humanly possible?"

I swore. In the legal sense.

"Because I am NOT supposed to do this. If anyone asks me, I'll have to tell them there was a mix-up or the machine failed or … something."

Mechanical error as the go-to excuse for an airline did not make me comfortable. But comfort was not going to put a refund on my credit card.

"Works for me," I whispered.

"Punch your PIN in now," Matthew hissed.

After a few seconds, he slipped the card back into my hand and turned the key on his terminal.

"I'm afraid we are closed for the evening," he said, in a suddenly loud and somewhat stilted voice. "You'll have to return tomorrow, Madam."

"I'll do that," I replied equally loudly. "Thank you, sir."

The only person who could possibly hear us was the man rolling his cleaning trolley down the broad aisle between the empty waiting room seats. It didn't matter. The deed was done.

Matthew winked at me solemnly, picked up his bag of trash and his keys and flicked off the light that illuminated the airline sign.

I shouldered my pack and ran for the nearest bank machine. I had a withdrawal to make.

Sitting on a bus rocking through the Highland darkness later that night, I contemplated my situation. I couldn't see any other word for it.

I'd become a fugitive.

Of course, technically the money was mine, dogmatic airline rules aside. I hadn't taken the flight yet, and I'd agreed to re-book. Just when I'd be able do so, though ...

Well, as soon as humanly possible. And in order for that to happen, I had to have enough cash, right?

I looked down at the statement I'd printed off from the bank machine. I now had four hundred pounds on my credit card.

Four hundred pounds.

Even with my pathetic math skills, I was pretty sure that translated to nearly seven hundred American dollars. A person might live a long time in the wilds of the Scottish Highlands on that kind of money.

So, yeah. I decided that for the present, I could live with being a fugitive, if it meant I could stay a little longer. Keep trying to find my Fraser.

Maybe I was not so different from Susan after all.

Fickle Fortune…
10:30 pm, March 16
Inverness Airport, Scotland

Sudden, happy change of plans. Fortune has smiled on me! My circumstances have altered a bit, and the quest to find my Fraser carries on. Will report in at my next stop. Wish me luck!

- ES

Comments: 61

SophiaSheridan, Chicago, USA:

Well, thank god you're all right. We've been worried sick since hearing about the robbery. Why won't you call? Surely you will have to come home now. If you won't call, perhaps you'll send me an email?

Gerald Abernathy, Ft. William, Scotland:

Not sure you'll remember me, Emma, but we met a few nights ago at the Clava Cairns. I promised you I would give you more information if I could on the subject we both care about. Just wanted to tell you that I found the circle, but no—ah—inhabitant. I caught a terrible cold that night and I'm actually typing this from the lounge at the hospital here in Fort William. If you do ever make it down to this neck of the woods, look me up. I'll be happy to give you the information about the site. Maybe you'll have better luck. My email is GAbernathy@ge*rgiabell.com

HiHoKitty, Sapporo, Japan:

Very relieved to hear you are well, Emma-san. Book club send luck!

(Read 58 more comments here...)

I woke in the gray dawn, swimming up to consciousness through the shreds of a terrible nightmare. American agents had forced me onto a plane back to the US at gunpoint. We'd gotten somewhere deep over the Atlantic Ocean before I discovered that there was no one flying the plane. I had to take the controls. The plane dipped and weaved, and finally flew the entire distance about ten feet above the waves. A whale spouted in the water beneath us, we were so close. Sharks swam below us, keeping pace with the plane. One of them had a laser beam strapped to his head, but even that didn't give me pause. Land in sight, I brought the plane down safely to the rousing applause of the entire crew of the Pequod from MOBY DICK.

I sat up in bed, my body bathed in sweat, adrenaline pumping. The cockpit dissolved around me into the shape of a drab little room, about the size of my closet at home.

I wasn't in an airplane with Captain Ahab. I wasn't in America.

I was in the town of Fort William, Scotland, population unknown. I had a hundred pounds of Scottish sterling safe in an inner pocket of my backpack. I had nearly three hundred and fifty more transferred from my visa card to my current account.

And I had a journey to complete.

The previous night, after a quick stop at the cash point, I'd spied an Internet-access-for-a-pound computer in the airport, so I had sat down to scope out accommodation. I thought she might offer me some compensation, but Mrs. Henderson had vanished with little more than an apologetic smile at the police station, so I was disinclined to ever darken her doorway again. Still, nothing was going to bring me down. And just moments after I had posted the cheery blog entry, up popped the comment from Gerald.

With my sudden change of fortune, at least it was a place to start. I shouldered my pack and looked for the signs pointing to the bus stop.

Outside the airport, I ran across the parking lot and hopped on a bus that was idling but still had its door open. The driver informed me that he was heading north, but that a southbound bus should be arriving shortly. "It's headin' for Glasgae, mind," he said, "but it'll stop in Fort William for ye. Jes' make mention to the driver, aye?"

And that is what I did.

Forts & Friendship...
9:00 am, March 17
Fort William, Lochaber, Scotland

Today as I type these words, I find myself in one of the most beautiful parts of this country I've seen yet. Upstairs, through my bedroom window I can see the peak of Ben Nevis, Scotland's highest mountain. And just south of here are breathtaking glens that roll away for miles between jagged peaks. Last night I couldn't see any of this, but the bus driver filled me in on a few of the details, since it turned out I was the lone passenger.

Not much call for midnight bus service to Fort William on an icy March night, apparently. Fort William was named for Prince William of Cumberland, a fact most of the Scots around here don't really enjoy. "He were a goddamned butcher, 'at he were," was how the bus driver put it.

And yes—there is a hostel in Fort William. How can there not be when this is the center of all Scottish mountaineering? But I am not there. We pulled in long after midnight and the driver took me to his auntie's house before heading further south. I have already availed myself of a most excellent full Scottish breakfast cooked by the driver's proud Auntie Gwen, connected with you— my fine friends—on her home computer, and now, on this beautiful almost-spring day ... I go to see a friend in need.

– ES

Comments: 56

The truth was that Auntie Gwen's breakfast had put me into a food coma from which I didn't emerge until noon. I popped back onto her computer before I left for the hospital to see the comments had begun arriving pretty much immediately after I'd posted. They were almost to a letter all asking about how I was able to stay on in Scotland when I had been robbed. This made me a bit nervous. What if my nefarious deed got back to the airline? I decided that sticking with a general travelogue format on the blog was the best idea for the moment. It was important to engage my readers so I needed to keep the travel tips coming, but maybe I'd hold the more personal stuff to myself.

Even after all that time, I wasn't really clear on the finer details of posting to my blog about real people. I mean—was it okay to mention names? I'd been pretty careful about it so far. Even in the case of Gerald posting straight to my blog, I still wasn't sure about using his name online. I decided to check with him when I saw him. Better take the safe route.

Auntie Gwen's place was gorgeous, and still smelled of bacon and warm bread. I couldn't help feeling a pang of guilt as I headed out the front door, her hand-drawn map safely tucked into my pack. She'd risen at that god-awful hour to let me stay the night before, and even offered me winter rates, but the cost was still triple what I would have paid to stay at the hostel.

I decided I needed to sort out the money as soon as possible. But I also I knew I was going to have to find a job to make up the shortfall, anyway, so a night or two of totally reckless spending wasn't going to kill me. My ill-gotten gains had only fostered my rebellious spirit. I had no work permit, so under-the-table employment was going to be my only option. A pirate's life for me, yes? I laughed out loud at the thought.

Walking down the street, I could feel a real change in the air. There was a lightness to it that lifted my heart, even on the way to a hospital. The grass may not have been green yet, but I had a bit of my pirate gold in my pocket and the birds surely believed spring was on its way. The air was filled with feathered Bocellis, all singing their hearts out.

After a twenty-minute walk, the roof of the hospital arose just up the road. It was the standard three-storey affair that I would have known even without the address. What is it about hospitals that they look so similar, regardless of where in the world they are?

It turned out to be a good thing that I'd gone back for a post-breakfast nap, as visiting hours were only in the afternoon and the early evening. After taking a wrong turn into the maternity wing, I found my way into the ward where Gerald was staying. His bed was closest to the window, but he shared the room with three other beds, two of which were occupied.

He hadn't seen me at first, and my heart went into my mouth a little at the sight of his pale face against the pillow. The hospital smell didn't help. Disinfectant, mixed with ... what? Sickness and worry, maybe.

A nurse was adjusting his IV, and Gerald caught sight of me just as she finished. "Emma! I can't believe you're actually here."

His smile lit up his face, making me hope he was less proximate to death's door than he had first appeared. He patted the side of the bed, and the nurse returned to sweep a curtain around to give us a little privacy.

"Sitting on the beds is forbidden," she said sternly, and pulled in a chair from one of the other cubicles.

Gerald stuck his tongue out at her back as she walked away. "I don't like that one," he whispered loudly. "There's another who's much nicer, but not on today, sadly."

I perched on the edge of the chair. "What happened?" I murmured, as the curtain wasn't doing much to keep our conversation private.

He pulled a controller out from under the covers, and held a button down so that the head of his bed slowly rose to bring him more upright.

"Not much to tell," he said, once he'd found a comfortable position. "I found the circle without any trouble at all." He shot me a sideways glance. "Don't you worry, none. I've kept the map for y'all."

"Oh—I wasn't worried," I insisted. "I just came down here to make sure you're all right."

A wide grin spread across his face. "Ain't you the sweetheart? Well, I must have caught something on the bus ride. Some woman had her snot-nosed kid with her, and he coughed all over me the entire trip. I moved right up to the front of the bus, but there was obviously no escaping his germs, the little bastard."

He coughed a little himself, and then began again. "By the time I arrived down here in Fort William, it was mid-afternoon. I got myself settled and then hired a car to drive up to the circle."

"A car?" I began doubtfully. The whole no-driver's-license thing might become a bit of a problem.

"Oh, don't worry, hon. You can easily do it by cab. Anyway, I got there just at sunset, and sat there the night through."

"The entire night?"

"That I did, honey. And it was a whole hell of a mistake, because first off, ain't no ghost gonna come around when someone's coughing their lungs up inside a stone circle. And second—by the end of the next day, I had pneumonia. Ah'm asthmatic, so they didn't want to give me drugs and send me back to my hotel room. Been here since then."

"Oh, Gerald—I'm really sorry to hear that. Both of those things," I added, hastily.

He nodded and I could see that just the act of telling me the story had taken a toll on him. His hand was limply feeling around the bedcovers, so I leaned out of my chair and slid the controller within his reach.

"Thanks, Emma," he said, and pushed the button to lower his bed.

"Are you okay?" I asked, as he sank away.

He nodded. "I think I might just have a nap," he said weakly, and then waved his hand at the bedside table. "Go ahead and take the map. It's in the top drawer with my Ricola."

As I slipped the map out from under the package of throat lozenges in the drawer, his eyes fluttered closed. I shut the drawer as quietly as I could.

"I'll expect a full report," he said, his eyes still tightly shut.

"Of course," I replied, and walked over to the opening in the curtain.

"And not jes' online—in person, y'hear?"

"I promise, Gerald."

"Good." He turned his face away from me and I crept out through the curtain. His voice carried after me, his Southern accent so incongruent in this setting. "And stay away from any of them goddamned germy kids, y'hear?"

The nurse frowned at me and I hurried out the door.

It was wrong to feel exasperated with someone who is ill. But

I somehow managed it.

As I walked back along the road to Auntie Gwen's, I studied the map Gerald had given me. It was a printed map, the kind you get when you're staying at a hotel or sometimes a restaurant in a tourist area. It encompassed the entire region of Inverness-shire, effectively from Fort William along Loch Ness, all the way up to Inverness. There were no real notes on the map at all, beyond a few hieroglyphic-like notations in red ink, and whether they were for himself or for me was unclear.

Either way, they spelled trouble.

There were two locations marked on the map. The first I found must have been the stone circle he'd talked about, where he'd spent the night and managed to acquire pneumonia. It was near a little town called Drumnadrochit. As far as I could tell, this was halfway back up Loch Ness toward Inverness, which had to be at least an hour away by car. The other location marked on the map was not as far—but as his red X ran through a site labeled *Ainslie Castle,* I couldn't even tell if there was a stone circle at all.

I checked my watch. It was 5:00 pm—a kind of dead zone in terms of time in the Scottish countryside. Just about everything in this part of Fort William appeared to have closed down, including the only Internet cafe I had spotted on my walk. I leaned against a tree on the corner of Auntie Gwen's property and pored over the map again in the failing light.

A car pulled up on the road beside me, and the driver leaned across and rolled down the passenger side window.

"Need a lift?"

I opened my mouth to decline, and then I noticed the hand-painted logo on the side: *Alec's Cab—Inverness-shire. No trip too small!*

The wizened-tortoise face of an old man on a bus flashed through my mind. Could it be?

I slid into the front seat, putting the map on the seat between us. "Just a sec," I said, and yanked my wallet out of my pack. The cabbie looked at me expectantly. I fished around inside, pulled out a tattered card and held it up to him.

"Is this you?" I demanded.

He took the card and held it under the dashboard light. "Aye, tha's me, awright. But this is one of my old cards—where'd ye find it?"

"I met your dad on a bus-ride to Inverness, and he gave it to me."

He laughed. "Ye'd never believe how many ride's the old codger has gotten me. Auld Alan is a marketing machine, he is. So—where to?"

"It's a little odd," I began …

It was nuts. We both agreed—Alan's son, Alec-the-cabbie, and me. But when had that ever stopped me before?

CL, Gerald's notes read on the very margin of the map. **Tidal castle. Definitely haunted.**

CL? What did that mean?

Alec, who turned out to be as convivial as his father, could not decode the CL acronym, but filled in a few other details of what he did know as we bumped along the winding route.

"Ainslie Castle, eh? Aye, it's an auld 'un," he confirmed when I showed him the place on the map.

"Bi' of a sad story, actually. The Laird who owns this property is what you'd call a mite cash-poor. He's tried for years to get government money to help restore the place, but it's too far off the beaten track."

"Is it a complete ruin, then?" I asked, straining my eyes to see the road in front of us. The afternoon sky was lowering, and I hoped he could see the road beyond better than I could, as it twisted through the trees on the old mountainside.

"Aye, pretty much. Ye can't get inside the place atall—it's blocked off to stop tourists from having the walls come down on their heads. Nice ta spend the day there, if ye want a picnic in high summer, mebbe, bu' it's tiny, so no' much to see, for all that. An hour should give ye a' the time ye need."

I held the map under the flickering light shining out from Alec's broken glove box. "I'm pretty sure there is no circle here," I muttered. "But it's near Fort William and it's on a mountainside."

"Why not ring yer friend?" Alec asked, not at all put off by my conversation with myself. "Mebbe he can gi' ye his reasoning."

"He's in the hospital with pneumonia," I said, absently. "He's written something else here, in the margin. Cattle ... something. Thane? Maybe? Cattle thane—does that make sense to you?"

"Gi'e 'er here," said Alec, and without missing a beat he grabbed the map. To his credit, the cab wavered not at all while he squinted at the tattered page.

He thrust it back at me as we careened around a sharp curve.

"Cattle thievery," he said, firmly. "Though cattle thane does make a bit o' sense, as the lairds around these parts are known as thanes, sometimes. It was a title—kinda like an Earl, ye ken?"

"Right," I muttered, trying to hold my head steady. The narrow roads and great speeds, not to mention the whole driving-on-the-wrong-side thing was reintroducing me to my good friend nausea. "I remember a Thane in MacBeth," I said, to take my mind off my shaky stomach. "The Thane of Cawdor?"

Alec slapped the seat between us delightedly. "Righ'! Righ'! And there still is a Thane up in Cawdor, for all tha'! But I reckon in this case, yer friend wrote 'thief' or 'thieven'."

I thought back to the story. Cattle stealing made up the background behind a lot of scenes in the book. The opening scene, where Jamie is wounded and requires Claire's medical expertise—he was with his uncle Dougal and his men, who had definitely been up to no good. Stealing cattle may have been a part of that.

I also remembered how large a part cattle thievery had played in Jamie's rescue from the evil clutches of Black Jack Randall.

The car took yet another corner on two wheels. "There has to be a reason," I said, teeth clenched to keep the contents of my stomach down. "If Gerald marked it, it has to be important."

"Y'er sure ta freeze," Alec said, as I stepped out of the cab onto ground beside the dirt trail that passed for a road. "I've a rug in the boot—can I please jes' leave it with yeh?"

I glanced down at my watch again. It was nearing six o'clock and the sun was almost down. "I just need an hour," I said. "I only want to be here until dark. I'm sure I won't freeze in that time."

I pulled up my hood and jammed my hands in my pockets.

"Well, at least take my torch, then. And mind ye don't walk too near the far side. The drop's steep and it's straight down into a damn cold loch." He thrust a flashlight into my hands.

"Thanks. I'll wave it at you when you come back so you can see me."

"Righ', then. I'll jes' nip inta Mallaig for a dram an' be back for ye by seven, latest," Alec promised me. "Stay away from any wee ghosties!"

Mallaig was the last tiny, seaside village we had passed through, following the notes on Gerald's map. It was a testament to my newly acquired faith in the Scots constitution that I didn't even blink at the thought of the driver hitting the road after a 'wee dram'. I just clutched my copy of OUTLANDER to my chest and nodded.

As soon as he pulled away, the truth of his assessment of the weather became clear. I thought fondly of the extra sweater I'd pulled out of my pack at Auntie Gwen's place, to lighten my load on the walk to the hospital. Susan hadn't stolen that one from me, as I'd been wearing it the day we went to Culloden.

I wished I was wearing it again.

As I watched the cab bump off up the road, the insanity of the situation settled in my brain. It was Gerald who was searching for ghosts, not me. I was looking for a flesh and blood Scotsman. And I'd just had a very nice one *right beside me* in the car. The chances of meeting another in this windswept corner of nowhere were below calculable.

"You need to focus, Sheridan," I muttered to myself.

A thin line of yellow reflected off the top of the mountains to the West, but the last of the sunlight rode atop a bitter wind. Above me, a castle stood on a rise of land, perched like a tall box on the back of a turtle hunched by the sea.

Alec—who was appearing more fetching in my memory as every moment passed—had given me a brief history. The castle had been built in the fourteenth century, long before Jamie's time. As castles go, it was pretty tiny. I'd seen bigger mansions on Hollywood reality television.

When it was built, the rise of land it was on had served to protect it from the enemies of its Laird and people. Alec assured me that four hundred years ago the tide did indeed sweep in and cover the road twice a day, cutting the castle off from the mainland.

"But these days, the roadway has been silted up. Now it jes' serves as a route in for the Laird tae shoo his sheep along," Alec had explained. In his handsome Scottish way.

I kicked myself mentally, and kept walking. The place was entirely deserted. Above the castle, the craggy peaks in the distance were all snow-topped, and the wind carried every frozen degree down with it. I tightened the cord on my hood and started across the causeway.

The tide was out, but Alec had declined to drop me along the pathway closer to the castle. "It's protected passage, against motorized vehicles," he'd said. "Not to mention private property. I'll just leave ye here, and be back in a tick."

From the direction I faced, at least, the wind was behind me, and it pushed me along toward the old building, now haloed in light from the setting sun. The castle was much tinier than any castle had a right to be, but perhaps this was as big as they could make them in the fourteenth century. It stood sentinel on its small tidal island, with the loch lapping the far shore. The line of the high rock wall was tessellated, and unbroken even by arrow slits. There were two triangular-shaped protrusions at the very top that may have once supported a roof, which probably would have been made of wood. But it was long gone, and all that remained were the bones of the place, cast in ancient, gray stone.

As I approached, the corona of the setting sun rested briefly on the curtain wall of the castle, and for a moment, I was entirely bathed in golden light. With the light … came clarity.

"Leoch," I breathed. "Gerald, you devil—you thought this might be the Castle Leoch." Dougal's home. Home, in fact, to Jamie's mother and her politically astute brothers, who together had ruled the entire MacKenzie clan.

Book in one hand and Alec's torch in the other, I began to climb the slope toward the old monument.

Walking briskly, I circled the building in under five minutes, at least the parts of it that did not hover on a cliff above the water. Along that side, as Alec the winsome cabbie had noted, the curtain wall rose three stories above the cliffs, most of it constructed with carefully placed rocks. Very little, if any, mortar was in evidence, and I had a sudden pang of sympathetic vertigo for the young stonemasons who climbed those long-ago heights and had put this jigsaw puzzle of a wall together.

One corner of the curtain wall was covered in vines that were lush green even in the teeth of the icy weather, and which crept down the cliff face to intertwine with the heather below. I stepped into the shelter of the castle wall. The sun had sunk below the line of the mountaintops,—and the sky had taken on a particular color that I'd only ever seen in the Highlands. It was an otherworldly combination of purple and blue and black, bringing thoughts of kelpies and other more malevolent Highland faeries somehow nearer.

The path wound around behind the castle, but still in sight of the road. I figured I still had at least ten minutes of twilight left, so I continued on, keeping a close eye on the ground so as not to stumble. Craning up on my toes, I looked over at the castle to see fingers of fog beginning to wrap around it from the loch-side.

I turned and scanned the roadway. Still no headlights in sight. The blue light on my watch showed 7:10. My cabbie's dram had kept him late, and strongly reduced any appeal I'd felt earlier. A decent man doesn't leave a lady—or anyone for that matter—waiting. I shivered and cursed the Scots predilection for drink, and cabbies in general, and turned to walk back toward the roadway.

That was when the moaning started.

If it had come from the castle it would have been bad enough. But the fact that it was coming from right under my feet would have caused me, under any other circumstances, to pretty much jump out of my skin, my coat and all my underclothes before dying of fear on the spot. Fortunately, it was too cold for that, so I kept everything on and decided to get the hell out of there, instead.

Forget waiting. It was less than a couple of miles to the nearest village, plenty of time to work up a speech guaranteed to sear that cabbie's ears right off his pleasant-faced, dram-drinking head. I had his torch. I could make the walk.

Years of ankle-wrenches and knee-scrapings had given me a certain inner caution against running along any path, so instead of a full-out bolt in the nearly total dark, I limited myself to a barely-contained hysterical scurry, muttering a mantra of "Don't-run-its-not-a-ghost-don't-run-it-can't-be-a-ghost-don't-run-you'll-trip-and-kill-yourself," or something along those lines.

Which is why I saw the hole in the ground open up at my feet before I could fall into it. I stopped so suddenly, the toes of my Converse sneakers kicked pebbles into the darkness. And squinting up through the hole, into the beam of my flashlight was a face I could not quite believe I recognized.

"Jack?" I said into the pit. "What the hell …?"

"Aye," came a puzzled voice from beneath me. "How d'ye know my name?"

I dropped to my knees and shone the light into the hole.

It was Jack Findlay, all right. I could see his face, pale and a bit squinty in the light, looking up at me. He was wrapped in what looked like a sheet of tin foil, sitting on the rocky floor of the strange little room beneath me.

"It's me, Emma," I said. "What are you doing down there?"

"Emma Stuart?" he said, holding up a hand to deflect the light. "Or … Emma Angus? Whichever one of you it is, can ye please no' shine the light ri' in my eyes?"

I flipped the switch on Alec's torch, and Jack and his small room were immediately swallowed by darkness. "Emma Sheridan," I said. "You know—from the floor of the hotel bar last month?"

Shit.

"I—I mean—we shared a cab in Philadelphia. I'm the one with the blog?"

"I'll be damned," he said. "Emma Sheridan of the blog. I can't believe it. I'm still readin' it, y'know. Every time ye post somethin' new. Ye got robbed!"

I smiled a little to myself. It pleased me more than I could have expressed that an actual human was following my blog, but it was definitely the wrong time for basking.

"Never mind that, now. How'd you get down there? Are you hurt?"

I could hear his sigh echo in the darkness. "Through the hole yer hollerin' down, o' course. And yes—I've hurt my foot. Cannae walk, anyway."

I felt a moment of smugness, not having fallen through the hole myself. But the seriousness of the situation won out.

"I—I don't know if I can climb down to you," I said. "I don't have a rope or anything."

"Oh, ye needn't climb down," he said, his voice indicating shock at the very idea. "Jes' walk round the way ye came. Here—flick the damn torch on again and I'll show ye."

With the light carefully aimed away from his eyes, I soon saw what he'd meant. The small room held nothing but Jack, and a large charred patch of ground in the center of a pebbly floor. But just to one side of him was a full, doorway-sized opening in the stone. I got to my feet, followed the path down the side and was sitting beside him in under a minute.

His face was creased with pain, so I directed the flashlight away.

"Fact-checking," he explained, when I asked again why he was there. "It's an old sentry station. They'd keep the fire burning low here, in the hearth, while they watched the loch for sea-borne enemies. That's why the path rings round to the doorway." His voice dropped in embarrassment. "The bit I fell through was the chimney hole."

I felt shame wash over me at my earlier smugness. If it hadn't been for Alec the cabbie's flashlight, I would likely have taken the quick route down into the hole, too.

"If I put my shoulder under your arm, do you think you might be able to walk?" I asked. "I'm supposed to have a cab coming for me, but he's late."

"Oh, that's grand," Jack said, wincing as he struggled to stand. "And I am right grateful for his tardiness." He placed his arm around my shoulders, and took a tentative step.

"I reckon I can manage, if I don't put all my weight down on it," he said. "Here—gi' me yer pack, so ye don't have to carry that and me, too."

"It's okay, I can manage," I said, but he slid it off my shoulder and onto his own.

"No' much in it, now yer laptop's gone, eh?" he said, as we awkwardly shuffled toward the sentry-room opening.

"So you read that bit?" I gasped. The man was heavier than he looked. "It was a pretty awful day."

"I can imagine."

We continued our slow, shambling progress along the path leading down to the causeway, pausing every few feet for one or the other of us to catch our breath.

Above us, a low moon hung over the craggy dark line of the mountains. The hoot of an owl rang out, and some distance away, another echoed in the dark. The sound seemed so old a primal shiver worked its way through me.

"You're cold," he said. "Hold up a bit."

"No—no, I'm fine," I said, lying through my chattering teeth.

The brilliant moon spoke to a crystal clear sky and though the wind had stopped, the air felt like a solid wall of ice. With one arm, he grabbed the edge of the strange silvery blanket he was wearing and pulled it around my shoulders. I stood there a moment, enveloped in his warmth. "That better?"

My teeth were still chattering, but I nodded. SO much better.

"It's a space blanket," he explained. "Helps a bit, aye? I did think to bring a safety kit, but no food or phone. Daft."

We started along the path toward the road again. My face was still exposed to the icy air, but if we moved carefully, the blanket created a sort of a circle of warmth that surrounded us both.

In the distance, a set of headlights jounced into view.

We stopped to rest against a big rock near the castle-end of the causeway. "Can you make it across here?" I asked. "The cabbie said he wasn't allowed to drive on this bit."

"Yeah, yeah. It's much easier on the flat."

The light of the moon showed me he was lying just as surely as I had been when I declared myself warm. His jaw was tightly set with pain, but I could feel him trying to bear more of his own weight as we inched forward again.

"What were you doing there in the first place?" I asked, more to take his mind off his pain than anything else. "I thought you were working on some secret project after the BBC gig."

"Yeah, well, not much of a secret now, is it?" he said, stopping to rub his good leg, which was clearly getting pretty sore. "I could kill Rebecca for suggesting it, too. The plan was to stand the watch for the length of time a sentry would have done."

"A sentry?"

"Yeah. The man I'm writing about had some experience as a soldier in the fourteenth century, and I wanted to make sure I captured what it really felt like to stand guard all night."

We'd made it about half way across the causeway, and we paused to stop and gasp a bit. I thought about asking him who Rebecca was, but got distracted when he tucked the blanket more closely under my chin.

"I planned to stand eight hours—a full shift," he said quietly, "but I'd only been here two and a half or so before I fell, like an eejit."

I thought about this a minute, stalling in order to bask in the warmth under the magic blanket. Even with our slow progress, any movement swirled the cold air around our legs and upward.

"So, the idea was that if you experienced what your character went through, you'd be able to tell the story better?"

He laughed—a short, sharp, pain-filled sound. "Aye—perhaps a little too thorough in my research, aye?"

We stepped off the edge of the causeway just as the cab came roaring up to the end of the road. It screeched to a stop and I waved my flashlight at it weakly.

Alec leapt out, talking before he'd even made it out of the car. "Ach, I am right sorry, Miss. My car had a flat and I had to travel back half way to Fort William ..." he began, and then stopped short at the sight of Jack.

"I am SO happy to see you," I said, teeth chattering.

He hurried over. "Are ye injured, Miss?"

"Not me—my friend has hurt his foot," I said. "Can you take us to the hospital?"

"Nae problem—ah can have ye back there quick as a wink. Here, let me..." He came around and transferred Jack's weight onto his own shoulder, and half-dragged, half carried him to the back of the cab. He got Jack tucked inside, and then opened the front passenger door for me.

"Looks like ye found yerself a wee ghostie, aye?" he said, with a nod to the back seat. "No' so wee, but lookin' damn pale for all that, aye?"

"No kidding," I muttered, and slid into the delicious embrace of the warm cab.

"You thought I was a ghost?" Jack said, as the cab jounced down the road to Mallaig. "I feel we live in such a cynical age, no one believes in ghosts anymore."

I shrugged, still shivering even in the overheated taxi.

"I was alone on the wall of a fourteenth century castle," I said. "And if you had said something sensible, like maybe 'Help me!' or 'Over here!' instead of moaning, I would have been less likely to assume the worst."

"I don't remember moaning," he said, reflectively. His foot was propped on the seat, but he winced every time the cab hit a bump. "I'm sure it was probably just in your imagination."

He leaned his head back into the corner and closed his eyes. I watched the pale reflection of his profile against the window glass. It was a fine profile, but I looked away. We'd met twice, and this 'Rebecca' had come up both times.

"You didn't say why *you* were there, Emma," he muttered, interrupting my roiled thoughts. His voice was laced with pain and tiredness. "Searching for your Fraser, were you?"

I felt my face flame in the darkness. Susan was the only other person I'd discussed my quest with face-to-face, and that had gone nowhere good. And I did not feel open to sharing with a writer I'd only met once before on a continent three thousand miles away.

"I—I was just having a look around."

"She's trying to find a wee ghostie for a friend," Alec the cabbie added, helpfully. He careened around a corner and the very hospital I had been visiting earlier in the day sailed into view. I looked over my shoulder and found Jack had opened his eyes again. He was smiling, but strangely enough, did not mock me.

"Seems to me we're even," he said quietly. "I believe I helped you out of a rough spot in Philadelphia."

"That you did," I said.

"And you most definitely did the same for me tonight. Much more, in fact."

Alec swung wide and brought us up to the emergency room doors.

"Isn't this reserved for the ambulance?" I said, nervously.

"Ach, it's A&E—and this is both," said Alec, recklessly. "I won' pull in or nothin'. They'll gi' us a hand here, is all."

I climbed out of the car, my legs still stiff from the cold, and just as the cabbie had said, a couple of nurses came out, wheeling a chair. In no time, Jack was whisked away, calling out that he'd be in touch.

I dug in my pack for my wallet, but Alec would have nothing of it.

"I practically abandoned ye out there in that godforsaken ruin," he said. "Auld Alan would slay me if I took a pence off yeh. Now ge' back in and I'll take you to yer B&B."

So that is what I did.

Following Figments…
Noon, March 19
Fort William, Inverness-shire, Scotland

Those of you who have followed my journey from the beginning will know I had a pretty clear route planned. I was going to walk in the footsteps of Claire Beauchamp Randall Fraser, as traced upon the map to be found inside the cover of my copy of OUTLANDER.

There have been a few bumps in that plan, and for all who have posted worried comments, please know I am okay. I've solved the worst of my financial issues for the time being, and I am back on track.

This week, on the advice of a friend (hi Gerald!) I traveled from Fort William to a ruined old castle in the West Highlands. The friend assured me the castle was haunted. And indeed it was.

Let's talk about ghosts, shall we? I am not hunting a ghost myself, but if you are ever on the hunt for a figment or a phantom, then this is the right country for it. And here are a few brief thoughts for those who might want to hunt a Gaelic ghost:

If out of doors, seek a sacred circle or shrouded shrine. Move only by moonlight and search solely in starshine. Ghosts melt away in the rain.

On days of prohibitive weather, seek out charismatic crypts, apparitions in apses and stained-glass specters.

And the best part? Even if you never spy the ghosts you seek, the beautiful old spaces and places in this country will haunt your heart forever.

In spite of my friend's highest hopes, I did not meet an Outlander ghost, nor any of the colorful denizens of the ancient Castle Leoch. I did meet another writer, deep in the research of his own tale. Ankle deep, you might say.

I have one more stop in search of a stone circle, but the truth is, even if I never do find the inspiration for *Craigh na Dun?* I can in no way call myself disappointed. Adventure awaits behind every standing stone.

- ES

---

kc dyer

Comments: 31

HiHoKitty, Sapporo, Japan:

If stone circle begins to hum—run!

MagischeSteinkraus, Berlin, Deutchland:

Nein! Step through...step through!

(Read 29 more comments here...)

I t was just noon by the time I finished the blog post. The Internet cafe had a special on sausage rolls, so I scarfed two of them down and called it brunch.

Being so deeply cold somehow at the castle seemed to justify the need for a recovery day. I'd spent the day after my latest adventure traversing the distance between my big soft feather bed at Auntie Gwen's and the giant, steaming iron tub down the hall.

And in the bath? I read OUTLANDER.

I also put in several hours monopolizing Auntie Gwen's home computer, searching the history of the wee castle where I'd found Jack.

However, after a day of sloth, I was beginning to get a bit anxious about finances. My flagrant spending since cashing in the return ticket in Inverness had seen the lovely large balance dwindling far too rapidly for my liking. I decided that once I had checked out the circle, I'd turn around and head south. Back to Edinburgh, the land of the coffee shop. My greatest area of expertise, and hopefully a decent source of under-the-table cash.

But before any of that, I needed to go visit Gerald. See how he was doing, find out if I had guessed right about his belief the ruin was Leoch. And get more information about the circle.

I arrived at the hospital thirty minutes too early for visiting hours. The nurse who sat at the information desk had the bristling blonde version of the Scottish unibrow, and her gaze when I suggested popping in a bit early was like thunder.

"I'll no' reckon so," she said, arms folded across her ample bosom. "It's two on the notice, and ye'll not get past my desk until that wee clock on tha' wall ower there tells me ye can."

I crept away, knowing full well that if I had a tail, it would be tucked between my legs.

The nurse at the registration desk was not as frightening, but her news was even less welcome. "Findlay, Findlay. Yes, here he is. Are you immediate family?"

"Uh—yes. I'm his—uh—his American cousin."

She tapped her pen on the desk and shot me a wry smile. "Well, Miss American Cousin, yer Scots relative has been discharged. Surprised he didn't let you know before he left, him bein' yer cousin, and all?"

"Oh… well, I—I guess he must have had someone else pick him up. But he was okay, then, when he left?"

"We aren't generally in the habit of letting our patients leave when they are not—as you say—*okay*."

I left the skeptical registration nurse behind and wandered back toward Gerald's ward. If I couldn't find out what had happened to Jack, I could at least bring him up to date on my adventures at the castle. It was ten past two by this time, and the scary unibrow nurse was no longer at her station, so I hopped in the elevator and sailed up to the third floor.

Unlike the previous visit, the ward was empty, except for Gerald's bed. He was sitting up, laughing, with a young man who was himself perched on the bed. I felt quite scandalized at the sight, given the dressing-down I had received for sitting on the bed, and even more so when the young man stood up and I caught sight of the ID card clipped to his waistband.

"Emma—come in, come in! This is Nurse Goodfield—I was hoping you'd get a chance to meet."

The nurse stood up slowly, clearly not troubled at all with the protocol. "Nice to meet you, Emma," he said with a crisp English accent, and shot a grin at his patient. "I'll leave you Yanks to talk in private. Back to check on you later, Mister Abernathy."

Gerald rolled his eyes at me. "They're so formal around here; all Mister this and Miss that. Still—I kinda like it."

"He didn't look so formal to me," I said, pulling up a chair. "I caught hell for sitting on the bed yesterday. This nurse is more of a rule-breaker, maybe?"

Gerald's eyes twinkled. "Jes' the way I like 'em ," he said. "Now—tell me. Did you get to the circle? What happened?"

"No, I did not get to the circle. It's almost two hours away from here—halfway to Inverness!"

Gerald looked crestfallen. "I know that. But I thought you'd hop in a cab and be there before dusk."

"Well, I plan to do that today, after I see you."

This news brightened him up considerably. "Oh, I can't wait to hear what happens," he said, happily.

"Well, in the meantime, I did go to your haunted castle," I said, digging around in my pack for the map. I found it and smoothed it out on the bed.

"Leoch," he breathed, reverently. "Did you ..."

"Leoch my eye," I interrupted. "I checked it out online, Gerald. Jamie's Leoch must have been based on Castle Leod, which is the actual seat of the clan Mackenzie. A real place—not this little wee ruin in the middle of nowhere."

He narrowed his eyes. "Where did you hear that?"

"I told you. On the Internet. I found pictures and everything."

He folded his arms across his chest. "Well, damn. No wonder I didn't see a ghost. Although I did hear tell that a piper has been known to haunt the battlements ..."

I cleared my throat. "So—you know we're not really looking for ghosts here, right? Anyway, I didn't find one either, unless you count a writer with a broken ankle."

Gerald nodded his head appreciatively as I told him the whole story. When I mentioned Jack's name, he let out a little shriek of joy.

"Jack Findlay? Not *THE* Jack Findlay? Did you just about die of excitement?"

"Um—no. He's a pretty nice guy, though. He was doing research at the castle. I think he lives around here, somewhere. How do you know him?"

Gerald actually fanned himself. "Girl—you need to get yourself an education. Have you not read his Dragon Thane books? The man can *write!*"

I shrugged. "Haven't read a word. They're good, are they?"

"After OUTLANDER, they're my favorite books. Let's just say he keeps a decent amount of swash under his buckle. Action, romance, a sprinkling of magic—they've got it all. I can't believe no one's told you about them, you bein' such a Jamie and Claire fan and all."

"I'll make sure to read one as soon as I can," I promised.

"Well, you might want to wait. Rumor is a new book is comin' this year, about Braveheart. It's gonna be *hot,* honey."

He squeezed my hand, and I stood up.

"I'd better run if I'm going to make my bus," I said, and stuffed the map into my pack.

"Write it all down, girl. I need to hear about every detail of that circle, y'hear? I'll be checking the blog every day."

"I promise." I hurried to the door, relieved that Gerald was looking so much better. I flashed a quick final wave, ran out into the hallway and right into the arms of the dark-haired nurse. Unfortunately, those arms were carrying a tray loaded with cups of juice.

Not a single cup was saved.

"I am so, so sorry," I kept repeating, as I helped chase down the paper cups, which were rolling in all directions.

The nurse smiled bitterly and waved over an orderly. "Can you arrange a wet-mop cleanup, Nelita? Thanks so much."

He stood up, the tray in one hand and surveyed the front of what had, moments before, been a pristine uniform. He was soaked from chin to ankles.

I handed him the stack of mostly crushed Dixie cups. Apart from a splash on the toe of one of my shoes, the wave of juice had entirely, uncharacteristically, missed me. "I am *so* sorry," I said again, rendered inarticulate by the magnitude of the disaster.

He glanced through the open door at Gerald, who was doubled over laughing, and then grinned at me, a little more earnestly than before. "Well, you've clearly amused our patient, and that's something. And luckily, I'm washable."

"Oh, thank you for being so understanding," I stammered. "I—I have to run for a bus now, but if there is anything I can do—pay for the cleaning—anything." I pushed one of my cards into his hands.

"Nonsense," he said, tucking the card into his pocket. "All in a day's work. I've another set of scrubs down in my locker. I'll just make sure Gerald hasn't laughed himself into an injury, and then go change."

He made shooing motions. "Now, run along. Don't worry a bit."

I did what I was told.

Halfway down the hall, I spied a final Dixie cup beside a thin trail of juice. Marveling at my ability to maximize a mess, I scooped it up and ran back to add it to the pile I'd given the nurse earlier. Just as I was about to step into the ward, though,

I caught sight of him standing at Gerald's bedside, holding his hand.

Not to be confused with taking his pulse.

I couldn't hear their voices, but their heads were together in close conversation. I dropped the stray cup into a nearby trashcan and tiptoed away from the door. Where I came from, fraternizing with patients was a firing offence, but the look on Gerald's face made me happy to keep anything I had seen strictly to myself.

March 19, 4 pm

North along Loch Ness

Notes to self, since even though there is Wi-Fi on this bus, I can no longer use it as I haven't a laptop. Thank you, Susan.

1. *Remember to check email to see if Jack connected re his ankle.*

2. *After circle, find Internet cafe to put up blog post*

3. *Think about getting a JOB*

4. *Keep eye out for Monster!!!*

I'd run out of the hospital without further incident and had made it to the bus stop just as the bus was pulling up. I felt sad about missing Jack—or at least not having a chance to say good-bye. Our shared experience at the ruined castle made me feel something of a bond with him. A fellow writer, anyway.

I sighed. He would have made a most excellent Jamie-contender, apart from the whole 'Rebecca' problem. I remembered the solemn—if somewhat drunken—pinky-swear with Jazmin after the Egon heartbreak—I would be no-one's Tiffany. NEVER that.

As the bus jogged alongside the waters of Loch Ness, I pushed all thoughts of Jack the writer aside and thought instead about Gerald. He was definitely looking stronger. I wondered if that had anything to do with Nurse Goodfield. And that he was still reading my blog made me happy, too.

The irony of having—apart from my small but faithful overseas contingent—two men as followers of the blog was not lost on me. Maybe chivalry is not dead after all? Or perhaps I just needed to consider being less sexist, myself.

Besides, Gerald was likely only reading to see if my luck at the second stone circle would be better than his. I had to admit, the thought of chasing down another deserted monument was beginning to wear on me, but I had promised and besides, the bus I was riding was headed there, anyway. I vowed to make future plans more Fraser-focused.

With the note-taking and scanning the waters for Nessie, it seemed like no time at all before the driver announced my stop. I stepped off the bus at Drumnadrochit just after five in the afternoon. The bus station was not really much more than a pole on the street, near a small hotel. I'd hoped to pick up a cab at the station, since according to Gerald's map, the stone circle was still about a twenty minute drive away, but as the bus pulled out, there was no line of cabs waiting to meet it.

Not even a single cab.

It had begun to rain lightly, anyhow, so I found myself a small hostel room and lay down to sort out my plans.

I woke at ten the next morning with my copy of OUTLANDER on the pillow. Turned out I had slept on the map. A hint of purple ink traced across one cheekbone as I gazed in the mirror while I brushed my teeth.

Clearly, all the travel had begun to catch up with me. But I knew it couldn't last—I'd have to return to the city and find a job, very soon.

I had a cup of tea while the hostel supervisor banged dishes together in the kitchen, and then headed out toward the bus station to see if I had better luck locating a cab than I had the night before.

Down the street I found a little parking sign with a taxi symbol on it, and planted myself there. If there was a cab to be hailed, I was going to be the one to hail it.

An hour later, not a single taxi had passed.

Not a single car had passed, as a matter of fact. My stomach rumbled and I began to think about finding something to eat. But what if the cab came when I left my spot?

Finally, after another twenty minutes, I spied a lady walking her dog. She smiled at me warmly when I stepped forward.

"Ach, no love—we do have a local taxi-driver, but last I heard his transmission needed an overhaul. We migh' try callin' up tae Inverness, but it'll be a fair wait, I'm sorry to say."

I must have looked disappointed, as she reached out and patted my arm fondly. "Where're ye off to, pet? Here to see family?"

"No, not exactly. I'm looking for—well, I'm looking for this." I held out the very-creased map to her.

She switched the leash to her other hand and pulled on a pair of glasses that had been dangling around her neck on a chain. After a moment, she glanced up at me over the rims.

"Are ye sure, pet? Them stones are ... well, are ye *sure*?" Her voice had dropped to little more than a whisper.

I nodded, and decided to risk the truth. "I'm really just checking it off my list. It's a—it's a bit of a long story."

She pulled her glasses off and they slid down her chest with a quiet rattle. The wind whistled around us a little, skittering last year's leaves along the ground. She looked down at her wristwatch and muttered. "Half-twelve. Should be enough time ..."

Her gaze returned to me, over the top of her glasses. "Well," she said, "if ye *are* sure, then best I drive ye, pet. Come along—it's just this way."

The little terrier on the leash gave me a short, sharp bark as if to say 'get a move on', and we were off.

Valerie Urquhart, for that was her name, had lived in Drumnadrochit all her life, as had her father, and her father's father. "The family's got property in the area," she said. I later discovered that the entire region was in the realm of Clan Urquhart, including a nearby castle on Loch Ness that had been in her family for generations. Whether it was modesty or for some reason I never learned, she shared none of these details with me.

What she did share, however, was her gift.

We were in her small Volvo, rocketing along the road less than ten minutes after I'd first met her.

"It's all right, pet," she said, expertly gearing down to take a sharp corner. "I knew right away you were a good person. I read faces like books, aye? An' when ye showed us the map, well, it was clear I had to help."

The countryside was primarily farm fields, each lined with low rock walls that wound up the hillsides. Any forested patches were mainly peppered with deciduous trees, so the area still had a bit of a bleak, pre-spring look. I could see alders and willows and even a few elm trees through the windows as we whipped past. And there was the barest trace of green to the blur of trees going by, showing spring weather might not be too far away to hope for, at least.

The little terrier, whose name was Wullie, stood on his hind legs the whole way, front paws balanced expertly on the back of the front seat as we rounded the corners. Gerald's map indicated the distance as twenty minutes from the town. Valerie had the car parked and was hopping out with the dog in under twelve.

My heart sank. I could see before I even got out of the car that this area was flat, again— not on a hillside, and not really even among the trees. Sheep placidly grazed one field over, beyond a ragged rock wall.

The small parking lot was entirely empty, and Valerie had stopped to wait for me by the path leading to the stones.

"So, ye've seen the stones at Clava, I take it."

I nodded and stepped past her onto the path, but she put a hand on my arm. "Emma—your family. Before they went to America—were they Scots?

"Not that I know," I said. "My dad's family was Irish, and I may have had a great-grandmother from Aberdeen, but I think that's it."

"Ach, that's Celtic on both sides, then," Valerie said. She reached out and took one of my hands in both of hers, and then closed her eyes.

We stood there in a most awkward silence, me desperate to withdraw my hand but not wanting to offend the kind lady who had, after all, driven me well out of her way. And she, standing still, humming softly to herself.

After what seemed like an eternity, she opened her eyes and looked at me earnestly. "There is a great longing in you, Emma. And yer willin' to work hard fer what ye want, there's nae doubt about that."

She was still holding my hand, and she unclasped hers from around mine but did not quite let go. Instead, she turned my hand around, so the palm was open and facing up. "Sometimes the best thing is to jes' hol out yer hand like this, in yer mind's eye—p'raps when you are about to drift off to sleep or even jes' when ye have a quiet moment. Hold out yer hand and picture what you want in it—in your own grasp."

We both looked down at my palm, held out between us. And for an instant in my mind's eye, I saw a hand there, clasping my own. My fingers curled inward to a fist, involuntarily, and she patted it softly before releasing me.

"That's the way," she said. "Now let's see about these stones, shall we?"

I hadn't said a word about my travels, or my intent regarding visiting the ancient site, but after our brief moment in the parking lot, I felt almost as if I had no secrets from Valerie— as though she had some weird grasp on my inner life. But instead of making me feel self-conscious and ridiculous, I felt strangely at peace.

That didn't last long.

We stepped off the path into the clearing, which I could see had been fenced away from a farmer's field. Just along the neat footpath was a collection of rusty red Highland cattle alternately grazing and staring into space. The circle of stones, eleven in number, was startlingly similar to the ones near Culloden. It surrounded a pile of rocks, indented on one side, with a rounded hollow center.

"It's a cairn," said Valerie. "Long deserted. Robbed, in times past, of any valuables. But something still remains."

She crossed her arms over her chest. "'Twas the old 'uns that built this cairn, and the ones at Balnuaran, too," she said, quietly. "Aligned with the midsummer moon, but not jes' any moon. The entrance lies in the path of the rare, long moon, wha' comes but once a generation."

She stepped to the edge of the cairn. "Did ye walk through the ones up north?" she asked.

When I nodded, she gestured toward the low entrance. "Those at Balnuaran are open to the sky, but this one still has its roof. It's corbeled, y'see, strong enough to hold those rocks in place for millennia."

Pointing at the middle, she walked back over to where I lingered near one of the low standing stones. "When the archeologists finally went in, there were no remains of the body. Just a sort of stain on the stone, showing how they'd placed her, face out to see the moon as it waxed full on all her children and theirs, each in turn."

"It was a woman?" I asked. "I thought these old monuments mostly revered kings and warriors and so on."

Valerie smiled. "Oh, they've no proof, o' course, as there were no remains found to test. But I've had my hand on that center stone." She pointed to a large slab that rested to one side of the opening at the top. "And I can tell ye, I feel her still, or what she once was."

We stood silently together and watched the wind create weird shapes in the dead grasses sown across the roof of the cairn, each lost in our own thoughts.

"Can you climb down through there to get into the center?" I asked her, at last.

Valerie nodded. "Oh, aye—it's called a passage grave for a reason, y'know. But I'd not like to do it m'self, I'll tell ye, as it is a wee low ceiling. I'm too claustrophobic for that sort of thing these days, though I done it enough when I was a young'un, up to no good here with the other boys and girls." She chuckled, eyes distant.

I walked over to the entrance, a dark smudge of shadow amid the gray stone. "It was here that the ghost stood," I blurted. "At Clava. I saw him and another man—a friend who was there—saw him, too. I could see his kilt in the moonlight, but not much else. Heavy boots, maybe."

Valerie, walking up to join me, burst into delighted laughter. "Ach, girlie, someone's havin' ye on. Ye'll see no tartan-clad ghosties at these sites. The spirits of any who remain here— even those of the warriors who may have guarded them— came long before the plaid. Long before the bonnie sort of folk you'd recognize these days. It was the old 'uns that made this place. Tha's why I came with ye today. Whether ye're of the Celtic blood or no', it doesn't do to come unlearned before the old 'uns."

I opened my mouth to argue with her. And then I remembered. "My friend who was here—he stayed all night hoping to see the ghost."

"And …?" She crossed her arms then, waiting for me to finish.

"He's in the hospital," I admitted reluctantly. "He caught a chill and it turned into pneumonia."

Valerie nodded, tracing a finger along the surface of the standing stone. "American?" she asked, though from her smile, I felt she must know the answer.

"From Georgia," I said. "But his mother's family came from England."

She shrugged. "Who's to know what's at play?"

We both stood quiet a moment, and then Valerie raised her head. "I don't have a sense of him, I'm sorry to say. But I hope he'll be well again soon."

"I think he's doing much better," I said.

She nodded, and stepped back onto the path. "And glad I am to hear it. But for you, though … have ye seen enough? Is there anything else I can answer for ye?"

Looking back over the low cairn, I could see the old stones standing sentinel around it. Behind it fields dotted with red cattle spread across the landscape, completed by the white coats of sheep on the nearby hillside. The only sound I could hear, apart from the cars on the motorway in the distance, was the jagged cawing of a crow as it flew overhead.

I turned and walked back to Valerie. "This is such a beautiful place," I said quietly. "Just looking around here, it takes my breath away. I can understand how your family has stayed here for so many generations. You must never want to leave."

She whistled sharply for Wullie and then smiled at me as he came bounding up. "For all that's true, pet, I *am* fond of a wee jaunt to Pamplona in February. The winters here can be a mite dreich."

Future Feelings…
9:00 pm, March 20
Drumnadrochit, Scotland

Just back from an amazing visit to another set of standing stones. This time, my guide was someone who *knows* things. Her heart and her blood are in this soil. And she taught me the Scots word for the constant rain and mist, too.

We did not see a ghost, or find a Highlander to

sweep me off my feet. But she has reminded me that my dreams are always within my grasp.

First, though? I need to find a job.

– ES

Comments: 13

Gerald Abernathy, Ft. William, Scotland:

Nothing?

Nothing?

Ah, well … at least you didn't get sick. Email me, y'all!

Jack Findlay, Edinburgh, Scotland:

Don't have an email address for you, Emma, so I thought I'd just drop you a quick note here on your blog to let you know all is well. Ankle is broken, but plastered and I'm back down to Edinburgh for re-coup and a chat with my editor. Thanks again for your help, and Godspeed.

Jack

(Read 11 more comments here…)

I leaned back in my seat and sipped the last of my almost-cold tea. So Jack's ankle was broken. I felt a spasm of guilt as I thought about him taking that long walk all the way from the castle to the road. But at least he was okay. Still writing. When my life returned to some semblance of normal, I would have to stop and buy one of his books. Gerald certainly thought he was a great writer. And speaking of Gerald, wherever I ended up next, I needed to email him. He clearly wanted all the details from the trip to the circle.

Not that I had a lot to share.

By the time I'd read the last of the comments as they rolled in, the woman at the front of the cafe had cleaned off all the tables and was looking at me pointedly. I gathered up the remains of my biscuit and backpack and stepped outside. The bus stop was right next to the coffee shop. A solid, dreary rain had begun to fall and I'd been hoping that the cafe would stay open for shelter until the bus arrived, but no joy on that front.

I pulled up my hood, waited for the lights of the next bus and thought about Valerie. About the moment when she'd held my hand. The circle of stones hadn't been *Craigh na Dun*, I'd known that all along. And even as star-struck as this voyage had been from the start, I had no real expectation of a Highland warrior suddenly manifesting for my approval. I couldn't quite remember just what I had been thinking at the onset of this journey, but the route I had taken had provided dreamy young Scottish men in distinctly short supply.

I had to face facts. In spite of the rain, and the cold and my inability to find a reasonable facsimile of *Craigh na Dun*, the country was beginning to take a hold on me. The Scottish grip was squeezing tightly on my heart. But finding my Fraser had not happened. I needed to earn enough to buy the plane ticket as promised, and go home.

A pair of lights swung round the corner and the bus pulled up at last.

Filleting Fish…
8:00 pm, April 3
Glasgow, Scotland

Been here for almost two weeks now, having caught the bus down from Drumnadrochit. Have to admit to having a bit of a struggle finding a job. As pretty much expected, it seems that a visitor's visa generally doesn't allow a person to work while they are visiting. At least not legally. So for your edification here are a few thoughts on things you should *not* do while looking for work while away from your homeland:

1. Don't be a linguistic loser: Affecting a Scottish accent in order to convince potential employers of your local status is not recommended. They can tell. They really can.

2. Pathetic principle: Do not turn down a position as a street-hawker with a haughty "I can do better", only to return and apply again when it turns out you can't. Because they remember. They really do.

3. Fatal flaw: And above all, do not overstate your skill set, particularly as a salesperson of seafood comestibles, as—and trust me on this one—it leads only to a back room, an apron that smells of fish guts, and a plethora of scaling-knife wounds.

From these tips you may be able to tell I found
something last week at last. I was going to call
myself a piscine executive, but the truth is I
have been cutting up fish for a man who owns a
shop here in Glasgow. However, twelve-hour days
of chopping and gutting don't leave much time for
blogging. Or Fraser-finding. Hoping things will
loosen up a bit, soon.

- ES

Comments: 6

HiHoKitty, Sapporo, Japan:

Emma-san! I too work in a factory. Chin up—
twelve hour days do not sound that bad. I work
fourteen each day, plus English class and violin
practice, yet I still find time to read your blog.
Is your new employer handsome?

(Read 5 more comments <u>here</u>…)

Flogging Fiction...
1:00 am, April 15
Glasgow, Scotland

So—ah—the fish-processing job didn't work out, in the end. My supervisor was … well. It just didn't work out, is all.

Anyway, I've got another job, selling speculative fiction magazines door to door. Starts tomorrow. There's a really small quota—I think it's going to be perfect. More time to blog, anyway, and if I'm going door to door, I'll get to explore the city as I work, and maybe meet a few people!

- ES

Comments: 6

SophiaSheridan, Chicago, USA:

Emma, I can lend you the money you need. You can pay me back when you get a decent job here. Chopping off fish heads? Direct sales? And I thought nothing could be worse than your coffee-shop drudgery. Come home!

(Read 5 more comments here…)

Financial Flagging…
11:00 pm, April 30
Glasgow, Scotland

Glasgow is an amazing city. But, you know? I'm re-thinking my role in direct sales. I suspect I lack what my sister would call the correct skill-set. Or financial acumen. Or the ability to sell anything except maybe a decent latte.

‐ ES

Comments: 0

I logged off long before my money had run out and gently rested my head on the edge of the desk. Now that I had the time to blog again, I couldn't find any words to say. My enthusiasm for writing had dried up, along with my quest. Glasgow *was* amazing—I wasn't lying. But it was a city—a fairly big city—with all the attendant city issues. Like expensive housing. High jobless rate. Creepy employers.

The truth was, the entire month of April had been a blur, with one terrible job morphing into another. I'd had two—no, three—jobs, all of which I'd had to run away or be fired from.

The fishmonger job had looked perfect at first, apart from the whole fish angle, until I went to wash up at the big sink in the back after a shift and found my shift supervisor doing the same.

Except he was not wearing his uniform—or anything at all, really.

It became immediately clear that our expectations on my job description differed.

Luckily, since one of us was naked, it only took me ten minutes or so to lose him on Crown Street. The fact that he didn't seem worried about chasing after me through his neighborhood, crying and calling my name—while stark naked—led me to believe it may have happened before. The public thoroughfare didn't slow him down any, either, but once I made it onto the Albert Bridge, I could no longer hear the telltale sound of his junk whacking against his legs as he ran. Who knows? Maybe his feet got cold …

I've said it before. Fish make people crazy.

Running through the streets of Glasgow in my bloody apron had left me sweaty and freaked out, so I spent the rest of the night in an all-night diner, going through the classifieds of a discarded *Daily Record*. I thought about going to the police, but decided that my own illegal employee status might not make me the most credible witness.

The lone waitress in the place came up with her coffee pot and filled my cup. "Ye want anything to eat?" she asked, giving my apron the side-eye.

"No, thanks." My stomach was still in knots from the unexpected, lurid street-race.

She shrugged and went back to filling saltshakers. By the time she made it around to my table again, I'd crossed off just about every listing. My only area of expertise was working at a coffee shop, and there wasn't a single job listed.

"Is there another paper?" I asked, as she refilled my coffee cup.

"Yeah. But no' much in the way o' work, aye?"

I sighed. "I tried being a fish monger, but it didn't really work out."

"Ah. That explains the smell then."

"Oh—yeah. Sorry about that."

In the end, the waitress had taken pity on me and sent me off to a "fella" she knew who was running a deal to sell science fiction magazines door to door.

A week later, though, he'd given me the boot, since I hadn't sold a single subscription. The Scots were canny about value, and everyone I'd approached indicated puzzlement as to why anyone would buy a magazine when the facsimile was available online.

I'd had no good answer.

So.

I'd run away from paycheck number one. Struck out on paycheck number two—*"Commission only, luv"*. My last attempt was a job I had managed to land only that morning. It involved holding a cardboard sign mounted on an unfinished wood stick, entreating passersby to eat 'New York-Style' pizza. I also had leaflets to hand out.

I rubbed my eyes, and thought about logging on again, to take advantage of my last couple of minutes of time online. I'd only come in because my feet were sore, anyway. But my comments had dwindled. Even the faithful HiHoKitty had been silenced by my increasingly desperate posts, so I needed to think of something optimistic to say. Maybe I should consider a post on how to run from a naked employer?

I'd just flexed my fingers to type again, when a shadow loomed over me. It was the Internet café manager.

"Oi! Wot's that, then?" he demanded.

"It's my sign." I tilted it so he could see. "I've tucked it in out of the way."

"No, no, no. Yeh cain't have tha' in here, aye?"

"I can't …?"

"No soliciting on the premises."

"Oh, I'm not …"

"Out wit' yeh. And mind yeh don't leave any of them flyers behind. I know yer kind—leavin' that crap all ower the place. Out wit' yeh!"

I took my flyers and fled.

Outside, I crossed the street and sat on a bench by the bus station. I stacked the flyers neatly on the seat beside me, and tilted the sign against the back wall. The gray mist of Glasgow settled onto the flyers, which began to curl at the edges almost immediately.

In front of me, a bus pulled up. Emblazoned on the side was an ad with a very large man in a kilt throwing some kind of huge stone boulder into the air. Behind him the sun shone with a warm yellow glow. Above the man's swinging kilt was printed *Gather Your Clan At The Nairn Games*.

I hadn't seen a man wearing a kilt since I'd arrived in Glasgow. My heart lurched.

The door of the bus opened, and I stood up. Didn't even look back at the flyers or the 'New York-style Pizza' sign.

"Where're ye headed, young lady?" said the bus driver, as I stepped inside.

I pushed off my hood and wiped a handful of wet hair away from my face.

"Nairn," I said, and paid the fare.

It only took me a minute or two to sort out the controls. If I'd known driving a carriage was this easy, I'd have picked it up long ago. But even though I held on tightly to the leathers— and who knew reins would work exactly like my Xbox?—the horses still raced toward the cliff.

I looked behind me for help, but both Elisabeth Bennet and her mother were dead on the floor. The door to the carriage burst open and the entire rest of the Bennet family was there, all screaming at once. I leaned back with all my weight on the reins and the carriage slowed a little, the wheels skimming just inches away from the cliff, shooting pebbles off the precipice. Iron-gray seas thrashed in foamy fury below.

One of the reins snapped in half and Mr. Darcy screamed like a girl.

Fried Food...
10:30 am, May 1
Nairn, Scotland

I have been trying so hard to do the right thing while I am here. To follow my map. To stick to the plan. But the plan has a way of not working, somehow.

Last night, I got onto a bus and left Glasgow. And today, I'm in Nairn, a seaside village in the Highlands; a place of great beauty and deep history. I've had a deep-fried Mars Bar for breakfast, which has banished the terrible Jane Austen dreams that came as a result of last night's mystery meat sandwich, and am about to embark on a research session to learn more of this place. Of its people.

Of the Nairn Highland Games.

Plan be damned. My journey is now back in the hands of fate.

Wish me luck!

- ES

Comments: 23

SophiaSheridan, Chicago, USA:

Wish you luck as you put yourself into the hands of fate? Emma, you've really lost it. After a month of trying, you can't even manage to hold down a job to earn the money to get home? I just can't read this any more. The stress is too much.

Jack Findlay, Inverness, Scotland:

Been buried in final galley corrections for the new manuscript, so I'm just catching up on your adventures today. Wonderful to see you back in the Highlands again, though I'm not sure the job prospects will be any better than Glasgow, to tell you the truth. At any rate, wanted to wish you a happy first day of summer, such as it is. May the sun shine down on your adventures while you are here.

Jack

(Read 21 more comments here...)

I shook my head and looked out the window of the library. It was May Day—how did *that* translate to the first day of summer? Jack had to be nuts—or making some kind of twisted Scottish joke.

That had to be it.

But he was right about one thing. The sun *was* shining in this wee town, and it was so good to be out of the Glasgow gray.

The dream I had awakened from on the bus had been brutal. And the inside of my mouth had tasted like a grease-slicked fry pan. But a wander through the town in the crisp, early sunlight had cured so much of what ailed me. Over my odd breakfast, I'd read through my copy of OUTLANDER yet again.

I couldn't recall if Claire had ever made the journey to Nairn, and I wanted to check it out. I had flipped pages, scanned and read some more, but the text of OUTLANDER proved no help. Claire had obviously not made Nairn a stop in her travels, at least in the first book. The map inside the cover was even less help, since the town name was nowhere to be found, and at that moment, I wasn't quite sure exactly where I had ended up. Had I taken a bus to nowhere?

Luckily, the man at the chippy had handed me a creased and dog-eared copy of a leaflet cheerily titled 'Welcome to Nairnshire'. The back half of the leaflet was missing, but it at least gave me a place to start. Then he pointed me to the Tourist Center, which shared space with the town library and actually offered use of a free Internet terminal for visitors.

I walked out into the street, feeling hopeful for the first time in what felt like weeks. This was, after all, the land of the hardy Highland Warrior. The Nairn Games. Another chance to complete my journey. Forget the ghosts that Gerald had me chasing—I needed to find my very own Fraser. Mind you, I needed to find a laundromat first. If I did come across my

Jamie, he'd probably like me better in clothes that had been recently washed.

But still. I felt so welcome already.

Inside the library, I learned that the town itself had a population somewhere north of 8,000 people, and that the locals considered their wee metropolis to be the center of golfing excellence, with two large courses nearby and more than forty others within a sixty mile radius. I wondered briefly about a golf-playing Jamie, and then rejected the thought.

I needed a guy who had time for noble pursuits. Like the pursuit of Emma, for example.

The brochure went on to note that other than being a seaside village with many popular tourist amenities, Nairn also hosted one of the largest competitive games events in the Highlands.

Of course. I'd known that from the kilted man on the side of the bus. Seeing as there were fewer clan wars in the twenty-first century, and cattle poaching had become almost unheard of, the Highland Games seemed as good a place as any to carry on the quest for my personal version of Jamie.

Unfortunately, a quick search of *Nairn - Highland Games* brought me a more complete story. While it turned out the dog-eared little brochure from the chippy man was correct, and there *were* Highland Games in Nairn every year, they were held in late summer. Which made perfect sense. It can't be easy to toss a caber while slogging through a muddy field.

I logged off the computer with a sigh.

At least some of my commenters had returned. But aside from the cheery note from Jack and the diatribe from my sister, all the comments came from overseas readers. All asked, in a range of dialects and with varying degrees of subtlety, when the hell I was going to find my Highlander and fall in love, already.

Since my last experiences with men had been a naked fishmonger and an irate café owner, I obviously needed more practice.

So there I sat, months away from the Games that drew the muscle-y Highland boys, one of whom might be my own personal Fraser. I had no idea what to do next. From the way my comments were going, it was clear the outside world was losing patience in my quest. And the dwindling contents of my wallet were dragging me down worse than the light blog traffic.

I decided to take a look around the place, anyway. I was, after all, deeper in the Highlands than ever before. I could at least allow myself a day to play the tourist before addressing the twin evils of facing up to my financial situation and heading back south to find work. And who knows? Maybe there would be a singles bar in Nairn.

Beside the computer terminal was a tourist information bulletin board, which was speckled with bent pushpins and old messages. After reading every torn page, it soon became clear there was no hostel in the town, or at least not one open in the off-season. Since the bulletin board and the computer desk were the full extent of the tourist information section, I wandered up to the library front desk and picked up a pamphlet detailing local accommodations.

Even at off-season rates, there wasn't a bed and breakfast anywhere that could match hostel rates.

Finally the lady behind the desk leaned forward on one elbow and looked up at me over her glasses. "Try Missus McGuinty, down Lochloy Road," she said, with a serious nod. "I've heard she'll give travelers a special rate in springtime, especially those who are willing to look after themselves."

"My budget is just ten pounds a night," I repeated.

"You try her, pet. She's got a lovely spot out there, facing the firth. Ye won't be disappointed, I promise."

It felt like destiny.

On the library lady's advice, I tried to banish my bad memories of earlier experiences and rented a bicycle from a garage across the street. After a twenty-minute ride into the teeth of an extremely brisk wind, I found myself at a deeply rutted driveway marked with the McGuinty's B&B sign.

Ominously, beneath the name, a little wooden plaque reading NO had been hooked on before the word Vacancy. I hopped off my bike, anyway, and pushed it carefully into one of the mostly-frozen ruts in the drive.

Inside the fenced yard off the lane, an epic struggle unfolded before my eyes. A squat old man, his iron-gray hair slicked back from a face the color of a fire engine was fighting a losing battle with a giant orange bull.

I'd never seen anything like this animal before. Huge horns on either side of its head spread out as wide as the handlebars on a Harley. A mane of long, curly red hair cascaded down the creature's forehead, obscuring its eyes. Completing the picture was a comparatively small pink nose, which at the moment was blowing twin bores of steam straight into the face of the small farmer.

The bull, massive testicles swinging, was pulling the man backwards by virtue of a rope harness the farmer had somehow tangled around the animal's head. The other end of the harness was clutched tightly in the hands of the farmer. The old man had his heels dug deeply into the mud, but I could see by the twin channels in the dirt behind him that the bull's tactics had proven successful for quite a distance already. The farmer's jaw was set, though, and there was no aura of defeat about him. I stood beside my bicycle, not sure what to do, but he didn't spare a glance for me.

"Ye'll no beat me, yeh wee bastard," the man hissed, but the bull pulled him steadily on toward the open gate to the road.

"Would you like me to shut the gate?" I called out, helpfully. I certainly wasn't going to offer anything else. That bull was a monster, taller than the farmer by nearly a foot.

"O' course I dinnae want ye to close the blasted gate. Jes' get yerself and yon bicycle ou' of the bluidy way."

By this time, the bull had picked up a bit of speed, as far as slow-motion tug-o-war contests went, and I could see the man's arms shaking as he clutched the harness for dear life.

Reasoning that I could be more help if I went up to the farmhouse to fetch Mrs. McGuinty, I did as the old man said, and pushed my bike further along one of the deep ruts. I could hear the bull blowing and the man grunting with exertion behind me as I hurried up the lane.

But when I got to the house, no one came to my desperate knock.

I heard a cry behind me and turned to see the bull had pulled the harness at last out of the old man's hands, but instead of the animal running along the road, it was charging up the hill into the field beyond. The old man, having closed the gate behind the animal, was stumping up the laneway toward me.

"I'm so sorry I couldn't find anyone to come and help," I said, as the farmer strode up and began cleaning his boots on an enormous iron scraper beside the front door.

"No help to be had or needed," he said, and having scraped his boots, put a hand on the door. "I manage on mah own jes' fine, thank-ye-very-much."

The bull, still trailing the rope harness, was by this time frolicking up a small hill behind the farmhouse. The farmer stared up at the bull, a smile of satisfaction on his still-rosy face. "Did tha' wee bastard right," he said, chuckling a little.

"How did you get him to go that way?" I asked. "I thought he was going to head straight out onto the road."

"'Sa kissin' gate," the old man said. He tapped his temple with a muddy finger. "It's all abou' the brains, y'know. The young fella wouldnae gone through that gate for any money, less I told 'im he wasnae welcome."

"So—you pulled him along to convince him he wasn't to go that way?"

"Aye, did that, indeed. And yer the sharp one to figure it out, aren't yeh?" He nodded at me approvingly. "Sure enough—lookit him up there. He'll be safe up away from the ladies down ta lower pasture until he's welcome."

"What about the harness—won't he trip himself on that?"

The old man opened up the front door of the cottage and shrugged out of his overcoat. "Nah, nah—won't hurt the wee bastard for an hour or two. Be needin' to halter train 'im for the show this summer, anyroad. 'Reinhardt's mah prime stock, for all his stubbornness."

"Reinhardt?"

"Aye. After an ol' beau, an all." He paused and looked me up and down.

"What'll you be needin' then? Directions to Nairn?"

I came back to myself. "No—no. I think I'm at the wrong spot, actually. I was told to find Mrs. McGuinty's place. There's no hostel in Nairn and I'm looking for somewhere to spend the night. I heard she offers good rates."

The old man jutted his jaw at me contemplatively for a moment. "Lookin' fer a place, are ye?"

"Uh—yeah. But the library lady told me to speak to Mrs. McGuinty, actually."

"She did, eh? That Katy is full of well meanin', now, ain't she?"

By that point I was starting to think the lady at the library hadn't been so well meaning after all. "I guess so. If you can just point me in the right direction …"

The farmer paused again, and then barked so loudly that I jumped a full foot backwards. He slapped his knee furiously and I realized he was laughing.

"Well, Missy, yer lookin' at 'er. I'm Morag McGuinty. Come inside—we'll have a cuppa tea and discuss terms, shall we?"

And that's how I found myself living in a converted cow barn in Nairn, Scotland.

Once Morag McGuinty had peeled off several layers of rain gear, she turned out to be not only more female than her first impression left me with, but also younger. She'd taken over the farm when her father had died and had run it since, all on her own.

"I'll be fifty next year. Never married," she chuckled, over a cup of steaming tea and a plate piled high with raisin scones. "Though not for want of suitors, I promise ye." With the twinkle in her eye, and that strong back, I had little doubt she was telling the truth.

After the hot tea and scones, she threw on her coat again and took me out the back of the farmhouse to a long outbuilding. It was gray stone with a clay roof, neat and trim.

"Built by mah great-great granda," Morag said, as she swung open the large wooden door. "Been kept up, o' course. His ghost wouldnae allow me otherwise."

Inside the barn, the walls had been whitewashed and a long trough ran the length of the room. We walked past several stalls, each smelling redolently of cow and hay. Morag stopped to peer over the top of one gate. Inside, a hornless version of the bull Morag had battled earlier lay in quiet composure, her back tucked against the wall of the stall. Alongside her, in a mound of fresh hay, nestled a tiny, fuzzy version of his mother, his coat a slightly paler shade of red.

"This 'un arrived las' night," she said, her voice glowing with pride. "He'll be a braw 'un, jes' like his father."

She gave a final fond glance to the calf and his mother and then stumped up to a door at the far end of the barn. "Here we are," she said. "See what y' think."

The tiny apartment set up in her cow barn was perfect. The room was only about fifteen feet square, but it had space for the bed tucked under a dormer window and a tiny kitchen counter with a hotplate and even a microwave. Fitted in beside the sink was a half-sized fridge. One door led into the barn, and the other into a compact bathroom.

"I can't believe you can offer this for ten pounds," I stammered, feeling guilty for even asking. "Maybe the woman at the library gave me the wrong rate?"

"Nae, nae," Morag scoffed. "The hand sleeps here in t' summertime, bu' I havenae hired anyone for the job, yet. Yer safe here for a month, at leas'."

"Oh, I just need it for the night," I assured her. "I have to head south to Edinburgh and find work in the next day or two."

When she closed the door and stamped off back to the house, though, I took a moment to stretch out on the bed and feel my back crackling with the comfort of it. This bike ride had been so much more satisfactory than the last, and it was nice to feel that no matter what happened, it was unlikely I'd have my things stolen by my roommates.

The cattle mooed their agreement through the wall.

7:30 am, May 2

Nairn, Scotland

Notes to self:

Remember to email Gerald. I feel like he's got something going on with that nurse...y'all.

I woke from a deep, dreamless sleep to the sound of banging in the barn.

Apart from the distinct smell of animal in the vicinity, I lay there and felt completely, strangely at home. I'd slept as well as I could remember. The rental bike wasn't due back until the end of the day. And for all its remarkable mod-cons, Morag's barn did not have a computer, so I couldn't even go online to be yelled at or frozen out by my sister.

It was the most deliciously freeing feeling.

I rolled over and wrote the reminder to myself regarding Gerald and then headed for the bathroom. While I was busy inside, there was a sharp knock at my door. When I emerged, I took two further steps through the wee flat and stuck my head out into the barn. There was no sign of Mrs. McGuinty, but on the low table beside my door was a tray groaning with eggs and ham and toast and sausages and marmalade.

I fell on it like I hadn't eaten in a week.

Afterwards, after I'd gratefully returned the dishes to the kitchen, Mrs. McGuinty shooed me out into a strangely sunshine-y morning, refusing my offer to help wash up. I squinted up at the blue sky and thought about riding back into town to find an Internet cafe. I could even return and use the library's computer. But I had the bicycle rented for a few more hours, and I had saved the map Mrs. Henderson had given me in Inverness. There was an old fort nearby, and that meant I had enough time to go exploring.

Fort George bristled belligerently on an outcropping into the Moray Firth in a place called Ardersier. It took me about an hour to ride over there from Mrs. McGuinty's farm, through winds that must have blown straight in from an iceberg-laden North Sea.

When I'd read the bit of history on the fort that I found in my mangled Nairnshire pamphlet, and it seemed so near, it felt crazy not to go see it. But by the time I'd finally gotten there, I had reason to be happy for every calorie I'd downed at breakfast.

There were only a couple of cars in the parking lot as I approached, and I was so grateful at the prospect of getting out of the biting wind that I didn't feel at all intimidated by the large, military drive leading up to the place. I pedaled across a sturdy drawbridge over a gorge of a moat that must once have held water, but these days was only filled with closely mown grass. A few specks of green showed here and there, but the grass was mostly frozen—just like me.

Inside the front gate, I sighed in relief to be out of the wind, and paid a little more of my rapidly dwindling cash reserves to tour the place.

The huge fort was about as different as possible from the battlefield at Culloden. With the enormous stone walls and carefully laid-out grounds, it felt almost like a modern military installation, which, in fact, it turned out to be. It was hard to wrap my head around the idea that men who had fought the Scots on the broken, barren fields of Culloden had returned to build this enormous place. Designed to quell Scots rebellions and the Jacobites in particular, the fort built by the King's men and soldiers had never fallen, and continued to be home to a battalion of soldiers.

I wandered around, mostly sticking to the inside exhibits because of the chill wind. I peeked inside the brew house and the bakery to get a feel for how the soldiers of Jamie's time ate and drank in such large numbers. After I tired of examining rows of iron pots and pans, I left the kitchens and stuck my head inside the little chapel.

It turned out to be not so little. The place was completely empty when I crept inside, but the bright, spring sunlight shone in through one of the most beautiful stained-glass windows I had ever seen.

I took a moment and slipped into one of the pews near the back. It was cold inside, and profoundly quiet. I leaned back on the bench, stared up at the glass and let my mind empty.

This fort hadn't left me with the deep feelings I'd had in Culloden, but there was a certain peace to be found, bathed in the dancing light coming through the glass. Those windows had been there since the time Jamie had joined the rebellion.

"Am I interruptin'?" said a quiet voice in my ear.

I jumped a little, and instinctively slid a bit along the bench. "No—not at all. Just looking at the lovely stained glass."

The young man who sat beside me was in uniform, but not period-style. He was dressed as a full-out modern soldier.

"Aye," he said. "It is, at that. Until you're assigned to clean it, and then all them wee panes suddenly seem more like work."

I laughed. "Yeah, I guess that's true. Do you have to clean it often?"

"Nae, on'y once for me. Bu' tha' was enough, believe me." He held out a hand. "And you are …?"

"Emma."

"Brian Morrison," he said. "Corporal."

His hand was very warm. It's possible I held on a moment longer than he expected, but covered by grinning at him. "You pronounce your first name Bree-an? I've never heard that." (*In a boy...*, I thankfully managed to not say aloud.)

He smiled back at me and broadened his accent further. "Ach, weel, ah'm from Glasgae, ye ken, an' we have our oon way of dooin' t'ings."

I'd never have been able to understand that accent two months earlier, and I felt a moment of pride that I'd mastered what practically amounted to a foreign language.

I also felt a little flushed, to tell you the truth, as I looked into those brown eyes.

The eyes of a warrior.

I gave him my sweetest smile, and then almost immediately blew it. "Glasgow? Ah—you don't know any gnomes, do you? By the name of Rabbie?"

He looked puzzled, and dropped the broad accent. "Did you say 'gnome'...?"

Dammit. How could I bring up the Rabbie fiasco at a time like this?

I shook my head. "No—no. Never mind. It was just a very strange person I met from Glasgow. He's a— a—little person."

"Glasgow has more n' half a million souls who call it home, aye," he said, thoughtfully. "I couldnae possibly know all of 'em . Cept you'd think I'd remember a gnome ..."

"It's okay," I said, hastily. "So, you work here?"

"Stationed here, aye. About a year now."

"So ... on active duty? What do you do around here, then?"

He crinkled his eyes at me and Scot-ified himself again. "Ach, if I tol' yeh, American ally or no, I'd have tae shoot ye, lass."

I think I may have looked a little too eager at the prospect. Anyway, my expression made him laugh. "Mostly training, actually," he said. "Wha' about you? A bi' early in the season to be touring about, isn't it?"

"Yeah. It's sort of a long story."

He got to his feet. "Righ'. Well, I'm off."

I jumped up, too. "Off? I—I was hoping you'd be able to—ah—show me around a bit."

"Sorry, Miss. I've duty down in the mess at fourteen hundred. If ye stop at the front desk, though, we have some seniors who volunteer their time."

"Sure—no problem. Thanks so much," I babbled.

He turned away, proving the view from the back was just as impressive as from the front, and then stopped suddenly. "I should give you this, if you want it," he said, reaching into his back pocket.

"Sure, oh for sure," I said, still babbling. I really needed to practice that talking to nice men thing.

Corporal Morrison pulled a slightly shopworn pamphlet out of his pocket and handed it to me. The ring on his left hand glinted briefly in a ray of light coming from the windows. "We're supposed to give 'em to the tourists—glad I remembered!"

I thanked him and he left. The light that had shone so pointedly on his wedding band faded behind a cloud, which made the pamphlet hard to read, but I could see it held a brief history of the fort. I tucked it into my pack for future perusal and stood up.

The chat with Corporal Married had been lovely, at least until I saw the ring. The whole country was lovely. But as the cold winter light shone through the stained glass, all I could feel was doubt.

What was I doing there? I was like—an American trout flapping around in a Scottish pond. As soon as I opened my mouth, my accent told my whole story to every person I met.

Foreigner, it said. *Visitor. Tourist.*

I looked around at the cold, stone walls and shivered. If Jamie had been here, he would have been shackled and bound, probably in some part of the fort that the public never got to see.

And who was I kidding, anyway? Jamie had never been here. Jamie had never been anywhere, except in the imagination of a vivid storyteller and the pages of her books. Could such a man even exist in the twenty-first century? Maybe I was on the world's wildest Scots Gander chase, following in the footsteps of an ideal man who had never really existed.

Maybe it was time to go home.

Feeble Finish…
4:00 pm, May 2
Nairn, Scotland

After today, I believe it is time to bid adieu to Nairn. This is a country of strong weather and rare beauty. I may not have found my Fraser, but I have found something of my soul here, and it was worth finding. It is a feeble finish to my grand plan, but my next step must take me away from my beloved Highlands and back down to Edinburgh. I hope my luck will be better there than it was in Glasgow, as I need to make enough money to pay for my ticket home.

- ES

Comments: 5

Gerald Abernathy, Fort William, Scotland:

Hey girl, if you do head south this week and pass through Ft. W, come see me. I'm feeling a mite tetchy still, and have decided to accept medical advice and take up residence in a rest home here until I am well again. Love to see you if you are passing through…

HiHoKitty, Sapporo, Japan:

Sad to see journey come to end. がんばって

(Read 3 more comments here…)

Clearly the bloom was off the rose. I sat by the monitor for nearly an hour, but to no avail. My comments had fallen almost to zero, with my loyal HiHoKitty one of the last remaining. The rest—apart from Gerald—had returned to selling me erectile dysfunction medication.

I signed off with a sigh, and waved to Katy behind her monitor at the front desk as I headed out the door. The next bus south was not until midnight, so I decided to wait and go the following morning.

The evening was clear and cold, and as I pushed my bike down the walk, I thought about Gerald. A rest home—what the heck was that? The words conjured up images of stately Edwardian manors and starched aprons. It seemed odd that he hadn't wanted to return to the warmer climes of his southern home. Presumably, though, he had to take the medical advice he was given. I felt badly for him, being so sick, so far from home. If there was any way for me to stop and visit him on my journey south, I vowed to try and do it.

I shivered a little with the cold, and walked my bike across the street to the garage to ask about the cost of keeping it until the following day. In the back I could hear pounding and clanking, accompanied by someone singing.

"*Bar-bar-bar-bar-barbara-ann ...* "

I leaned across the grease-covered table that stood in for a desk and tried not to touch anything.

"*Come take my ha-ha-hand,*" crooned the voice.

"Hello?" I called, hoping to save myself another verse.

Sure enough, the door to the back swung open and man I had met the day before came out, wiping his hands.

Unfortunately, the singing continued from the back.

I tried to ignore it, and pitching my voice over top, asked the garage owner if he would mind if I kept the bike another day. He waved a hand at me, told me I could keep the thing for a week and shooed me out into the street.

"Ye look fair frozen, Miss," he said, kindly. "They'll give ye a spot of tea at the cafe to warm ye up before ye head back to Morag's place."

I was feeling more like a cup of hot chocolate than tea, but his advice seemed sound, and I was starving, besides. Perhaps a Nairn scone would solve at least that problem, for the moment.

By the time I had walked my bike across the street, the sky had a lowering look I didn't like at all, and I decided to make it a quick drink and maybe a sandwich to take away with me. I stepped inside and the wind caught the door, so I needed both hands to pull it closed. As I turned back into the cafe, the warmth of the place enclosed me for a single, welcome moment.

Then I got hit by what felt like a freight train, in the form of a young, blonde woman.

Screaming.

"Ay-ay-ay-ayiiiiiiiiiii," she yelled, as we hit the ground. I say "we" loosely, since it was I who hit the ground first. She literally bounced off me onto her knees. I ended up flat on my back on the rain-soaked mat by the door, the wind entirely knocked out of me. But instead of helping me to my feet or apologizing—all the things one would expect to happen after being suddenly and unceremoniously bowled off one's feet, instead she grabbed my arm and wailed again.

I took a whistling gasp to try to suck air back into my lungs, and the woman continued to clutch my arm with what felt like a death grip.

I sat up and managed an "Ooof," not really having enough oxygen left to express the true nature of my shock and outrage. Her fingers squeezed like a vise on the flesh of my upper arm.

It was then I realized she was pregnant.

And not *just* pregnant.

"Oiiiiiii … ," she cried, neatly ripping the collar off my jacket with her death grip. "It's COMING."

I looked around wildly. It was not yet five, but if this place had a late-afternoon rush, it hadn't materialized. The cafe was deserted.

By this time, we were both on our knees and I realized the mat might not be just rain-soaked after all. The woman had my jacket collar bunched up in one hand, and the other hand still clenched around my arm.

"Uh—hello?" I called, now that the breath had been shocked back into my lungs. "Anyone? We need some help out here!"

"Unnnngggghhhhh … ," the woman groaned. "Don't leave me. The bairn …"

"I—I won't leave," I said, trying not to freak out. I wasn't even an auntie yet, and I'd had zero experience with birthin' babies.

The woman let go of my torn collar and clutched her midsection, groaning. I noticed with some shock that, though she was clearly well along in the pregnancy, she wore a waitress uniform. It was buttoned to the waist and she'd unbuttoned the lower half, covering the baby bump with a voluminous white apron.

"Is there anyone in the kitchen who can help?" I asked her, but she was beyond answering for the moment. Her head was down, and she was panting urgently.

I heard a door slam in the back, and a cloud of cigarette smoke floated gently in through the serving window. "Hey, hey—we need some help out here," I yelled in the direction of the smoke, trying to keep the panic out of my voice.

A startled face appeared around the corner of the kitchen wall.

"What the hell …" he said. The face disappeared and I heard the door slam.

The woman groaned again, and started rocking back and forth on her hands and knees. "Too soon—it's too soon," she panted.

I'm not actually sure what I said at that moment, to tell you the truth. All I can remember is seeing a wash of blood on the floor and then pretty much a black wall of panic closed in. The next thing I knew a young man in chef's whites was on his knees beside us.

"Cara," he said imploringly to the woman. "Are ye all' righ'? Is the baby comin'?"

"Uh—yeah, I'm pretty sure that's what's happening here," I said. "But it seems so fast—aren't these things supposed to take forever?"

I revised my estimate of the man—he was more like a boy, maybe sixteen or seventeen, max.

He looked at me as though he'd not noticed me before. I could see panic in his eyes that I was sure was reflected in my own. "Ah've no fookin' idea," he gasped. "She's the only one on until seven. What do I do?"

My arm had already gone to sleep—there was no way this woman was going to let go of me any time soon. "Get help," I said. "Call 911!"

He looked at me like I was crazy, and then a light dawned in his eyes. "It's 999. I can do that!" He jumped to his feet. "And I'll run to Jacquie's," he said. "She's just across the street. She'll know what to tell them."

"Wait! Have you got a towel or a blanket or anything I can put down—just in case?"

He nodded and dashed into the back, returning seconds later with a giant stack of dishtowels. "We havenae anythin' bigger," he said. "Righ'. Back in a tick."

He put his hand on the doorknob and the woman—Cara—groaned. "Get me some help, Ash," she said, through gritted teeth. "Ah cain't bloody do this alone."

Ash was yelling into his cell phone on his way out the door, so, "I'm here," I said, as soothingly as I could, all the while wishing to hell I wasn't.

But Cara's one spell of lucidity had passed. She began panting in a way that I didn't like at all. It reminded me of the birth scenes I'd seen on television. Without the tidiness. And the doctors.

My hand had gone a grayish shade, all feeling lost.

"Cara," I said. "Just hold on. Someone is going to be here any minute. It's going to be all ..."

Her face snapped up to look at me, and I thought her eyes were going to pop out of her head. Her mouth opened so wide I could see she had three silver fillings on one side—but not a sound came out.

We stared at each other for a single long moment. Her eyes slowly closed, and she let out a perfectly gentle, relieved sigh.

And behind her on the stack of dishtowels, was a baby, with a tangle of fabric around one leg.

"God in heaven, that were fookin' brutal," she said, glancing over her shoulder. "And she's ruined ma' knickers, ta boot."

The door behind me blew open, hit me in the ass and a mob scene took over.

After that, in spite of the mob, things unfolded in a much more comfortable fashion. Someone got me a chair, and pushed a cup of tea into my hand. A pair of ambulance attendants neatly scooped Cara and her lustily crying baby onto a gurney and rolled her out the door. Even the pile of dishtowels vanished, somehow.

The kid in the kitchen whites arrived, grinning, at my elbow, and poured a generous tot of whisky into my tea. We toasted each other silently, and he took a long slug from the bottle.

"An interesting day," he said.

I nodded and sipped.

"You a tourist?"

I nodded again, and sipped some more. "I'm leaving tomorrow," I clarified.

He pointed at the ground. "Here? Or Scotland?"

I shrugged. "Here. I need to head south to find a job, to earn money for my ticket home."

He was silent a moment, as the ambulance, siren on, drove away. A collection of chattering people stood around outside the cafe, laughing and smoking and waving their arms in the air.

"Well, if ye're not set on headin' south, it looks like we need a new waitress. And yeh seem pretty good at thinkin' on yer feet. Want the job?"

I looked at him and blinked. It seemed my time in the Highlands might not yet be at an end, after all.

Flabbergasting Fate…
Noon, May 15
Nairn, Scotland

In a flabbergasting twist of fate, I'm actually working now, and at a job I like. I still haven't got a computer of my own, which makes regular posting pretty tough.

On every other front, though, life is good. The people of this little town have taken me in and made me feel like I belong. I've found a job in a cafe, and I even helped a baby come into the world—which I would blog about in more detail if the experience hadn't been so disgusting. Let me just say, when I met the baby again after she was all cleaned off and dressed, she was a beautiful, perfect little human being. I'm meeting all kinds of other amazing humans here, too. No sign of my Fraser, yet, but I still hold out hope!

— ES

Comments: 3

SophiaSheridan, Chicago, USA:

Working? Well, I suppose actual employment is a good thing. At least you are taking responsibility for yourself. How long will it take for you to earn enough to come home? A month? Six weeks? If you will be so kind as to let me know, I may even be able to arrange to have Paul meet you at the airport.

(Read 2 more comments here...)

To: EmmaFindingFraser@gmail.com
From: JackFindlay@*range.co.uk
May 15

Hey Emma,

Thanks for the email. Nice to have your email address. I feel special!

And yeah, around here, summer starts in May. Midsummer's Eve is on the solstice, ye ken? It's only you Americans who are crazy enough to insist summer begins at the very time the days start getting shorter!

The ankle is mending quickly, judging from the infernal itch right at the spot I can't reach with even my longest pencil. The book prep seems to be going well at the publishing house. My editor tells me it should be out late this summer.

Hope your quest continues apace. If the Highland warrior falls through and you do end up down here in Edinburgh for a bit, let me know. I'd love to take you for a 'thank you' cup of tea.

Jack

Katy the librarian began to make closing-up noises, so I quickly logged off, after sending Jack a quick note suggesting he use a ruler rather than a pencil to address his itchy ankle. A broken leg on my first attempt on an Adirondack ski hill as a teenager had given me a plethora of experience on how to best deal with the discomfort of six weeks in a cast, and I was fairly certain things hadn't changed much in the technology of scratching an itch in that time.

My first couple of weeks in the new job had been far less eventful than the first hour, but I have to say that I liked it that way. It was kind of reassuring to get back to the routine of regular employment after the series of disasters in Glasgow. Whoever said that the Scots are cheap had obviously never worked in this cafe—my tips were accumulating in the jar on the wee counter of my flat very nicely.

And—for the time being, at least—I got to stay in my beloved Highlands.

It turned out the kid in the kitchen whites was the owner's son, Ashwin. Ash's dad was named Sandeep Patel, who was, in his turn, the son of Indian immigrants who had moved to Scotland during the time of partition. Sandeep had a Glaswegian accent as strong as Rabbie the Gnome. Our first conversation had been tempered both by his suspicion of me as a foreigner and his relief that I actually had experience as a barista in the US.

"We'd thought we'd hae plenny o' time afore Cara's babby arrived," he said, kneading the dough for tea biscuits as we spoke. "Another month, at least. I were halfway to Glasgow on mah supply run when I go' the call from Ash. Turned aroun' fair quick, I did! As for findin' another girl, I havenae even posted a note on the board at the local Jobs Center."

He punched the dough viciously with his flour-coated hands, and then rolled it flat and began cutting out rounds using one of the drinking glasses from the dishwasher. "So yeh worked at the Starbucks in Chicago, did ye?"

I nodded. "Can make a caramel macchiato with the best of 'em," I said, proudly, thinking it pays to trumpet one's accomplishments to one's new boss.

He rolled his eyes. "Ach, there'll be none of that shite here, luv. Jes' serve 'em the coffee out of the perc and change the grounds every coupla hours, and it'll all be fine."

That had been the full extent of my interview. After a bit more than two weeks, it turned out that the job was seventy five percent serving and the rest of the time wiping tables and lugging dish trays. Pretty much zero percent barista, in fact.

I didn't mind a bit.

Fins in the Firth…
2:00 pm, May 31
Nairn, Scotland

Spent an amazing, glorious day chasing a pod of dolphins along the shores of Moray Firth. Dolphins!

I've never even seen one dolphin, except on television. Today, there were thirty or more of 'em, bobbing and dancing and playing in the distance. I counted dorsal fins, and it was hard to keep track but still!!!!

There were a few other people out walking along the shoreline. The rain has been falling pretty much every day, but today was supposed to be fine, and it was my day off. I headed over the shore on my bike, following Morag's directions, just planning to read and catch a little sun. But when I got to the beach, I could see a young family hurrying up the shore, the two kids leaping up and down madly.

So exciting to see. And to think—in Scotland!

I overheard the mother of the young kids insisting it was good luck to see dolphins, so when I went back home after they had swum away, I asked Morag to confirm.

"Ach—that's a pile o' nonsense," she sniffed. "They're here all the time, rain or shine. Some tourist's story, nothin' more."

Still—I like to think the dolphins might auger something special.

Why not?

- ES

Comments: 3

HiHoKitty, Sapporo, Japan:

Dolphins do bring luck. To old sailors, seeing dolphins mean land was near, but I think they carry spirit of joy inside. Do you still have joy even though you have no Jamie, Miss Emma?

(Read 2 more comments here…)

W ell.
   I hadn't heard from HiHoKitty in a few weeks, so I was delighted to see her name. I totally agreed with her take on dolphins, too. The last sentence set me back a bit, though.

Strangely enough, when I really stopped to think about it, I did still have joy, even with no Jamie. I had found a nice rhythm, riding to and from work every day. The owner, Geordie, of the garage across from the cafe gave me a generous deal on the bike, essentially waiving any charges "until I found my footing" as he called it, with the new job.

The cafe turned out to be great. I enjoyed the people I worked with, and I was learning how to help Morag on her farm. On top of that, I was making money, which I needed so desperately. And with little to worry about apart from the three pieces of crockery I'd broken in a minor dishwashing disaster, the rest of the month seemed to fly by. I couldn't believe when I put up my post that it was almost June already. June!

I'd collected my first two paychecks, and managed to set a decent amount aside toward my flight costs home before disaster struck hard.

But this disaster? Best. Silver. Lining. EVER.

Katy strode back to her desk, shooting me a glare as I slunk away from the public terminal. I was going to have to find another place to post my blog, as her patience for me tying up the only free computer station at the library was wearing thin. Plus, I was waging a passive-aggressive seat war with an old dude who came in every single day to play solitaire on the computer. Mind you, if Katy caught him at it, she threw him off immediately. Tough broad—she would do well in Chicago.

Anyway, now that I was working, I guessed I could afford to pay the two pound fee at the only Internet cafe in town.

It's just—I felt kinda bad going in there, since they *were* our competition. They sold their coffee out of a vending machine. Also, the place was pretty sketchy-looking, and smelled like Lysol.

I made it into work with a couple of minutes to spare, but ran straight into the back to get my apron because it was so busy. Sometimes the lunch crowd runs really early in Nairn, where everyone seems to get up before dawn for some reason.

Things went fine until the stroke of twelve noon. I'd managed to wipe down all the empty tables, and Ash hadn't burned anything for at least an hour. Up front, I had a young couple in one of the booths, and was just about to pour coffee for them when their baby leaned forward and smacked his mother's cup off the table. The mom pulled her baby back into his seat, the dad retrieved the cup and I managed to swoop my carafe back in time so as to not scald anyone at the table.

Unfortunately, the guy at the next table was not so lucky.

As I swung my arm away, the competing forces of gravity and arm momentum took their toll on the lid of the carafe, which flew into the next booth. Centrifugal force kept most of the coffee inside, but the steam that had condensed under the lid poured down the collar of a man sitting with his back to me.

"Christ Jesus," he roared, and jumped out of his booth, frantically trying to brush the steaming droplets away from the back of his neck.

I didn't know who to handle first, so I quickly turned to check that the young couple were okay, before dealing with the man still swearing behind me.

"I'm so sorry, " I began, as he swung around to face me—and I stared at him while his features clicked into place. It was Hamish.

Hamish of the bar in Edinburgh. Hamish of the spilled beer in lap. Hamish with the well-muscled forearms.

Hamish, now freshly scalded. By me.

"You!" he choked. "The American girl from Edinburgh."

"Em—Emma," I said. "I'm *so* sorry—are you okay?"

"Yeah."

He untucked the dishtowel from my apron and wiped the back of his neck with it.

"No harm done," he said, and then hummed in a slightly strangled voice: "It's all right—to be a redneck ..."

"No—no, it's not. It's not all right. It's all my fault, is what it is. Let me at least get you some ice, okay?"

He put his hand on my arm. "I'm grand, Emma. I promise yeh. Now, tell me how it is yeh come to be here in mah own town?"

The lunch rush had gotten in the way, but Hamish had promised to come by after work, and he did. He told me that he worked across the street in Geordie's garage. And how he never ate at the Nairn Cafe but his favorite Chinese takeaway happened to be closed that day. We walked through Nairn and talked about how much I loved his country. He told me how he'd yelled at his boss for not telling him that he'd rented the bicycle to a lovely American. I made him repeat the words "lovely American" several times, just to be sure. Then we talked about how much he loved my country.

Afterwards, we went for dinner at the Chinese takeaway, where it turned out the owner had just slept in that morning. And after dinner ...

He took my hand as we walked over to my bike, which was leaning up against the coffee shop. He had long, square fingers that fit just perfectly between my own. The air was quiet and balmy—the first truly warm evening I had experienced in Scotland.

"I'm so sorry about splashing you today," I said, to the sound of our feet on the gravel.

"It doesnae hurt a bit," Hamish said. "An it means I can welcome yeh to mah town properly, aye?"

Before I could ask what he meant, he leaned down and made himself clear by kissing me. A dizzying, head-spinning, perfectly wonderful kiss.

And I pedaled off into the moonrise as purely, sweetly, and divinely happy as I had ever been in my life.

Part Three: The Finding

Fraser Found...
4:00 pm, June 8
Nairn, Scotland

I'm not sure I believe in love at first sight.

But I might.

And Sophia? I may never come home. Bite that, will ya?

- ES

Comments: 70

Gerald Abernathy, Fort William, Scotland:

DETAILS!!!!

(Read 69 more comments here...)

S o.
Now that it had come to pass, I felt strangely reluctant to blog about it. Like telling the story might let the magic out, somehow. Even my longing to rub my sister's nose in

my success was tempered by a sudden need to keep things private.

The massive number of comments over the week following my reunion with Hamish was a bit daunting, as well. Most of them were variants on Gerald's theme. What does he look like? How does he act? Will there be a hand-fast? A wedding? How was your first night together?

Things had changed. The blog had changed. I had no intention of posting his picture. And describe what he looked like? How we were together? It was—it was just not what I wanted to do any longer.

Besides—what if he ever saw it?

I began to think about taking the blog down.

He was away on deliveries for most of a week before I saw him again. But on the Tuesday, there had been flowers waiting for me on the front counter. And on Thursday, a very sour-faced Ashwin had handed me a note. The envelope it came in was torn.

I read the note, (*Miss U, cant wait to see U soon,* it said), and asked Ash about the envelope.

"It came that way," he said, and stalked off for a smoke behind the cafe.

I just smiled, and tossing the envelope, tucked the note into my bra, close to my heart. I missed him, too, that I did.

That Friday, when Hamish stuck his head in the cafe just before closing, and told me he had only one job to finish before he was off work, and would I care to go for a walk again?

I had every table wiped in under a minute.

We'd headed out right after he finished changing the transmission on the local vet's van. I'd ridden my bike to work, but we left it leaning against the back wall of the cafe and strolled down the road, instead.

For just a moment, I closed my eyes, walking beside him, and thought about where I was. In the most beautiful part of the most beautiful country in the world, walking under the stars with Hamish.

I thought my heart might just stop beating out of sheer happiness. But when I opened my eyes, my large Scottish male companion was scowling up at the sky.

"Bad enough there's now't tae do in this dull place, and now the weather's gone smirrey."

"Smirrey?" I said, as a smattering of raindrops smacked me in the face.

He looked at me and rolled his eyes. "It's hell on mah hair," he said, touching the blonde tuft in front gingerly. It did look a bit more limp than usual.

I pulled up my hood, and he took my hand and curled it in his.

"I hate the rain," he said, and circled us around back toward the cafe. "In California, it's sunny most of the time, did ye know?"

I shrugged. "I've gotten kind of used to it, actually. Besides," I added innocently, "I'm sure there's lots of things we could come up with to do inside."

He nodded resolutely, and lengthened his stride as we walked past the cafe door. "You're right. I'm famished—I'd slay an army for a bi' o'curry. You?"

"I—uh, okay," I replied, as he dropped my hand and pushed open the door of the chippy beside his garage. I hurried in behind him, relieved to be out of the wet, but disappointed that my hinting skills seemed not to have improved since my long-ago relationship with Campbell.

We'd stepped outside an hour later, and that time Hamish held the door for me. It had been a spirited meal, as Geordie and another mechanic had been inside and had waved us over to their table. Hamish had taken a fair bit of ribbing over keeping company with the new American waitress, but on the whole it had been—if not exactly what I'd hoped for in a date—still pretty fun.

I stepped out into the rain, and Hamish followed me across the street as I went to collect my bicycle. The gel spikes had fallen out of his hair in the damp, and he pulled a baseball cap from his pocket and jammed it on backwards.

"Hair's ruined in the dreich, anyroad," he said.

It had been a long time since I had walked with a male wearing a ball cap on backwards, but I peered up at him through the misty darkness. "California Angels?" I guessed, squinting back at the logo.

"Aye!" he answered, delightedly. "They're mah team."

I flipped the switch on the bike lamp and it created a damp puddle of light on the ground in front of us. "I guess I'd better head home," I said, reluctantly. "Thanks for dinner."

He burped gently, smothering it in one large fist. "Better up than down," he said, cheerfully, and put his hands over mine on the handlebars. "And why would ye ride, lass, when I can take ye?"

I pretended I hadn't heard the burp and grinned up at him. "No reason I can think of," I said. I followed him over to his van and waited while he loaded the bike in the back.

He came around the side, the rain creating dark patches on both his shoulders. "Plannin' to take the wheel, are yeh?" he said, and gestured at the van.

I realized I was standing on the drivers' side. "Old habits …" I muttered, and scurried around to the other door while he grinned at me through the rain-speckled glass.

I slid in beside him and the warm air from the heater enveloped me. Hamish wiped his long arm across the seat between us, sweeping a collection of paper cups and wrappers onto the floor at my feet.

"Sorry 'bout that, luv," he said. "Two deliveries to Fort Augustus and one to Inverness."

"Are you on the road often?" I asked, over the roar of the engine.

He nodded and shifted gears, as the road to Morag's place lurched beneath us. "Aye, quite a bit, actually. No' really my favorite part of the job, but good practice, for all that."

"Good practice?"

He shot me a shy smile. "For mah green card application. Though' I migh' try mah hand at long-distance truckin' in America."

"Ah." My heart lifted a little. He so loved America. Maybe that meant he could fall for an American girl?

I'd never really pictured myself with a truck-driving guy, but—what was I thinking, anyway? That my Jamie and I would live happily ever after in Scotland? I told myself to quit being so judgmental and just learn to enjoy the moment.

Gravel crunched under the wheels of the van, and he pulled off the motorway at the end of Morag's lane.

"She's locked the gate," he said, peering into the darkness. "I'll wheel the bike up for ye."

I jumped out and walked around to the back of the van.

He flung open the doors and hoisted the bike over the gate in one smooth motion, and then patted the seat. "Yer chariot awaits, milady."

I slipped through the swing door of the gate and lifted my leg across the seat. He stepped through the gate and, with his arms holding me safely in place, wheeled the bike up the path to the house.

The gray stone of the old farmhouse loomed at the end of the drive. The rain had stopped, but a silvery mist crept up from the damp hollows. A lamp burned low over the rear door

---

of the farmhouse and another over the barn door, but apart from those, the landscape was completely dark.

"My room is in the barn," I whispered, and we skirted the pool of light from the farmhouse and headed for the thatched-roof building off to the left. As we closed the distance to the barn, my heart was pounding like an autumn drum.

I had my feet on the pedals, but Hamish was essentially doing all the work, pushing my bike up the slight rise in the path. We rolled up to the barn door, and I stood up to swing my leg off, but he caught me under the arms and lifted me down. With no one holding the bike, it teetered and fell, and inside the barn, one of the residents lowed, cranky at being awoken at such an ungodly hour.

I glanced over my shoulder guiltily, scanning for movement at Morag's window. She had to be up at five—an hour that was truly ungodly—but the window remained dark. I turned back to look up at Hamish, and found his lips, warm on my own.

My gasp of surprise was nicely muffled, and we stood there in the dark beside the fallen bicycle. He kissed me, and I kissed him back without any trouble at all.

When we both finally had to pause to breathe, he smiled ruefully down at me. "I've got to leave again tonight for a delivery down in Fort William," he said. "But I wanted to see yeh 'afore I left, even jes' for a bit."

"I'm— I'm so glad you did," I managed. I ran my hands over his jacket and up to clasp around his neck. "Would you—can you come inside, for a few minutes?"

He pressed his mouth down to mine again, and groaned softly into the corner of my lips. "Geordie's waitin' for me at the shop, and I wouldnae put it past him tae come an' haul me bodily away. I would stay if I could—ye know that, aye?"

Um, yes. And knowing how he felt—*feeling* how he felt—did not make his leaving any easier. It's possible my desperation showed in my voice.

"Really? *Really?* Not for two minutes?"

He shook his head and stepped away, and the cold swirled around me like a living thing.

"Never want to say goodbye ..."

He was through the gate before I realized he was singing. It said something about the state I was in that even the fact he was just a little off-key didn't affect the level of my ardor.

The cow inside the barn lowed again, and I only had time to lift up my hand before Hamish was gone.

Faraway Fellow...
8:00 pm, June 21
Nairn, Scotland

Well, here it is, my favorite day of the year, because it's the longest. At home, we call it the first day of summer, though here (or so I've been told) this day is considered Midsummer. Anyone care to refute this bit of lore?

I would be spending it with my stalwart Scots boyfriend, but he is once again on the road, delivering auto parts all around the north. I miss him!

But now I am late for work, so I will save news of any celebratory bonfires and so on for another post.

- ES

Comments: 23

HiHoKitty, Sapporo, Japan:

Your love is all we speak of in our book club, Miss Emma-san. You are an inspiration to us all. But still you have not shared the truth of how the fire burns between you. This we long to hear.

Gerald Abernathy, Fort William, Scotland:

Well, girl, I think maybe your dreams have actually come true. From your email it sounds like he's certainly big enough to be Jamie, and a good kisser, too. Don't sweat the blonde tips and gel—nothin' wrong with a California boy wanna-be! And maybe all that singing will land him a spot in a boy band!

As for me, I am out of the rest home, feelin' fine. I've decided to stay on here in Scotland for a while. My nurse—you might remember him?—has a sweet little B&B, and when he's not nursing people back into the land of the living, he's cooking full English breakfasts in his little cottage. He's been showing me around a bit, and as there is so much more to see, I've decided to stay awhile.

Stay happy, Emma! I am.

Gerald

Jack Findlay, Edinburgh, Scotland:

Well, I will certainly defy anyone who dares to step forward and refute! For you are most well-informed. When measured properly, summer runs from May Day to Lammas on August first, with the end of June therefore being midpoint.

It's clear from your other commenters at least, that your quest has been successful. In that regard, I wish you both the best. If you plan to be down near Stirling any time soon, I will certainly be delighted to do so in person.

Jack

(Read 20 more comments <u>here</u>...)

I logged off and looked around. Up front, Katy was just packing up her things. I checked my watch. Right on schedule. Now that I wasn't blogging as often, she didn't seem to mind seeing me in the library, as long as one or both of us was on our way out when we met.

After getting to know Hamish a little better, I'd learned that he didn't even own a computer. I was a bit sad to hear he wasn't interested in reading anything, but at least I didn't have to worry about him seeing my writing online. I just—I just wasn't ready to give it up, yet. I felt so connected to my online community. They were all, to a person, completely delighted for me—well, perhaps not to a person. Jack's comment had sounded a bit stiff and formal, but I put it down to pre-occupation. He must be getting ready for his new book to come out. And since Hamish had been away, I had been reading my way through his backlist. Katy had a whole shelf devoted to Jack Findlay titles, right up at the front of the library, near her desk.

I gave her a wave and leapt onto my bike to head back to Morag's. Nothing good came of dwelling on my absent boyfriend, so I spent the ride trying to think cheerful thoughts about Gerald. Staying at a B&B run by a cute English nurse? It sounded to me like he was definitely on the road to recovery.

But try as I might to focus on Gerald and his happiness, my mind still turned magnetically to Hamish. I aimed my bike at a pothole in the road and bounced through it viciously. What could I say to HiHoKitty and the other commenters who demanded details of our first night together?

Up to that point I'd managed to avoid admitting how little time we had actually spent together, but things were getting ridiculous. I wanted to be with him. I knew he liked me back from the way he'd kissed me. And riding at high speed over the rutted lanes on my bike was a poor substitute for what we could actually do with some decent time alone together.

I decided to make plans for the next day. I could just whip over to the garage on my break, and all of this worry would be put to rest. We were both consenting adults. We just needed enough alone time to let things develop naturally. My stomach clenched with anticipation. Things were going to work out just fine.

I'd reached a good rhythm, driven by these pleasant thoughts, as I pedaled past the cafe. I'd almost ridden right on by before I noticed the black smoke pouring out the front door. Screeching the bike to a stop, I didn't even bother to flip out my kickstand, but hopped off and tipped the bike against a wall. I ran to meet Ashwin, who was walking out the front door.

"Is there a fire?" I gasped, as he stepped out to meet me.

He rolled his eyes. "The percolator blew up. I told Da it was on its way out, but you know ..." His voice trailed off, and even through the closed door of the cafe, I could hear his father yelling into the phone. Ashwin nervously pulled out a cigarette and lit it.

I peered into the front window. Sandeep was in the back, a pall of smoke hovering above his head in the kitchen. Nothing else appeared to be damaged.

"We had only one couple in the place, so I'd nipped out back for a fag," muttered Ashwin in my ear. "It turns out, the coffee machine boiled dry without anyone on hand, which was probably a good thing, seein' as it shattered into murderous shards that snowed down over everythin'."

I couldn't help feeling relieved my shift was long over and there was no way I'd be blamed. "Everything?"

He took a long drag, his eyes slitted and staring into the distance. "The sink, the big bin of sugar, the vat of chocolate powder—ever'thin'."

"How mad was your dad?" I whispered.

Ash shuddered. "If he could've actually flayed me alive using only his voice, I would have no skin left. He yelled for about an hour, then he closed the place down, kicked me out and cleaned the kitchen himself."

His fingers trembled a little as he lit a new cigarette. "This whole 'family business' thing ..." He shook his head. Through the window I could see Sandeep slam down the phone and grab his raincoat. Seconds later, he came storming out the door, jamming one arm into the coat. He caught sight of his son and stopped in his tracks.

I could see Ash physically brace himself—eyes half-closed, shoulders hunched.

Sandeep took a deep breath and looked at me.

"Set yer alarm, Emma. I need yeh to consult on the new equipment. We're headin' tae Edinburgh in the mornin'."

kc dyer

He jammed a catalogue into my hand and stabbed a finger in his son's face. "And yer driven', if ye can manage it without blowin' up the fookin' van!"

Sandeep's van was parked at the foot of Morag's driveway by the time I emerged at eight the next morning. With all the bus travel, I had become completely used to driving on the wrong side of the road, though the roads seemed so much narrower when driving in the van. Still, it turned out keeping my eyes closed meant I shrieked less at the sight of giant trucks bearing down on us on the impossibly narrow roads, so I mostly tried to nap.

In all, the trip went very smoothly. The roads were clear, Ash kept his head down and his speed under the limit, and his father spent most of the time ignoring the fact I was trying to snooze, and waxing rhapsodic about the new espresso machine he planned to buy.

Once we passed Fort William, I gave up trying to sleep. Sandeep seemed a little disappointed that I didn't know the difference between the brand names. I explained that I knew how to run the machine, but the relative manufacturing merits were beyond the scope of my barista experience. I'd read through the catalogue and picked out the one that I thought would look nicest in the shop, which managed to thoroughly disgust Sandeep.

In the end, he decided that since I would be no help in the decision process, I would be allowed an hour to explore Princes Street while the men went and collected the new equipment.

No argument from me. I didn't have any available funds, but at least I could window shop. And besides—hadn't Claire spent time in Edinburgh looking for Jamie on her return in DRAGONFLY IN AMBER? It wasn't technically an

OUTLANDER detail, but trying to puzzle out the location of Jamie's print shop would be a fun way to kill time.

As we drove toward the city over the Forth Bridge, Sandeep had Ashwin pull off and took over the driving. Ash grinned at me and slid into the back seat.

"It's a madhouse drivin' this city," Sandeep muttered, and I had to agree. It took us almost an hour to get into the heart of the city, mostly due to construction and slow-moving traffic.

As we wove through the city streets, I kept my nose glued to the window, watching for a glimpse of the castle. Soon enough there it was, looming through the misty day like a huge guardian on its mammoth pile of granite above the city. I craned my neck to look for the bar where I'd first met Hamish, but it was lost in a puzzle of streets running off at strange angles. I was pretty sure I'd never be able to find it again.

Sandeep's van pulled up to a red light right beside a huge, soot-blackened structure on Princes Street. He pointed out the window.

"Tha' ugly thing is the Scott Monument," he said. "This should only take me an hour, but with traffic it could be as long as two. So how about we meet right here at four, to be safe?"

"I'll be here," I said, and hopped out of the van. He honked moodily and rolled forward a couple of feet before stopping again. I walked by his open window.

"Damn tram lines," he said, and shook his fist at the sky.

I waved goodbye and headed along Princes Street. It was Edinburgh's main street, filled with shoppers despite the dreary day.

I stared at all the lovely spring outfits and shoes that I could not afford in the shop windows and thought about Hamish, delivering car parts today somewhere far north of me. We both were in the same boat, in a way, earning money to go to America. Except he was desperate to go, and I—I wasn't so sure any more.

I didn't want to think that way. I'd found my Fraser, right? A big, beautiful Scot—not really a red-head, but close enough. And if he wanted to see my homeland, too—all the better. After all, Jamie and Claire had ended up in America, and for both of them it had been the most foreign of lands.

I leaned against the cool stone of a shop exterior, and pulled my copy of OUTLANDER out of my pack. Flipping open the cover to look at the map, I was horrified when it came away in my hand. I stood there on the street, staring in blank shock at the naked book in one hand and the torn cover in the other.

"Ye can git another jes' oop the street, lass."

The man speaking to me was sitting on the ground, leaning against a pole. His dog was asleep on his lap and propped against one knee was a sign that read Destitute and Hungry. I took a moment to be impressed with his facility with the written word, Austenesque capitalization and all, but then he spoke again.

"Wha'za matter? Ye deef? THERE'S A BOOKSHOP JES' OOP THE STREET."

The sheer volume made me jump back a little. "Yes—ah—thank you, sir," I babbled, backing away. I jammed my hands in my pockets and hurried off, embarrassed that I hadn't had the presence of mind to drop a coin in his cup.

Two doors up I discovered the well-educated panhandler was correct. It was a bookshop. I stepped inside, feeling just as torn as my copy of OUTLANDER.

Of course I could buy another copy. But this copy had brought me all the way here from Chicago. It was filled with my notes. It held Gerald's map, folded neatly in between the pages. Inside the torn cover, it held my own travel plan in passionate purple ink, alongside the signature of the author Herself.

I couldn't bear to give it up.

But maybe one of the clerks would have some tape I could use. I wandered over to the front desk, to find the cashier talking on the phone.

"An God, he was SO drunk, I tell ya I laughed me arse off …"

She caught sight of me and put her hand over the receiver. "Can I help yeh?"

"I've just torn the cover off my book—do you have any Scotch tape?"

"Nah—sorry. Got some cello, if ye want it."

She slid a roll of what was clearly Scotch tape over to me and turned back to her phone call. I spent ten minutes carefully repairing the damage. When I was done, it looked like it might hold, but most of the tape was gone. As I slid the dispenser back across the desk to the cashier, I remembered Claire's quest.

The cashier was still talking, but I finally caught her eye and she replaced her hand on the receiver again.

"Thank you so much," I said, handing her the dispenser. "Listen, I'm looking for an old book makers nearby here. Do you know of one?"

She paused, twisting her mouth in concentration. "Dunno," she said at last. "But this here is a book *sellers*, no' a book *makers*. Cheers, aye?"

She showed me her back and returned to her call.

"Eh, sorry, Gert. So he's drunk, mind, and I'm right tipsy meself, and 'e says 'have another', and I'm like, 'don't mind if I do, luv,' and he's like, 'fair play to yeh' …"

I cleared my throat.

This time she was glaring as she swung back to face me. "I'm sorry, d'ye still need summat?"

"Look, I know you sell books. That's why I came in here. But I'm looking for a place that *makes* books— binds them, and so on. Like with a printing press."

"Oh! I thought you was havin' me on, and you were lookin' for the bookies—them guys you make bets with, yeah?"

"No. It would be an old shop, you know, or an old collection of buildings where they bind books."

She shrugged and chewed the end of her ponytail. "Most of the books we sell is printed in China, from wha' I can see," she said. "Bu' if ye look on that shelf ower there—unner the plaid banner, see? There are books about Edinburgh neighborhoods. Historical-like. Maybe that'll do?"

I nodded and she smiled with relief before turning back to her phone. I headed over to the shelf she'd indicated and propped my hands on my knees in the universal technique for reading spine titles on low bookshelves.

I'd just pulled one out of the shelf that looked promising: A HISTORY OF BOOK-BINDERIES IN SCOTLAND, when someone walked right into my personal space. I shuffled back to get out of the way, before looking up into the eyes of Jack Findlay.

He was carrying a book in one hand and was wearing a cardigan—and a kilt. It was a dark green and navy plaid that cut nicely over his narrow hips and down to just above the knee.

And before I knew what was happening, he'd wrapped his arms around me and kissed me.

Twice.

One on each cheek.

With the second kiss effectively right on the corner of my mouth. I found myself completely speechless.

He smelled so good—like wind and wood smoke and ink. Not even a whiff of machine oil.

"I can't believe you came, Emma," he said, stepping back with his hands still clutching my arms. "I am *so* happy to see you."

"I was just—hunting for books," I babbled, when I found my voice at last. "But look at you! You look great! How's the foot?"

A strange light dawned in his eyes and he dropped his hands hurriedly and stepped back.

"Oh, of course, hunting for books, right, right. It's a bookstore—that's only natural. What a coincidence!"

Honestly, as an embarrassed babbler, he had me totally beat.

Finally he acknowledged my question and pointed down at his feet. He wore a heavy boot on one foot, complete with the hilt of a dagger peeking out above his wool sock. The other foot didn't look quite as dashing.

"Still in the walking cast, as you can see. I thought it would be off by now, but it's taken its time healin'."

There was a long, awkward silence, where we both tried not to look right at each other and instead listened to the cashier regale her friend on exactly how drunk she had become the night before.

"Well," he said at last, "I'd better ..."

As he spoke, I suddenly caught sight of a poster on the pillar behind him with a picture of his face on it. "A reading..." I interrupted. "*You* are here to do a reading, then? Is your new book done already?"

He shook his head. "It's done, or nearly, but not out yet. This is a reading for the one that came out last year."

"The one about the dragon bones?"

He sighed and held up the book in his hand. "That's *bane*, not bone. It's not about dragon bones. It's a Scots legend, re-imagined."

"Um, okay." I glanced at the poster again and then up at the clock. "Weren't you supposed to start fifteen minutes ago?"

He flipped through his book nervously. "Ah, yeah—just waiting to see if the crowd would—ah—grow any larger. But, as it hasn't, well ... See you sometime, aye?"

His voice trailed away has he turned and walked toward the front of the large, open area behind us. I could hear the girl at the desk, still on the phone, shrieking with laughter and assuring her conversational companion that "Yeah, she really *were* that drunk."

I hurried after Jack as he walked down the aisle between the chairs set up for the event.

At least fifty chairs.

In them, sat three people. Including me. And judging from the smell, the guy hunched in a chair at the back may well have been out with the cashier the night before. He had long, dirty hair, and his beard was actually braided and fastened with a yellow rubber band. I recognized him right away as the man who had directed me here in the first place. His dog was asleep beside him on the floor.

The man himself was out cold.

I took a seat about half way along the right hand side, out of scent-distance from the panhandler and far enough up so that it would make the room look a little more ... occupied.

Jack stood up at the front of the room by a podium with a microphone attached. He took a deep breath and then squared his shoulders and stepped in front of the podium.

"Uh—thanks for comin', everyone. I'm here tonight to read from my last book, BANE OF THE DRAGON-LAIRD. So—ah—if no one has any objection, I'll jes' read a selection from the first chapter."

The old lady sitting in the front row on the other side of the aisle waved her hand at him. "Ach, Mister Findlay—a wee moment before ye begin?" She set her large handbag down on the seat beside her and using her cane, pulled herself to her feet.

"Aye jes' wanted ye to know I loved this story. It's even better than the last one, lad. Well done. Well done." She beamed at him like a fond auntie.

Jack gave a little half bow. "Thank ye, Missus McCarthy. I'm glad ye liked it. Is there any part you'd 'specially enjoy hearin' tonight?"

The old lady waved her cane, having settled back down in her seat. "Nae, nae, laddie—ye jes' go on and read the bit ye chose fer us. I'll be delighted wi' whatever ye read, son."

Jack set the book on the podium, and gave a last hopeful look toward the front of the store.

No one else appeared.

"Right, then," he said, and pulled a pair of glasses from his pocket. "Here goes."

He cleared his throat. "Sleet slashed across the cast iron sky and collected in tiny glass pebbles around the body at his feet. He knelt carefully, the …"

The old lady suddenly made a loud Scottish noise at the back of her throat.

"Ye know, lad, I've only jes' thought of it," she called out from her spot in the front row. She waved her copy of the book at Jack. "What about the bit where he meets the peasant girl in the rain?"

Jack closed the book with his finger marking the place he'd been interrupted. "Ah—all right, then, Missus McCarthy. Shall I finish this bit first?"

"As ye like, as ye like, pet. It's on'y—ye *did* ask the question. Go on, go on, finish this bit first, o'course."

He nodded and cleared his throat again, a little painfully to my ear. "He knelt carefully, the …"

"Because it's the sexy bit, innit? All yer books have a little rumpy-pumpy, aye?"

Jack sighed and flipped through the pages. "I'll jes' read it now, since you are so looking forward to it, shall I?"

"If ye like, pet."

The panhandler at the back awoke with a snort. He looked around blearily and focused on Jack, who was still flipping through pages at the front.

"I hear yer next book is about the Wallace, lad," he yelled from his seat at the back. "Dozzat mean yer acquainted with that there Gibson fella, then?"

"Aye—tha' Gibson fella, he's a sexy one, too," added Mrs. McCarthy.

Yeah, things went pretty much downhill after that.

"I'm sorry you had to see that," Jack said, afterwards.

I'd let him buy me a pot of tea in the shop next door, and we sat at a small table in the back, cups steaming.

"It wasn't so bad," I said. "You sold a few copies, and ..."

"Two. I sold two copies. One of them to you, which, with your financial situation, I should force you to return."

He closed his eyes and breathed in the steam from his cup. Eyes still closed, he said, "Take it back. They'll give you your money. The mercy buy doesn't apply when you weren't even expecting to find me here."

I nudged his arm with my hand and his eyes opened. "Look, you made sales and a few new fans today. Your discussion with that man on the flaws in Braveheart was fascinating. I had no idea there were so many historical errors in that movie."

"He was a drunk, Emma."

"Okay, I did know that," I admitted. "After his racist rant awhile back ..."

"Not the actor. The man at the reading was a drunk. He was just here for the refreshments. He did know his movie trivia though ..." His voice trailed away, and he tapped one finger lightly on the table as we sat in silence.

"Right," he said at last. "Let's talk about you. Sounds to me like you've found your Fraser. So—mission accomplished for the blog?"

I could feel myself blushing. I fought it down. "Yeah—no—I don't know," was all I could manage.

He smiled. "Oh. Sore subject? No need to be embarrassed. It seems to me you deserve a little happiness, after all ye've gone through to get to this godforsaken country."

"Don't say that. It's an amazing place. I love it here. Did you read the post about the stone cairns?"

"Aye. That I did. And the truth is, I do hope ye keep at it— the writing, I mean. You've a flair for storytelling. Those cairns are a bit before my era, though I've done my time at plenty o' Historic Scotland sites. I've more of a Middle Ages focus, I guess, so when I read your post, I learned something, and enjoyed it, too."

"Hamish told me he thinks the pre-historic monuments are good for nothing except pulling down."

"Ah," he said, looking pointedly at something in his cup. "It's Hamish, is it? So he's the one, then? Ye've hardly been postin' to yer blog at all since ye've made his acquaintance."

I felt strangely tongue-tied again. "He's—yeah, he's pretty wonderful," I said. "And anyway, I *am* still blogging. It's just been slower since my laptop was stolen."

He grinned wryly. "Hmm. I don't know about that. It seems these days the content leans more toward a paean to the country than it does a description of your fella. Your fan base certainly seems to be demanding more details. I reckon they are ready to marry you off to the man."

I snorted. "My sister is convinced that I've made them all up, just to show her that someone out there thinks I'm not crazy. Which—I would have, if I'd thought of it. But they're just … I dunno …"

"Living out their dreams vicariously?" he finished.

I nodded.

He fell silent a moment, and we both sipped our tea.

"As long as you have found your dream, Emma," he said, at last. "I mean, commenters aside, it's *your* dream that's important here."

I looked up at him, but as soon as I did, he dropped his eyes. "Well, anyway," I said, hurriedly. "We're supposed to be talking about you. This is your event. Look at all the amazing books you've written."

He raised an eyebrow. "Each one has had its struggles, no doubt about that."

"Well, it doesn't show. I've been borrowing your books from the library and enjoying every one."

"Really?" His eyes lit up.

I traced my finger over the silhouette on the cover of my new book. "Yep. And what about that old lady? She has to be your biggest fan. Do you know her lips were moving when you read her favorite sexy bit aloud? She's obviously committed the whole passage to memory."

He allowed himself a half smile. "She literally *is* my biggest fan. She's president of the Scottish chapter of my fan club."

"See? I didn't even know you had a fan club! I will join the American branch, for sure when I get home."

"There *is* no American branch. There's just the Scottish branch, and I'm pretty sure Mrs. McCarthy is the only member. But thanks for the thought."

"Well, for what it's worth, I'm with Mrs. McCarthy. I like the sexy bits, too. Except ..."

"Except ..." His face took on a look I remembered. From the time he was trying to walk on a freshly broken foot. I mentally punched myself in the head a few times.

"Nothing—it was fantastic, really. I can't wait to read the whole thing."

He closed his eyes and sighed. "It's okay, you don't have to tell me."

"It's not that big a deal, really."

He opened his eyes again. "I'm sorry. I didn't mean to make something of nothing. It's just—I don't know. Hearing how wonderful the book is doesn't sell copies, you know? There *is* something I'm missing. Something that I've not managed to capture jes' right. I'd like if a few more people wanted to read my books than just the sum total of the Scots fan club, aye?"

"I get that." I thought for a minute and then plunged ahead. "I mean, I haven't read this book all the way through, obviously. And I know your stories take place in an historical context where things were different. But I've kinda noticed that your heroines are always so perfect. Like, *too* perfect. They are gorgeous, they are sexy, they're great in bed, and—well, like this one tonight was even a fantastic hunter. So they're—not really human. The one you read in the book tonight is a goddess. But in the end, he still has to rescue her."

His expression was puzzled, but since this was so much better than hurt, I kept going. "In one of my—uh—*other* favorite books, the best part is that the female lead gets to help out the hero once in a while, too. There's a bit of balance, somehow. A partnership. If you can write your female characters a little less physically perfect and a little more like rounded humans who can actually have a role to play in their own destinies, you'll have it nailed."

He took a big swallow of his tea and managed a smile.

I reached over and squeezed his hand. "The story was fantastic," I said. "I can't wait to read the whole thing."

The color in his neck flushed right up his face. "Thank you, Emma. Your standards may even be higher than Rebecca's, and that's saying something. I think you may have offered the kindest slam any of my books has ever received. And now, I'm afraid, I have to run."

He got up, paid the bill—gave me a wry smile and a wave, and was gone before I could say goodbye.

Fabulous Findlay…
4:00 pm, June 22
Edinburgh, Scotland

I've spent the last few weeks reading books written by Jack Findlay, a Scottish writer I met in—ah—extraordinary circumstances before I left the US.

These are marvelous stories. You can find out more about them at his website. And a little blackbird has told me that another one is due, based on the life of Scottish hero William Wallace. Watch for it soon!

- ES

Comments: 153

HiHoKitty, Sapporo, Japan:

Jack Findlay is second favorite writer to Herself. His books romantic and adventure. You SO lucky to meet him! You live my dream, Emma. But still—we wait patiently to hear of your true love. Does he ride horse?

(Read 152 more comments <u>here</u>…)

After tea with Jack, I managed to find an Internet cafe to make the blog post and still be only twenty minutes late for Sandeep. No chance to read all the comments, though – they were coming in so fast and furious. For a guy who had so many empty seats at his reading, he sure had a lot of fans.

Sandeep spent the entire drive home raving about all the features on his new machine, so at least he wasn't angry with me for being late. Ash slept in the back, curled in the one corner of the van that wasn't filled with giant espresso machine parts. I listened to his father rave on, and thought about Jack Findlay.

I felt like I had spent two hours (and twenty-five minutes, according to my boss) kicking a puppy. I mean—bad enough that no one had shown up to Jack's reading event. But then I had to add insult to injury by giving him my expert opinion on what was wrong with his books? His broken foot still hadn't healed, he was clearly struggling with self-confidence issues and I had stomped all over the female character in his story.

The blog post was the only remedy I could come up with.

I'd missed seeing my boyfriend, AND ruined Jack's day all in one.

I tried to take my mind off Jack by thinking about Hamish. About how I'd persuade him that a night out didn't need to involve Geordie and the boys. About how much fun we could have, just getting to know each other better.

But even the idea of seeing Hamish soon couldn't banish the look of pain on Jack's face as he walked out of that tea shop. Well, maybe he could go home to his Rebecca for comfort. I'd actually forgotten her existence until he mentioned her again, just as I'd forgotten to look to see if he wore a ring or not. So, after all that time together, I still didn't know if he was married or not. Not that it mattered—it had to be a pretty committed relationship, with the reverential way he referred to her.

As Sandeep chirped on about his new machine, I slumped in my seat and considered how big a vat of espresso I'd need to drown myself.

Five hours of winding roads and a major two-hour traffic jam brought on by an errant collection of sheep and a cranky farmer brought us back to Nairn just after ten. After helping Ash and Sandeep unload the enormous machine into the back of the cafe, I headed home to Morag's on my bike. Sandeep had looked at me like I was crazy to refuse a drive, but my backside was tired from all the sitting, so it was a relief to stand up on the pedals and stretch out my legs. It looked like it might have been raining earlier in the village, but the evening brought a light breeze that cleared the sky, and a blanket of stars lit my way home.

The clean air smelled like spring, and I thought about sneaking some of Morag's leftover bannock for a midnight snack before bed. My stomach rumbled at the thought.

I'd made it just past the outskirts of the town when I bumped through a pothole in the dark and my front tire began to make an ominous hissing noise. I tried to keep pedaling, but after a revolution or two the tire was completely flat. I hopped off and rolled the bike forward, hoping the valve had just been pinched or something, but the evil shard of green glass gleaming up at me from between the treads removed all hope.

At least the rain stayed away. I contemplated pushing the bike back to town, but with Hamish away with Geordie, the garage would be locked up tight. I decided to finish walking the route to Morag's and beg a ride in her truck in the morning to get the tire repaired.

Even at that late hour, the inky sky was tinged purple at the eastern edge, and, with a strange pang in my gut, I thought about leaving. Another month and I would likely have enough money saved for my return ticket. As comfortable as I felt with my life in Nairn, I could hardly bear the thought of returning to all the unknowns back in Chicago. I'd sold everything. I had no apartment to go back to. And what about my life in Nairn? Even just imagining the return home made my stomach ache.

As I pushed my bike along the edge of the road, bits of gravel shot into the ditch with little *tings* as the rim rubbed against the road. I pulled my hood up against the evening breeze and leaned forward to flip the headlamp on. Its comforting beam shone a clear path down in front of my wounded wheel as I pushed the bike along.

My mind wandered back to Hamish. With his broad shoulders and long, muscular frame, he was everything I'd dreamed about when seeking my Fraser. His hair was fair, not red, it was true, and the baseball hat was not a look I'd choose, but he could be talked out of it eventually. Maybe. He was kind and funny, and I was pretty sure he liked me as much as I liked him.

Pretty sure.

In spite of my best efforts, his erratic work schedule meant we'd not managed enough alone time to prove his interest without a doubt. I'd not seen him in a kilt yet, either, but if he pulled it off half as well as Jack Findlay had, I was ready to have my socks knocked off.

Anyway, if he was content to take things slow, I was happy to oblige. I was only really worried about one thing. He'd made it clear since we'd met—really even from that night in the bar in Edinburgh—that his ultimate goal was to make it to America.

That should be a good thing, right? I had to go home soon, myself.

Didn't I?

My bicycle rim thudded rhythmically on the road, as I tried to sort out what I was really feeling. I hadn't come to Scotland planning to stay. But now that I had to seriously think of leaving—well, it had me feeling panicky. The irony of panicked thoughts at a *return* to the US wasn't lost on me, either.

A set of headlights washed over me from behind, and I automatically moved off to the side of the road. Luckily it wasn't too deep a ditch. And I was at least halfway home.

Home.

My stomach clenched. It was the first time I'd thought of my little place at Morag's as home. Chicago seemed in another lifetime. A whole world away.

I realized then that the headlights hadn't swished by me, as expected. I turned to look, shading my eyes from the brightness, to see the vehicle had slowed to a walking pace directly behind me.

I lifted my hand to wave. "Hamish? Thank God! I've blown a tire. I'm so glad you're here!"

No answer.

I stopped, and the van slowed to a stop, too. Right in the center of the lane, idling.

My heart started beating a little faster. If not Hamish, who would stop behind me? The road was not a minor one, but it was nearly midnight on a weeknight. I'd seen fewer than a handful of vehicles, mostly heading to local farms.

I stared into the headlights long enough that they left twin spots on my retinas.

Something wasn't right.

I turned and started pushing the bike again, my whole body tingling with adrenaline. The van didn't move—just sat behind me, idling. I started to run, still pushing the bike. It didn't even occur to me to leave it behind.

I'd been running a full ten or fifteen seconds when I heard the van's engine rev. My heart roared along with it, especially when I heard the gravel spitting out from under the huge tires. In less than a second, the van was beside me.

My legs turned to water. I had time to be grateful that I hadn't tossed the bike in the ditch, as without it I could never have remained standing when the window rolled down.

Hamish stuck his face out.

"Hey babe," he said. "Thought 'at might be you. Want a lift?"

It only took a few minutes to sort out. I was furious—beyond furious—that he would frighten me like that, and told him so, in no uncertain terms.

"But babe, I was just listenin' to a song," he said, "on mah way to see yeh."

He pointed to his iPod, sitting on the dash. "Beachboys 'Surfer Girl'—look, yeh can see for yerself."

Sure enough, the menu was still rotating across the screen.

"When I spotted yeh in the road, I slowed down righ' away."

"I waved to you and called ..." I said, still feeling wobbly-legged, even though I was sitting down.

"And I waved back, and pointed to mah headphones. I didn't know yeh couldn't see me. I didn't even realize you were frightened until I had to hoist yeh into the van because yer legs gave out."

At least I didn't wet myself, I thought, grateful for small favors.

We drove on in silence until his headlights lit up Morag's farm sign in the distance. "I'm sorry I yelled at you," I said, at last.

He nodded affably. "I understand. You were frightened. Look, let me make it up to yeh. I'll keep the bike in the back and we'll mend it in the shop in the mornin'. And I'll come back and drive yeh in to the cafe, aye?"

As it was long past midnight by that time, I nodded gratefully. Hamish pulled his van into the yard, and I jumped out to get the gate, but he put a hand on my arm.

"Wait," he said. "I'll leave the van out here on the road, and tha' way it won't wake the old lady."

I felt a strange tingling somewhere south of the pit of my stomach. And the wave of tiredness that had washed over me receded instantly. The bit of my brain that was still angry at him for the stunt on the road called out weakly in protest.

"So—ah—you want to come in, then?" I said, my mouth strangely dry.

He grinned. "Well—if you'd care to show me around ..."

I was out my door in a flash, the tiny, admonishing part of my brain instantly crushed by something that had nothing to do with logic.

He took his time, putting on the parking brake, and checking the bike was safely stowed in the back before he walked around the front of the van to meet me by the gate.

He took one of my hands in his. "Emma, I'd like to formally apologize for frightenin' you," he said.

I looked up at him. "Accepted. And I for yelling."

"Aye," he said. "Our first fight, resolved."

He leaned down and kissed me then, slowly. The tingly feeling took up permanent residence.

This was Not a Bad Thing.

Stepping quietly, our fingers still twined together, we walked through the gate and up the path directly to the barn, skirting the farmhouse. There were still lights burning in the kitchen. As we walked, I realized that Hamish's lips had been on mine while I leaned against Morag's kissing gate. I felt that somewhere, someone was ticking an item off a list with my name on it.

We walked through the barn, giving it no more than a cursory look.

"Yep," he said, as I pointed out the stalls, "Hay, animals, smells like shite—it's a barn a'right. Where's your digs, lassie? Is tha' it?" He pushed me up against the door to my room and kissed me again.

Then he undid the top button of my coat.

I grabbed his lapels and pulled him inside.

The thing about getting naked fast in a late Scottish springtime is—well, it really can't happen. There are just too many layers. And multiplied by two people who are in somewhat of a hurry, but still mindful of not being quite in the financial position where torn clothing can be easily replaced ....

Let's just say that in seconds, there were raincoats on the floor at my feet, and shoes, and his shirt and my sweater. Hamish had made his way down at least three buttons of my uniform, when the door behind me flew open.

Morag stood in the doorway, the light from the barn framing her Mackintosh-clad form. Her hair was sticking straight up and she had a streak of blood down one side of her face. "Emma," she said. "Allison has a problem. I need yeh."

I clutched the top of my uniform closed as her head turned to take in the pile of clothing at our feet. She looked up at Hamish.

"Ach—nice tae see yeh, young man. We might have use fer a man who's good wi' his hands. Ye'd best come, too." She thrust a flashlight at him, scooped up an armful of dry hay and headed out the door.

"Who's Allison?" hissed Hamish, as we scrambled back into our coats.

"I'm not sure," I whispered back. "Maybe one of her cows is stuck in a ditch ...?"

But we followed Morag's bobbing flashlight upward, so there could be no ditch involved. It was hard going with the ground covered in prickly heather bushes, chasing a farmer who was deceptively round. In pitch-blackness.

Perhaps she could move so quickly because she was low-slung.

In any event, we made it, panting, about half way up the big hill behind the barn to the spot where Morag's flashlight had stopped moving. We found her on her knees, spreading the straw she'd been carrying on the ground. She had propped her flashlight against a heathery shrub and the light shone down on a small sheep, lying on its side and clearly in distress.

As we approached, the animal bleated a little and kicked her legs weakly. Morag ran her hand across the wooly flank and made soothing noises as she tucked handfuls of the straw around to make a bed.

Hamish shone his light on the tail end of the sheep, which was awash in mud and blood. He made a little gagging noise in his throat. Morag made her own disapproving Scottish noise in return. "Righ' man, you don't have to linger at that end. Jes' hold her head steady—I can do the rest."

I knelt down near the head. "Will she bite me?" I asked, a trifle nervously, and remembering my experience with Cara all too clearly.

"Nah—she'll be fine. Jes' take ahold of her front legs there, young man, and you grab her head, Emma, gentle now ..." The rest of what she had to say disappeared in a flurry of grunting and bleating.

I couldn't tell who was making which sound.

What I could tell, as I put all my weight down on the sheep's head to stop her from whipping it around, was that Hamish wasn't doing his job. I could tell this, because one of the legs he was supposed to be holding smacked me, hoof first, square in the ear. My glasses slipped dangerously down my nose.

"What the hell..." I sputtered. I leaned my left elbow down on the sheep's head, and tried to feel for the damage with my right hand. My hand was mud-covered when I inspected it in the beam of the flashlight, but there didn't seem to be any blood. Luckily it had been a glancing blow, and my glasses hadn't broken either.

"Hamish," I gasped, "Can you try to grab her legs?"

"Ugggh," grunted Morag, and the sheep bleated anxiously in unison. She yanked her head out from under my forearms and I could feel the wind as her teeth snapped shut beside my right cheekbone.

"I thought you said she didn't bite," I yelled at Morag.

"We'el she never has done before," came the tense reply. "But as I've got mah whole arm inside her now, I reckon she's a mite uncomfortable, aye?"

She grunted again, and then the animal lay still for a moment, head down, flanks still trembling.

"Nearly there," said Morag, through gritted teeth. "Yer boyfriend's run off, then, has he?"

"What?" I yelled, whipping my head around. "Hamish?"

Sure enough, I could see a flashlight bobbing halfway down the hill.

"I'll see yeh in the mornin', Emma," came his voice, floating through the cool night air. "Somethin's come up!"

"Arsehole," muttered Morag. "Men are useless at this sort of thing, anyhow. No stayin' power."

The sheep bucked its legs, but I managed to dodge beneath the hooves.

"Aye—atta girl," said Morag, approvingly. "Yer learning, ain't yeh?"

I didn't have even a moment to think about Hamish, as the sheep suddenly began whipping her head back and forth, frantically.

"Jes' hold her head, luv," Morag panted. She was on her knees by that time, her hands busy doing something I was just as happy not to see. The sheep stirred distractedly under my grip and then suddenly jerked her head as if to sit up.

"Hold 'er, hold 'er," cried Morag. "Almost got it ... now!"

The sheep closed her eyes and grunted, and the farmer was suddenly awash in a tangle of legs and head and blood and ...

I focused on the mama sheep for a minute, until the night sky stopped spinning.

But Morag was beaming, and took up a great handful of straw to swipe the gore off a tiny, mini-sheep. When she'd cleaned it to the point of it looking more like a wet rat than anything, she lifted it carefully over the mother's back leg and the baby immediately nestled in, nursing.

The mama sheep began straining under my grip again. "Ye can let 'er go now, Em," said Morag, so I did. The mama nosed her new offspring with a tired kind of interest, and I felt badly for holding her away.

"Whoops," said Morag, and vanished from out of the flashlight beam. The mama sheep and I both peered through the dark, trying to see what was going on. I got the impression of something whirling through the air, and when Morag reappeared, she was beaming and wiping off a second arrival. She placed the other wee lamb in beside the first, and leaned back on her haunches. She was bloody to the elbows on both arms, but she slapped her hands onto her knees and grinned at me.

"I should have seen tha' comin', but it's such a late delivery and this mama's so tiny. Couldn't sort it out until the second wee one poked out his nose."

Morag got to her feet wearily and I realized I could see her face without the flashlight. The sun was near to rising. She slapped me heartily on the shoulder.

"Feel like some breakfast? A good lambing always gives me a roaring appetite for eggs and bacon."

I nodded and stood beside her, looking down at the new arrivals busily gobbling their own breakfasts. The mama sheep was flaked out on her side, nearly asleep with exhaustion, but all signs of distress gone.

"I'll head back up after we eat to take care of this mess," Morag said, indicating the pile of bloody straw with the flashlight.

We started down the hill together.

"Will the lambs be okay out on the hillside like that?" I asked. "I can help you carry them down to the barn, if you want."

Morag shook her head. "Nae—they'll be jes' fine, the little beggars. I'll have the vet up later in the week to check 'em for scour and so on. If I was worried at all, I'd bring 'em in, but they both latched on jes' fine."

We walked into the main barn door, and Morag headed straight over to the giant stone sink. She sluiced the blood off her hands and arms, scrubbing with a soap whose antiseptic smell wafted across to where I leaned against the next stall.

I walked over to close the door to my room. We must have left it open in the rush to follow Morag up the hill. I also tried very hard not to think about Hamish. About what had nearly happened inside my room. Or about what hadn't happened up on the cold hillside. Inside my head the thought *Jamie would never have run* seemed to be on repeat.

Morag was striding down the barn toward the door to the farmhouse. I followed along, staring at my mud-boots as they shushed through the straw. "That's three babies since I've been here," I said, more to myself than anyone. "This is a weird habit to be forming."

Morag grinned as she dried her hands on an old piece of sacking. "Are ye sure it's a habit, Em? P'raps it's more of a … calling."

The look on my face made her cackle, and still chuckling, she walked out of the barn to see about making breakfast.

Farm Family…
11:00 am, June 25
Nairn, Scotland

It seems some Scottish warriors are at a loss when it comes to babies——even baby lambs! Okay, just kidding. But my landlady Morag's new lambs are gorgeous, and she tells me the wee farm family will feature at a Highland Games sometime this summer.

Today the sky is a thin, clear blue——no rain in sight, and I'm hoping my warrior returns soon.

- ES

Comments: 63

(Read 63 comments <u>here</u>…)

To: EmmaFindingFraser@gmail.com
From: JackFindlay@*range.co.uk
June 25

Hi Emma,

I want to apologize for being such a gomeril the other day in Edinburgh and dashing off on you, so I thought email might be more private than posting a comment to your blog.

Still, I would like to hear more of the lamb story, next time we meet. You have a way of giving just a tantalizing tid-bit in your posts that leaves your readers wanting more. You are a fantastic storyteller—keep at it! This is a skill I need to learn with my books, which brings me to my next point.

Thank you also for your kind words on the blog, flogging my books, and for helping me get past a problem that's been worrying at me with the new story. Your honest assessment has been more valuable than I can articulate.

As always, wishing you and your warrior the very best. I am a sucker for a happy ending.

Jack

PS I also want to apologize for the perhaps slightly over-enthusiastic greeting I gave you at the bookstore. These events can be very trying and—well, it was just lovely to see a friendly face. So—sorry.

PPS To clarify, I am not sorry for the kiss itself—or kisses, if you want to get technical. I am, however, abjectly sorry if I crossed a line or startled you in any way.

PPPS Right, so I do know I crossed a line, kissing you when you are already in a relationship, but just to be clear, it's very customary in places like Europe for people to kiss each other on greeting. Edinburgh is a very European city.

However, I think I'd better just stop now before this gets even more humiliating. Thanks again for coming, Emma, even if it was by accident.

JF

Summer may have come to the village, but I soon learned that summer in this part of northern Scotland, at least, meant the occasional sunbeam, quickly murdered by rain-filled clouds and a piercing wind.

So essentially, the same as winter.

But somehow, I didn't mind it at all.

Since I was on late shift that day, I spent the whole length of Katy's coffee break in the chair at the library, reading and re-reading Jack's email. I wasn't sure just what to make of it. He had been happy to see me, yes—but something in that kiss felt different. Before he knew I'd only stumbled upon his reading. I stared at the screen until my eyes were sore, replaying that kiss in my mind. Of course he knew I was with Hamish. And he was with Rebecca. He was just happy to have a friendly face to read to. Of course he was.

Still …

When Katy marched over to throw me out, I made her happy by paying the twenty pence to run off a copy of his note to stick into my pack.

On my afternoon break, I leaned against the fridge in the back and read the email again, until Sandeep came in and threatened to cut my break short. So I threw on my coat and dashed across to see Hamish.

Which turned out to be the Right Thing To Do.

Hamish emerged from the back of the garage, wiping the grease off his hands on a rag. He kissed me, and began a somewhat convoluted apology explaining his dislike of blood, which involved a dead squirrel and an accident on his bicycle when he was seven. He just reached the part where the bike, with him on it, was in mid-air above the poor, doomed squirrel when Geordie walked in, raised an eyebrow at me and ordered Hamish to "quit ditherin and get back tae tha' bleedin' engine."

Which he did.

And that was okay. It had to be okay, right? I mean, you can't blame someone for a real phobia. Of all people, I should understand a panic-driven reaction.

But that voice in my head shouted me down. *Jamie wouldn't have run.*

I pushed the voice away and walked along the street for the rest of my break, trying to focus on the warmth of the late afternoon sun. Hamish wasn't on the road at the moment, and we'd soon have time together again.

To finish what we'd started.

Besides, I was busy myself at work. Sandeep was in heaven with his new espresso machine, and I'd spent many hours going through the differences between a cappuccino and a latte—not to mention Americanos and macchiatos—with him and Ash. He'd taken copious notes, and as I left each night it had made me smile to see him carefully dusting coffee grounds out of the components.

After my walk, I returned to the cafe to find Ashwin in the back, holding a piece of paper between his fingers.

"Yer boyfriend left ye a note," he said, and waved it under my nose.

I snatched at it, but he pulled it away and held it behind his back.

"Give me that," I said, indignantly. "It's private!"

Ashwin looked defiant, and took a step backwards. "Are ye in love wi' him, then? Because he's no' right for ye, Emma."

I took another unsuccessful grab at the note. "Ash! It's none of your business."

His face fell, but he took a second step back. By that time he was up against the wall that separated the kitchen from the seating area.

"It *is* my business," he muttered. "Maybe I care what happens to yeh, aye? Hamish Lewis has gone ou' with nearly every girl in Nairn, and walked ou' on as many, too. He dropped one when he met you—didja know that? Eilidh MacAdams. Left 'er like an ol' shoe out in the rain."

He crossed his arms over his chest, the crumpled note still in one hand. "I wouldnae want it to happen to you, is all." His face had gone red with this speech, but he still hadn't handed me the note.

"Hamish already told me he'd broken up with someone recently," I replied. "He didn't keep it a secret."

Ashwin jutted his jaw at me and didn't budge. As I stared at his flushed face and red eyes, something clicked in my brain. "Ash—how old are you? Sixteen?"

"Nearly eighteen," he said, defensively.

I reached over to him and patted his shoulder. "I didn't know you felt so protective of me," I said. "I'm really okay, honestly. I can look after myself. But thank you for watching out for me. It's very— brotherly of you."

"I'm no'—" he spluttered. "It's not like tha' …"

We both stood there for a long second, then he sighed deeply and handed me the note.

"I'll be here when he breaks yer heart," he muttered, and stalked outside to puff moodily on cigarettes for the rest of the afternoon.

I turned away quickly to hide my smile. To tell the truth, I was kind of flattered. I'd never been the subject of anyone's unrequited crush before, even that of a seventeen-year-old boy. It was very sweet.

Hamish's note sobered my mood pretty quickly, though. Apparently he had to go pick up auto parts in Glasgow, and would be gone for at least a couple of days.

But it was the last line of the note that really left me freaked out.

We'll get together when I get back, he'd written. *I know you need to go home to America soon—and I've been saving my own money. Let's talk about travelling together …*

He'd signed the note with a little heart, and his name.
Love, Hamish.

That's what it meant, right?

I love you and I want to go home to America with you. Right?

And even though I was considered the expert barista in the place, I messed up the next three lattes while I tried to figure out how I felt about that.

Ash was speaking to me again by the next day, and things seemed to be pretty much back to normal. We had a bit of a rush in the cafe in the morning, when a busload of tourists stopped for coffee.

The noise level rose the way it always did when Americans came in. The people from the tour bus were mostly European, but sure enough, two Americans were at the end of the line. Their delight at having "coffee like Starbucks" meant that they tipped me lavishly.

"Best mocha I've had since leaving Boston," said the man. He wore a plaid tam that reminded me uncomfortably of the stripper in Philadelphia.

His wife nodded eagerly. "You've got the touch, honey," she said, and threw another two pound coin into the cup with the chipped handle we used for tips. Then she blew her nose.

"Are you having a nice visit?" I asked.

The woman took a long, appreciative sip of her coffee. "Oh, yeah. I been cryin' all morning after visiting that battle site. SO sad."

The man nodded. "First Braveheart, and then that Bonnie Charlie—it was a sad time to be a Scot, and no mistake."

"Oh, Braveheart ..." I began, but the lady jumped in.

"Now THAT man was a hero if I ever saw one." She swatted her husband's arm. "Why can't you be like that, Barry?"

He grinned at her. "What? Run around in a kilt with blue paint on my face, and then get cut to pieces in the end?" He bent his knees and brandished an imaginary sword.

"That wasn't ..." I tried again, but the wife squealed at her husband's antics and he squeezed her tightly before hustling her back out to the bus. Historically inaccurate, maybe, but I was pretty sure that couple's role-play was benefitting from their Highland tour.

It wasn't until long after the bus had gone and the morning rush was over that I realized they had not recognized me as a fellow American.

I stuck my head in the kitchen. "Where's your dad?" I asked Ashwin, who was pulling his cigarette pack out of his jacket pocket.

He shrugged. "Left. Think mebbe's he's gone for more beans—those tourists drank all the coffee in the place."

He kicked open the back door and lit his cigarette.

"Ash, do you think I sound Scottish?"

He snorted at me and blew smoke out the door.

"Seriously. Do I still sound like an American to you?"

"'Course ye do, eejit. Ye've on'y been here a month, aye? Anyway, Americans never get the accent righ'. They allus sound like themselves."

I counted on my fingers. "Nearly *two* months here, actually. And four since I got to Scotland in the first place."

He shrugged. "We'el, ye still sound American to me. Prolly allus will do, too."

I walked back into the cafe, thinking.

An older man I didn't recognize sat down at one of the booths. "Coffee," he said to me, as I walked up. "And noon o' tha' fancy crap, mind. Jes' plain coffee—black as mah soul."

He shook open a newspaper and began to read.

I filled his cup from my carafe and turned to go collect up the dishes from another table, when a fleeting glimpse of a photo on the back of the paper he held caught my eye.

Without thinking, I grabbed the newspaper out of his hands.

"Oi, that's mine," he said, jumping half out of his seat.

"Calm down, you'll spill your coffee," I muttered, scanning the story underneath the photograph.

"Watch it, lassie, or I'll have a word wi' yer manager," the man demanded, huffily. I pulled the outer page of the newspaper off and tossed him the sports and celebrity sections.

"Very sorry, sir," I said to him, scanning the page. "I just need to read this one story. You read those sections first. I'll be done in a second."

He narrowed his eyes at me, pushed out of the booth and stomped over to the cash desk where Ash had returned and was playing a game on his mobile phone.

"Sorry, sir," he echoed, dead-pan, and then added: "She *is* the owner."

He dropped his voice to a stage whisper. "And she's righ' crazy, so I wouldn't mess with her. She stabbed someone with a plastic fork just last week."

"A—a plastic fork?" the man said, looking over at me, nervously.

"Yeah, and you would not believe the mess. A carving knife woulda made cleaner work of it."

The man slapped a few coins on the counter near the cash and, clutching the remains of his paper, dashed out the door.

"Thanks, Ash," I said, absently.

"No probs," he said. "Chasing zombies on my phone—fair inspirational, aye?"

The article was very short. The picture at the top could have been a mug shot, but on further reading it turned out to be a passport photo. It was better than mine, too—she didn't look like a serial killer.

She looked like Susan.

I took a deep breath, and read the story again.

American Actress Behind String of Thefts

AP Glasgow

Lothian and Borders Police continue to search for a fugitive who is thought to be behind a series of crimes throughout Inverness-shire and other Highlands districts over the past year. American actress Gail Lee Duncan, known for her facility with accents, is accused of masterminding a string of thefts with losses amounting in the tens of thousands of pounds.

"The woman is a chameleon," said Chief Inspector Milton Garda of the Inverness Force. "We had her in our custody, but she was released on bail prior to her hearing."

That bail is now forfeit, as Miss Duncan has not been seen since leaving the Inverness Police station.

"This accused is accomplished at switching identities and has mastered several accents," the police officer added, "though it's true her Irish accent is a particularly poor imitation, and in fact it was that which led to her initial capture."

Duncan, who also is known to go by the aliases Susan O'Donnell and Gaily Dee, is due to stand trial on a long series of offenses ranging from theft to impersonation. Police believe she has fled the country for one of the larger cities down south."

"*I* bought her Irish accent," I muttered, and looked over the paper to find myself staring straight into the substantially irate face of Sandeep.

"What's this I hear about you stealing newspapers from our customers?" he asked, snatching the page out of my hands and brandishing it at me.

I looked over at Ash, but he'd stowed his game and was ringing through a customer's bill. I couldn't quite manage to catch his eye.

I tried to grab the page from my boss's hands, but he held it behind his back. "It was a mistake, Sandeep. I just—just borrowed it to—ah ..."

"Read crap during work hours?" he said, silkily. "Or perhaps learn the techniques required for threatening my customers with a plastic fork?"

I stared at him, speechless.

He shook the paper in my face. "Do NOT let this happen again!" he roared, and stomped off into the back.

"He's going to read that while he's taking a shit, aye?" said Ash, pulling his phone out again.

"Probably so," I muttered, letting my breath out at last.

Susan. Even reading about her got me in trouble. "That woman is poisonous," I said, to no one in particular. "If I never see her again, I will be a happy person."

"If I ever get coffee again, I'll be a happy person," said an old lady at the counter.

I poured the rest of my carafe into her cup and went off to wipe the tables. But I could not get that photograph out of my mind.

Freaking Felon...
8:30 am, June 27
Nairn, Scotland

Have to type quickly here—the Supposed-to-be-Free Internet Gestapo is marching over from the periodical section toward me at this very moment. I just want to link to this news story. Took me a few days to find it online, but if you ever see this woman—WATCH OUT. She's the one who stole all my things!

BBCNewsLink-American-Crime-Spree-Suspect

- ES

Comments: 67

HiHoKitty, Sapporo, Japan:

What a terrible criminal to steal from you and other peoples. Her face must be burned in your memory. Will your Hamish hunt her down and put her in hands of police?

GenesieFanGirl, New York, USA:

Hey Emma,

You probably don't remember me, but we met last

winter at an OUTLANDER Fan Fiction event. I've been following your blog since then, and have to admit it's been pretty entertaining. But since you haven't posted in a while, I figured you might well have given up the chase, having found your Jamie Fraser clone and all.

But in case he turns out to be a dud, (I mean—have you even *slept* with him yet?) I thought you might like to know the rumor here is that your friend Jack Findlay is retelling the Braveheart story, and it's all the buzz. Now, William Wallace is truly a man worthy of chasing down! Maybe you'd have more luck getting it on with Braveheart…?

- Genesie

(Read 65 more comments <u>here</u>…)

Genesie. I couldn't believe she was actually reading my blog. After all, we hadn't parted on the greatest of terms. If she was still upset with me, though, she'd certainly gotten her own back with the crack about Hamish.

I slipped out of the library before Katy even had a chance to give me the stink-eye. I had bigger worries than Katy, anyway. Outside, the sun had begun to shine like it really might be summer. A breeze swirled up from the Firth, cooling the heat that had sprung to my face reading Genesie's comment.

What if she was right? Was Hamish a dud? Or worse—what if I was? I counted backwards as I pedaled toward the cafe. I'd spilled the hot water down his neck almost a month ago. Almost a month. And the closest we'd come to getting naked together had been thwarted by farm animals.

Cute farm animals, but still.

Maybe Genesie was only pointing out what I hadn't been willing to face. Why hadn't I pushed harder to get alone time with Hamish?

And why should I have to push, anyway?

The minutes until my lunch break ticked by more slowly than tenth grade physics class. Sandeep flicked his fingers impatiently at me when I asked him for the third time if he thought the worst of the rush was over.

"What's so important that you have to race out of here?" he demanded.

"I'm—I'm just going to run across the street a minute. I have to ask Geordie a question. I'll be back right away ..."

He rolled his eyes and viciously dug coffee grounds out of the strainer. "Geordie? More likely Hamish, aye?"

"No—well, maybe. I just want to find out when he's coming back."

Sandeep snorted. "In the old country, girls don't chase after boys. They let their fathers handle the arrangements."

I untied my apron and cracked open the back door. A blast of warm air swirled in. "I'm not chasing anyone. Just asking a question. Besides, weren't you born in Glasgow?"

"Close the fookin' door," he yelled, and I bolted.

Less than a minute later, I ran into the garage office. Genesie's comments had made me more desperate than ever to see Hamish. Seeing him would quiet that doubting voice in my head, I knew it. Earlier in the week, when I had stopped by and asked Geordie, he said Hamish would be back in a day or two. It felt like an eternity since we'd been together.

When I burst into the office, I was surprised to see Hamish standing inside the first garage bay, large as life. He and Geordie were laughing uproariously.

"You're back!" I said, and threw myself into his arms.

Geordie gave me a sideways glance. "Two minutes, man," he said to Hamish, and grabbing his coffee cup, stalked into the office. Hamish picked up a rag and began to wipe the grease from his hands.

"Don't worry about that," I said, and leaned in for a kiss.

He gave me a little kiss on the tip of my nose, and then hurriedly stepped back, still wiping his hands. "Ach, ye'll no' want this grease on yer uniform, lass," he said, and walked round to the far side of the small car in the bay.

"Okay, you're probably right," I said, reluctantly. "I missed you so much, though. It feels like you're always away."

He nodded, and started digging around under the hood of the vehicle. "It's been a bi' of a busy season," he said, his voice muffled.

I stepped closer, and stuck my head under the other side. "So … where'd you go?"

"After the pickup in Glasgow, I had to turn around and head to Fort William. It's down south a bit."

"I know it. I have a friend there. Maybe I could hitch a ride with you the next time you go?"

"Mebbe," he muttered, and dropped the wrench he was using inside the engine. "Aw, fer fook's sakes," he said, and dove in to try and reach it. "Em, ye'd better get back to work, hadn't yeh?" he gasped, as he felt around inside. His voice reminded me of Morag the time she was dealing with the mama sheep.

"Okay, I'll go," I said. "But I feel like we haven't spent any time together lately. I miss you."

He grunted loudly and then held up the wrench triumphantly. "Got the bastard!"

Geordie stuck his head in from the office. "You still here?" he said to me.

"I'm leaving, I'm leaving," I said. "But since I never get to see my boyfriend any more, maybe next time you send him away on a weekend, I can go along to navigate?"

Hamish was making wild hand gestures at me, but Geordie crossed his arms over his chest and stepped inside the door.

"Aye, well your *boyfriend* is makin' a short trip tomorrow evenin' all the way doon to the fine municipality of Dores. I'm sure you'd be a welcome distraction to his drivin', if yer free."

I nodded eagerly. "I'm off at five. That would be perfect!"

He turned to Hamish. "Weel, now that's settled, mebbe we can get a little godDAMNED WORK DONE AROUN' HERE?"

I blew Hamish a kiss and fled.

I didn't have a chance to see my favorite mechanic before work the next day, but when things slowed down after the lunch rush, I followed Ash outside to ask him where Dores was, exactly.

"It's a wee place, doon the south shore of the Loch," he said, shielding his cigarette from the rain. "Bou' forty minutes drive, give or take. Plenty o' time fer a booty-call, afterwards."

"Never mind about that," I said, hastily.

"Wha—ye think I don't know what's goin' on wi' you two?"

"Well, it's none of your concern," I said, primly folding my arms across my chest.

An incredulous look spread across his face. "Fer fook's sake, Emma—don't tell me ye haven't done the nasty, yet? What's the matter wi' yeh?"

I punched him in the arm. "Shut *up*," I hissed. "I have no intention of discussing this with you. You're—you're just a *child*!"

I stomped back into the kitchen.

"A child who's plainly gettin' more than you," he yelled after me.

I refused to speak to him for the rest of the day, but his stupid remarks—in chorus with Genesie's—kept replaying in my mind. By the time I needed to leave, I had myself worked up into quite a mental frenzy.

What was the matter with me? Hamish was gorgeous, especially without the baseball cap, and I wanted to see more of him. But whenever we were together, something always seemed to get in the way.

Ash was right. He probably *was* getting more than me. For God's sake, Morag was probably getting more than me, since what I was getting was a big, fat zero. But I was convinced all I needed was less talk and more getting-to-know you time with Hamish. He was everything I was looking for in my Jamie—tall, strong, handsome. And, if you thought about it, having come all the way from America, I was even more of a Sassenach than Claire, right?

Right?

Sadly, driving a truck down what was little more than a country lane turned out to be less than ideal for a bonding-without-chatting time. As I climbed into the passenger seat, Bob Seeger implored me to take my old records off a shelf. I leaned forward to turn the volume down a little, and nestled into the seat beside Hamish. He grinned at me, and cranked the volume again.

"*I love that old time rock n' roll,*" he crooned, using both hands to push me back into my own seat.

"Um ..." I began, but he patted my hand reassuringly.

"Need yer belt, pet," he said, buckling me in place. "It's not such a winding road, but safety first, aye?"

Aye.

Once I was fully buckled and Bob had finished his song, Hamish ground the gears, and we were off.

"Ah love that man," he said fervently, as he flipped the volume down. "He represents everything that's right about America. Hard work, success—believin' in yer dreams ..."

"I'm pretty sure he's a grandfather by now," I said. "You don't actually hear his music that much any more."

Hamish waved his hand dismissively. "Yeah, I know he's mostly on the oldies stations, but—good music like tha' will never die."

He shifted gears—literally—and then launched into a dissertation about how he'd saved his money for years, waiting for an opportunity to move to America. This opportunity had finally presented itself in the form of, apparently, me.

"Don't you need a work permit ..." I began, but he waved my concern aside.

Or maybe he was just conducting the Silver Bullet band.

"Jes' a formality," he said, grinning. "They're always looking for good mechanics in California." He shifted gears and looked over at me. "When is it ye have to return?"

"I'm not actually sure," I said, glumly. "I guess I'd better look it up. Sometime pretty soon, I expect."

Hamish's face took on an anxious expression. "Will it still be summer in California by then?" he asked.

I nodded. "And in Chicago, too. 'Cause that's where I live, y'know. I need to save enough for my ticket home."

He smiled happily, and flipped on his signal. "Ach, maybe Sandeep'll give yeh double-shifts. By then, ye'll have enough cash to get rid o' those glasses *and* move to LA!"

I was still feeling a little burned by the glasses remark by the time we pulled into Dores. I mean, I hated my glasses, too, though I'd gotten pretty used to them since Susan had made off with my contacts. Still. I didn't think they looked that bad. And according to all the fashion magazines, four-eyed nerds were finally in.

Weren't we?

The village was nestled on the shore of Loch Ness, along a narrow road that wound through farm fields before swinging back toward the water. As there was little to be seen other than a scattering of houses, Hamish dropped me near the village inn.

"Is this where you are going?" I asked. There didn't seem to be any commercial buildings at all, apart from the inn. "I don't see a garage."

"It's a private home," he said, looking through his papers. "Called—ah—Sunshine Motors. Must be a fella workin' in an outbuilding behind one of these houses. I won't be long—the place cannae be hard to find in this wee town."

The little splatter of rain that had fallen while we were driving seemed to have cleared, and to the west the sky began to wrap itself in faint pink streaks. I hopped out at the end of the road and he drove off, promising to be back in fifteen minutes.

The breeze off the water caressed my face as I walked along the shoreline. With the cool air, the embarrassment about the glasses faded and my good intentions returned. I just needed to spend some time NOT talking with him, I reasoned. That was the whole purpose of this little jaunt together. And this was the fabled Loch Ness, after all.

I hadn't even had a glimpse of it before, when I'd traveled in the dark to Drumnadrochit to find Gerald's stone circle. It was amazing to see now, and another 'Claire site' that I could check off my list. I decided to scour the park for a romantic spot where Hamish and I could watch the sun set together.

Within five minutes of wandering down the lane away from the inn I had found the ideal location. A section of low, flat rock lay just above the waterline, out of sight from any prying eyes on the road above. An old log had floated up on the shore and jammed itself on the rocks. Perfect for leaning against.

I sat down on the rock, pulling my jacket beneath me to cushion the surface a bit—and decided it was just right. Private enough for a little canoodling, especially now that the light was failing. It was time I took matters into my own hands and move things forward, to see if Hamish and I were as physically compatible as I believed—I knew—we would be.

At that very moment, a small child covered in equal parts dirt and scabs came tearing out of a little lane that emerged behind some of the larger houses.

"Hide me!" he demanded, and dove behind me.

I jumped to my feet.

"What …? Who are you running from?"

The child grabbed my coat and dove under it.

"Big Bunny," came his muffled reply. "Big Bunny's gonna get me."

I looked around wildly, half expecting to see a giant pink rabbit bounding up. Instead, a weary-looking woman came jogging out of the lane.

"Have you seen a …?" she began; when she caught sight of the wriggling creature, unsuccessfully trying to hide his lower half under my jacket.

"Ach, Ruardh, yeh little shite. I've got yeh now."

She reached down and, grabbing the fugitive by the arm, looked up at me apologetically. "Ah'm 'is auntie," she said. "He's bolted on me three times this afternoon alone. My sister owes me big time, I swear."

She handed me back my jacket. "Ice cream, Bunny?" the little boy pleaded, as she scooped him up.

"Yer ma can give ye sweeties, laddie," she said. "Auntie Bonnie's all tired out."

They walked a few steps, and then she paused and turned back to me with an odd expression on her face. "Y'er not sittin' down here by yerself, aye?"

"Oh, I'm just waiting for my boyfriend," I said. "Why?"

But at that moment, the boy gave a joyful shout and wriggled loose. With a cry of despair, she broke into a run. The two of them disappeared back into the thick green foliage of the lane.

I listened for a moment, but the echoes of the little boy's giggles and his auntie's threatening shouts soon faded away into the shrubbery. I folded my jacket to sit on again, as the peaceful evening enveloped me once more.

The water was completely calm, and I stared out across the surface, my eyes following the gentle ripples left by the evening breeze. The loch itself was long and narrow, but my little section of beach was in a bit of a protected inlet. Across the water the yellow afternoon light briefly gave a golden glow to the trees on the opposite shore.

I had just leaned back against the log experimentally, imagining Hamish's body pressed against my own, hot and insistent ...when I heard a little splash. I opened my eyes and scanned the water. Had the kid made his escape again? It couldn't be him—everything was completely silent.

A low fog was rolling in with the dusk. And breaking the surface—just at the forefront of the twilight creeping across the loch—was a head. I rolled up onto my knees and peered through the gloom. Maybe it was a dolphin, like the ones in the Moray Firth?

A long, white head was emerging from the dark green waters of the loch.

Not a dolphin head.

I scrambled to my feet, staring. Was it—could it be ...?

Jumping up onto on the log I'd been leaning against, I rubbed my eyes and blinked, but the head didn't disappear. It came closer. My heart pounding like a bodhran, I stood frozen with fear atop that splintery bit of log.

The nostrils belonging to the head snorted out a blast of water and steam. The head turned, and huge brown eyes blinked as it swam toward me.

There was nowhere to go. I was on top of the log, with my back against the rock wall that I had been valuing for its privacy just moments before. I opened my mouth to call for help, but nothing came out.

In seconds it was over.

The head, which turned out to be attached very firmly to a neck and below that to a body, emerged from the water's edge. It belonged not to a disembodied monster after all, but to a fine, white horse, draped in a bit of lake greenery. After arising like Venus from the cool waters, the horse paused to shake itself from head to tail. Small fragments of algae or seaweed littered the pebbly shore at its feet. The animal stood a moment, regarding me, and then blinked its eyes once before trotting into the bushes that lined the lane leading off from the main road.

A horse—in the waters of the Loch?

The feeling came back into my legs just as I heard gravel spatter above me, and I ran as if my life depended on it up the hill to meet Hamish's truck.

"Sorry I was a bi' long, luv ..." he began, but stopped when he caught sight of my face. I blathered out the whole story to him, stumbling over my words, but was so caught up in the magic of it all I could hardly articulate.

When I was done, he chuckled.

It was not a "laughing-with-me" kind of chuckle.

"Yer havin' me on," he scoffed. "I've niver heard of a horse swimmin' in the loch. It's too deep, for one, and it's near freezin, still, innit? Now jump in to the lorry, will yeh? I'm right starvin'. Let's go see if we can find a McDonalds, aye?"

I climbed in the truck. "No—no, wait," I cried, but he'd already spun the truck back onto the main road.

kc dyer

"But—I found a nice little place we could have a picnic," I pleaded. "I could show you the splash marks from where the horse came out. Then you'd know it was real."

He jammed his hat down on his head. "It's a quarter-pounder for me, luv," he said, shifting gears on the truck. "Dontcha know that's what every McDonald has unner his kilt?"

He slapped his leg and roared.

"I haven't had a chance to find out," I said mournfully, but he'd pushed a button on his dash and Springsteen came on to drown me out, singing *Tunnel of Love*.

Fantastic Figment…?
7:15 pm, July 3
Nairn, Scotland

Morag is making noises about getting Wi-Fi at her farm. I am encouraging her in the direction of getting a computer, too, because the lightning moments in which I can actually post a blog here at the library and Tourist Center are getting fewer. But I believe I just have time to share a magical moment I had last night on the shores of Loch Ness.

Yes, *that* Loch Ness.

I found the perfect setting for a romantic picnic with my Highlander, and while I was waiting to him to arrive, a beautiful white stallion arose

from the water. He had been swimming in the loch!
He trotted out of the water and shook himself
before running off.

Has anyone ever heard of a horse doing this?
Swimming for the sheer joy of it? It was a
beautifully warm day, apart from the little bit
of rain that fell. Maybe he just wanted to cool
off.

Another mysterious Highland memory for me.

– ES

Comments: 23

HiHoKitty, Sapporo, Japan:

Oh, Miss Emma. It must have been the water horse!
Claire's beastie! Your picnic sounds so romantic.
To have true love such as you and Hamish share is
a rare wonder. I envy you.

(Read 22 more comments here…)

To: EmmaFindingFraser@gmail.com
From: SophiaSheridan@angstandarg*t.com
July 3

Emma,

I'll get straight to the point. I've had it with
communicating only through your blog. Jollying
you along has not worked, and I insist on a
proper reply to this email. I expected you'd be
back long before this, but your stubbornness has

won out, as usual. I fully assumed your little jaunt into madness would last two weeks—three at the most. And here it is July!

I hope you are not taking our parents' tacit acceptance of your bizarre behavior as some kind of approval. NO one is happy about this abandonment of your family responsibilities, trust me. Regardless, your six month tenure is nearly maxed out and you will have to return sometime in the next four weeks, or sooner. I'm writing to tell you that, in spite of all the worry and anxiety you have caused Paul and me, you are still my sister, and may stay here until you find a new job and get back on your feet.

I hope you recognize this for the generous offer it is, and accept with good grace. Please let us know when your return flight is expected to arrive.

Sophia

To: EmmaFindingFraser@gmail.com
From: JackFindlay@*range.co.uk
July 3

Dear Emma,

Well, I must say it was a big relief to receive your email after the crazy one I sent you recently. I was quite thrilled with your story of the water horse emerging from the loch, and that you shared it with me before posting it to your blog made me feel strangely privileged.

But no luck, alas. I scanned the daily papers, but could find nothing referencing a lost animal. Of course, this may well be because I am in Stirling at the moment. (My editor allowed me the addition of a small re-write, and at last the new book is now at the printers.)

Have you had any luck with the more local newspapers? Will let you know if I hear anything, although I am sure it is just as you surmised; a young steed that needed to cool off. Keep your eyes peeled, though. If it is possible for anyone to see a mythical beast, I have no doubt it will be you.

All best,

Jack

The ride home after I'd posted to the blog seemed much longer than usual. The day had been hot—truly hot—and even the road seemed to be steaming at me as I pedaled the last mile. It was a huge relief to swing myself wearily off my bike at the kissing gate at last. I pushed the bike through and walked it toward Morag's barn. I could see her on the hillside above, as she and her new farmhand walked the fields, checking the sheep. She'd hired the farmhand a couple of weeks earlier, and since he lived in the next town over, he didn't need a place to stay. My spot as a boarder was still secure.

I felt bad about taking the room and not being more help around the property, but when I'd said so, Morag just shushed me down.

"When yer a burden, lass, ye'll know it, for ye'll be out on your arse on the road there, bicycle an' all."

She'd said this with a sly grin, but I didn't doubt it for a moment, so I made an effort not to add to her work, at any rate. I swept out the barn whenever I had the energy, and had learned where all the various harness parts were stored in the low shed nearby.

It had been a long day at work, and Sophia's email arriving just seconds after I'd posted did not make me feel better. However, my latest blog post about the creature in the loch had met with a huge flurry of interest, so I cheered myself up by answering as many of the commenters as I could. And Jack's words had made me feel better, too.

I didn't reply to Sophia.

But that didn't mean she hadn't got me thinking. It hadn't really occurred to me that there might be a limit on my stay, beyond the eight weeks I had originally planned for. Of course, there had to be some kind of timeline of how long a tourist could stay. But ... only six months? That couldn't be right.

I swung open the large barn door, deep in worried thought, and walked right into the chest of one Hamish Lewis. I hadn't seen him for nearly a week, so the touch of his body on mine flooded me with ... mixed emotions. I wanted to feel only relief—and his skin on mine—but I felt a bit sick, and a bit worried, too.

Sophia and her threats vanished for the moment, anyway. I reached up to wrap my arms around his neck, but he held up a hand to me.

I stopped in my tracks, arms still in the air.

He was wearing earbuds attached to his phone, and his head bobbed gently for a moment, before he flicked the screen with his thumb.

"Important call?" I asked, reaching up again.

He shook his head and gave me a sheepish smile. "Springsteen. 'I'm On Fire'. That song slays me every time. I jes' had to hear the end."

He leaned down to brush his lips on mine. "Miss me?"

I kissed him back with everything I had.

"Ooh," he whispered. "You're on fire, too, baby."

"Yeah, I guess." I'd always been lousy at playing hard to get, even if it meant I was second fiddle to The Boss. "I *am* pretty hot."

"Tha' you are." He pulled out a paper bag from behind his back. "Brought you something. It's a special night, baby."

That old tingly feeling flooded back, tsunami-style.

He pushed past me into my room, and flopped onto my bed, before tossing me the bag. "Go on. Open it."

Inside was a small paper American flag. On a stick.

"Tomorrow's Independence Day," he said. "That makes today Independence Day Eve. And I want to spend it wi' you."

"Um. Okay." I smiled and waved the flag at him. "Thanks. It's just …"

I was going to say that Independence Day Eve was not really a thing, but I couldn't get it out, because he kicked his boots off one at a time and beckoned me over.

"Come to Uncle Sam," he said, and patted the bed. I was beside him in an instant, and he reached over to pull my face down for a kiss.

"Hey now baby, is he good to you?" he hummed, and his fingers toyed with the buttons on my shirt.

I closed my eyes. This moment had been so long in coming; I was prepared to even dismiss the Uncle Sam cracks.

Hamish sat up on the bed, his baseball cap on still backwards, and unbuttoned his shirt. All the saliva dried up in my mouth. He looked *good,* but whether it was the heat of the day or my own hormone rush, I was having trouble articulating.

"I—I …"

"It's all righ' lass," he interrupted, reaching into his pocket for a small foil packet. "No worries. I thought ahead."

He rolled past me and stood up beside the bed. The torchlight gleamed off the pale skin of his chest. He leaned down and tilted my chin up toward his face with one hand. With his other hand he took my hand and placed it on his flat stomach.

He grinned down at my expression. "Wha' de yeh think of 'em?" he asked as he gently lifted my glasses off.

"Them?" I said entirely befuddled by the feel of actual male skin beneath my fingertips. "Think of who?"

He chuckled softly and dropped to his knees beside the bed to kiss me again. I actually had to lean against him at that point. Turns out it's not only fear that makes my legs wobbly.

But his words brought my head back into the conversation.

"Mah abs. No' bad, eh? I've been doing sit-ups at the gym, but ah'm not quite to a full six-pack yet. When we get to California I want to make sure that I've got the righ' look."

I thought they had the right look already, but it gave me a moment's pause that it was he and not me pointing out his assets.

He kissed me again, which took my mind off just about everything, and then paused to slide my windbreaker off my shoulders.

I put my hand on his stomach again. I had to admit, his abs did feel pretty good. As a matter of fact, I could not remember ever having felt such good abs. My weak knees agreed. I closed my eyes and tried to lock the sensation in my memory forever.

He began to unbutton my shirt. I took a moment to thank whatever gods were out there that I had worn my prettiest pink bra that day. Kissing me again, he held me close, so that I was kneeling on the bed, feeling the skin of his stomach on my own for the very first time.

"There's a girl's section at the gym, y'know," he whispered.

"Ah … a what?" The blood was rushing away from my head at that point, so I wasn't hearing all that clearly.

"A girl's section. Fer' if yeh want to get yerself a bit more bikini-ready. There's still time, aye?"

His lips trailed down my neck.

More bikini-ready?

This stung enough to get through the lust haze. I mean, since I had come to Scotland, I had been walking or riding my bike everywhere. I was in the best shape of my life.

For a brief moment, I wondered how Claire would react if Jamie had ever told her she needed to do sit-ups. And then the parts situated below my brain decided that maybe it was not the best moment to take offense.

Pulling my hands away from where they had been feeling the muscles on his back, I quickly tucked my shirt between us so it covered my stomach, while strategically allowing the pink bra to show to its best advantage.

But something was niggling.

His ear was beside my mouth at that moment, so I took the opportunity to whisper in it.

"Uh—Hamish? Still time for what?"

He leaned back and ran one finger along my bra strap. I felt a surge of relief that his attention was off my abs for the moment.

"Before we go to California. Together."

He beamed at me. "I've sorted it all out wi' Geordie, after we talked on our drive. I can make this happen, babe. We'll soon be hittin' those Los Angeles beaches together, aye?"

I closed my eyes and sighed. As I did, he leaned forward and kissed my collarbone. I felt my will power melting away. What was so wrong with going to California with this gorgeous man?

And yet somehow, my mouth kept talking.

"It's just—I hardly ever see you lately. And when we do get together, it seems the only thing you ever want to talk about is going to America. Living in California. And—I don't live there. I don't even live *near* there."

He flopped down on the bed. "I cannae help if I'm interested in where ye come from, Emma. Chicago can't be that far away from Los Angeles. Think o' them beautiful beaches, aye?"

He undid the top button on his jeans and pulled me down beside him.

The problem was, I couldn't think of anything while he was touching me—not clearly, anyhow. And while part of me—most of my lower half, truthfully—wanted me to quit talking and just enjoy, the teeny part of my brain that was still functioning demanded clarification.

"Look, I know I came here on some kind of wild goose chase in search of someone who—someone like you. I didn't really know what I was doing. But since I've been here—Hamish, I've found a home. A place I love. *This* is that place. I have friends here. I helped a baby come into the world here. Three babies, if you count those lambs, right? I've seen the weather at it's worst, and I still love it. And I found you, Hamish. That is—we found each other. *This* is where I want to be. Here in Nairn. With you."

He sat up and swung his legs over the side of the bed. "You're an American, Emma. Yeh can't stay here forever."

"I—I know that. I need to sort it out, somehow. But Hamish—America is a very large country. And Chicago is nowhere near California. It's like from here to Madrid—maybe further, actually."

We stared at each other in silence a moment. The electric torch light on the wall suddenly seemed to cast a far harsher glow than it had just moments before. I nervously pulled my shirt across my stomach.

Hamish reached out to squeeze my hand.

"You'll look fine in a bikini," he said softly. "We'll get yeh a spray tan before we go—that'll cover up all the problem areas. Everyone looks better with a tan."

I opened my mouth, but was saved from replying by the sound of his phone, buzzing from inside his jeans pocket. He stood up and flipped it open.

He glanced at the phone, smiled wryly, and then looked down at me as he refastened the button on his jeans.

"Emergency at work, pet. Apparently Alec McGuffin's chrome fenders are ready and Geordie needs me to run into Aberdeen with him. Sorry. I gotta head in."

"Now?, Hamish. Seriously … not right *now*?"

He pulled his shirt on over those serrated abdominal muscles and jammed the damned baseball cap back on.

"Look, babe, mah work has to come first, aye? And I'll be back by tomorrow night." He reached over to my wee bedside table and slipped the condom packet back into his wallet.

A little part of me died right then.

As he went to close the wallet, a stiff piece of cardboard stuck out.

"Ach—wouldja look at that," he said. "I found a spare pass for the gym."

He snapped the card on the table then reached down and pulled me to my feet. "A couple of weeks on the weight machines will do yeh a world o' good," he said, kissing my neck. "The endorphin rush alone will change yer mind about the whole California thing."

He kissed me again and then pulled on his jacket. He stood at the door to my room, the barn night-light emitting a low glow that bathed him in what appeared to my near-sighted eyes as a halo.

"*Don't worry, ba-by,*" he crooned. "*Everything will turn out all right.*"

He closed the door softly and I buried my face in my hands.

kc dyer

I stood in the shower a long time that night. The water had cooled more than my ardor— it allowed my brain to think again. And after the shower, I lay in bed and contemplated the Jamie-shaped hole that I'd been trying to stuff Hamish into. Maybe the fit wasn't as skin-tight as I had first hoped, but I could make it work. I knew I could.

Hamish stayed true to his words and gave me some space. The problem was, after a few days of thinking things through, I didn't want to any more. Thinking had given me little beyond sleepless nights, and a pretty decent resentment built up against any mention of spray tans and gyms. But it didn't change the way I felt inside about my Jamie. Besides, I wanted to touch those abs again.

I woke up a week to the day after our last encounter determined to tell him so, but the morning didn't start well. Pedaling to the library left me feeling woozy and confused. Katy arrived before I even had time to log in, so I had to leave without posting.

Within ten minutes at work, I dropped a whole stack of plates as I was unloading the dishwasher.

There was no greater sin in Ashwin's world than breaking a clean plate, and he elbowed me aside imperiously to sweep up the mess. Even Sandeep yelled at me.

I crept away into the back to get ice, and to my embarrassment, leaked a few tears as I reached into the freezer.

"Get ahold of yourself, Sheridan," I muttered into the frozen silence. It felt so good in there. So cool. I decided to go out and apologize to Sandeep. I couldn't afford to lose my job over something as stupid as a couple of plates.

I pulled my head out to see Ashwin, staring at me.

"You're talkin' to yerself," he said, shortly, but then his tone softened. "And your face is rare flushed."

I wiped my eyes. "I'm okay. I just have a bit of a headache. I'm sorry about the plates, Ash."

Holding the bag of ice in one hand, I turned to leave the kitchen, but Ashwin put his hand on my arm. "Ash ..." I said, but he reached up and touched my cheek.

"Either yer just entering puberty, or ye've got the chickenpox," he said. "Yer face is covered in spots."

"Don't be ridiculous. I had chickenpox in fifth grade," I said, and fainted dead away.

I have a vague memory of a conversation with a doctor, though I have no recollection of how I'd made it to his office.

"Young lady, I'm afraid you have indeed succumbed to chickenpox," he said, washing his hands. I stared at the water sluicing across his long white fingers. "When were you exposed?"

"I have no idea. Maybe at work?"

He dried his hands on a paper towel. "Aye, perhaps. I'm surprised to see it, in truth. Most people get it over with as children."

"I don't have any children," I mumbled. "I'm never around children."

The doctor spoke to someone behind me. "The confusion is normal, I'm afraid. This'll be no easy week," he said, and I turned to see Morag sitting there. "It's fair serious for an adult to go through."

She nodded at him and smiled at me kindly, and then suddenly we were in her truck.

My glasses knocked against the side window as she drove.

"I'm sorry, Morag," I whispered, so my head would not fall off my neck.

"Can't be helped, pet," she said.

The doctor was right.

I cannot remember ever having been so sick. I think I may have slept that first night curled around the toilet on my bathroom floor. All I know for sure is that the visit to the doctor began what I remember as my month of darkness.

It was a bad month. And it was not lost on me that it was pretty much the only warm month of the year in the Highlands.

July 12

Notes to self:

It's Wednesday, possibly, or maybe Thursday. I have a vague memory of Morag bringing me a wet cloth sometime recently. I found it a few minutes ago, under my pillow.

I also made the mistake of looking at myself in the bathroom last night. My glands are swollen, so my face is completely round. Round and covered with red, oozing blisters. I'm hoping this thing just takes me. I can never go out in public again.

July 13, I think.

Dreamed of the water horse. The kid who hid behind me on the shores of Loch Ness was covered in scabs, wasn't he? What had his auntie called him ...?

Oh yeah—the little shite.

She was right.

July 16

Woke up thinking of Hamish. I must have infected him. I pulled a t-shirt on over my pajama top and staggered out to get my bike. I nearly made it to the kissing gate before Morag caught me.

"What in the name of all that's holy...?"

She seemed kinda out of breath. I think maybe she ran all the way from the kitchen.

So I told her that I needed to see Hamish. What if I'd made him sick?

She wrested the bike from my hands and told me I was delusional. And all the way back to my room, I tried to talk her into letting me go to him. As sick as I was - he would be so much worse for being so big.

But Morag was having none of it. She tucked me back into bed – literally jamming the sheets under the mattress so that I was trussed flat as a pack of cello-wrapped chicken.

I gave it one last shot. "What if he gets scars on his abs?"

This last thought made me burst into tears.

Morag looked alarmed, and she promised to call Hamish at Geordie's before she turned out the light.

Sometime later that night, I remember her sticking her head into my room. "The great bastard's had them," she reported.

Relief washed over me. "Oh, that's such good news," I said into the darkness. "He'll be safe, then."

"Safe as houses, pet," she said, and closed the door.

July 18

Up this morning, and feeling well enough for a bit of guilt to seep through. I hadn't mentioned a word to my sister, and cranky as she is, she might be worried at my radio silence. Checking the coast was clear on the Morag front, I gingerly pedaled my pockmarked face, (shrouded in my biggest hoodie) into town. I figured no one would recognize me at the Internet cafe, but discovered that sometime over the time I had been sick, it had closed down.

I slunk into the library to post a quick note to my sister but was immediately caught by Katy.

She looked so horrified by the sight of my face that I turned and fled in shame. As I pedaled home, I thought about her expression and felt a wash of relief that I hadn't run into Hamish.

But as I wrestled my bike through the kissing gate, I thought - why hasn't Hamish run into me...?

To: EmmaFindingFraser@gmail.com
From: JackFindlay@*range.co.uk
July 20

Dear Emma,

Haven't seen any new posts from you in a while. I hope that means you are settled and happy, with no time to write, now that your quest is over. It is over, yes? Things haven't changed?

Anyway, just wanted to let you know that the first

advanced copies have come back from the printers. My agent emailed me the day after I sent the manuscript to her, saying she'd stayed up all night reading it. Never had a response like that from her before, so hoping it's a good sign. She tells me they are fast-tracking it, whatever that means. I'm just glad she liked it.

Thank you again for your honesty.

And…you *are* well, yes?

Jack

Finally Finished Fever…
12:15 pm, July 21
Nairn, Scotland

So, it turns out that a person can have the chickenpox twice. I clearly remember being very itchy and missing a few days of school when I was in the fifth grade.

Apparently it was not enough.

I have to say, that memory doesn't really compare with what my life's been like for the past couple of weeks. It's been brutal. But I am feeling better now. It takes more than a kid's disease to bring me down for long.

Unfortunately, it's set my earnings back a bit,

but that is soon remedied. I'm looking forward to life returning to normal.

- ES

Comments: 7

HiHoKitty, Sapporo, Japan:

Be well, Miss Emma. So good your Highland warrior can nurse you back to health.

(Read 6 more comments here...)

I'd wakened in the morning actually feeling like myself again. I'd kicked off the covers in the night, so I lay there and took a good long look at myself in the first light of dawn. The blisters had all scabbed a few days earlier, and it seemed like most of them had finally dried up or fallen off. My body was still red and speckled, but I no longer looked like an active plague victim. And not only that, but from the angle I was lying, I could have sworn I could see the shadow of one hip-bone.

I'm fairly certain *that's* never happened before.

This cheered me enough to send me into the shower, and then to take another ride into town.

I got lucky and arrived as Katy was lying outside on the lawn, taking in the sun on her lunch break, so I had time enough to make the post and send Jack a quick reply, telling him briefly what had happened. Then I headed back out into the sunshine to see about getting back to work.

The long ride had left me a bit winded, so I walked my bike the three blocks or so between the library and the cafe.

And while I walked, I thought about HiHoKitty's remark. I did have a somewhat vague memory of Morag announcing that Hamish was immune to chickenpox.

So why hadn't I heard from him? Not even a phone call to Morag's?

I wasn't about to go see him, especially in my speckled state. But since my head had become clearer, I definitely needed to give my Highland warrior some further thought. I mean – even if he hadn't been immune, he could have sent flowers. Or even called …

And speaking of which, Sandeep was on the phone when I arrived at the cafe.

"Aye, now. Righ'. See yeh."

"I'm better," I announced, as soon as he rang off. "I'm ready to come back to work.

He took one look at me and dragged me back into the kitchen. "Like hell," he said.

"No, seriously—I am feeling better. And the doctor said I was only contagious a week, so …"

"So, yer not working here still looking like a poxy whore."

"Oh, very nice. No 'Welcome back, Emma!'. No 'How're you feeling, Emma?'"

"I'm sorry, luv, but yeh still look awful."

"Look, Sandeep—I can't afford to be off any longer. I've already lost, like, two week's pay."

He sighed. "I know. And ye've been missed. No one makes a latte like you do. But I can't have yeh driven' me customers away wi' yer face."

"It's not that bad, is it?"

He scrutinized me closely. "Well, it's fair hideous, still. But how's this? You are one of the family. And I don't want you to worry about the money, so if you stay home for another fortnight, I'll pay ye at half-wages, aye?"

"I guess so," I said. "But, please don't give my job away, Sandeep. I need …"

I stopped. I hadn't mentioned to Sandeep that I was going to have to return to the States soon. All the more reason for him to give my job away.

"Ach, dinnae worry. The ol' lady from the Internet Cafe is lendin' a hand."

"Bet she doesn't make as good a cappuccino as me," I muttered.

"She don't break as many dishes, neither," he said.

There was a rustling behind me, and Morag walked in. "Ye've got to quit making these escapes, Emma," she said. "It's playin' hell with mah schedule."

I stared at her. "How did you even know I was here?"

She nodded at Sandeep, and he tucked his phone in his pocket guiltily. "Look, lass—jes' take a fortnight off. Ye can help me wi' the garden, aye? A little sun will help that complexion."

"I hope so," Sandeep muttered, darkly.

I shot him a look. "Fine. I'll be back in a week. But you are going to miss me, I promise you."

Morag tossed my bike into the back of her truck as if it weighed nothing.

"I'm sure he will. In the meantime, this bicycle is mine for the present, aye?"

July 25

So, the truth came out on the drive home. Turns out it was Morag who suggested to Sandeep that I take the time off, and told him she'd waive my rent, while I was sick.

Argued with her about this long and hard, but deeply touched, actually. What a softie she is, though you'd never know it to look at her.

Also? It turns out a fortnight is actually TWO weeks.

She insisted I would work for my keep, and so that's what I've done. Weeded the garden, learned how to feed Reinhardt and the other cattle, and trekked the fields, checking on the sheep every day.

No sign of Hamish. I think — he might be truly done with me. Yesterday while weeding, I caught myself humming Beach Boys tunes. I miss him so much, but am haunted by one question: would Jamie have left Claire to recover from the plague alone?

July 30

Morag won't let me near the bike, so once again forced to write notes here in the hope that one day I'll get to my blog again.

I've spent this week mucking out the barn, which is just about as fun as it sounds. Unfortunately, all this labor has meant I have been eating like a horse. I've managed to acquire a pretty decent farmer's tan, and my biceps are looking _fine_. But I looked this morning and I can't find the shadow of my hipbone any more.

I complained bitterly to Morag, who told me that all decent men like something to hold on to. "Hipbones," she said, "are fookin' nonsense."

I don't think I've ever heard her use that word before!

Later...

I heard Morag yelling at her farmhand this afternoon. Apparently she caught him asleep in the haymow.

"Ye need to step spritely if ye're to earn yer salary," she said, "since mah boarder is doin' twice the work of you, yeh lazy sow".

I flexed my new biceps and beamed for the rest of the day.

Fondness in the Fields…
12:15 pm, August 3
Nairn, Scotland

Since I have little to discuss of my own life except that I am feeling better, I thought I'd share a quick story about someone else instead.

This person, whom I will call Mary, has title to her own farm here in the Highlands. Livestock, a huge garden and a few acres of crops. She's pretty much self-sufficient, and she works very hard, especially at this time of year, getting ready for the harvest.

No time for anything else, aye?

The neighboring farmer has a field of spring wheat that is harvested early in August each year. We'll call him Henry. Since I've been here, Henry and Mary have little more to do with each other than any other neighbors would. They help each other out with equipment once and a while, and that's about it.

Yesterday was Mary's birthday, though, and in the morning, as I walked the bull up to his pasture, I noticed something odd. Henry's field of spring wheat had been plowed. But only part of it. Only the middle.

In the shape of a heart.

When I pointed it out to Mary, she shrugged and

suggested I was inventing things. I replied that I was not, it was clear to anyone with eyes in their head that the field had been partially plowed, and the wheat that had fallen was in a heart-shaped pattern. She then insisted that it was I who was love-obsessed and it was making me see things. I then noted that the object of my affections had been unexplainedly absent for the duration of my severe and disfiguring illness.

Her response was only to make that very Scottish noise in the back of her throat and stomp off.

There the matter might have rested, had I not returned late last night to her kitchen, with an aim to steal one of the sugary doughnuts she had inexplicably produced in the afternoon. As I opened the kitchen door, however, I spied the following:

- one lit candle, jammed in old wine bottle, centered on large wooden table

- one new wine bottle, red, open

- two wine glasses, filled

- one plate piled high with afore-mentioned sugary doughnuts

And finally…

- the backs of two heads, tilted together, voices pitched low in conversation.

I leave you to draw your own conclusions…

- ES

The day before I was to return to work, Morag had actually agreed to let me take the bike out for a test ride. So, naturally, I'd headed straight for the library.

Katy had come over and offered me a polite hello. My shocked expression must have been evident, because she'd looked a little embarrassed and told me that I'd been missed. I'd grinned at her and headed straight over to the computer terminal, my head held high.

Writing about Morag and her neighbour Hendry (okay, okay, so I didn't do a great job of inventing aliases) took my mind off Hamish's disappearance. But it hurt. It hurt and I wanted him back. I still had that note he had signed with a heart. That had to mean something.

My spirits sank further when there was no email from Jack, but I chastised myself for it. It was Hamish I needed to concentrate on. I might be writing about romance Scottish-farmer style, but what I really needed was romance, Hamish-style. After I finished posting, I decided to walk across the street and talk to Geordie.

When I stepped inside the office of the garage, Geordie was there already, going through a pile of invoices. As soon as he caught sight of me, he quickly moved over to stand behind the desk.

"I'm not catching," I insisted. "The scabs have all fallen off."

"Charming," he said. "But there's no use you hanging about. Hamish is in Dores—has been all week."

"All week?" I said, relief washing through me. So *that* was why he hadn't been to see me, at least for the past week. He hadn't even been in Nairn. "Why?"

"It's a—a big job," said Geordie. He gathered his papers into a pile and scurried into the garage without even saying goodbye.

Which didn't explain why Hamish hadn't called or sent flowers. But it was something.

Fair Form...
12:15 pm, August 4
Nairn, Scotland

Back to work for me today, and feeling fine. Things are starting to feel normal again.

Almost completely normal.

- ES

Comments: 0

I didn't really have time to post, and only put something up because I was in checking for comments. But the site had fallen strangely silent.

So, yeah ... pretty much nothing felt normal. My relationship with my Highland warrior was over before it had really begun, and I hadn't breathed a word of it online. I had become a serial blog-liar.

Things picked up a bit once I started work, though. The cafe was busy all morning, and at one point there was an actual line-up for coffee.

My public had clearly missed me.

But the best part happened right in the middle of the lunch rush. The bell on the door jingled, and I looked up to see Hamish.

I rushed over for a hug, but he side stepped me.

"Keep it professional, aye?" hissed Ash, as he brushed by me to wipe off one of my tables.

Sandeep rolled his eyes and held up one finger at me, which I took for permission to go into the back for a minute with Hamish.

When we got into the kitchen, he took my head in his hands and gently kissed me—on the forehead.

"I'd heard you were a wee speckled hen," he said. His voice sounded so wonderful, I thought I might cry at the very sound of it. But then the words sank in.

"They won't scar," I said. "The doctor promised, as long as I don't scratch, and I've been super careful."

"Aye," he said, thoughtfully. And then again. "Aye."

I gazed up at his face, brown with the summer sun beneath his baseball cap. "I so missed you," I whispered. "Why didn't you call?"

"Ach, it's been rare busy," he said, and patted my arm with two fingers. "I must get back—Geordie only gave me a minute, aye?"

I nodded. "Yeah, me too. But when can I see you again? I'd really like to talk. Can we make a plan?"

"Oh, soon …" he said, his voice trailing off. "Maybe we could go to the gym sometime. Have ye been at all, yet?"

And suddenly, everything became clear.

He waved goodbye, and I stood at the back door and watched him walk across the road. A sudden hot fury swept through me, and I leaned out into the street.

"Claire never went to a gym in her life," I yelled so loudly it hurt my voice.

But the garage door had already closed.

I knew I wouldn't see him again soon, and I didn't. He didn't come in the café next day or the day after that. And when I rode my bike past the garage, his truck was never there.

The anger carried me for the next three days. I threw myself into my work at the café. I scrubbed every corner of the place, adorned every latte with cinnamon masterpieces. But sometime on day four the doubt began to creep in. I admit it. I'm weak. It got so all I could think about was the feel of those abs under my fingertips.

And then…? It became an obsession. Even though I was feeling myself again, I lost all focus except to try to find a way to make it work with Hamish. I spent every spare hour haunting the library, mostly staring at other women's abdominal muscles on the Internet.

In a way, Susan—or Gail or whatever her real name was— had saved me, because if I'd still had my laptop, I would never have left my room.

He had kissed me. We had nearly been together. *We could be still.* I just had to figure out how. I had so little time left— how could the time have gone so fast? How could I go home, knowing I had blown my chance with the only Fraser I had managed to find?

As days passed, a pattern began to develop. When I wasn't at work, I spent as much time as I dared scrolling through image files at the library. The only thing limiting me was my fear that Katy would think I was downloading porn. (I don't know how people watch porn. Even after only a week of looking at women's midriffs, they all began to look the same…)

At night, I stood on a milking stool I'd stolen from Morag's barn, in order to get the right angle to stare at my own stomach in the tiny mirror above the bathroom sink.

Then I'd lie on the floor, cry, and eat chocolate.

I'd had a boyfriend who wanted to take me away and live in California. As long as I managed to whip my abs into shape. And once my problem areas were spray tanned. And yet, even with all the obsessing, I still hadn't managed to find the time to make a trip to Hamish's gym.

Instead, I'd drag into work, sleepwalk through my shift, cross over to the garage on my break. Geordie (or the other guy, Jimmie, who only fixed transmissions and had one eye stuck in a permanent squint) would tell me Hamish was on the road or working in Dores. I'd go back to the cafe, finish my shift, then ride up to the library and monopolize the computer until Katy closed the place and I was forced to ride home and spend another night staring at my stomach in the mirror.

I'm not sure how long this pathetic circle of self-destruction would have continued—maybe forever—but one night, a little more than a week into my grim and blurry world of self-loathing, two things happened to change everything.

The first was Katy.

Fine, Fine, Fine…
6:15 pm, August 12
Nairn, Scotland

Things are much the same here. Everything's fine.
Just fine. The town is busy planning the upcoming
Highland Games, and the farmers are staring at
the sky and fretting over the weather. Harvest
time is near.

- ES

Comments: 0

arvest time is near? No wonder my followers were
dropping like flies. I had lost all ability to write anything
remotely compelling. Instead, I sat slumped at my terminal,
scrolling through pictures of a collection of starlets pre- and
post-cosmetic surgery, and thought back on my day.

Work had unfolded as usual. Sandeep was a little crankier
than normal, and Ash alternated between smoking furiously
behind the cafe and killing zombies on his mobile phone.
But sometime mid-morning, I'd spied Geordie's van parked
behind the garage, and that meant Hamish had to be around.

I ran over on my break, and as soon as I opened the door, I could hear yelling in the back. That was usually a good sign.

I rang the bell until the yelling stopped and Geordie appeared.

But his story hadn't changed. "He's no' here, I tell yeh."

"But the van is there. I saw it, parked in the spot behind the garage."

"Aye. He left it las' night. He's gone again, righ'?"

"Geordie, he's your mechanic. How can you survive if he's not here working on cars?"

"Weel—ah've got Jimmie, aye? And Hamish'll be back soon. He's just done a delivery for me to—ah—Aberdeen. Righ'." And he had stomped off into the back, where the yelling began again.

So yeah, same as usual.

The van had been gone again by the time I left work.

I sighed and clicked through to the next screen. Maybe he'd be back by tomorrow. If I could just talk to him again …

I heard a sudden scrambling noise, the sound of a chair falling and a rush of wind.

And in front of me? Stood Katy.

"Emma," she said, and I noticed that her hair had actually come free from the tidy knot she always wore at the back of her neck. "This has got to stop. You are no' alone."

"Not alone…?" I began, but by this time she had my shoulders clutched tightly in her hands. She gave me a shake and my chair rolled a little.

"It's no' so hard, once ye jes' accept it," she said. "We've all been there. Janey down at the chippy. Agnes in Tesco's. And Eilidh righ' before you—he really broke Eilidh's heart, I haveta say. She still hates ye for it, didja know?"

"Eilidh? I don't know anyone by that name …" I said, weakly. Even though I sort of did.

She carried on as if I hadn't spoken.

"I admit I thought you might be the one, bein' American an' all. And some might say—Eilidh for starters—that ye deserve bein' cast aside like this. But I was one o' the first, Emma. I've had time to get over it. And workin' here, I see you every day—how bad you're failin'. Everythin' has an end, Emma."

I stared at her face as a light shone into my own murky skull.

"No—no. It's not like that. He hasn't dumped me. We just have a few things to sort out. He's just been really busy, and—and I don't want to lose my Jamie."

She shook me again, gently.

"Just listen to yerself. You're babblin', girl. The man's name is *Hamish*. And maybe the person you are losin' … is not him." She dropped her hands to her sides.

"I've done all I can do here," she said, maybe to the universe. "All I know is that you're lookin' at more nearly-naked girls lately than the twelve-year old boys I have to shoo out of here during the school year. It's got to stop, Emma. Or you have to buy a computer of your own. I've go' tourists to deal wi', and I'm tired of having to clear mah browser cache!"

I hung my head. There was nothing left to say. I stood up, tucked in my chair and walked out quietly.

In the distance, I could see Geordie's truck parked outside the garage. And in Hamish's little apartment upstairs? The light was on.

So.

He *was* home.

I thought about everything Katy had said, and instead of running to throw myself on his mercy, I resolutely pointed my bicycle toward Morag's place.

A balmy breeze blew back my hair as I pedaled. The evening was so warm that part way home I had to stop and pull off to the side of the road to take off my hoodie. Maybe Katy was right. Hamish had been honest with me—how much more honest can you get then handing your girlfriend the business card of the nearest gym?

But… what kind of a dick move was *that*, anyway?

I tried to picture Jamie suggesting that Claire had *problem areas* and actually drove myself right off the road, gravel spraying, at the very thought.

I steered myself back onto the road, my glasses sliding down my nose as I pushed my pedals through the final uphill leg. Katy was right. I had been so worried about losing my dream Jamie that I had accepted behavior from Hamish that I would have kicked any American boy to the curb for.

I pedaled into Morag's driveway just as she stumped out of the barn, carrying a large stoneware pitcher.

"Been shifting hay all day," she said by way of explanation. "Think I need a little medicinal pick-me-up before dinner. Care to join me?"

"Why not?" I said, and followed her inside.

The pitcher turned out to be full of cream, freshly skimmed.

"Look," Morag said, as she set it on the table. "I've a mind to make buttermilk scones for mah dinner. What say we whip up a bit o' butter before you head over to the barn? It'll take yer mind off things."

I stared at her blankly. She looked heavenward and pulled a tall, slender ceramic jar out of a drawer. From the cupboard beneath the sink she removed a large bottle of scotch and slammed it on the table beside the jar.

"You use Scotch to make butter?" I said. "Is it an old family recipe or something?"

Morag barked a laugh and pulled a teacup out of the dish drainer. She slid it toward me along the scrubbed-smooth top of the wooden table.

"Scotch makes anythin' better," she said, "but only a clot-heid would put it *in* the butter."

She poured the cream from her pitcher into the ceramic jar and screwed the lid on tight. "Now take this and gi' it a wee shake, will ye?"

The jar was about the size of a large travel mug. Morag turned it on its side and showed me how to roll it back and forth on the table. Then she poured a finger of scotch into the teacup and slid it back in front of me. She collected another cup from the dish drainer—a much larger coffee cup—and poured two fingerfuls for herself.

"Ye can sip it, or ye can slug it back," she said. "Your choice entirely."

"What do you do?" I asked, eyeing the amber liquid doubtfully.

She blinked her eyes at me, and her cup was empty. I let go of the butter jar to pick up my teacup.

Morag gazed at me sternly. "Ye mustn't stop wi' the shakin' or t' butter won't be as sweet."

I hastily resumed rolling. She took the opportunity to pour herself another scotch, clinked my teacup with her own and downed it.

"*Sláinte,*" she said, and seized the butter jar from me. The ridges on the outside of the jar rumbled like thunder against the wooden tabletop.

"Yeh need ta put some energy in," she said sternly. "Now. Abou' this Hamish."

I swallowed the contents of my teacup.

"He's a good man," she said, eyeing the scotch bottle while she rolled her butter.

I poured her another and she beamed at me.

"A bit of an inclination toward the ladies, I'll admit, but 'e's nobbut a lad yet. On'y ta be expected."

I wasn't sure I agreed. "Katy thinks he's dumped me for someone else. And maybe that's not such a bad thing. When we were together, all he would talk about was moving to the US, and how I needed to get into bikini shape for California."

One side of Morag's mouth twisted upward. "Bikini shape, eh? Mebbe he jes' likes who ye are an' where ye come from?"

I toyed with my teacup. "Right—that's what I said. But, I can't help thinking he seems to have some odd …ideas about America. Or his concept of America—and—and what Americans should look like."

Morag snorted. "Far as I can tell, ye look jes' like Scots. P'raps a wee bit less pale. And I'd be hard-pressed to choose which is the fatter, wi' all them fried Mars bars we Scots have taken to these days. Present company excepted, of course."

"Oh, well you know Hamish. He's pretty fit, right? He seems to think that's a part of the American dream, or something. I'm not quite clear on it …"

Morag rolled the jar back and forth, back and forth. "He's never been to the States, I'm fair certain," she said, and neatly managed to pour us both another drink without missing a beat on the butter. "Picked up all his views from the telly, like the rest of us."

I finished my drink and then had to take my eyes off her mini butter churn for a bit, because the rocking was starting to make my head feel funny. "Have you noticed anything a little—odd—about the way he sings all the time?" I said, enunciating carefully. "About how he seems sort of influenced by American music?"

"Ah, American music," said Morag, sighing rapturously as she rocked her butter. *"We could have had it a-a-alll, Rollin' in the De-ee-eep!"*

She had an amazingly rich contralto, and dipped her head in a little bow when I told her so. I didn't tell her she was singing a song by a British artist, however. It wasn't the time to spoil her moment.

We sat in silence, but for the rocking of the butter jar, until Morag cleared her throat at last.

"Speakin' of having it all, my dear, I reckon you need to decide what it is you really want. If this young man is it, go after him." She leaned back, tilting up onto the rear legs of her chair. "I remember back in '85, I had a wee flutter for a fella by the name of Willie MacBride."

She licked the rim of her coffee cup contemplatively, her eyes distant. "Ach, the boy was well-named. He had a cock on 'im ten inches long and thick as a baby's arm."

There was a long moment of silence, as her last sentence had rendered me entirely speechless, and Morag was clearly lost in thought.

"We had some good times, me and Willie," she said at last, closing her eyes and smiling.

I set my teacup carefully on the table.

Morag's eyes snapped open and she slammed her chair legs back down to the floor. "But it came to nothin', for all that. It ended because he decided to step out on me, and no piece of man-flesh is worth that, girlie."

She leaned forward across the table and set the jar upright with a thump. "Ye have to love yersel' first, Emma. My greatest regret is that I walked away from Willie without chasin' him down and showin' him what he'd lost. I'd hate tae see ye make the same mistake, lassie."

She pushed herself to her feet and leaned over to twist the lid off the jar. "Perfect!" she yelled, and stumped over to the counter. She expertly poured the liquid off into a little stone pitcher, and scooped the remaining lumps of butter into a small bowl. She shook a little salt on it, stirred it around a few times and handed me the bowl.

"Fer yer porridge," she said, then she reached up with one hand and patted me on the cheek. "Follow yer heart, lass. If ye can work things out, it's all for the good. But if ye can do better, tell the bugger so."

I stood beside her, my heart full and the little pot of butter in my hand. The thought of her kindness overwhelmed me a moment, and I leaned forward to hug her.

The look of horror on her face stopped me in mid-air. Clearly even six shots of whiskey were not enough to entice her to indulge in such a physical display. Instead she thumped me on the shoulder, held open the kitchen door and waved the scotch bottle at me as I headed out into the dark.

As I stumbled down the path to the barn, I knew she was right. One hundred percent, absolutely correct. After all, what was this whole trip about if not following my dreams? I couldn't let my time with Hamish just melt away into the Highland mists.

The air was cool, now that the midnight hour was well gone. In this part of the Highlands at least, the heat of even the hottest summer day dissipated as dusk fell. But the fragrance of the warm grass and whatever else was blooming along the margins of the farmyard persisted. I gazed for a long moment up into the clear starry sky.

Morag was right. I needed to take her advice.

I didn't even stop to go inside.

Carefully placing the pot of fresh butter on a little wooden shelf beside the door, I threw a leg over my bicycle. The air held a chill that only someone who had been in the Highlands in August could truly appreciate, but I didn't feel the cold. The talk with Morag had given me a fire in my belly.

Not to mention all the single malt scotch.

The whole ride into town, I replayed conversations with Hamish in my head. The way he recited song lyrics—that was endearing. It was. What kind of cold fish didn't like to be sung to?

The recent rift was repairable. What good was falling in love with Scotland if I didn't have a man to love, too? After all, the whole reason I'd come here was to find my Fraser.

I followed the glow on the road cast from the headlight on my handlebars. Hamish had adjusted that light for me—made sure it shone straight and true. The road surface showed clearly ahead of me, and if my trajectory was not exactly in a straight line on that dark night, the light gave me notice so I could correct before driving off the edge and into a ditch.

That headlight was his way of showing his love for me. So what if he'd never managed to refer to love without it being a part of a song lyric? That was his way. Scottish men were a breed apart. Anyone who'd read the OUTLANDER books knew that. And I'd never told him I loved him either, so how could I judge him by such a harsh standard? I loved his country. I'd come there to find my Jamie Fraser, and I'd found him— or as close to him as I could hope for. Any problems we had were fixable.

Rolling into town, I began to feel a certain chill in my fingertips. Morag's fuel was burning low, and with the cold night air in my lungs, I began to think a little more clearly. I'd begun this journey on little more than a whim, but by the time I'd arrived in Scotland, I'd had a plan firmly in place.

What I hadn't really thought about—beyond tracing the journey in the front of the novel—was Claire's part in the love story. Claire's heart was true, but there was never any doubt that the woman had standards. Jamie literally lived through hell and more to meet those standards. Even living with uncertainty and chaos all around her, she knew what she wanted.

As I rode my bicycle off the High Street and into the lane that led to Hamish's flat, I noticed a light was still on in the back of the garage.

This stopped me in my tracks.

The light was off in his apartment, but still on in the garage.

The glow inside me from Morag's scotch increased once more. The man was so dedicated, he worked until the job was done. That was why people from miles around came to his garage. How many nights had he been working late recently? This was a *real* man.

I choked up a little at the thought that I'd doubted him—that I'd doubted *us,* and swung myself off my bike. It was a little bit of a wild swing, I admit, and my foot missed the curb. But in moments, I was back on my feet again and had the bike leaned against the wall of Geordie's shop. There would be no use trying the front door at this late hour, so I took the long way around to the back.

The lane was cobbled, and I had to concentrate on the footing. As I righted one of the bins I'd lurched into in the dark, I thought about a new plan.

A Hamish-friendly plan.

We needed to talk through what we both wanted—what was important to each of us as individuals, as well as together. I needed answers to a few questions, for sure. But after all that, if he still wanted to go to the US? We could go together. My allotted six months was nearing its end. Thanks to Sandeep and the tips from my Scottish customers who were more generous than the world gave them credit for, I had earned enough for my ticket home, with a little extra. Perhaps even enough for new contact lenses, as Hamish had suggested. We could start again, but this time in America.

And when he got homesick for his own beautiful country, which was sure to happen, I could be at his side on the return journey, too.

A perfect plan.

A foolproof plan.

Light shone around the frame of Geordie's back door. The chill in the air had finally worked its way through the alcohol in my blood and I shivered a little as I thought about sitting in the garage with Hamish as he finished his work.

It would be warm inside. I would tell him all my deepest thoughts, and afterwards?

Well, his little flat was just up the stairs.

As I reached for the door-handle, I silently thanked the ancient gods for Morag and her scotch-fuelled butter making. Without her, I'd never have known to follow my heart.

The light blinded me as I stepped into the delicious, oil-scented warmth of the garage, but the first thing I heard was Hamish's voice. He was still singing, god love him.

"I wish they all could be California Girrrlllllssss ..."

Though he had a little trouble staying on key, the man had a fine baritone. As my eyes adjusted to the light, I thought briefly how nice it would be to hear him singing with Morag. Stepping over a stray tailpipe on the floor, I walked into the repair bay.

In addition to his fine baritone, Hamish also had a fine, strong pair of buttocks. And they were the first things I saw as I stepped into the shop. A fine, strong pair of buttocks, leaning at a very odd angle against the hood of a car.

I watched them flex, and release, and flex again.

When I finally managed to drag my eyes away, I saw his work overalls were puddled around his ankles. My head was spinning a bit from the ride, and perhaps the scotch, so I was slow to take in the whole picture. But after a moment, it became clear that the pair of long, finely tanned legs wrapped around his waist were most definitely not his own.

Any remaining alcohol evaporated from my system in an instant.

"Oh, honey, you're right. We *are* the best," came a breathy voice from beneath Hamish.

That is to say, from the person lying on the hood of the car. Apart from the legs, all I could see was impossibly long, straight blonde hair draped over the new chrome fenders on Alec McGuffin's car. And a tiny Celtic cross attached to a narrow, silver chain around one ankle.

Final Farewell...
5:00 pm, Aug 14
Nairn, Scotland

Well, it's been a long, crazy ride, but it's over. I just noticed the date. I guess I am officially twenty nine and a half today. That is, if a person can still be allowed a half-birthday so far along into adulthood.

Thank you, each and every one, for your loyalty. For following me on all my adventures. For always asking the right questions, especially you, HiHoKitty. To all my followers in Japan and in Germany and around the globe, thank you.

I am a better person for having known you all through this blog. I am a better person for having been to Scotland. But my quest is over—I know it now to be the deluded, foolish thing my sister has insisted it was all along.

Time for me to go back to Chicago.

- ES

A better person.
I leaned back in the chair and felt nothing but relief that I'd managed to post something that actually sounded sensible.

Not broken-hearted at all.

I couldn't read more than a couple of the comments, though. They started flooding in almost immediately.

What about Hamish?

What has become of your Fraser?

At least the man had the decency to pull up his pants. In fact, as soon as Hamish had realized he wasn't just serenading the girl who'd wrapped her legs around him, he'd had his pants up right quickly.

"Aw, baby," he said, fumbling over his buttons. "I was gonna tell you about this, but—you know—*breaking up is hard to do.*"

He actually crooned the last line at me.

I would have thrown a jibe about Neil Sedaka being for grandparents—for GREAT-grandparents—into his face, but I was busy staring.

With my mouth open.

At the girl who had just pulled up her thong, smoothed down her skirt and adjusted white plastic sunglasses onto her nose.

In the middle of the night.

Now—who would do something like that? Wear sunglasses after midnight, even after being caught with her thong down?

I took a step closer and peered into her face. She opened her bag and took out a lipstick.

"Susan …?" I said. I could hardly push any voice past the giant lump in my throat, so it came out sounding pretty strangled.

"You must be mistaken," she said, in a perfect middle-American accent. "My name is Sunshine."

"As in *California* Sunshine," added Hamish, helpfully.

I couldn't tear my eyes from her face as she applied her lipstick. From her hair. She'd bleached it to an almost platinum blonde, and added the long extensions I'd seen draped across the hood of the car.

She looked *so* different. But there was no question in my mind.

"First my contact lenses and now—my Jamie?" I whispered.

"I'm sure I don't know *what* you are talking about. Who is this crazy person, Hamish?"

I was able to look him in the face at last.

"Aw, baby," he said. "I'm sure there's a way for us to stay friends. Yeh know I'll always ha'e a wee soft spot for ye."

"A wee soft spot?" I repeated. "Hamish, do you know who this is?" I'd found my voice somewhere, as evidenced by the way Hamish kind of wilted back from the volume.

Susan tried to redirect him. "Don't listen to her, Sugar. She's jealous of what we have."

But he answered me calmly, and with true conviction. "Her name is Sunshine, Emma. I met her the day we first drove to Dores. And we are goin' to California together."

"Aww, honey," Susan said. "That's so sweet!" Her lips were now a paler shade of pink than her skin. It gave me a moment's satisfaction to see how orange they made her artificial tan look.

I turned back to Hamish, sure my head was going to explode. I wanted to scream at him.

But somehow I found it in me to swallow it all down.

When my voice came out, it was strangely calm. "Hamish, this isn't Sunny Delight or whatever she's told you her name is. This is Susan; Susan O'Donnell. She is an actress and a thief. She stole almost everything I had and ran away. And she's skipped bail now, for stealing from other people too."

He was back in his coveralls, and had the grace to look uncomfortable. "You've got the wrong person, Emma. My sweet Sunshine could never do that to you. To anyone."

"Never," echoed a sincere voice from somewhere behind me.

I ignored Susan and took a step closer to Hamish. "You've always had my heart, Hamish, from that first night in Edinburgh. And even when you let me down, I still held onto hope. Even tonight, I wanted to give you a chance to talk things through. But we are done talking. We are just— done."

My voice broke, and I knew if I said another word I would sob like a baby.

"I'm sorry, Emma," he said. "Maybe we can talk it through tomorrow?"

I took a deep breath, and by the time I had exhaled, I knew one thing for sure. They deserved each other.

"The luck of the Irish to you both," I said, kind of regretting it as it came out of my mouth.

"Aw—ain't that sweet?," Sunshine Susan brayed. "Hamish, honey, ain't that sweet?"

I stomped to the door. Hamish's voice followed me, and I could hear where he was practicing the cadences of Susan's accent already. "It shore is, Sugar," he said, but then something of the Hamish I thought I knew kicked in.

He took a step toward me. "*I never can say ... good-bye,*" he sang, and then awkwardly added "*Emmaaaaaaahhhh.*"

I rolled my eyes. "Well, I can say it. Goodbye, Hamish."

And I slammed that garage door behind me, knowing my dream of ever finding my Fraser had just come to an end.

That was it, really. When I checked my email the next day, Jack had written to say he'd read my post and wanted to see if I was all right. Sweet of him. He also wanted to invite me to the launch of his new book, but I didn't even bother to click through to the details.

Gerald had written, too, expressing the standard condolences and asking me to at least come say goodbye before I left the country.

Reading their notes made me feel a bit better, but—well, the dream had died, and with it, a little part of my heart had died, too.

Morag took the news of my leaving stoically, though she did promise to "Gi'e the boot" to any field hand occupying her spare room in the barn if I ever decided to return. She tried to talk me into staying for the Highland Games, which were due to run in just a couple of weeks, even throwing the little lambs I had helped deliver into the mix as further incentive.

"They'll have a place of honor, Emma, and you'll get to see it happen!"

But she took my refusal pretty well, in the end.

When I gave my notice to Sandeep, he told me he'd accept it, but only if I'd stay until the end of the month.

"You'll be harboring a fugitive if I stay that long," I said. "I'm supposed to leave the country by the 25th."

"You got yer ticket yet?" he asked.

When I shook my head he smiled. "Then I'll have a fugitive making the best coffee in the place."

I think it was the first real compliment he had ever paid me.

Ashwin refused to acknowledge I was leaving. He just stood outside in the back lane, with an unlit cigarette in his mouth, viciously punching the buttons on his mobile phone.

Facing Forward…
12:15 pm, August 31
Nairn, Scotland

Saying goodbye to Nairn is just about the hardest thing I have ever done. But truthfully, compared to the panic attacks and nonsense that attended leaving the US to come here, things have been relatively calm.

I am facing forward with a steely resolve. This country has taken its place in my heart, and I know I will be back.

- ES

Comments: 1

HiHoKitty, Sapporo, Japan:

So sorry you cannot stay just a short while longer, Emma-san. For we—myself and the members of our book club—have taken you and your adventure into our own hearts. We face the great unknown ourselves…and are set to join you as world travelers. Perhaps one day, we shall meet. We wish you Godspeed, Emma Sheridan.

That HiHoKitty. Loyal to the end. I had to admit to being a little confused by her comments now and again, and this final one that arrived right on the heels of my posting, was no exception. But I could not fault her sincerity, and I was strangely grateful for her good wishes. They had sustained me for so long, I couldn't really imagine having done without them.

By the time I picked up my final paycheck, I'd been what the United Kingdom Immigration authorities apparently call an "Overstay" for six days. When I sat down and counted my money, I realized that if I passed on buying new contacts, I would have just enough to pay for my ticket home and still stop on the way to see Gerald. He'd sent me an address by email, and since it was walking distance from the bus station in Fort William, I would even be able to save the cab fare.

For all my talk of steely resolve in the blog post, when I climbed onto the bus heading south on that last afternoon of August, and saw Morag lift her arm to wave goodbye, I sat back in my seat and cried like a baby.

Clutching the address Gerald had sent, I walked up to the front door in Fort William, just as a warm, summer dusk was falling. Still, I could feel the cool wind slipping down the slopes of Ben Nevis, and I pulled my hoodie tightly around my waist as I waited for someone to answer my knock.

Gerald and Clarence came to the door together, and welcomed me into their home. Gerald introduced me properly to Clarence, and they shared the news he had been holding out—they were going to be married.

"None of this 'civil partnership' for us," Gerald said, after we'd clinked our glasses. "We're heading to Canada this fall and doing it right."

"And then," added Clarence with a grin, "perhaps a tour of the deep South."

Gerald snorted, and poured us more champagne.

We had a lovely evening, eating Brie and cranberries melted on crackers, and laughing about our first meeting in that stone circle outside of Inverness.

"It feels like a lifetime ago," I said, after Gerald had told his side of the story.

He smiled and squeezed the hand of his love. "I *am* a sucker for a happy ending," he said.

I grinned at him, knowing I'd heard that somewhere before.

The boys had insisted I stay over, but early the next morning, clutching a cup of tea and leaning against a rock wall, I waited for the bus that would carry me to Edinburgh. I stared through the window of the teashop, watching images flicker across the television screen on the wall inside. Two impossibly perfect-looking hosts bantered as they prepared some kind of elaborate breakfast dish. None of the sound traveled through the window, of course, and for a moment I thought it might be Good Morning America.

I leaned up closer against the glass and caught a glimpse of the UK Channel 4 logo in the corner of the screen, and realized my mistake. I also caught the eye of one of the servers inside, who looked a little alarmed at the way I was fogging up the glass with my breath.

I hurriedly stepped back, my stomach twisting inside me. I would be watching Good Morning America or one of its dozens of clones within a couple of days.

It was time to go home. But somehow the thought of America just—didn't feel like home any more.

I tried quelling the panicky feelings that rose up by focusing on the visit with Gerald. It had been great to see him looking so well, and so happy. We'd both been looking for a Highland warrior on that long-ago cold night, and in spite of the ghost-sighting, neither one of us had found him. But fate had sent Gerald into the arms of an English nurse named Clare. A happy OUTLANDER ending if ever there was one.

And I really couldn't complain. I'd had an adventure of a lifetime.

Inside the teashop, a sports clip had replaced the cooking segment and I stared idly at images of Glasgow Rangers fans, roaring their joy at a goal. The camera panned the studio audience, filled with delighted, screaming faces, and I had a moment to wonder how such a large group of people could look so awake at such an early hour, when the picture changed again.

The hosts were welcoming a guest, who strode across the stage with his hands up, waving at the clearly delighted audience.

It was Jack.

I bumped my chin on the window, and the people seated at the closest table jumped back a little. I shot them an apologetic smile and focused on the screen.

He wasn't wearing his kilt this time, and he looked a little startled at the audience reaction, as the camera panned back and forth. Many of them bore little Scottish flags that they waved in the air with enthusiasm. The hosts greeted him warmly, and along the bottom of the screen, the caption read: *Best-selling Inverness author Jack Findlay brings William Wallace back to life.*

I could see he still had a slight limp as he walked across the set, and I was trying to lip-read what the female host was saying to him when the bus pulled up. The driver allowed the bus to stand idling a moment, and then honked at me, so I was forced to tear myself away from the screen and jump aboard.

As I stepped inside the bus, I looked back. The teashop server emerged carrying a spray bottle and cloth, and shot me a nasty look through the window. The bus pulled out as I dropped my pack onto the floor and fumbled for my ticket.

So Jack's new book was a success. That was certainly quick.

"Oi—I need yer ticket, Miss."

I scrambled back up to the front, my warm glow at seeing Jack dissipating under the weight of the driver's scowl. "Sorry. Here it is."

He grabbed it from me, glanced at it, and shoved it back at me.

"Y'er on the wrong bus. We're fer Glasgow. Ye need to get off at the next stop. Or ye can pay me ten quid to change yer ticket."

I grabbed the handrail behind him as we careened through a roundabout. I wasn't about to pay extra for a ticket to somewhere I couldn't afford to go.

"Can I get out here, then? I can walk back and get the right bus if you let me off at this corner."

He didn't even look up at me, just tapped a little notice he had tacked up beside the swing arm to open the door. NO UNSCHEDULED STOPS.

"Well, what's the next stop, then?"

"Crianlarich. Ye can change there and go through Stirling to Edinburgh."

"Seriously? That's going to take…"

His glare stopped me in mid-sentence. "Yer lucky I'm not fer chargin' yeh. Pay better mind the next time ye get on a bus, aye?"

Duly chastened, I struggled toward the back to find a seat as the bus rocketed along the motorway. At least it was not likely to be a long detour.

The bus was almost full, but I managed to jam my pack into an overhead bin and fall into a seat beside a lady whose knitting needles were busily clacking. I apologized when I realized I was sitting on her bag, but she waved it off.

"Ach, niver mind, Miss. I shoulda been quicker to move it away when I saw ye comin'." She tucked the bag with the ball of wool inside between her feet and handed me a newspaper. "Here's your paper, dear."

"Oh, it's not—" I began, when I caught sight of a teaser on the front page.

"Thank you," I said, instead, and sat back to read an excerpt of my friend's new bestseller.

My plan to keep my eyes to the windows and drink in the last of the Highland scenery had washed away in light of the found newspaper. I'd hardly noticed anything of the trip to Crianlarich as we sped along the road, the sound of the knitting needles beside me competing with the belches and gurgles of the bus.

The piece was in the Entertainment section of the *Daily Scotsman*. Apparently they had been running sneak peeks for a week or so. This issue held an excerpt, an interview with Jack and a rave review noting that the new book had bumped Ian Rankin's latest thriller out of the number one spot on the bestseller list.

After the reception he'd received on that morning show, I didn't doubt it. The three articles, along with an ad for Irn-Bru, took up most of the lower half of the page. The interview focused on the political implications of writing a book about a Scottish hero at a time when popular opinion in the country was surging toward independence from Westminster.

The excerpt, on the other hand, looked like Mrs. McCarthy from Edinburgh had picked it out. It was a love scene, depicting Wallace's last night with his wife sometime before leaving to fight at Stirling Bridge. It was the steamiest thing I had ever read, apart from my favorite scene with Claire and Jamie in the hot springs. And I found it interesting that Wallace's wife was no red-head, but had "wheaten" curls and hazel eyes. She had a decent grasp of the dire political position her husband was in, too. I'd never read a love scene with quite so much intellectual foreplay. It was—thought provoking. And hot.

Which made me smile.

"Lovely piece o' writin', aye?" said the lady with the knitting needles as I put the paper down. I nodded, still caught up in the scene Jack had woven.

"I pre-ordered the book at Waterstones," she said from under a cloud of pale blue wool. "Been a fan o' his work fer years, but the man has really stepped up his game wi' this one."

With the clicking needles, her warm smile and the tight brown curls around her head, I was reminded of a pre-alcohol Genesie.

The thought of Genesie actually made me laugh out loud.

"Oh—I was just remembering someone I met in New York," I said in response to the woman's questioning look. "Your knitting reminded me of her. She loves Braveheart."

The knitting lady's brows drew together, reminding me even more startlingly of Genesie. She folded her knitting into her lap.

"You Americans," she said—quite scathingly, I thought— "Yeh allus get yer history wrong. Even the title o' that fillum was wrong. The Braveheart was the Bruce, not Wallace. Robert the Bruce, tae be exact, another giant of a man who died years after William Wallace. He'd tasked his friend the Black Douglas to take his heart to the Holy Land, but they were set upon and the Douglas were kill-et. Before Douglas died, he threw the heart toward the east, calling upon it to carry on bravely. That American fillum got it entirely wrong."

Having learned my lesson from Genesie and her knitting needles well, I sat quietly and nodded as the bus rocked side to side.

"And mind, I'm from Stirling, m'self, and I were there when that young movie star fella came to town to premiere the thing. You know he never stepped out of his big black car, not even the once? Kept them limousine windows dark as the devil's arse, never mind all them folk around, waitin' to see him, all who'd put their lives on hold while he filmed his movie."

She made a noise in the back of her throat. "He tries to claim he's Australian, yeh know, but the man is American through and through."

She nodded her head at this pronouncement; as if this was the worst insult she could come up with. Rant over, she gathered up her needles and the wooly project she'd been working on. The bus wheezed and farted and as we slowed, she reached down for her knitting bag, her former placid expression completely restored.

"Where ever yer headed, ye'd do worse than to stop in Stirling for an hour and visit the shrine tae the Wallace," she said, as I stood up. "It'll gi'e yeh an education, if now't else."

So, that's what I did.

A Fleeting Foray…
2:00 pm, Sept 1
Cathy's Café, Stirling, Scotland

A brief pause in the journey—a final fleeting foray into the past, as prescribed by a wise woman I met earlier today.

A few thoughts on the best way to spend the last days of a journey:

Let spontaneity rule the day, as you never know what's behind the next corner.

Look past the standard tourist fare and seek out locations where real people live their lives. Common ground can be found in the craziest places!

Listen——to any local willing to share a bit of their story. You will learn more than you think—— and you will thank me.

And now I go to learn more of the Wallace, and his role in the shaping of the country.

About time, wouldn't you say?

- ES

Comments: 0

I'd told myself when I stepped off the bus that I'd just take a quick look at the Wallace monument, and then head south again. But the first thing I saw when alighting in Stirling was an Internet cafe. I reasoned a quick look at my email wouldn't hurt. I had decided not to tell Sophia when I was returning just yet—prolonging the inevitable, I suppose.

I splurged and caught a cab from the bus station. Stirling was almost like a smaller version of Edinburgh; with a medieval center to its old town, topped by a castle at the end of a long, winding road. The castle looked interesting, perched above the city like a gray eagle. A single building stood out from the rest, shining like gold in the hot afternoon sun.

"It's grand, innit?" said the cab driver, as he wound me through the city and away from the castle. "It's called the King's Gold, but is really just a limestone wash. The whole great hall has been reconstructed, though—ye really ought to take time to see it."

"I have to get to Edinburgh today," I said, staring back over my shoulder regretfully. "But maybe just a quick look."

"Ach, weel, tha's a shame, tha' is," said the cabbie. "Enjoy looking around the castle. And as for the rest, yeh can allus return next year, aye?"

"Aye," I said, absently. "Aye."

It was the off-season rates that pulled me in. And the stories of the Bruce and the Wallace and all the other heroes who had tread the soil of Stirling, in its place between the Highlands and the Lowlands of this great country. I found myself a student again. Just trying to learn something before heading back to America.

It's amazing how quickly the days can pass, especially when one is already "an overstay"...

Ten days after I had first stepped off the bus in Stirling, I found myself among a crowd standing at the base of the Wallace Monument.

It was the last significant landmark remaining for me to visit in the area. I had spent several days exploring the castle and the town of Stirling, with its jails and its refurbished townhouses and interpretive centers. It seemed everywhere I wandered I could learn something new. But there, among a busload of late-season tourists listening to a man portraying one of Wallace's soldiers explain his part of the uprising, I knew it had to be my last day. I'd used up the last of the 'little bit extra' I'd saved over what a plane ticket would cost, which was at a premium since I was buying so last-minute. I had enough to catch the bus to Edinburgh, and perhaps buy dinner, if I was lucky.

I looked up at the tower, feeling faintly disappointed. I hadn't realized until I arrived that, by Scottish standards at least, it was practically new. Built in the nineteenth century by Scottish patriots who felt that Wallace had never been given his due, it towered above the surrounding countryside. But it was built closer to my time than his, and I felt a little sad that this comparatively new edifice would be my last experience in Scotland.

Still. The description noted that at least seven significant battlefields could be viewed from its turrets. It sounded impressive. It looked impressive. I climbed all the way up the crag to see these very views.

But I never saw a single one.

You'd think, being practically a modern building and all, the patriots would have thought to put a reasonable staircase into the thing. But no—Scots practicality won over all, and the only way to scale the two hundred forty six steps of the tower was by spiral staircase.

A tight, dark spiral staircase.

I would have been fine—or if not completely fine, at least able to make it to the top—if there had been a window half way. The stairway was clear when I started up, and I didn't run into anyone as I climbed. But the first room into which the stairway emerged was packed. Inside, a weird William Wallace hologram spoke of the battle. Across the room, admirers encircled the man's mighty broadsword in its illuminated glass case.

I could feel my heart begin to squeeze in my chest. I knew I was at least half way up the tower, and I knew the top would be open to the air. But in front of me, a large man clutching a melting ice cream cone lumbered toward the tight staircase. I couldn't take my eyes off the sight of his substantial buttocks bulging below a straining leather belt. A climb to the top meant his ass would be my view all the way up that tight, dark, twisting stair.

Before I knew what was happening, my legs had propelled me forward. I elbowed past the man and his ice cream and flung myself down the stairs. I pushed past at least two families on the way down, and one woman had to clutch her child's hand to prevent him falling down behind me. "I'm sorry," I muttered each time, but by the time I got to the bottom, I was in full-out panic mode. I ran out through the door, past the performer still in full voice as a soldier and down the winding path through the trees.

I'd run almost all the way down the crag before lack of oxygen and muscular exhaustion slowed me to a walk. I was panting and trying not to cry, and collapsed onto a bench near the entrance to the gift shop to try and collect myself.

I dropped my head into my hands, and went straight for the heart of the matter. My claustrophobia was one thing, but this had been so much worse. The kindly Genesie-clone, the cab driver—even the cranky bus driver. Every step that had taken me away from Nairn, away from all I had grown to love, was making me sadder and more desperate. Knowing this was the last stop before the airport in Edinburgh had obviously flipped some kind of switch inside my head.

I took a deep, shuddering breath. Going back to Chicago—I could no longer think of it as home—wouldn't be that bad. I would find a way to get back here.

I would.

And right then, the police arrived.

I'm not sure how it happened. One minute I was sitting on the bench, trying to get a grip on myself, and the next a police car had pulled up beside me.

Since the six-month tourist visa time limit had passed, I had been a little nervous when I caught sight of a policeman, but really? I wasn't *that* worried. If someone did find out I'd overstayed my welcome, I could always play the ignorance card. Sitting there on the bench below the Wallace Monument, I was, if anything, less worried than I had been since I'd left Nairn. I was, after all, on my way to the Edinburgh airport.

I did feel a little guilty, remembering Matthew, the sweet airport employee who'd refunded me the ticket money in Inverness all those months ago. But I was on my way, and his airline was still the one who was going to take my money and fly me home.

Of course it was.

So when the police car slowed down beside me and the window scrolled down, I couldn't have been less concerned.

"Are ye all right, Miss?" the policewoman asked me.

And I bolted like a rabbit.

I have no idea why. I've always wondered, when watching various cops and robbers shows, why the robbers would run for it, especially when there was never any question they'd be caught. On camera.

Didn't stop me. I took a straight right turn and headed into the field, the 'Bad Boys' theme ringing in my head. "Dammit, Hamish," I muttered, as I picked up speed. I hated to think the only thing I'd taken from our relationship was a pop-song fixation.

The field, I knew, backed into a wood. I'd seen it on my way up with the cab driver, and I'd run through part of it once already, on my way down from the monument. If I could make the wood, I could hide there until the police lost interest in me, and then hop a bus before they knew I was gone.

It was an excellent plan.

Behind me, I could hear a strangled cry, and someone yelling "Wait! Stop!"

I didn't stop.

As I ran, I saw a goat standing behind the low rock wall separating my field from the next. He had four horns on his head, and looked like someone had splashed his white coat with black paint. He seemed entirely unperturbed at the sight of a stranger blundering past.

For the past six months, I had been riding a bike twice a day, not to mention the miles walked between tables at the cafe and up and down the fields with Morag. I not only had panic on my side, I had a bit of muscle.

And I would have made it—I really would have—but for the kissing gate in the field.

Obviously, I knew kissing gates. I'd learned how they worked the very first day I'd met Morag, and I'd even been quite memorably kissed up against one. The gate below the Wallace monument attached to a stile on either side; perfect for leaping over if one was a human, less so for cattle. Or goats.

Not at all worried, I took a flying leap over the stile, but somehow managed to clip the toe of my Converse between the two sides of the gate. Seconds later, I was being sat-upon by a large policewoman, who was possessed of a substantial body mass, but was very damned fast, for all that. She pulled my arms behind my back and cuffed me. Considering I had just been through a major bout of panic-driven claustrophobia, I didn't take to the cuffs very well.

"I cannae uncuff ye, Miss, until ye give me yer name," she said, when I paused for breath.

This left me so confused that I forgot to feel panicky. "Don't you know my name?" I gasped. "Why would you arrest me if you don't know my name?"

"You're not under arrest, madam. That is—I would prefer if you' just assist me by telling me your name."

"It's Emma Sheridan," I said, hanging my head. "Can you please just take the cuffs off?"

"Look, luv," she said, kindly. "I dinnae know who you are, but even in America, ye must know that if ye run from the police we *will* chase you. No why would ye think I'd want to arrest ye on this fine day?"

"I—I've overstayed my visa. But I was heading to the airport today, I swear."

The policewoman looked thoughtful. "Well, I have to say we're not generally in the habit of arresting tourists, especially on their way home. But ye *did* run, so let's just walk back to the car and get this sorted, a'right?"

In the end, I was ignominiously perp-walked back through the Wallace Monument field. The spotted goat viewed me balefully, chewing. The police officer, whose name was Doris, carried my backpack and helped me over the fence to the waiting police car.

And standing beside the car was Jack Findlay.

I had used up my full capacity of adrenaline for the day. "What are you doing here?" I asked, as coolly as I could, considering the handcuffs.

"I was just about to ask you the same question," he said, raising his eyebrows at the sight of my shackled wrists. "I'm here to sign copies of my book at the gift shop." He glanced up at the tower looming above us. "My *Wallace* book. And you …?"

I didn't have time to answer, as something had come over my arresting officer.

"Hellow Mister Findlay," said Doris, simpering.

I stared at her, but she only had eyes for Jack.

"Er … hello," he said.

"I've read all yer books, Mister Findlay," said Doris, breathily. "But this last one about Wallace? It were a masterpiece."

"Well, thank you, PC—ah—Potts. Perhaps you can tell me why you have my friend here all trussed up?"

"I especially loved Missus Wallace, Jack. She was so—enamored with her husband, weren't she?"

I noted with alarm how Doris had moved so quickly into a first-name basis with her favorite author.

"She was indeed, PC Potts. I—I had a wee bit of historical freedom to develop her character, as so little is actually known. But, regarding my friend Emma, here. Can you tell me why she's being detained?"

Doris looked over at me as though she had forgotten my existence. "Oh, righ'," she said. "She tells me she's overstayed her visitor's visa, so I need to run her name through the system."

Jack's face cleared. "Oh, is that all? Well, I'm sure we can clear this up very quickly. Who is it we need to speak to?"

Doris shook her head regretfully. "I'm afraid there is no speaking to anyone, Mister Findlay, sir. If she is an overstay, I'll need to bring Miss Sheridan in to the Bannockburn station, and they'll hold her in a cell until she can be deported, sir."

"He—held in a cell …?" I began.

Jack put a calming hand on my arm. "It's okay, Emma," he said to me in a low voice. "I can handle this."

"I—I'm not sure I can," I said, wondering if I had it in me to drop-kick PC Doris and get away with my hands locked behind my back.

But she must have sensed my thought patterns or something, because before I knew it, she'd jammed me into the back of her car, and slammed the door shut.

I did not know, until that moment, that the rear seats in Scottish police cars are sound-proofed. PC Doris's car was, anyway.

Later, I was grateful for this.

But at the time, I just screamed.

Dear Emma,

Well, all I feared has come to pass. Detained by the police and asked to leave? Is that the same as being deported? Your email was conveniently unclear.

Emma, I...I don't even know what to say. We are your family, and of course will stand behind you, but...deported?

I will, of course, have Paul research the implications.

In the meantime, I suppose I should tell you that Starbucks is opening up a new location in my building downtown. Once you get back here safely, we can take you down to fill out an application.

Please, please try to stay out of any further trouble. It's only a plane ride. Send the arrival information as soon as you have it.

Sophia

PS. We do love you, Emma. See you soon.

I sat silently in the car as Jack pulled away from the police station and headed north. A doctor had been called and they'd given me something that left me feeling fuzzy-headed but calm. And a bit weepy.

They'd even let me check my email after I'd calmed down, but with the drugs on board, that had made me weepy, all over again. And Sophia's swift reply to my confessional email had not helped.

I clutched a tissue tightly in one hand. "I'm so sorry," I said, for the nineteenth time. "I don't know why I ran."

Jack shot me a sideways glance and swung expertly through a roundabout and onto the highway. "You ran because you didn't want to be locked away. You clearly don't like being locked away."

I hung my head. "I know. I'm sorry."

Twenty.

"Look, I don't like being locked away either. In theory, anyway, since I've never actually had the opportunity. Still, I'm sure it's quite terrible. So there's no need to apologize."

I took a deep breath and stared out the window as the green and gold Scottish countryside flashed by. "It's so flat, here," I said, resting my head back on the seat. "S'beautiful, but I miss the hills."

He laughed. "Those hills are our mountains, I'll have you know. And you'll see them soon enough."

He was quiet then, concentrating on driving. I turned my head and watched him as he did. With full sunlight on his hair, I could see glints of copper and rust woven in with the brown.

"Did you have red hair when you were a kid?" I blurted.

He jumped a little at the sound of my voice, but recovered quickly. "Vivid orange, sadly. My nickname was Rusty until I was seventeen," he said. "Thankfully it's darkened up a bit since then."

"Yeah it really has. I thought it was brown until now."

He smiled a little, and tapped a finger lightly against the steering wheel as he drove.

"I forgot you wore glasses," I said, idly. The truth was, I felt a little drunk and it was making me dizzy holding my head upright. So much easier to let it loll back.

"Usually only to read," he said, a trifle defensively. "But they seem to help when I drive, too. Signs and all."

"S'okay by me," I said, "since I wear 'em myself. I like my contacts better but ..."

"But?"

"She took 'em. Took 'em all. My contacts and my laptop ... and my Jamie."

I could feel a teardrop roll down my face and into my ear, and I swiped at it with the tissue.

Missed. The coordination hadn't quite come back.

"I know," he said, quietly. "I was there when you told the story to the police officer."

I turned my head to the window then, and we drove along in silence for a long, long time.

I woke up as the car slowed down, gravel spitting under the wheels. My head felt clearer, but I was still strangely exhausted. It was completely dark outside, and a cool wind whistled through the trees and made me shiver.

Jack wrapped a coat around me and took my hand to help me across the cobblestones. A lady held open the door for us, but didn't say a word as he walked with me inside, down a hallway and into a small bedroom.

"Are you well, Emma?" he said, when the door closed behind us. "Do you need help to the bathroom or anything?"

"No—no, I'm good," I said.

He turned to leave.

"Jack, I want to pay for my own flight home. I have enough money. I don't want the police or the government or whoever to pay."

"It's okay, Emma. I'm sure they'll be happy to let you do that."

"'Cause if they have to pay to throw me out, they might not want to let me back in. And I'm coming back, Jack."

"That's grand, Emma. I'm so happy you like it here."

"Back, Jack. I'm coming back. I'll be back, Jack." I started to hum. "Hit the road, Jack, but I'll be back ..."

Right about then, I burst into tears.

I think he lay down with me until I fell asleep, but I don't really remember.

I woke with the dawn the next morning, feeling completely back to myself again. And therefore? Humiliated.

Why had I run from that police officer? Why was I even still in Scotland? Why hadn't I just left and gone back to Chicago before my six months were up?

I had a long, hot shower and changed into the last set of clean clothes at the bottom of my pack. The famously unsuccessful pink bra, a tank top, jeans and my sweater. I couldn't find an elastic band or anything to tie my hair back, but there was a hairdryer under the sink, at least.

It wasn't until my hair was nearly dry that I remembered Rebecca. Events of the night before were still pretty fuzzy, but I surely would have remembered Jack's girlfriend, if she'd been waiting at the house. The lady who had answered the door last night hadn't seemed quite girlfriend material...

Maybe they didn't live together? The bathroom was clean and functional, but there were no telltale extra female products lying around. Even the shampoo in the shower seemed pretty— generic.

By the time my hair was dry and I was dressed, it was a quarter to eight and I could stall no longer. I took a deep breath and headed out into the hall.

Jack was standing by the front door. Alone. "Hiyeh," he said. "Are ye well this morning?"

"Way better," I said. "But I have a few gaps in what happened yesterday ..."

"That's to be expected. Think you can eat something? We could talk a bit over breakfast."

My stomach rumbled, answering for me.

"Right then," he said. "Breakfast it is."

I took a last bite of bacon and pushed my chair back. "That was awesome," I said. "I couldn't eat another bite."

"Grand." Jack smiled at me, and then handed his plate to a woman who appeared through a swinging doorway. "That was lovely, Mrs. Moorcock," he said. "Thank you."

She nodded, took my plate as well, and vanished.

The woman had gray hair done up in tiny curls around her head. Certainly not a look I would associate with the mysterious Rebecca.

I leaned across the table. "Is that ..."

"Mrs. Moorcock, my housekeeper," he answered.

"She looks so familiar," I muttered.

"I think ye may just be remembering her from las' night. She met us at the door?"

"I guess that's it." I took a shot. "Mrs. *Rebecca* Moorcock?"

He raised an eyebrow. "Gladys, actually."

I looked down at the spot where my plate had been, unsure of what to reply. Contrary to his earlier suggestion, our breakfast had been eaten in almost total silence, with the mysterious Mrs. NOT-Rebecca Moorcock delivering food and pouring drinks before vanishing through the green door by the sideboard.

Jack cleared his throat. "Would you like some more tea?"

"No, thanks."

The awkward silence resumed, until just when I thought I couldn't stand it anymore, we both broke it at once.

"What do yeh remember..." he began, while I said, "Can you tell me ...?"

We laughed together, and then said, "You first," in total unison.

It was almost worse than the silence.

After another moment, when it became clear he was going to wait me out, I tried again.

"I really *was* heading to Edinburgh to catch a plane," I said. "I have no idea why the police stopped me. I mean, why stop someone who is leaving anyway? It just doesn't make sense."

He took a sip of his tea. "Emma, I don't think they were planning to stop you. It's likely only because you ran off when the policewoman called over to you. They likely didn't know you were in violation of your visa until they looked up your name."

"I actually told her myself," I muttered. "I'm such an idiot."

He reached across the table and squeezed my hand. "Why were you in Stirling in the first place? You said in the blog you were just stopping there briefly before heading home to America."

I sighed and looked up at him. "I know—I hadn't even planned on going, really. I just—I caught the wrong bus, and had to change, and then—well, I just wanted to see the place you'd been writing about. So I stopped on the way."

I toyed with a spoon Mrs. Moorcock had left on the table. "But, I'm still not clear why I am here at all. I mean—here in Scotland, still. And also here ... in this house. The last I remember, Constable Doris said she was going to lock me up and then put me on a plane. And then a bit of screaming ..."

He shrugged a little. "Not so very much screaming. Their nurse gave you the shot almost right away."

I swallowed, trying to remember if I'd ever had a more embarrassing moment. The only one I could think of was the night I crawled out of the bar in Philadelphia.

And Jack had been there, too.

"You have a talent for showing up when things are at their worst," I whispered. "This is so awful."

He grinned. "Not for me," he said, lightly. "You know, I spend most of my days locked in a dark room, writing stories about heroes who are long-dead. It's a rare treat to be able to actually lend a hand to someone who needs it."

"I do remember the shot, I think," I said, slowly. "And you promised to …"

"Take you with me to the airport," he said, and gave me a slow smile. "My American tour is set to begin in a week or two, so I can move up my flight to New York with no problem. And we had a bit o' luck in that Constable Doris turned out to be a fan. I signed a book for her, and promised to have ye on a plane soon as possible. Besides, it'll make a great story for your blog. Your stories always make me laugh out loud."

Not likely, I thought, but I beamed at him, anyway.

He pushed his chair away from the table and stood up. "But first you need to call and book your ticket for tomorrow."

I stood, too. Mrs. Moorcock appeared at the door, and directed me through to a phone in the hallway. Thanks to the long-ago Michael, the airline had my name on file and booked the ticket in under five minutes. As I stepped out to the front door, Jack appeared, holding my pack and his own bag.

"I have one final commitment before we drive down to Edinburgh. I hope you don't mind?"

"I don't mind," I said, as we walked to the car, and then I decided I couldn't wait any longer. "Are you going to say goodbye to Rebecca?"

He shot me an odd look and shook his head.

"Nae, I've seen the last of her for a while, aye?" he said, unlocking my door. He tossed my pack in the back, and turned to face me. "We're goin' to the Games in Nairn."

The thought of going to back to Nairn drove everything else out of my head. After assuring PC Doris of my unquestioning obedience to the crown in Stirling, Jack had taken me back to his home just outside of Inverness. So by contrast to the long drive I could barely remember from the night before, our morning trip was a quick jaunt. The games were being held on the estate of the current Thane of Cawdor, just outside Nairn itself, but along roads I recognized instantly.

It felt like I was going home.

We pulled up and parked in an area beside Cawdor Castle. On the driveway below, a parade of pipe bands gathered amid a marching of the various Highland colors. The Laird himself led the parade, surrounded by a collection of gentlemen sporting plaids in all possible combinations, mostly topped with white shirt and tie.

I spent an entertaining few moments comparing sporrans— trust the Scots to have invented the original, most practical man-purse. Some of the younger men had gussied up their kilts with leather sporrans featuring embossed skulls, but most were of the traditional combinations of leather and metal and fur. Some were black and hairy and some were gray and hairy and I even saw one that sported the entire head of an ex-fox.

Not once did I see a man actually put anything in or take anything out of his sporran, though. A total waste of good space, to my mind.

After the trooping of the colors, it was time for Jack to head off to assume whatever duties a guest of honor is required to undertake. He asked if I would still be there as promised at the end of the day, with a flash of anxiety on his face I could see he tried very hard to hide.

I assured him I would, and when I say I meant it with all my heart, well—I did. I'd had enough of running. Sunshine Susan could have the fugitive life. It was not for me anymore.

Since the drug haze had passed, the memories of events at the police station had come a little clearer. I could recall Constable Doris standing beside a stern looking man who had clearly out-ranked her. He had glared at me and then turned to Jack.

"Well, sir, in that case we'll trust you," the stern cop had said. "But it'll be on your head if she don't show."

"She'll show," Jack said.

So, there on the field, I promised twice, just so he knew I was good for it, and Jack was whisked away.

Most of the morning I'd just meandered, enjoying the sunshine and the spectacle. There were caravans parked all around the grounds, delineating the space, and the blue and white-striped awnings were everywhere. I wandered from one to the next, taking in the various exhibits.

Tiny, kilted dancers took turns on a stage, toes pointed and legs kicking as they skipped and twirled, then bit their fingernails nervously afterward, waiting for the results of the judging.

I spent a few anxious moments worrying that I would bump into Hamish, but thankfully the first person I ran into that I knew was Katy from the library.

"Now, this is a surprise! I'd heard ye'd left to go back to America," she said, after giving me a hug.

"Yes, well, I'm on my way," I managed.

"Grand, grand," she sighed. "I'd love tae see America. I've been to France a few times and Spain once, but niver across the pond, aye?"

"It's a big pond," I said, and then quickly tried not to think too closely about the crossing of it.

"I s'pose ye've heard that Hamish has finally gone too, then, the big dunderheid? He and that new hen o' his."

"Hamish is gone? To America?"

She nodded emphatically. "As he allus wanted. And good riddance to the lad, aye?"

I didn't know what to say. Part of me wished happiness for him, but mostly? I kinda hoped his Sunshine screwed him as thoroughly as she had me.

"Weel, have a lovely time today," said Katy, sincerely. "Ah can't believe ah'm sayin' this, but I miss seein' ye at the library. Haven't had to clear out a single cache since yeh left. No—wait, I'm lyin'. The Jones boys were in lookin' up pictures of the Duchess of Cambridge—that time before the babies when she were in France, ye know. I did have to clear those out righ' quick." With a final kind pat on my arm, she bustled off.

I wandered over to watch the older girls compete in Highland dance, whirling in clean right angles above the swords placed beneath their feet. From there I headed over to watch the sporting competitions, from wrestling to hammer throw.

I arrived just in time to see a long row of men in kilts get dragged through the mud in the tug of war finals. Among the members of the triumphant team, I saw Ashwin running around in jubilation. I waved at him and he leaped the rope barrier and came over to wrap me in a giant bear hug. It was a definite improvement on our last meeting.

"Congratulations," I said, after extricating myself.

"Thank yeh verra much indeed," he said, proudly. "We won because of mah new fitness regimen."

"Fitness regimen? So you've quit smoking?" I asked, delighted.

"Don't be daft! I've shifted from lager to ale. Geordie tol' me it'd make the difference, and damned if he wasnae righ'!"

"Ah." I decided to change the subject, just to be safe. "I've never seen you in a kilt, Ash. It suits you."

He shrugged, still beaming all over his mud-caked face. "Usually only for events like this. Me mum's clan are the MacKenzies, so it's her family plaid."

The rest of the team appeared to be clearing the field. "Oi—Patel!" someone shouted. "Quit kissin' that girl and come fer a pint!"

Ashwin's face fell. "Guess I'd best be off," he muttered, and turned to go.

I grabbed his arm and planted a big kiss on one muddy cheek. "See you soon, Ash."

His mouth dropped open, then he gave a whoop, which momentarily deafened me. "I wasnae kissin' her—she were kissin' me!" he yelled, as he ran back to join his team.

I waited until they were well into the beer garden before I wiped the mud off my lips and wandered over to the next event. He hadn't even seemed surprised to see me, but if that boy's heart was going to be broken, it wasn't me who would be responsible.

A large set of wooden seats had been erected to watch the heavy events, but I skirted them and stood near the fence to one side. Seeing the huge men throwing their enormous hammers, I remembered the picture on the side of the bus from early in the springtime, and my high hopes then of finding my Fraser from amongst their number. The memory was threatening to erase the happier mood I had been in since kissing Ashwin, so in the end, I decided it was better to hang out in the agricultural exhibits. Fewer regrets there, anyhow.

Sometime after lunch, I looked up to find Jack beside me.

"Have you had enough to eat?" he asked anxiously. "I've been in the main tent over there all day, signing books with the others."

"There's plenty to eat," I assured him. "Pasties and meat pies and bannock ... Not that I'm very hungry after that giant breakfast."

"A full Scottish breakfast does stick to your ribs," he admitted. "But honestly—are you enjoying the day?"

"Yes, of course," I said. "I've wanted to see these Games since I got here. I can't believe I actually get a chance to be here in the end. Thank you for bringing me."

He shook his head impatiently. "You don't need to thank me. Coming here was just an obligation I couldn't get out of. But if it makes you happy, then I'm happy, too."

"It does," I said. "I just feel sort of—I don't know—poignant? Nostalgic? I SO hate to leave."

"Look," he said intensely, and he took one of my hands in his. "If you want to be here, we will find a way to make it happen. You'll have to go home first ..."

"To Chicago," I interrupted, thinking of the little wee room at Morag's.

"Yes," he went on, not really noticing. "But we will get you back. I promise."

My eyes followed him as he walked over to the big white tent, and it occurred to me that I had never seen Hamish in a kilt. But I suddenly doubted that he could cut a finer figure than Jack did at that moment, striding off into the afternoon sun.

I thought about telling him so, for about half a minute. I even walked a few steps in the direction of the tent. And then I saw the sign. Not from above, though it might well have been. No, this sign was right in the middle of the field. It was a direction sign.

Author Event, it read. *Meet our Guests of Honor.*

Guests.

I took a step back, shaded the slanting rays of the afternoon sun from my eyes, and peered at the tent. A long line of people carrying books snaked out the door and around one side of the field. Inside the tent was pretty dark, but if I squinted my eyes, I could just make out the outline of Jack, sitting up on a raised platform, signing books.

And beside him?

A woman with dark hair, dressed like a vivid butterfly in blue.

Herself.

How had I missed this? I should have known …

The tinny public address system gave a squawk, which made me jump.

"Ten minutes to final presentations at the main stage. Ten minutes."

In the distance, I could see the top of a huge log moving behind the white special-event tent. Suddenly the log disappeared, only to reappear, flipping end over end. A roar went up from the crowd.

"Ach, I knew yeh couldn't stay away. Still got yer room fer yeh, should ye want it, aye?"

I turned around to see Morag's smiling face. She had two leggy young sheep in tow, one in a harness of red and the other green.

I grinned at her and it felt good. I was pretty sure I hadn't really smiled since the last time we'd clinked teacups that night making butter.

"Maybe not right away, Morag. But I will be back."

She beamed. "I know it. Yeh comin' to the presentations?"

"Yes." I reached down to pat one of the woolly sheep. "Are these …?"

"Aye. Them late twins you helped deliver. Tole' ye I were savin' 'em for summat special, righ'? They are to go to the guests of honor, after they finish presentin' the prizes."

I laughed. "I imagine they will be thrilled," I said.

"Damn well should be. These are fine pedigreed sheep. They'll make a fair decent lamb chop, I'll tell ye that."

Oh, I did *not* want to think of those sweet fuzzy things as chops. "Maybe they can be wool producers instead?" I said pleadingly, which made Morag laugh.

She pushed one of the leashes into my hand. "Come gi'e me a hand, would yeh? You can hand Wallace here over to that fine lookin' writer lad."

I hastily handed the leash back. "Oh no—no. I couldn't do that. I'll just watch from the crowd. But wait a minute. If this is Wallace ..."

"Yep. Named 'em special for the guests, o' course. This little fella is Wallace, 'named special for Mister Findlay's new book."

She held the red leash up and the lamb at the end capered a little. "An' this one's for the lady. Called 'im Fraser, righ'?"

I stared at her, mouth open.

"After a character in her books—name o' James Fraser. Yeh mus' read 'em, if ye havenae, lass. Lovely tale-teller, she."

Morag bent down, scooped the lamb up, and held her out to me. "Sure ye dinnae want to help hand him over? Ye did find him an his brother in the field that night, aye?"

In a bit of a daze, I stepped forward and she thrust the lamb into my arms. I couldn't come up with any words, but there was no question Morag was right. I guess I had found Fraser, after all, though he was not exactly the one I was looking for. I nuzzled its soft wool a moment before it lurched its head back suddenly and bashed me in the chin.

"Whoah there, Fraser—careful now. Ye dinnae want tae hurt the lady who helped ye into the world, do yeh?"

I set the lamb down on the grass and handed his harness back to Morag. "You're very sweet, but I think it's best if you do the presentation. I'll cheer you on from the audience, okay?"

Morag shrugged. "Suit yerself. Ye know where tae find me when ye return, aye? Or yeh could drop me a line sometime—I jes' had them put in the router this week. Got mah own Wi-Fi channel now, and a new MacBook tae boot."

"I'll do that," I said, and rubbed my sore chin as she and her two woolly little charges hurried over to the stage.

The sun set over the main platform as the final presentations wrapped up. The winner of the caber toss that'd I'd seen behind the main tent turned out to be Geordie, and I had a minute to congratulate him as he stood afterwards, holding his trophy. He told me Hamish had said he was never coming back to Nairn.

"He were full o' some nonsense about sun and fun. But I've no doubt he'll be back." He took a long drink from the cup of his trophy, and I realized he'd filled it with beer. "Really thowt yeh were the one fer him, there. But that blondie he ended up with? Yowza!"

He leered blearily at me until a tsking lady organizer walked by. She grabbed the trophy cup from him, dumped the beer into the grass and led him away.

In the final act of the evening, a small child stepped on stage, tugging the lambs along, and presented them in turn to the guests of honor. I cowered, watching behind one of the heavies in the crowd. And then in a flurry of smiling and thanks, it was all over. The crowds streamed toward the exits and to the overflowing beer garden that had been set up nearby.

In a moment, Jack was beside me again.

"Would yeh like to meet her?" he said, catching me peeking up at the stage. "We can go up now, before her car comes."

I shook my head. "No. I—I can't bear facing her again."

We walked along toward the exit. "What happened, Emma? You wouldn't tell me that night in Philadelphia. And you've never put anything on your blog."

"I swore to myself I'd never mention it again. And I haven't."

His voice dropped a little. "What could be so terrible? Did you vomit on her or something?"

I paused beside a blue-striped tent near the exit.

"Nothing like that. It's just—I'd waited in line for her the whole day, and when I finally got up to speak to her, she was so kind. She smiled up at me, and I wanted to tell her everything. To confess what I was about to do, and to ask her where—where she thought I should look to find my Fraser."

I had to stop for a minute and catch my breath. I was ashamed to realize my eyes were tearing up, just at the memory.

"In the end, there were just too many questions. I opened my mouth to speak to her, but instead of saying anything, I just burst into tears. She handed me a tissue, very kindly, of course, but I still turned and ran away."

Jack gave me a bit of a strange look. "Emma," he said. "I thought *writers* were bad about living inside their own heads! You worry too much. Listen, people cry about my characters all the time."

I sniffed a little. "Really?"

He paused a minute. "Well, not really. I can't say anyone has actually burst into tears over my writing. But I get it. As a fellow author, I really get it."

I took a deep breath. He was right. It was time to find my way past it.

"Anyway," he went on, "she's marvelous. You'll love her. Please let me introduce you."

Looking up at him, something else surged in me. The hero worship that had haunted me for so long would never really leave, but for the first time, I was conscious of feeling something else in its place. I thought back to the kiss—the kisses, really—he'd given me at the bookstore. Suddenly I wasn't so sure I wanted to share any of the time we had left with someone he thought was so lovely.

Even if I thought she was lovely, too.

"No—no, I don't think so," I said, and turned and walked toward the exit gates.

To: EmmaFindingFraser@gmail.com
From: PCAlthrop@l*thianandb*rders.p*lice.uk
September 13

Miss Emma Sheridan,

This is to acknowledge receipt of your email, including your booking number and itinerary for your return to Chicago, Illinois, United States of America on September 14.

We have been in touch with our Stirling colleague PC Doris Potts, and appreciate your timely follow-up with our office. With receipt of this email, you have met all requirements as outlined by that precinct.

Please remember to check in with one of our officers at the Edinburgh terminal prior to your departure. Failure to do so will result in a permanent notation to be placed on your United Kingdom immigration file.

Thank you for your cooperation,

Police Constable Lawrence Althrop

Jack had let me use his phone to check my email. I'm pretty sure he was as relieved as I was when I read it out to him, as we drove into the dark. The soft warmth of the summer afternoon had given way to a cool wet evening with an edge to it that I recognized. A swirl of leaves blew across the windshield as the car pulled out. It would soon be fall. I realized with a jolt that it would be the only season I'd not lived through in Scotland.

I had no idea when Jack's flight was due to leave, but my flight was scheduled just before noon the following day. However, the celebrations after the Games had gone late into the night. We'd been stopped at the gates at our first attempt to leave, and dragged into the Beer Garden tent by Geordie and a collection of the winning tug o'war team.

Every time we'd tried to head out, Jack had been drawn back into the merriment again, to raise a glass to someone's triumph on the present-day Highland battlefields. That Jack was drinking Irn-Bru (Scotland's *other* national drink, according to Geordie), was our saving grace, in that it allowed him to finally elude the grasp of the scotch- and beer-slowed revelers sometime after two in the morning. The sounds of the celebration roared on in one of the tents behind us as we slipped away at last.

When we got to the car by the Castle, he'd apologized for the late start.

"We'll not have time to stop home at this hour, I'm afraid. It's a bit of a journey all the way down to Edinburgh. I can make up a wee bed for yeh in the back seat, if ye like," he'd said, but I waved the offer off and sat beside him. The chances were I'd snore less sitting up, anyway.

Not that I did.

The car's engine was the only sound as the miles rolled away under our wheels. It turned out that my snoring worries were all for naught anyway, since I didn't sleep a wink.

I spent the drive thinking over all the mistakes I'd made, beginning way back with my first boyfriend Campbell. I realized I had been casting men in roles they didn't suit; trying to make them each fit my image of what a boyfriend should be, all the way through to Egon. Sure he was a philanderer, and that was entirely his to own, but hadn't I secretly known that part of him existed? Hadn't I thought I could make him change? And because Hamish reflected some of the physicality of my ideal mental image of Jamie, I had pretended the other parts of him didn't exist until it blew up in my face. I needed to learn from all these bad choices. These were choices Claire would never have made.

For a long time, when sleep wouldn't come, I looked over and watched Jack driving the car. After all my time in Scotland, and all the friends I had found, it was he who was the one I had come to most depend on. And even though in the dark I could see there was no ring on his finger, the fact that there was a Rebecca in his life meant that I needed to learn from all the bad choices I'd made in the past. I turned and stared out into the darkness as the road took us away from everything I had grown to love.

Sometime just before dawn, the car shuddered a little as we pulled onto a side road. I'd been drifting—thinking again about Jack's kindness since I'd met him. Before my arrest, and especially after, he'd gone out of his way to make sure I'd felt safe and comfortable. And now he was driving all night to make sure I didn't get arrested again.

The car slowed a little with the change of roadway and I lifted my head to see he was looking at me. His face appeared a little worried in the lights from the dash.

"Ach, I'm sorry Emma," he said, his finger tapping against the steering wheel. "I dinnae mean to wake yeh. It's just— there's somethin' I thought ye might like tae see before you catch your plane."

I sat a bit more upright, and surreptitiously wiped the side of my mouth. "I wasn't asleep," I said. "Where are we?"

He turned a sharp corner and then pulled the car to a stop.

"When I was growin' up, my cousins had a place near here. We used to come as children, to play on the stones."

He peered out the window at the sky. A thin gray line showed the shape of a dark hillside looming above us. "I believe it's stopped raining," he said. "Would yeh like to step out with me?"

The circle of stones stood silent in the near-darkness. I was still panting a little from the climb, but it was much easier to see now than it had been when we'd left the car. Leaves swirled underfoot and around our ankles as we walked up the path. Jack had taken my hand and held it through the long climb in the dark, but he dropped it then and stepped forward into the circle.

"Holy smoke," I breathed.

The dark gray stones seemed to materialize out of the air around us—solid but somehow out of time. The air was crisp, and a curled brown leaf skittered across the dew-studded grass in front of me. We were in a clearing that had no right to be where it was—a flat, sort of oval space somehow carved out of a wooded hillside. Unless you stumbled upon this place, I don't know how anyone could have known it was there.

I spun around, trying to take it all in.

"Is this more like the place you were looking for?" Jack said, his voice hard to hear above the wind.

"Yes. Definitely."

Unlike the earlier circles I'd visited, this one had no cairn at its center. There was a collection of eight small stones forming a sort of ellipsis, encircled by a group of twelve much larger, more evenly-spaced stones. A single stone connected the two groups.

I walked over to look more closely. Of all the stones, this was the only one that had the same cup marks on it as the cairned circles at Clava and Drumnadrochit. I traced one of the marks with my finger, wondering.

The trees above us were rimmed in pink. I looked up to see Jack watching me as I walked around the ancient, sacred space. I could see his face clearly for the first time since the car. He looked anxious and—something else I couldn't read.

"This is *amazing*," I said. "I'm so happy I got to see it before I had to leave."

"I'm glad," he replied. "When I read the post you'd written about your search for the circle, I remembered this place. I hadnae thought about it in years."

I lay my hand against the cool stone with the cup marks. "Do you know what these mean?"

He shook his head. "No. We mostly used this place to hide from the adults when I was young. We'd play cowboys and Indians from the programs we loved on American television. Not terribly politically correct these days, but the coolest thing ever, back then."

He walked over beside me. "I'll wager this is the sunstone, so maybe whoever placed it here marked it this way as an indicator. We used to lie on the grass and watch the sun move over it, as I recall."

I looked up into the lightening sky. "Do you think the sun will rise over it this morning?"

He leaned against the rock. "Maybe, though I'm fair certain it marks the midsummer sun, somehow. Or—it might be the moon."

"The moon was out the night I saw the ghost warrior, but I didn't really notice where it rose. Too busy chasing phantoms."

Jack cleared his throat uncomfortably. "Ah—yeah. About that night ..."

He folded his arms across his chest and stared somewhere into the distance over my left shoulder. I looked at him expectantly.

"I believe I have a confession to make," he said, at last.

I pushed my glasses firmly up my nose, but it didn't really help me read his expression any better. So I just waited.

"I think it's possible—I'm not totally sure, mind—but it's slightly possible … thatImighthavebeenyourghost," he blurted.

"Pardon?"

He shot an anguished look at me. "I didn't actually put it together for quite a while, but one night when I was reading over your back blog posts …"

"You read over my back blog posts?" I interrupted. I felt so completely thrown by the direction the whole conversation had taken, I grabbed onto what I could. "I don't think even Genesie does that, and I'm pretty sure she's cyber-stalking me."

He shrugged. "Hey, I'm only one of your followers. In my case it's—well, maybe just a bit more literal."

I thought about how grateful I had been to see him at the Wallace Monument. "Okay, never mind. You were saying …?"

He took a deep breath. "Well, I was at a cairn one night in March—the one near Culloden. It was late. I always go late to avoid having to deal with the tourists, same as with Ainslie Castle. So, I think it may have been me you saw. I know I left as soon as I heard voices."

I leaned back against the cool silvery rock and felt a little shiver tingle up my spine at the thought of that night. "But why—why were you there?"

He crouched beside me, staring into the circle of stones, silent for a long moment. In the distance I heard the cry of a bird, clear against the dawn sky. He looked up then.

"A golden eagle," he said, and turned round to search out the source. "There!"

When it became clear I couldn't see anything, he stepped behind me and turned my shoulders. His arm reached around me, pointing high above the woods behind the center of the circle. "Right there—can you see her?"

And I could. The eagle glided high on the morning wind and then stalled abruptly and shot downwards. I lost sight of her against the trees.

"Breakfast for the wee ones," he said, with a smile of satisfaction. "Full Scottish breakfast, if I'm not mistaken."

With the eagle gone, he stepped away, and I shivered again as the warmth of him against my back disappeared. But he'd crossed his arms and leaned against the stone beside mine.

"I was there to pray," he said, abruptly. "Or rather, to find a spot where Wallace might pray. I'd taken him through the fighting and anger. The war years—the deep triumph at Stirling Bridge and the sorry rout the following year. He had been a man on top, but over time, it had all burned to ashes in the flames of politics and deception. I'd finished writing the book, but Rebecca wasn't happy with it. I was …"

"Just a minute," I said. "Rebecca wasn't happy with it?"

He shrugged and smiled a little. "Aye. I'm so lucky to have her, y'know. She's a tough critic, but she's honest. Ye need that in an agent, aye?"

I held up my hand again. "Wait a sec. Rebecca—is your *agent*? Not your girlfriend?"

He laughed aloud. "Well, she's sixty, and has been married herself for thirty-some years, so no, she's not technically my girlfriend."

A warm glow that I could not attribute to the weather began to work its way through my body from somewhere south of my sternum. Jack had stopped telling his story, and was looking at me with a curious expression.

"A—about that circle," I said, not really caring any more at all.

A gust of wind swirled Jack's hair around. "Right. Well, I was reworking a scene not long before the end—or before the betrayal that led to the end, anyway—and somehow, I couldn't find Wallace any more. I knew the fighter and the tactician, but I'd lost the man."

I jammed my hands deeper into my pockets. "When you talk about the story, you get this inward look. It's like you can see it all playing out inside your mind."

He grinned at me. "Well, that was the problem, y'see. Because I *could* see it all so clearly. Until the final days—his final days. Then it vanished. He was totally gone from me. I wrote it anyway, but when I handed in the final draft, Rebecca called me on it."

"Rebecca," I said again, not even caring that I sounded like an idiot. "Rebecca, your agent."

He grinned at me. "Yes. Rebecca my agent called me on it. So I headed to the circle. It wouldn't have been one Wallace would have found—I was too far north, writing near home, but it was of a similar look to those down south. The problem was all the damnable tourists, of course. So that's why I left, in the end."

"Yeah —I hadn't expected to find that bus there, either. Or Gerald, for that matter."

Jack raised an eyebrow. "Gerald?"

I grinned at him. "Oh, just someone I met who was looking for his own Scottish warrior."

"Ah. Well, I'm sorry how that all turned out," he said, quietly. "Or rather, for how unhappy it made you. I didn't want to add to it."

"I'm okay," I said, lightly. And as I said it, I knew it was true. "I have to go back to Chicago, but I think I really did find what I was looking for here, after all."

He leaned against the ancient stone. "And ye'll be back someday, aye?"

"I hope so."

"I do, too." He smiled at me then, and brushed the sleeve of his coat. "Well, we'd best be off, before the Lothian and Borders Police start combing the countryside for ye."

"Just a minute," I said, and in two strides I was in front of him with his jacket lapels in my hands. I believe I actually muffled his startled exclamation when the kiss began, but he got the idea pretty quickly. When I pulled away from him so we could both catch our breath, he clasped my hands in his.

"Emma Sheridan, I did *not* see that coming," he said, and his slow smile erased the worry he'd been wearing since we'd climbed the hillside.

"I just wanted to see if it would be as nice as the last one," I said.

"And?"

I thought a minute. "Well, you do taste a bit of Irn-Bru and— maybe peppermint? But it's a surprisingly nice combination at this hour of the morning."

He kissed me again, then, perhaps to give me the opportunity to solidify my opinion, and the chill of the morning suddenly fell away. The eagle cried out in the distance once more, and a sliver of yellow daylight shone down and touched the top of the sunstone.

"So, all this time, ye thought Rebecca was my girlfriend?"

"Well, only since I determined you're not wearing a ring. Before that I thought she was your wife."

He laughed a little, low in his throat. "No wife," he said. "No girlfriend, either. Not for a while, anyway." He brushed my hair away from my face, and tucked a loose strand behind my ear.

"I *have* read the book, y'know."

"The book? OUTLANDER, you mean?"

He nodded. "Twice, in fact. And just to be clear, I'm no Jamie Fraser." He crinkled his eyes at me. "I'm not exactly a virgin, for starters."

I thought for a moment. "Well, as long as you bear no resemblance to Black Jack Randall either, I think I can live with that."

He clapped a hand over his heart. "Ye wound me, Emma. And I'll have ye know, that man's name is actually Jonathan."

"It is indeed. Jonathan Wolverton Randall, to be exact."

I grinned up at him, and using the flat of my hand, pushed him back against the mammoth stone. Holding him in place, I leaned back and ran my other hand down the front of his coat. "So, you know what She says about why women love men in kilts?"

"She?"

"Yes, She. With a capital 'S'. As in Herself. Your lovely friend the author."

He smiled down at me. "Okay, I'll bite. What does *She* say?"

"She says it's because we know in the back of our minds that you can have us up against the nearest wall in under a second."

He grinned, and spun me around so the cold stone pressed against my back. Undid the top button of my coat and kissed me under the line of my jaw.

"I might have heard her tell that story," he said, his lips warm on the skin of my neck.

And it turned out—he had.

Much, much later, as we walked down the hill from the circle, I decided that my blog audience would just have to do without the full story of the discovery—at last—of my own *Craigh na Dun.*

Channeling Claire…
Somewhere in the Highlands of Scotland
10:00 am, September 14

As this leg of my journey ends, I think what I have taken most from this trip has been the importance of friends.

And perhaps the discovery that sometimes Highland Warriors wield pens, not swords.

I may have begun this journey with the sole objective of finding my own Fraser, but I am much happier that the person I found, instead, was my own inner Claire.

I'll be back soon…

- ES

Comments: 0

Hi Emma,

It was with great relief we received your email noting your arrival details. I've arranged to get the time off, so Paul and I will be there to meet you.

By the way, I received the strangest email from a friend who works at a publishing firm in New York. Apparently they'd like to speak to you about a blog-to-book deal. I have no idea what that means, but if it's a chance to earn a few dollars, I hope you do the sensible thing and take them up on it!

Sophia

Reporting in to the police station at the Edinburgh airport was unnerving. We pulled up to the terminal and Jack pointed to the small sign.

"It's just over there. Don't worry about a thing. I just need to sort out my ticket, and then I'll meet you on the other side of the security gates."

I got out of the car and walked around to the driver's side. Jack rolled down his window. "Listen—it may take them a bit to run the paperwork. Hold on ..."

He rustled around in his computer bag, pulled out a book and handed it through the window. "Somethin' to do while ye wait," he said.

"Thanks."

I tucked it into my pack beside the copy of OUTLANDER, but it didn't really make me feel any better. The kiss he gave me before I stepped inside the door marked with the stark POLICE sign helped quite a bit more.

In the end, the visit to check in with the police was entirely anti-climactic. After assigning me to a chair, they left me sitting outside the office door for almost an hour before calling me in. While I was waiting, I paid out one of my last pound coins to use the airport wifi to make the blog post and read my email, but that only took a moment or two. I was grateful for the copy of Jack's book, as it at least gave me something to think about other than my imminent arrest.

I skipped right through the entire first couple of chapters and headed straight for what Mrs. McCarthy would call the juicy bits. When the police did call me, I'm pretty sure they had to say my name twice.

It was a good book.

Inside, I handed over my letter, which they stamped with great formality, and tucked into my passport.

The policeman on duty shot me a quizzical glance. "Yer not even a full month overstay, it says here," he said, reading off his screen.

"Yes—it was more of a mix-up than anything. I don't know why everyone got so upset."

He shrugged, and then peered at his screen before looking up at me.

"'Pears you've got yerself an enemy, Miss. Says here you were reported—by anonymous call. Full description of yeh, too. It's uncanny ..."

"Anonymous call..." I repeated slowly.

"Well, I wouldn't worry about it, Miss. They'll not bother to flag this. It prolly won't even show up if you try to return to the UK."

I thought of Sophia's note. "Oh, I'm coming back," I said.

"Let's get ye through to yer plane, then, aye?"

He swung open the door into the terminal, and I walked through.

After signing off with the police, I hurried toward the security gates and spotted Jack almost immediately. He was still on my side of the gates; craning to look through the crowds. My stomach clenched a little at the sight of him, still wearing his kilt from the festivities at the Games. I thought about our brief trip to the circle on the hillside, and immediately felt my face suffuse with heat.

I hate being such an easy blusher.

As I walked up, he turned and caught sight of me. His look of anxiety was swept away by a relieved smile. "Oh, thank god. I thought I'd missed ye."

"You could always have found me on the other side of security. You know my gate, right?"

"That I do. Since it is mine, as well."

It took me a minute to catch on. "You've changed your flight?" I said, slowly.

"Indeed I have." He stepped into line behind me, and the guard waved us through to the scanning machine.

"What about New York? The tour?" I put my backpack on the conveyor belt and automatically began unzipping it, when I remembered I had no laptop to pull out.

Jack put his things on the conveyor belt after mine and followed me up to the metal detector.

"Come through," the woman said, so I did.

The machine lit up like a Christmas tree, so they pulled out the scanning wand.

"I've made a slight change," he called, as he walked through in his stocking feet. Naturally, the lights did not blink even once. He'd replaced his shoes and put away his computer by the time they'd finished wanding and swabbing me for suspicious powders.

"I don't know why they always pick me," I muttered, as we waited for my pack to be x-rayed. "I lead the most blameless life ever."

He grinned. "Perhaps ye always look guilty. And besides, it's the blameless ones who carry the deepest secrets, aye?"

That might well be true, I thought, as I collected my pack and swung it up onto my shoulder. We turned down the long hallway leading to the gates.

"So, didja have a chance to begin the book?" he asked, with a certain casualness that rang utterly false.

"No— no, too busy dealing with the cops..." I began, but I totally caved as his face crumpled in disappointment. "Of course I read it. William's love interest seemed—ah ..."

"Human?" he asked, eagerly. "More realistic?"

"Umm-hmm. And kinda—familiar."

His face creased a little as he tried to smother a smile. "Ah. You noticed, then."

I opened my mouth to reply when a collection of heated voices rose up behind us. As we turned to look, there was a sudden explosion of activity at the very security station we had just come through.

Two guards—I couldn't tell if they were policemen or not, had come marching down the other wing of the airport, escorting a handcuffed prisoner. One of the guards had his hand on the prisoner's head as they ducked backwards through the security line, when the person shook free and ran right for us.

There was no time to react, apart from registering that the person wore enormous, white plastic-framed sunglasses and had long, flowing blonde hair.

"Susan?" I whispered, but not surprisingly, she didn't stop to respond.

It was a futile attempt, in the end, as she only managed three or four strides before the guard tackled her to the ground, essentially right at our feet.

"Brutality!" she screeched, before landing a decent kick right under the guard's kneecap with one five-inch platform shoe. "I'm goin' to sue you cocksuckers, one and all. See if I don't! This is fuckin' police brutality! Is this the way you treat all your visitors?"

Jack and I joined the throng of travelers who were backing away as quickly as possible from the scene. By this time, a second guard had arrived and was actually sitting right on top of Susan, trying to avoid her flailing feet long enough to zap-strap them together. In the end, the woman who had patted me down dropped her equipment and held Susan's heels together long enough for the guard to truss her up like a turkey.

As the final strap was tied, a large figure pushed through the security line.

"I'm wi' her," he cried when the woman with the wand tried to stand in his way. "They're arrestin' mah fiancée!"

"Hamish, Hamish—make them untie me," Susan screeched.

In the melee, several of her extensions had come away and were wrapped around various body parts of the guards, who were by this time struggling to get her upright. As both her hands and her feet were tightly bound, it seemed unclear to me why they were doing so, since there was no way she could walk on her own. But they pulled her to her feet, and Hamish stood beside her, helplessly collecting knotted strands of blonde hair from off the floor and the guard's uniforms.

"Look," Hamish said earnestly, peering down into the very red face of one of the guards. "There mus' be some mistake. We're gettin' married. I cannae leave without her! They'll no' let me stay in America!"

A line of police officers moved silently through the security line behind Hamish.

"Sir, I reckon you'd better come with us. This woman is Gail Lee Duncan, and she's needed to assist our enquiries into a series of thefts from Berwick to Thirsk."

The crowd watched in silence as Hamish's face went a shade of deep scarlet that I recognized with a pang of dread. "There mus' be a mistake," he repeated, his hand closing to a fist. "This is no Gail Thingummy. This is mah Sunshine—mah wife to be."

He raised a hand to the guard and there was a gentle sizzling sound for a moment before Hamish slid to the ground.

"Strap him up, too, Sammy," said the police officer, holstering his Taser as Hamish groaned and tried to sit up. "We're gonna need two gurneys for this lot." He looked up at the crowd, still standing in silence. "Now't to see here, folks. Move along to your flights, now—move along, tha's right."

"Holy smoke," I said, and took a great gulp of air.

I realized I'd been holding my breath through the entire ordeal. Susan—I couldn't bring myself to call her Sunshine—and Hamish. Maybe there was trouble in paradise, after all.

"Hey, wasn't that...?" began Jack, staring after the police, but I pretended not to hear and hurried down the long airport hallway.

At the gate, a couple of airport employees were dismantling a Visit Scotland display. Several large posters—including the one for the Nairn Games—lay partially furled on the ground beside a large plastic claymore and a collection of gray Styrofoam stones. The workers stood together beside the largest of the standing stones, having a heated argument over which screwdriver they needed to finish the job.

Just then a group of perhaps eleven or twelve dark-haired young women came milling through the door from the Customs area. They giggled at the sight of the stone circle, and in the end, one of the workmen took pictures for them as they all flashed a peace sign.

Every woman clutched a copy of OUTLANDER in her hand.

Jack skirted the largest of the stones, dropped his computer bag onto a chair, and turned to me, his expression puzzled.

"About that fella..." he began, when his mobile phone rang, deep inside a coat pocket.

"Odd," he said, fishing around for it. "Who's callin' me at this hour?"

"Is it the police again?" I asked, feeling a moment's irrational panic.

"Nae, my guess is they're busy enough with that blonde woman for the moment," he muttered, grabbing the phone at last.

It stopped ringing just as he pulled it out of his pocket.

"Unknown number," he read. "Damn—I hope it's not one of those 'You have just won a free cruise' calls."

He smiled at me apologetically and pushed the button. "I'll just check if they left a message ..."

After a few seconds listening, all the natural color drained out of his face. Ear pressed to the receiver, he reached with his free hand for the arm of the chair and sank down. A moment or two later, he pulled the phone away from his ear and touched the screen.

The airport demolition crew packed up their tools, and gave up, leaving the tumbled circle of stones standing by the airline gate. As they drove off, a "Thank you for Visiting Scotland" banner blew out of the bin on the back of their gently-beeping golf-cart and lay crumpled on the floor beside the archway.

"Are you okay, Jack?" I asked, sitting beside him. "Is it bad news?"

Wordlessly, he hit the replay button and held it up to me. The message began to run again before I could get the phone to my ear.

"...el Gibson, calling. I've just read yer book, mate, and I want the rights. They're to go to no one else, got that? I've a script treatment in mind already—it's clear as day in m'head; clear as day. I need this book, Findlay. It'll mean my redemption, man. I've taken so much shit over the years—it's time for me to atone. The Braveheart shall rise again, as God is my witness! Call me, babe."

I stared at Jack, open-mouthed. He took the phone from my limp hand, and brushed his lips against my cheek. "Fancy a trip to California?" he murmured. "I might need to talk to a fella."

There was nothing I could think of to say.

They called our flight, and as we walked toward the gate that marked the way to our airplane, he took my icy fingers in his warm hands.

And I swear on my tattered, worn and well-loved copy of OUTLANDER, as we stepped hand-in-hand through that stone circle, I felt the air begin to hum.

The End

Acknowledgements

How lucky am I?

Well, I'll tell you. I realized just the other day that the production of this book has been, from start to finish, only in the hands of friends. To clarify, I've always had a very friendly working relationship with the publishers and staff of the traditional houses who have produced each of my earlier books. But this one? Different. I wrote this book for friends. It was beta-read, edited and copy-edited by friends. The cover was designed and shot and photo-shopped by friends, and the text was digitized by a friend. I can't tell you the name of whoever digitized the text for SEEDS OF TIME or A WALK THROUGH A WINDOW. But I have eaten dinner with every single person who worked on FINDING FRASER. Every one is an industry professional, all at the top of their game.

And me? I am one lucky writer.

So thank you, Kathy Kenzie, for being my regular writing buddy, for encouraging this book and holding my hand every step of the way.

Thank you, Pamela Patchet for being a weirdo-magnet (especially in elevators!) and the BEST storyteller evah. Sharan Stone could never have existed without you. It is not lost on me that I likely, in fact, qualify as principle weirdo…

To Laura Bradbury for talking me into this publishing adventure in the first place, and offering sweet support from afar.

To Tyner Gillies, for word-racing me through part of the first draft (though NOT for the chicken suit you made me wear when I lost…).

Thank you to my editor Eileen Cook and copy-editor Mary Ellen Reid for eagle eyes and razor-sharp talents. [NOTHING gets by these women!]

To Martin Chung for photographic genius and a brilliant eye for detail.

To Lee Edward Födi for cover design and expertise. The force is strong with this one...

To digital wizard Crystal Stranaghan, the tech genius behind both book and websites.

To Rob MacDonald for good sportsmanship – and the kilt! – and to Tricia Barker for making the connection.

Thanks also to Peter Dyer, Alicia Kingsland, Meaghan Dyer and Jurgen van Wessel, who each play their own part in coping with Having A Crazy Writer in the family.

To the Scoobies for keeping it weird.

To Julie Kentner and all the other denizens of the CompuServe Books & Writers forum; friends, supporters and flag-wavers from the start.

To Diana Gabaldon and Jack Whyte; friends and mentors always. Two more generous writers I could not name.

And a final, special word of thanks to all my SiWC family. This book could never have come to be without the camaraderie and craziness behind our annual gathering; and you, my friends, must share the blame!

photo credit: Alicia Kingsland

kc dyer resides in the wilds of British Columbia in the company of a wide assortment of mammals, some of them human. She likes to walk in the woods and write books.

Contact kc [or Emma!] at kcdyer.com or FindingFraser.com.

If you liked this story, please review it!
Go to Amazon, Goodreads, or your favorite book-blogging site and share your thoughts on Emma's adventures.

Thanks for reading!

CPSIA information can be obtained at www.ICGtesting.com
Printed in the USA
LVOW06s2353110915

453920LV00021B/529/P